CW01669811

First paperback edition June 2022.

Book design & typography by Glynn Williams.
Produced by Manton House Printing Ltd, Derbyshire DE21 5EG.

About the Author

"Stanley Thomas is a Very Bad man" is Katie Trinder's debut novel.
Katie was born and bred in Nottinghamshire, growing up in Kirkby-in-Ashfield and now living in Mansfield.

Katie's career began working as a radio presenter and journalist for Mansfield 103.2, where she still hosts weekend shows. She's also worked for stations all over the country (and world!), including BBC7, and BFBS.

Katie's main job is working as a celebrant across Nottinghamshire, officiating at funerals, weddings, vow renewals and naming ceremonies; a job she loves.

In her spare time, Katie has seven dogs, loves going to concerts (she's seen Bon Jovi 16 times and Matt Goss 8 times) and is a huge Mansfield Town fan.

For Dad and Uncle Lou.

Chapter 1

Stanley Thomas wasn't a bad man; he just wasn't a very good one.

Chapter 2

1953 – Nottingham Prison

Stanley Thomas knew what was coming; he'd known the moment he'd been arrested. The moment the copper had pinned his arms behind his back and put him in handcuffs, and spat in his ear, "You'll swing for this Thomas".

Yeah, yeah, yeah.

The judge had at least pretended to listen to the evidence. But Stanley knew he'd sat there stroking the piece of black cloth on his desk, willing the outcome.

The moment the foreman of the jury had stood up and said they'd reached their decision and it was unanimous, Stanley saw the flicker of a smile dance across Judge Haynes lips.

'Do you find the defendant Stanley Thomas, guilty or not guilty of murder?'

'Guilty' replied the foreman of the jury.

For a moment the courtroom fell silent, the foreman of the jury sat down before Judge Haynes had the chance to tell him too.

The silence was broken by a single cheer coming from one section of the courtroom, that cheer battled with jeers and shouts of 'cunt' from another.

The sobbing of Stan's wife Hannah eventually drowned them all out. The tears she had held back finally bursting through. Stan knew her tears were for him, for herself and for their boys and the life that was being taken from them. It wasn't the first time he'd made her cry and it probably wouldn't be the last.

The Judged silenced the courtroom. He wasn't even bothering to hide his smile now. Reaching for the piece of black cloth, Stanley half expected him to stand up and start wanking from all the excitement. Instead, he placed the cloth on his head and said in his most solemn voice, 'You shall be taken to the place from whence you came, and from there be taken to a place of execution. You shall be hung by the neck until you are dead. Take him down.'

Judge Haynes: the man who would claim credit for getting rid of Stanley Thomas and breaking up the Merry Men... What a cunt.

Chapter 3

1953 – Nottingham Prison

Stanley Thomas lay on his bed. He knew it was happening today, he could hear movement in the next cell, them getting set up, making their preparations. Making sure it went without a hitch. From what he knew of Old Man Rope, everything would run as it should, he didn't make mistakes.

Every so often someone opened the window in his cell door to peer through at him. What did they expect to see? Him huddled in a corner in tears, scared to die? Angry Stanley, smashing up his cell swearing vengeance?

Fucking mugs.

Stanley Thomas lay on his bed, smoking, he'd quite have liked the radio on, but he supposed there was little chance of that.

Stanley Thomas looked like he didn't have a care in the world, he certainly didn't look like a man who had a date with Old Man Rope.

Chapter 4

1953 – Nottingham Prison

At nine am, the partition wall to his cell swung open and in walked a smartly dressed man, who handed him a glass said, 'Now then son, let's make this quick and with no trouble.'

Stanley's hands were bound, he was marched quickly to the gallows, the partition door swung shut.

Stanley Thomas wasn't a bad man; he just wasn't a very good one.

The Fixer

1953

The Fixer blended in with the crowd outside the prison. They'd been there since the previous evening, stood in amongst the huge mass of people who had gathered, some holding placards proclaiming Stanley's innocence, others holding boards saying they were glad he was being hanged.

There was singing, chanting, crying, swearing.

The Fixer stood in amongst them, just a nameless face.

As the clock on the prison wall edged nearer to 9am, the pro-Stanley crowd, held hands and started singing hymns, the Fixer noticed a few ladies crying loudly and proclaiming how much they'd miss "their Stan".

The Fixer doubted they'd even met him.

As the clock struck nine am, the crowd fell silent. The Fixer held their breath and closed their eyes.

Thirty minutes later a notice was pinned to the prison gates proclaiming that Stanley Thomas had been hung by the neck until he was dead. Some of the crowd cheered, others cried. Putting up their hood and sticking their hands in their pockets, The Fixer walked off, just a faceless person in the crowd going about their business.

Chapter 5

1988 – Television Centre, London.

Henry Mason straightened his tie, patted his greying hair down and rubbed his beard, smiling at his reflection in the mirror. The new glasses he'd bought really suited the shape of his face, his wife Maisy had been right, but then she always was!

He smoothed out the lines of his brand-new suit. He never could resist the cut of a good suit. Maisy had said it was silly spending so much money on a suit, but Henry had ignored her; with all this press coverage, he had to look the part.

At sixty-three, Henry wasn't by any means an old man. In fact, one of the journalists who'd interviewed him had described him as a 'silver fox' and he'd noticed that women had started to be nicer to him. Some even flirty. It made him laugh. He knew it made Maisy uncomfortable seeing women flirt with him, but as he kept telling her, not many women would understand his past and even less women would be happy about him going on every TV show in the UK to talk about it!

The memoirs had been her idea. When he'd retired from his job as Governor of Nottingham Prison, she'd been worried he'd get bored. She knew better than anyone that pottering in the garden growing prize lettuces wasn't going to cut it for Henry Mason!

Initially he thought they'd just be the ramblings of an old prison officer, who'd started his career as an assistant hangman, following in the footsteps of his father. Jerry Mason had been Chief Executioner between 1930 and 1953. He'd earned the nickname Old Man Rope and had been the best in the business. When Henry had shown no signs of doing anything useful with his life, Jerry had suggested he follow in his footsteps and those of his grandfather. It wasn't so much of a suggestion, more of an instruction! Henry had been reluctant at first, but he'd soon changed his mind when he realised it was good money for very little work.

After hanging had been abolished, he'd started work as a prison guard, but had very quickly risen through the ranks and found himself back at Nottingham Prison, only this time as the Governor.

The book had gone ended up being more about his time as an executioner than anything else; people couldn't get enough of his first-hand encounters with some of the UK's most notorious criminals.

Adam Belvedere, or "the Sparkle Killer"; Stewart Wilson and Ruth Carson. They'd all met their fates on the gallows. And then there'd been those like Daniel Parkes. Parkes was still one of the most hated men in Britain, Henry thought he must be in his 70's by now, with no hope of ever getting out of prison. Parkes had got a life stretch for killing two 10-year-old girls. The story had dominated the papers for months and Parliament had been lobbied to bring back the death penalty. He'd taken a beating every day of his sentence and Henry had made sure his officers had let it happen.

Then there'd been the Merry Men. Everyone, but Sidney Longshaw had passed through his nick at some point, although some had enjoyed shorter stays than others.

It was his connection to the Merry Men that had sent the publishers into a frenzy: any mention of them and the media still went crazy. It had been thirty-five years since their leader Stanley Thomas had been executed, but yet another film was coming out about them.

Some big Hollywood actor, who'd never have even heard of Mansfield – let alone be able to do the accent, would once again try and portray Stanley as a real-life Robin Hood and his boys as actual Merry Men, who robbed from the rich and gave to the poor!

The Hollywood versions never came close to depicting the real Stanley.

The phone call from the publisher to invite him for a chat about the book had come as a complete shock to Henry. Not many people knew about his real past, he'd always kept it from his friends and his children. By the time his kids Philip and Anna had been born, hanging had been abolished and he'd been working as the Governor of Nottingham Prison, so hadn't seen the point in telling them.

Before he knew it, the book was being published and he'd had to explain to his kids about his past life and that of their granddad.

Now, here he was stood in a suit, waiting to be interviewed by some more morning TV presenters, who'd press him for the salacious details about Stanley's death and then get him to comment on whether the death penalty should be bought back, before they flicked to a feature about how to wear floral.

It wasn't having to tell his children he minded. Once they'd got over their shock, they'd actually enjoyed the book. He didn't even mind being tagged 'The Handsome Hangman' by one newspaper. It was quite flattering for someone in his sixties. He was even a little bit tempted by the offers to have a TV series made about his life.

He just couldn't stand answering any more inane questions!

Chapter 6

1988 – Television Centre, London.

'So, Henry, when did you first want to become an executioner?" The male TV presenter with his shoe polish black hair learned forward as if to add weight to his question.

'Well, Russell, my dad, Jerry was Chief Executioner from 1930. No one outside me and my mum knew what he did. To everyone else he was landlord of The Wagon and Horses in Kirkby-in-Ashfield. When I got older and needed a job, he suggested I follow in his footsteps, it was a career that ran in the family, my grandad and great grandad had both done it, plus it was good money."

The female presenter, Caroline, took over now, giving him what she clearly thought was an engaging smile. 'Hardly a traditional Saturday job Henry?' She turned to her male co-host and giggled. He reciprocated the laugh and then in a well-rehearsed move they turned to Henry and waited for him to join in with the implied hilarity.

Henry was bemused. If there'd ever been a case for bringing back capital punishment, these two were it.

He lent back on the pastel green sofa and folded his arms; Caroline's question didn't really warrant a response.

The female presenter obviously sensed that Henry wasn't going to respond to her "Saturday job" comment. She shifted uncomfortably in her chair, someone was clearly yelling in her ear to shut up and move on, so she ploughed on with another line of questioning.

'The first execution you were a part of was that of notorious gangster Stanley Thomas. Can you talk me through the morning of his death?'

Henry had been asked this question so many times now he could pretty much roll off a stock answer. The nervous producer, however, had warned him not to go into too many graphic details: 'Sometimes we have poorly kiddies, who are off school ill watching. We don't want to give them nightmares, do we?'

Henry took a deep breath. "It was like the morning of any other execution really, except for the huge crowd that had gathered outside the prison, some of them had been there for days. They were holding banners and placards, some in support of Stan, some not, but apart from that, it went just as I was told it would. Dad and I had prepared the execution suite the day before, the drop had been worked out and everyone who needed to be there was ready and in place. The only thing that would have been different for some people was me being there.

'The fact it was Stanley made no difference. The aim was to make things as quick and as painless as possible. Everybody, no matter what they'd done, deserved respect and dignity in death, my dad taught me that'

Russell, the male presenter with the very black hair took over the questioning next. Henry had to remind himself not to get transfixed by his and Caroline's hair colour. It was like the ITV hairdresser had done a deal on black hair dye.

'Stanley was and still is quite the celebrity. Do you remember the moment you first came face to face with him?'

'I never viewed Stanley as a celebrity, he was a criminal, who'd been sentenced to die by the courts because of the crime he'd committed. My dealings with him were strictly professional. I assisted the hangman with his duties.'

Henry knew what they wanted him to say. They wanted stories of Stanley swearing at them all, promising to haunt them, trying to make a run for it, his gang turning up to bust him out of prison, being the rebel till the very end. It hadn't been like that at all.

It had all been very quick and gone to plan. To Stan it was, what it was – an adventure.

Henry was dragged away from his thoughts by the female presenter pushing him for details of Stanley's last words.

Henry had to stop himself from smiling, Stanley's last words had always made him laugh. As the door to the cell had been pulled back, Old Man Rope had said, 'Now then son, let's make this quick and with no trouble.'

Stanley had simply stood up, looked Henry directly in the eye, saluted Old Man Rope and said, 'Alright fuckers, let's do this.'

He'd then said, "Till our next merry meeting" and then that was that – Stanley was no more.

The version Henry told during interviews had to be slightly edited.

At the end of the interview, he shook Russell and Caroline's hands and thanked them as they told him his insight had been 'fascinating' and then moved on to a feature about how to wear a shell suit with a pair of heels.

The Fixer

1988

Morning TV wasn't The Fixer's normal choice of TV viewing, but they were interested in what Henry Mason had to say for himself. It had irritated The Fixer greatly that Stanley wouldn't stay dead. They had long since accepted that a documentary or a film about Stanley reared its head every few years, but this was taking the piss.

The Fixer clicked off the TV. Till our next merry meeting Henry Mason!

Chapter 7

1988 – St Pancras Train Station, London

Out of all the TV interviews, he'd done, Henry had hated that one the most. Daytime TV made it difficult to talk about what had really happened the day of the Stanley Thomas' execution and idiot TV presenters made it even harder!

Henry decided to grab a beer before going home. Maisy wouldn't mind, he'd phone her.

Finding the nearest phone box, just punching in his home number made him feel calmer.

'Alright duck, it's me.'

'How did it go? They didn't seem to know their arses from their elbows.'

Henry smiled; his wife was very to the point. 'It was OK, just not a lot you can say on daytime TV. I'm going to nip for a pint, so I'll get the two o'clock train home.'

'Alright love. Oh, there's a parcel arrived for you. I've left it in your office.'

'Thanks. Love you.'

'Love you.'

Henry hung up and wandered into the pub nearest the train station. Ordering a pint of mild, he settled himself in a booth. As he took a sip of his pint and the malty liquid slid down his throat, he pushed his glasses onto the top of his head, closed his eyes and leaned back against his chair. He could feel himself start to slowly relax.

Sometimes, Henry wished he'd never written the book, it was only meant to be a way of him trying to get out of his head some of the things he'd seen and done. He thought if he wrote it all down, everything could live on in the pages of a notebook and not in his head, but now he was having to talk about it day in day out with everyone wanting to know every single detail about Stanley.

Occasionally one of the other executions he'd been involved with got a mention; they were passing thoughts to some people, but to Henry, they were etched into his soul.

Aaron Belvedere had met his fate in 1957. The press had dubbed him "the Sparkle Killer". He'd been a nightclub host, who'd worked in a gay club in the West End. Belvedere had been twenty-three at the time of his death, six foot two, ginger and physically very fit. He'd been convicted of luring older gay men back to his flat, torturing them over the course of a week before killing them and having sex with whatever was left. A nasty piece of work if ever Henry had met one. On the gallows, Aaron had pontificated and proclaimed his innocence, wailing about miscarriages of justice and a corrupt police force and how he was being persecuted simply because he was gay. If he was honest, Henry had been quite relieved when he'd pulled the lever and shut him up for good!

Stewart Wilson was a man he'd executed in 1961. Stewart had been convicted of the murder of his wife and children and had shown no remorse. The press had dubbed him "The Family Man".

Wilson had woken up one day decided he no longer wanted to be a husband or a father and spent the next three months plotting his family's deaths. He went out organised himself a new passport, somewhere else to live and set up a new bank account. He then purchased a gun and some petrol. Once everything was in place he'd returned home, told his family he was leaving, shot his two children in front of his wife, shot his wife and then burned his house down.

The police had tracked him down living the "high life" in Southend on Sea. He'd pleaded guilty and, on the gallows, his last words had been, 'Well that didn't go to plan, I was meant to be in Spain by now.'

Finally, there was Ruth Carson, she was executed in 1962 and her death had always bothered Henry. Ruth had been convicted of killing her boyfriend, in what had been deemed a crime of passion. Throughout her trial, she'd been painted as a scarlet woman, who'd been fast and loose with her morals, sleeping with anyone who gave either the time of day or money. Her fate had been sealed as soon as the jurors had seen her; there was no way a jury was going to find an attractive woman with peroxide blonde hair, red lipstick and tight-fitting clothing innocent.

The truth for Henry was actually far more harrowing.

Yes, Ruth had been those things, but she was a woman who'd been horrifically abused over the years, both physically and sexually by, pretty much everyone she'd ever met. Starting with her dad, being continued by her stepfather and the many 'uncles' her mum had introduced into her life and finally ending with her own string of lovers. She'd been pimped out by her mum from the age of fourteen and undergone numerous backstreet abortions. By the time she murdered Lance Kay, she carried scars and wounds so deep that they lacerated her soul and being hanged had been a blessed relief for her.

Henry had always felt that if she'd committed the crime in more modern times, she'd never have been convicted. Instead, she would have received help and ended up a modern-day heroine.

Ruth hadn't made any bold statements on the gallows; she'd simply thanked Henry for his kindness.

If hanging hadn't been abolished a year later, Henry would have quit anyway.

And yet, all anyone cared about was Stanley... It always came back to bloody Stanley.

Chapter 8

1988 – Berry Hill, Mansfield.

Henry put his key in the front door, took a deep breath and opened it. 'I'm home' he shouted.

'In the kitchen,' came Maisy's reply.

Henry hung his coat on the peg, kicked his shoes off and headed to the kitchen.

Maisy was sat at the table, surrounded by recipe books and with the radio on in the background; it was playing a pop song about heaven being a place on earth. Maisy was tapping her foot along in time with the music as she thumbed through the books, making notes as she went.

Henry walked over to the table and planted a kiss on her cheek. 'Alright love? What are you planning?'

She smiled up at him. 'We're having a dinner party to celebrate your success. I've invited a few friends over at the weekend, that OK?'

Henry nodded.

It wasn't alright if he were honest, he'd have to spend yet more time satisfying the ghoulish curiosity of people who wanted to know all about his memoirs and his former life. Being friends, they'd think they could get away with asking him more personal questions, things such as:

QUESTION: 'Did you throw up the first time you killed someone?'

ANSWER: 'No and I didn't kill someone, I assisted in their lawful execution.'

QUESTION: 'Was Stanley really scared? Could you see it in his eyes?'

ANSWER: 'He really didn't seem bothered.'

QUESTION: 'Were you scared of reprisals from his gang the Merry Men?'

ANSWER: 'No.'

Then there'd be questions about who cried the most on the gallows, who had the funniest last words, who shit themselves and then who he'd wish he'd executed.

In all honesty, he'd rather spend his Saturdays watching Mansfield Town play and then coming home, putting his feet up in front of the TV, drinking a pint of Mansfield and falling asleep in front of the telly.

But he smiled at his wife and said he was looking forward to it.

'Did you say a parcel had come for me?'

'Oh yes, I put it in your office, it came recorded delivery.'

'Thanks, it's probably something from the publishers, they said they were sending me more copies of the book to sign. Then joys of being a famous writer.' He could hear Maisy giggling as he headed to his office.

This room was his sanctuary, it always had been the place he'd retreat to when his kids Philip and Anna had been little, and he'd needed some peace, the place he still came to when his grandchildren Toby and Rebecca came over and he got fed up of playing with Pound Puppies and Sylvanian Families and refereeing fights over Rubik's Cubes.

It was the place he shut himself away when he wanted to listen to football commentary as his beloved Mansfield Town played or watch some old John Wayne film.

It was the place where he'd written his memoirs, Derek Jameson on Radio 2, a pot of coffee on the go, a pack of biscuits on his desk. It all seemed a long way from where he was now.

It was the place that hid his secrets.

Wandering over to his desk, he sat in his big leather chair and examined the parcel. It didn't have any labels that suggested it was from his publisher, in fact it had a Nottingham postmark. Taking a pair of scissors, he cut along the tape.

Henry cut away the bubble wrap that encased it as it became clear what the item was. He dropped it on the desk, the item rocking back and forth, its gruesome expression mocking his fear.

It was a death mask.

Revealing that whoever the face belonged to had suffered intolerable horrors in their final moments on earth, their face contorted in equal measures of pain and terror.

Henry noticed a note had fallen out onto the desk. It read...

"Till our next merry meeting."

Chapter 9

1952 – Mansfield.

"I don't give a fuck, what you think, I didn't ask you to fucking think!" Stanley stood up from his chair and slammed his fist on the desk. "When I tell you to fucking do something, you fucking do it! Now get back out there and tell that cunt I want his money and I want it now!"

Sidney "Babyface" Longshaw scuttled back out the room, at fourteen he was the youngest member of the Merry Men. He had the lanky, skinniness of a youth that hadn't yet grown into his limbs, but when he did, he was going to be devastatingly handsome, big baby blue eyes, blond hair and a smile that somehow managed to be menacing and endearing all at the same time.

Stanley had taken Sidney under his wing for several reasons; he was bright, he was devious, and he was his brother-in-law. Hannah wasn't happy about Stanley's enthusiasm for her little brother or the fact he apparently had what it took to join the Merry Men. Hannah would have far rather he'd have studied hard at school, played football with his mates and then gone to work down the pit like their dad and every other honest man in Mansfield.

But Sidney Longshaw dreamed a different dream. From the moment his sister had first started dating Stan, Sidney had idolized him. Stan was feared and respected by everyone who knew him, he wore the sharpest suits and had the prettiest girls on his arm. Sidney's dad was a nice man, but nothing remarkable, he could walk into a room, and it could take you twenty minutes to notice him. Sidney wanted far more out of life than working down the pit and a pint of Mansfield on a Friday night and if that meant demanding money with menaces and beating people up, then that's what he'd do. The Longshaws had long since washed their hands of him. 'Boys will be boys,' his mum would mutter as soon as Hannah broached the subject, his dad would simply say, 'Speak to your mother,' and go back to reading his paper.

Today, Sidney, or Babyface as he was more commonly known had mucked up royally. He was meant to collect some money from a shop keeper called Mr. Gatsby who had fed him a line about needing to pay for some treatment for his mum. Normally this sort of line would have fallen on Babyface's deaf ears, but for some reason on this day he'd taken notice and said Mr. Gatsby could have an extra week.

He might have got away with it, had Stanley not seen Mr. Gatsby in the bookies placing a large bet and bragging how he'd told the Merry Men where to stick their threats.

Babyface and Mad Larry Yates were on their way to pay Mr. Gatsby a little visit.

'Get in the car Babyface, we ain't all dancing to your fucking tune,' snarled Larry.

Babyface got in the car and put his seatbelt on, which almost seemed a fruitless exercise as no seatbelt could protect him from Mad Larry if he decided to turn on him.

'If he doesn't pay, then we are just going to belt him.'

Babyface nodded, he knew better than to try and suggest something else. He also knew that the threat of a beating from Mad Larry was normally enough to make even the hardest man pay up. He hoped Mr. Gatsby wasn't going to be stupid.

Mad Larry Yates may only have been five foot five, but anyone who decided to mock his height, soon learned the hard way that, that was a mistake. Stanley had first found Larry when he'd been working as a bare-knuckle fighter. Mad Larry appeared to never feel pain and would continue beating his opponent long after they'd surrendered.

Larry had the charm of a bulldog that had been abandoned by his owner on the street and left to fend for himself. He was from one of the only black families in Nottingham and life hadn't been easy for them. They'd moved from Jamaica to St Anns with the belief that life would be easier for them. Larry's Dad, Burgess, or Pappa B as he was known, was a hardworking god-fearing man as was his wife Zekia, Mama Z. They'd moved to Nottingham and opened a shop, where they were popular with the local community and attended church every week. But life wasn't always easy for them and although Burgess and Zekia would ignore the stares as they walked into a room full of white people or pretend not to see the customer who walked into their shop, realise it was run by black people and then walk out, their son was less forgiving.

As a result, from a young age, Larry had been in countless fights and had a nose that sat at a jaunty angle on his face from all the times it had been broken. He also had a scar that ran the entire left side of his face and a mop of brown curly afro hair. When he relaxed, his big brown eyes would sparkle and if you were ever lucky enough to hear Mad Larry Yates laugh, then his big bellowing guffaw was something special to behold.

Today, there was bugger all chance of Sidney getting a laugh out of Larry.

Larry was in charge of dishing out the more "intricate" of the Merry Men's punishments and would almost relish the opportunity to come up with something that would inflict even more fear and pain on his victims. If Mad Larry came knocking, you were generally fucked.

Mad Larry stopped the car outside the Gatsby shop, reaching into the glovebox he took out two pairs of knuckle dusters and handed one to Babyface.

'Here, put these on and don't be afraid to beat the fucker if he needs it.'

Babyface put them on and got out the car.

Mr. Gatsby looked shocked as the door to his shop swung open and he realized what was about to happen. The colour drained from his face and Babyface noticed that he gripped the counter to steady himself.

'Now then Mr. Gatsby, you and I need a little chat. It has come to our attention that you've been shouting your mouth off whilst putting a bet on. It will come as no surprise to you, to find out that Mr. Thomas is not happy about the situation, isn't that right Babyface?'

'That's right Larry, Mr. Thomas finds it disrespectful.'

'And how, Babyface, does Mr. Thomas like people who disrespect him dealing with?'

'Well, Larry, he's not an unreasonable man, so I'm sure if Mr. Gatsby were to pay what he owes and maybe a little something else as a mark of his respect, then the matter will be considered closed.'

Gatsby went pale, "How much are we talking?'

'Ten pounds should set things straight.'

'I'mmmmm nnnnnot sure I can get that right now,' Gatsby stammered.

Larry took his hand out of his pocket and started to look at the knuckle duster that adorned it, the brilliant gold glinting against the blackness of his skin. 'Oh dear Mr. Gatsby, then we may have a problem.'

Gatsby frantically opened the till and started counting out notes and loose change. 'Here take this and I'll see what's in the safe out back.'

'Now that's more like it.' Babyface opened the door to the back. 'After you, Mr. Gatsby.'

Gatsby walked by him, Larry and Babyface following. Babyface could see the shopkeeper shaking as he started to move the dial on the safe. Eventually it swung open to reveal bundles of notes.

Larry pushed Gatsby out the way. 'Now then, what do we have here?' Taking out one of the bundles, he began to count. 'Lot of money in being a shopkeeper then Gatsby?' He put one of the bundles in his jacket pocket. 'That'll do Gatsby. Mr. Thomas, will be very pleased with the respect you've shown him.'

Gatsby let out the breath that he appeared to be holding in and followed Babyface and Larry back into the shop.

Larry turned. 'Mr. Gatsby, thank you for your co-operation, I shall report favourably back to Mr. Thomas, but if you ever fuck with us again, we won't be so reasonable.' And with that Larry punched Gatsby in the stomach. As he fell to the floor, Babyface started kicking the shopkeeper in the ribs.

They both laughed as Larry shouted over his shoulder. 'Just a little parting gift to remember us by.'

Chapter 10

1952 – Mansfield.

Mad Larry and Babyface walked into the room where Stanley was sitting with the rest of the Merry Men, Billy Potter and Richard "Dicky" Richards. The table was littered with cups and ashtrays, there was a fug in the air.

'Get it?'

'Yes, Stan, we got it and then some, let's say Gatsby got his too.' Larry laughed at his own joke, his bellowing rumble filling in the room. Taking it as sign he was forgiven, Babyface joined in too. Larry threw the bundle of notes down on the table.

'This all come from Gatsby?'

'Yes, it would appear our friendly shopkeeper has a bit of a goldmine on his hands.'

'Right, Babyface, next time you collect tell him his insurance went up.'

Babyface nodded and took a seat at the table next to Billy.

Babyface was a bit in awe of Billy Potter. Billy and Stanley had been friends since school and were both tall and imposing, but that's where their similarities ended. Stanley was blond haired with blue eyes and a somehow managed to smile at you in a way that made you want to go to the wall for him, but also told you he could devastate your life in a manner of ways you couldn't even imagine. Billy had a mop of ginger curly hair, laughing green eyes and a face full of freckles. Whereas Stanley was all fire and ice, Billy was calm and reasoned, no less ruthless, but he ruled with his brains, not his brawn.

Billy was the one who would talk Stanley off the ledge when he needed it, and to whom Stanley would listen. Babyface was keen to learn from him, he wanted to be as important to Stanley as Billy was. He daydreamed about the day Stan put his arms around his shoulders and said, 'Now then son, I'm stepping back from the business and there's no-one but you that I trust to take over the running of it.'

Then he, Sidney Longshaw would be the most revered man in Mansfield, nah, Nottinghamshire, Sidney wanted an empire, he'd expand the Merry Men.

Billy took a drag of his cigarette. 'Stan, now Gatsby's sorted and everyone on Ladybrook is in line, we need to look at dealing with the other matter.'

'Dorrell?'

'Yes Dorrell'

"He's getting a bit gobby for my liking, pay him a visit, explain our terms of business and make sure he knows they're non-negotiable. I won't have him and his whores thinking they're in charge. Get yourself to the brothel on George Street.'

'Want me to take Larry and Dicky?'

'Nah, take Dicky & Babyface.'

Babyface looked up from the sofa where he'd been drinking a cup of tea. 'Me, boss?'

'Yes, you, time you saw a bit more action.'

Dicky Richards got to his feet and straightened his jacket. Standing at six foot six, with jet black hair and eyes to match, he'd been described him as a wicked version of Cary Grant. Dicky's presence was very often all people needed to see. He was, however, the epitome of the old saying, "Derbyshire born, and Derbyshire bred, strong in't arm and thick in't head." Along with Mad Larry, he was the muscle of the Merry Men, but whereas Larry was known for carrying out intricate and deviant forms of torture, Dicky was known for his ability to break a man's arm with a gentle touch and generally giving them a good old-fashioned beating.

Dicky had been in and out of prison his whole life, normally for some form of GBH, he'd known Stanley and Billy for years, having met them during various stays at Her Majesty's pleasure.

Billy, Dicky and Babyface headed out.

The Fixer

1988

The Fixer watched as Henry Mason opened the door to his guests, kissing the women on the cheek, pumping the men's hands up and down, welcoming them into his home. No doubt he'd spend the evening regaling them with his stories of prison life and executions... And of Stanley.

As The Fixer drove off, all they said out loud was, 'Henry Mason, you really are a very stupid man.'

Chapter 11

1988 – Berry Hill, Mansfield.

'I'll get it.' Henry headed to the door ready to welcome the guests he didn't really want to be spending his Saturday night with, but it was important to Maisy.

'Frank, Sheila, Sue, Lou how lovely to see you, come in.'

Henry welcomed his guests with the utmost grace, kissing cheeks and shaking hands, taking their coats and bottles of wine they'd bought; these were his friends, they were pleased for his success and wanted to celebrate.

Henry decided he would stop being miserable and would enjoy himself tonight. After all, Maisy had gone to a lot of trouble and the evening would be all about him and his success. He'd relax and allow his friends to praise and bask in his glory. He took his guests drinks orders and headed into the kitchen to fix them.

He wandered back into the lounge, to find Maisy hugging his guests. 'Dinner's nearly ready, so in the meantime make yourselves comfy and enjoy your drinks.'

Lou raised his glass. 'To your success, my friend, we're all so bloody proud of you! I was in the Boy Pub the other night and you're all anyone in the pub could talk about Mr. TV star. I swear they're going to re-name it "The Hangman' after you.'

Everyone laughed as Henry knocked his glass against his friend's, smiled and tried to look modest.

Lou continued, 'But tell me the truth were those TV presenters really as bloody useless as they looked?'

Henry laughed, Lou had been his friend for many years, and he'd never been one to beat about the bush. 'Worse!'

They all laughed, and Maisy ushered them all into the dining room for dinner.

The laughter and conversation continued over dinner and Henry was pleased that Maisy had invited their guests round. But soon conversation turned back to Henry's book.

'I see that Dicky Richards was on a TV show the other night talking about the Merry Men and Stanley. Did you meet him, Henry?', asked Sue.

'Once or twice, he was in Nottingham Prison when I was Governor, thick as pig shit, and violent. I'm surprised he's managed to string enough words together to do after dinner speaking.'

'It was quite interesting what he was saying, he made Stanley out to be a hero. I just remember him beating everyone up when we were at school together. Scared the shit out of me. I had to sit next to him once in assembly and he thought it was funny to smack me in the balls during the Lord's Prayer, I got a weeks' detention for that.'

They'd all heard Lou's 'smacked in the balls by a gangster' story a hundred times, but they made their obligatory sympathetic noises.

Henry rolled his eyes and took a slug of wine. 'Hmmm, all about perspective I think.'

Frank joined in. 'Doesn't that Billy still run that pub in Kirkby?'

'The Duke? His daughter's in charge now." added Frank's wife Sheila. 'They do talks there about the Merry Men, I think Mad Larry and that other one, the good-looking one are doing a talk there soon.'

Henry could feel his resolve to have a good time disappearing.

'You mean Sidney "Babyface" Longshaw?' Henry made quotation marks as he said Babyface.

'Oohh that's him, there's something dangerously handsome about him.'

'We should all go.' said Frank.

Henry glanced across the table at Maisy, who mouthed the word "sorry" at him. Doing what Maisy always did, she stepped in to sort out the situation. 'I don't think it would be right for Henry to go to something like that, so we probably wouldn't go.'

'Not right?' asked Lou.

'Well yes, Henry was one of the executioners who was there at their friend's death and then he was Governor of Nottingham Prison where most of them served time at one point or another.'

'But that's all water under the bridge surely?' asked Frank.

'I'm not sure stuff like that ever will be, it'll hardly be a pleasant reunion, remember the time I put you in solitary for sticking that inmate? Ooohh how we laughed, good times and high fives all round. I don't think so!' Henry got up and started to clear away the plates.

Sometimes it was easier when people just wanted to hear stories about Stanley and not try and organise a reunion with his nearest and dearest.

Chapter 12

1988 – Berry Hill, Mansfield.

'I'm so sorry.' Maisy put her arms around her husband. 'I didn't realise how bad they'd be or stupid! Suggesting we go along to a talk by Dicky and Sidney Longshaw! Can you forgive me?'

Henry planted a kiss on the top of his wife's head. 'Nothing to forgive.'

'I'm going to bed. You coming?'

'I think I'm going to have a brandy and watch a bit of TV, that OK?'

'Course, night, love you.'

'Love you.'

Henry went into the kitchen and poured himself a large brandy. He took it in his study and opened his desk drawer, removing a piece of paper. He put his feet on the desk and rubbed the scar just below his knee that was aching tonight, and he lent back in his chair.

Ever since the death mask had arrived earlier in the week, he'd read and re-read this note over and over again.

"Till our next merry meeting"

Stanley's last words.

The only people that knew about those words were those in the room that day.

Henry turned the bit of paper over in his fingers, seeing if there was anything hidden away, any clue as to who'd sent it, but there was nothing.

Henry got up and crossed to the cupboard where he'd hidden the death mask so Maisy wouldn't see it.

He carefully took it out it's wrapping, studying the look of pain on the man's face, he traced the contours. It was as if every stroke of the mask revealed the torture this man had suffered in his final hours, the moments before the wax filled his nostrils and hardened in his throat. The relief he must have felt as his final breath left his body, and he knew his suffering was finally over.

Henry had done some research on death masks, they were normally made after someone had died, so they could be used to create a portrait or an effigy. He also knew they'd been very popular with Stanley and his gang the Merry Men. Rumours had always persisted that every time they'd killed someone a death mask had been made of their victim's face as they took their final breaths.

These had never been found anywhere, but they lived on as part of the many myths that still surrounded Stanley and his boys.

Henry studied the face. It was hard to tell from a death mask how old someone was, or even when it was made. Henry ran his finger over the curve of the victim's face.

Nothing.

Not one clue.

Henry turned it over, running his finger around the inside. He tried to ignore the thought that the last time someone spent this long touching this side of the mask it would have been the victim, condemned to take their final breath in a waxy mask. Henry lifted the mask up to his own face and held it there, breathing in and out slowly. The mask had held its waxy smell and there was still a faint lingering of the iron of blood.

Henry moved it away from his face, as he did, he noticed the light caught something on the bottom of the mask, the glow of his desk lamp betraying the masks secret.

The initials W. D.

'Dorell!' exclaimed Henry, as the mask dropped to the desk it smashed into a thousand pieces.

Chapter 13

1952 – George Street Brothel, Mansfield.

Walter Dorrell was one of life's losers, only he didn't realise it.

In Walter's head he was The Man: he was as handsome as James Dean, had the brawn of Marlon Brando and the charisma of Frank Sinatra.

He didn't.

Walter Dorrell was a loser; he'd been born a loser and would die a loser. He had a scrawny frame of five foot seven, mousy brown hair, pale green eyes and sticking out teeth. Everything about him was unmemorable.

Walter was the only son of John and Betty Dorrell, he was a dustman, she was a cleaner, good, decent people.

The Dorrells also had a daughter, Pearl. Pearl was the opposite of Walter, she was attractive, with long brown hair, blue eyes and a slim, but strong physique. At five foot eight, Pearl turned heads, she was smart. She was quite remarkable.

The Dorrells died within two weeks of each other. John was knocked over and it was said Betty died of stress cardiomyopathy. Although others say her broken heart was aided by an overdose of tablets and gin.

Walter was left in charge of his sister Pearl, who at the time of her parents' death was just sixteen years old.

Walter was twenty-five and despite many attempts to impress Stanley and the rest of the Merry Men, he was generally considered an idiot. He'd tried everything to establish himself as Mansfield's number one not-to-be-messed with gangster. He'd tried demanding money with menaces but had come unstuck when he'd picked on the wrong group of OAPs and had found himself with a broken arm and a black eye after a group of old ladies had given him a beating. He'd tried drug dealing but had lost the drugs on the way to do a major deal. And then he'd tried breaking and entering but found that was too much like hard work and he couldn't work out how you could make a quick getaway if you had a to carry a toolbox and a ladder to commit the crime.

After each attempt, Stan and the Merry Man would laugh in his face and speculate about the next thing he'd try.

Walter decided it was time to make Stanley and his boys come to him. Quite literally. Walter started to run a group of girls, who he claimed could cater for any man's needs. Once his parents died and he was left in sole charge of Pearl, he added her to his "girls" and turned the family home into a brothel.

Stanley tolerated the George Street brothel, but only on two counts: Firstly, Walter paid Stanley for the privilege of operating his business, and, secondly, Stanley and the Merry Men could pop in and have their pick of the girls whenever they wanted.

Walter obliged with Stanley's requests, but as demand for his girls grew and he added some boys to cater for other needs, including his own, he believed Stanley owed him respect. The Brothel was highly successful, and Walter wore the finest shoes in the whole of Nottinghamshire; he travelled to Bond Street in London to have them specially made.

Why wasn't Stanley begging him to be in the Merry Men? Asking him for advice on how to keep Mansfield in order? Paying him money? Asking who his tailor was? Begging him to reveal who made his shoes? Respecting the fact that he ran Mansfield and not the other way around?

Walter thought it was time things changed.

Chapter 14

1952 – George Street Brothel, Mansfield.

Pearl Dorrell sat at the table of the George Street Brothel, cupping her mug of tea with both hands. Her brown hair tied up in pigtails, wearing a short, pleated skirt, a white unbuttoned blouse and her old school tie. Her stockings visible under the hem of her skirt.

Walter wanted her to cater for those who wanted someone younger.

Pearl hated her brother; he was an idiot. Giving it the big 'I am' everywhere he went, pretending he was a gangster, making her dress up in this shit and deal with the sorry excuses for men that came into the brothel.

'Want a biscuit?' May, one of the other girls offered her the packet.

'Nah, I best not, my shithead of a brother will have a fit if he catches me eating. Says I've got to stay slim for the punters, otherwise I'll start to look old.'

May took a biscuit and dunked it in her tea. May was a petite brunette, in her twenties with long curly hair. She was one of the girls who lived in the house. She said very little about her past, but Pearl knew from her accent that she was originally from London and had moved up to Mansfield with a bloke. That had gone wrong and somehow, she'd met up with Walter who'd convinced her that he was the answer to all her troubles. He offered her a room, food, friendship and then promptly put her on the game.

May seemed to attract the older men. She never moaned about anything, but was pleasant to the other girls, she never even slagged Walter off, which was unheard of in the George Street Brothel.

Pearl liked her.

They heard steps coming down the stairs and then the sexy voice of Cheryl purring at her client, 'Oh no, sugar, the pleasure was all mine, I'll see you really soon.'

With that, the door closed, and Cheryl stormed into the kitchen wearing thigh length boots and a silk robe. She switched the kettle on.

'Need a top up?'

Pearl and May shook their heads.

'God, I hate that man, slimy bastard and a real kinky fucker too.' Cheryl shoved a teabag into a mug as she spoke, she was virtually spitting out the words.

Cheryl was like this every time she had a punter. She appeared to hate everyone and everything. Pearl took the bait. 'Which bloke was that Chez?'

'That politician man, the old guy, grey hair, big stomach, bulging eyes.'

'Oh him, does he still like a finger up his bum?'

'And the rest!' Cheryl sat down at the table, and May offered her a biscuit.

'I don't think I've had the pleasure.' said Pearl.

Cheryl replied through a mouth full of biscuit. 'You're not missing anything. I don't think your brother pays me enough to deal with perverts like him. Why do I get him every time? May, can you do him next time?

'No chance, I'm not his type apparently; my hands are too little, he couldn't feel my finger up his bum.'

'He's moved on from fingers let me tell you. Speaking of which I best go tidy my room and change the sheets. I've got another punter in an hour.' Cheryl took her tea and headed back upstairs.

Pearl got up to wash her mug. 'Is it just the three of us in?'

'No, Geraldine and Shirley are having a threesome with Randy Roy, apparently your brother didn't have enough cash to pay him so he's taking his payment in other ways. Gerard and Dennis have gone shopping, they're helping your brother organise tomorrow night's party.'

'Walter never has any cash; I think he spends it all on those poncey shoes of his. He thinks they're his signature. Little does he know they make him a signature twat.'

May put her fingers to her lips in a shushing motion and lowered her voice. 'Malcolm the Mug is outside, you know how he reports back to Walter on everything.'

Malcolm the Mug was the George Street Brothel's 'security guard'. He idolized Walter and was mean and spiteful. He reported back to Walter on everything, especially if it was something that might get one of the girls a beating. If it was Pearl who got the beating, then that was the best result.

Malcolm spent his time either sat outside the front door smoking, if the weather was nice, or inside the front door smoking if it was raining.

Pearl shrugged her shoulders. She was sick of Walter, sick of living in the George Street Brothel and sick of her life.

The door to the brothel opened and Malcolm popped his head round the kitchen door. 'Pearl, punter.'

Pearl smoothed down her skirt, undid another button and got ready for work.

Chapter 15

1952 – Mansfield Town Centre

Walter strolled through Mansfield Market Place, smoking. He had on a new pinstripe three-piece suit, his thinning mousy hair was slicked back, and his signature handmade black and red shoes were shining. He was the man! This was his manor and people should be showing him some respect.

As he walked towards The Boy pub to meet his friend Barry, a woman stopped to attend to a crying baby in a pram. She was standing right where Walter wanted to walk, a clear act of disrespect. As Walter approached, he pushed them out of his way and flicked his cigarette ash into the pram and pushed it out of his way, uttering the word 'slag' as he did so.

No-one got in Walter Dorrell's way.

Barry Fox was sat in a booth with two pints in front of him. He waved over to Walter as he walked in.

Walter nodded to the landlord behind the bar and walked over to sit with Barry.

'Cigarette.'

Barry dutifully put one in between Walter's lips and lit it. 'There you go boss.'

'Now, tell me, what's the latest?'

'Well, we're all set for the party tomorrow. Gerard and Dennis are sorting it out. Thought it best to get the poofters to decorate the room, they've got an eye for that sort of thing. The girls all know what they're to wear tomorrow and also that anything goes, no questions asked. Guest list is sorted. All on schedule boss.'

'Good, good, what about Stanley and the boys? Are they coming?'

'Not heard owt, they've not replied.'

'Rude bastards, that fucker better start treating me with respect or shit's about to get real for them! No-one disrespects Walter Dorrell.' Walter banged the table with his fist to emphasise his disgust and get people's attention.

No-one turned around.

'I know, boss. Word on the street is that there's rumblings on Ladybrook, Gatsby stopped paying his bill and Stan's lads gave him a kicking. Has anyone said anything to you about not paying?'

Walter watched as Barry shifted uncomfortably in his seat. Walter loved seeing the power he had over Barry. Barry had been working as a barman at The Boy pub when they'd first met. One day Walter had decided to invite him round to the George Street Brothel, Barry ended up having sex with one of the girls, but because he was so stupid, he didn't realise that she was a prostitute. Barry actually thought the girl liked him. Walter had laughed his head off when he'd told him that he now owed him money. Barry didn't have him, so Walter, very kindly said he could work off his debts by running a few errands.

That was 6 months ago, Barry had quit his job and was now working for Walter fulltime.

'No, Stanley's a pussy, he knows not to mess with me. It won't be long before he's paying me.'

Barry nodded and took a drink from his pint.

Chapter 16

1952 – George Street Brothel, Mansfield

Walter walked around the George Street Brothel making sure that everything was just as he wanted it, and everything met his high standards.

There were buckets full of chilled champagne, more in the fridge. Bottles of red wine lined the table in the kitchen, mixed in with cans of beer. There was plenty of food and Bing Crosby blared out from the record player.

Gerard and Dennis were putting the finishing touches to a cake. They were dressed ready to entertain, both wearing tight gold shorts and nothing else.

Geraldine and Shirley were putting out glasses. Geraldine was dressed in a black see-through baby doll nightie and red high heels. Shirley the good cop to Geraldine's bad, was wearing the same outfit, but in white. Walter knew that the vicar would definitely want a threesome.

Cheryl came storming into the kitchen, wearing thigh high boots and a corset and carrying a whip in her hand. Cheryl was the only one he was slightly scared of. He couldn't help but think she might beat him to death in his sleep. Still, she was a hit with the punters and the politician loved her.

May followed her in poor, sweet, stupid May. She'd been so easy to recruit to work for him and she never gave him a moments trouble. And she was a hit with the Governor. She was dressed in frilly pink knickers and a matching bra; a lacy pink dressing gown and fur high-heeled mules completed the look.

'Need me to do anything Walter?'

'Just check how Geraldine and Shirley are getting on. Where's Pearl?'

'I don't know, I think she's still getting ready.'

Walter stood at the bottom of the stairs and yelled, "Pearl, get your fucking arse down here now"

Sometimes his sister really took the piss. Just because they were related, she thought she could get away with murder. Once this party was done, he'd teach her a lesson. It would serve two purposes, one, it would remind Pearl who was boss, and two, it would also scare the others into realising they couldn't do what they wanted and that he was the man in charge.

He decided to make sure he was wearing his shiny black and red shoes as he kicked her.

Chapter 17

1952 – George Street Brothel, Mansfield.

Pearl lay on her bed. She could hear her brother screaming for her to come downstairs. She ignored him and continued her fantasy of Walter being brutally murdered. Pearl thought that with every passing day, it became more and more of a possibility. Walter was a sorry excuse for a human being, so someone was bound to want to do away with him, although if he didn't shut up, she'd murder him herself.

Pearl hated these parties that Walter threw. They were a monthly affair, where he invited the Great, and the Perverted of Nottinghamshire to come to the George Street Brothel and do whatever they wanted. They were charged a hefty fee to come along. They'd spend the afternoon fulfilling whatever perverted fantasy they wanted, all washed down with plenty of free booze and food.

Little did they know that as they got their kicks, Walter was compiling a list of their perversions, along with photos and documents that could be used to blackmail those that attended should he need to.

Pearl heard her brother screaming up the stairs, 'Pearl, get yourself down here now!'

Pearl and her murder fantasy duly obliged.

Chapter 18.

1952 – George Street Brothel, Mansfield.

'About fucking time!' Walter dragged his sister down the last couple of stairs. 'What have I said? When I shout you, you fucking run! Now, open more buttons, you've got to look like everyone's schoolgirl fantasy. You know the Doc and the Hon like them young.'

Pearl duly opened more buttons and blew a bubble with her bubblegum.

'Better, make sure you take that gum out when you suck them off, I don't want them moaning about sticky pubes. Gum in the bush is not easy to explain to the Mrs.'

Pearl took a seat on the sofa next to Cheryl. 'Another afternoon at the fun factory.'

Cheryl laughed sarcastically. 'Yeah, it's going to be a real hoot this afternoon, I can't wait to spend it sticking various items up that fat fucker's arse"

Pearl laughed. 'Well at least you won't spend it saying. 'Are you going to punish me again sir?' while some sweaty twat sticks his cock in your mouth and the other fucks you up the arse. Respectable members of the community my arse. Dirty, sadistic perverts the lot of them.'

Pearl and Cheryl laughed. Sometimes in her fantasy, it was Cheryl who beat Walter to death, using her whip to lacerate every last bit of skin he had and then finally putting the heel of her thigh high boot into his miserable throat.

Malcolm the Mug came into the room. 'Walter says stand by, people are starting to arrive.'

Cheryl got to her feet, cracked her whip. "Showtime."

As the guests started to arrive, Walter walked around the room, Lord of all he surveyed. Champagne was flowing, and the guests shovelled the food into their mouths as quickly as they could or allowed themselves to be fed by his boys and girls.

Pearl looked around the room. The usual suspects were there. The Sheriff, the Hon, The Gov, the Rev, the Doc and a couple of other faces. No Stanley though, this really wasn't his or his boys' scene, no way he'd turn up to this. Firstly, Stanley would know it was a trap and that Walter would be arranging to blackmail him; and secondly, Stanley thought Walter was a prat.

Pretty soon, the guests started to make a move to the girl or boy they wanted to play with, some headed straight for the bedrooms, others started off in full view of everyone.

Pearl could see the Gov with his hands down May's pants, the Rev was watching, one hand down his own pants, while the other shovelled sausage rolls into his face.

Gerard was kneeling in front of the settee sucking the cock of a man who Pearl had never seen before, while Dennis was sat next to him with the man was wanking him off.

Cheryl was screaming at the Politician as she marched him upstairs. There was a series of 'Yes mistress, no mistress,' mixed in with whip cracking. She winked at Pearl as she dragged him up the stairs with a dog lead.

Before long the Doc had made his way over to Pearl. Pearl forced herself to smile sweetly and gently leaned forward.

'Now then little girl, are you being good?' He ran his hand up her thigh and started clawing at the top of her legs so he could stuff his fingers inside her. His fingers were sticky and greasy from the food he'd been eating, and she could see beads of sweat forming on his top lip as the excitement started to gleam in his eyes. Pearl's skin started to crawl, and it took every ounce of strength she had not to spit in his face and strangle him with his tie.

Instead, she smiled and obligingly opened her legs. 'I'm not sure Sir, you know how hard – 'Pearl paused and twirled her pigtail with one hand and put her hand on the Doc's groin, ' – I try to be good, but sometimes I need someone to keep me on the straight and narrow.'

The Doc took her hand. 'Maybe we should go and have a chat.'

'Maybe we should.'

Pearl saw the Hon, who was on the other side of the room, notice the two of them move. Normally the Doc and the Hon insisted on a threesome.

'Should I ask the Hon if he wants to join us and dish out my punishment?'

The Doc nodded. 'Go and ask him.'

The Hon was sat the other side on the room wanking himself off whilst the Gov fingered May.

'Hon, do you want to join me and the Doc?'

The Hon nodded. Pearl very often wondered what the criminals who stood before him would think if they could see him, glass of champagne in one hand, his cock in the other. 'Not guilty your Hon!'

Pearl made her way upstairs with them.

At least whilst she was being fucked, she could amuse herself with her Walter-being-murdered fantasy.

The Fixer

1952

The Fixer watched as people started to leave the George Street Brothel, walking out of the front door and back to their respectable lives as if they hadn't just indulged every perverted fantasy they'd ever had.

Back to their jobs. Back to their wives.

It made the Fixer sick to their stomach.

Chapter 19

1988 – The Homesteads, Kirkby-in-Ashfield.

'Mum, Dad... It's me.' Henry opened the door to his parents' home.

Jerry and Joyce Mason were now both in their 80's and both as sharp as tacks. They'd moved into a retirement village, 'The Homesteads', eight years ago and loved it there. They had their own space, but there were plenty of their friends there and a centre where they could play cards and meet with each other. They also had a bar there, so Jerry could partake in his afternoon pint and Joyce a gin and tonic. There were always staff around so that if either of them needed help or had an accident, there was someone on hand to help, which put Henry's mind at rest.

Jerry and Joyce had been publicans. They'd run the 'Wagon and Horses' pub in Kirkby-in-Ashfield until they'd retired in 1965, when they'd gone travelling. Joyce liked to refer to it as 'travelling', but they'd really just had lots of holidays. The knickknacks from these trips adorned their home; a small replica of the Statue of David was in the garden; a photo of them standing by the Trevi Fountain adorned the mantelpiece in a novelty frame, a sombrero hung on the wall, a pair of castanets lay on a bookshelf. Their trips made them both happy and seeing his parents happy and relaxed and enjoying life made Henry happy.

As well as being a publican, Jerry had also had a more secret job. He'd been Chief Executioner between 1930 and 1953. He'd had the nickname 'Old Man Rope' because he'd treated everyone who found themselves on his gallows with kindness and compassion. In total, he'd executed five hundred and ten people and could still name all of them and their crimes. Unlike his son, he had no intention of writing his memoirs. For Jerry, what happened on the gallows stayed on the gallows.

'Henry, I'm putting the kettle on, do you want a brew?' shouted back his mum.

'Yes, please, milk no sugar and a biscuit if you've got one.'

His dad came walking through, his steps aided by a walking stick. 'When does your Mum, not have biscuits?' Jerry Mason hugged his son. 'Nice to see my TV star son, you did well the other day. Those presenters were bloody stupid though, didn't know their arse from their elbow either of them.'

Henry laughed and followed his dad through to the lounge. His dad had always been straight to the point. His small stature was deceiving, but Henry knew that deep within him was a steeliness that wasn't for messing with; it was why he'd been so successful both as an executioner and a landlord. No sob story ever got to him, and he treated everyone as they deserved to be treated. His small frame, grey hair and moustache very often made people think that he was a gentleman who could be manipulated, but the steel blue eyes behind his glasses told a very different story.

'I must admit, I didn't think my book would get this much attention.'

'It's you that doesn't know his arse from his elbow then! You know how many people still think Stanley was some sort of folk hero, him and his bunch of scrotes."

Henry shook his head. 'What happened to your saying, "What happens on the gallows stays on the gallows." and that an execution was the ultimate way of being absolved of your sins?'

'I got older and wiser! Plus, the others escaped my rope, so I can still call them scrotes! Did you see that Dicky Richards is trading off your book now? He's some kind of bloody after dinner speaker now! Who wants to hear that thick prat wax lyrical, he could barely string a sentence together, spoke with his fists! And Mad Larry Yates is a bloody vicar now! Some church in Edwinstowe, I mean I ask you?'

Just as Henry could sense his dad was a roll, his mum walked in with a tray of cups and a plate of biscuits. 'Are you banging on again about Stan and the boys? It's all I've heard for weeks! Now shut up and drink your tea. I've told you both many times, I don't want that man's name mentioned in my house. Do you hear me?'

Henry knew that Joyce had never much approved of her husband or her son's choice of career, she'd been far happier being a landlady and had been even happier when Jerry had quit his role of Chief Executioner in 1953.

A few years ago, Jerry had been taken into hospital with a burst appendix, Joyce had been so worried that she'd had too many gins and tonics to steady her nerves. As she and Henry sat waiting for news, she'd confided in her son about his dad's nightmares, how that even after all these years they still haunted him, and he'd wake up in floods of tears. Jerry had quit his job after Stan's execution. Joyce wanted to know if Henry suffered in the same way, he told his mum quite clearly that he didn't.

Henry recognized his mum's distraction techniques; she was now stuffing him full of tea and biscuits and launching into a blow-by-blow account of the plans she had for her latest cross stitch!

Joyce Mason was a real pocket rocket, her grey perm was beautifully styled around her round smiling face, twinkling eyes were lined with just a hint of mascara and her lips painted with the palest pink lipstick. Her 'day look' she called it. Joyce would never be caught without her slap on. She'd been an incredible landlady, knowing how to deal with the more troublesome customers in a firm, but fair way and always having a sympathetic ear for those who wanted to talk, while gently sending those who'd had one too many on their way. Joyce Mason, Henry knew had room in her heart for everyone.

'Henry, get yourself a biscuit and tell me how those gorgeous grandchildren and great grandchildren of mine are doing. Isn't it Toby's birthday soon? What does he want? What do you buy a six-year-old these days? I asked your dad, and he said a football. Does Toby like football, or are you and your dad trying to turn him into Mansfield Town's next star striker?'

'According to Eve, anything with Ghostbusters on is a winner. We've got him a Slimer figure, I think.'

Joyce looked disapproving. 'Ghostbusters! Jerry, have you heard this? Our gorgeous great grandson wants to bust ghosts. Whatever next?'

Jerry rolled his eyes. 'I told you to get him a football. He can be the next Kevin Kent.'

'Eve asked me to remind you that she's having a birthday party for Toby at their house on the Sunday, me and Maisy can pick you up.'

'We'll be there.' Joyce sat back in her chair and took a sip of her tea; this was all the gap that her son needed to bring the conversation back to Stanley.

'Dad, did you say that Mad Larry was a vicar in Edwinstowe now? Any idea what Church?'

'St Mary's, I think... Mad Larry a bloody Vicar, I mean... I know they say God forgives all sins, but I'm not sure even the Big Man has enough forgiveness for that mad black bastard.'

Henry couldn't help but smile to himself as his mum started talking over his dad again. 'Do Eve and Philip need us to bring anything?'

It was clear that there was to be no more talk of Stan and his boys this afternoon.

Chapter 20

1988 – St Mary's Church, Edwinstowe.

Father Yates stood in front of his parishioners. 'Go in peace to love and serve the Lord.'

He smiled, as the gathered congregation replied, 'in the name of Christ, amen.'

Father Yates knew his words had filled them full of joy and hope, he also knew that his congregation had been a lot fuller than normal because of that book, Tales from the Gallows.

Larry's parishioners had long since come to terms with their Vicar's murky past. As far as they were concerned, he'd fully repented for all his sins and since he'd found the Lord in 1970, he'd worked tirelessly to help those who might have been about to follow a similar path, and those who'd taken a wrong turn and needed his guidance.

Initially he'd been called to inner city churches, where Larry had worked tirelessly. It had been tough, but gradually the Afro-Caribbean community that had settled in Nottingham had started to trust him, which was largely helped by his parents Pappa B and Mama Z being on the front row every week. Gradually, irrespective of colour or culture, Larry's churches were packed to the rafters and a sense of community filled the streets of even the toughest areas of Nottingham.

Larry's mop of curly brown hair was tinged with grey, the scar down the left-hand side of his face had gradually faded over time, but the twinkle in his eyes shone brightly and his big bellowing laugh would echo through the old wooden beams of his church. His desire to inflict pain on others had most definitely faded into the depths of his soul over time.

As he approached his sixties, Larry had been called to a somewhat quieter church in the Nottinghamshire village of Edwinstowe. The irony had not been lost on either him or the congregation that one of the modern-day Merry Men was now a vicar where the latter-day Merry Men had once roamed. In fact, sometimes he thought the Bishop was having a laugh at his expense.

Where once he counselled, and guided the troubled souls of criminals, he now spent his days eating cake baked by the Mothers' Union and listening to plans for various village fetes.

'It was a wonderful sermon, Vicar, truly wonderful. Now, will we see you for tea and cake at Tuesday's meeting?'

'Yes, Mrs. Kirk, I'll be there, especially if you're going to bake that wonderful Victoria Sponge again.'

Mrs. Kirk giggled, 'Oh I will, I promise! Don't forget to bring Moses with you, will you?'

Larry shut the door behind a skittish Mrs. Kirk, and for a brief second, he longed for the days when he had a whole brothel full of whores to choose from, who he could shag and leave. However moist Mrs. Kirk's Victoria Sponge was, sometimes being the poster boy for the Mothers' Union wore a bit thin.

Larry pushed the thought from his mind. Maybe it was time for some repenting of his own.

One of Larry's favourite times of the week was on a Sunday when the congregation had left. The doors of the church were bolted, and he could sit in quiet contemplation. He could chat to God about whatever he wanted. Sitting on a pew at the front of the church, Larry closed his eyes and started to pray.

Chapter 21

1988 – The Commodore, Aspley Road, Nottingham

'And I said to Stan, no way, not on a Sunday.'

The room erupted in laughter. Richard "Dicky" Richards paused so he could lap up the adoration and take a swig of whiskey.

Since he'd begun his career as an after-dinner speaker ten years ago, he'd been very much in demand. His weekends were spent regaling groups of drunken businessmen, sportsmen evenings and, ironically the Law Society with tales of his time as part of the Merry Men.

Dicky had been their muscle and had been involved in some of Stanley's trickier 'negotiations'. He was tough and strong and could break a man's arm with a gentle touch. He'd once been the most feared muscle in the whole of Nottinghamshire. He'd spent his fair share of time in prison but had always avoided the hangman's noose. He'd mainly spent time inside for GBH, ABH and there'd been a ten stretch for manslaughter, but since then he'd gone straight. Once known as an evil version of Cary Grant, Dicky was still a good-looking man, although hair dye was responsible for his black hair these days. His dark eyes a six-foot six frame still sent many a lady into a frenzy.

Once Dicky realised, he could make more money talking about being part of the Merry Men, rather than actually being one of them, he was happy to retire. Although, if anyone asked the Merry Men had died the day Stanley had dropped through that trapdoor.

As the laughter quietened down, Dicky finished his speech 'Whatever you've read, seen or heard about Stan, he was my friend, my leader and he was a good man and that's why his legacy lives on and why it will always live on. Thank you.' He raised his glass to the audience, and said, 'To Stan.'

The audience raised theirs back and said, 'To Stan.' The room then erupted in applause and Dicky took a little bow.

As Dicky was stood at the bar having a drink, he noticed a red-haired woman standing by the side of him. She looked over at him, smiled, and then coyly lowered her gaze as she ordered a glass of wine.

'Let me get that, and another whiskey, duck, too.'

The barmaid hurried off.

'Thanks, that's very kind of you.' The redhead stuck her hand out. 'I'm Diane.'

Dicky took her hand and kissed the back of it. 'Dicky. I thought his was a no birds allowed event?'

Diane smiled sweetly. 'It is, but I'm here to pick my brother up, so I thought I'd treat myself to a glass of wine whilst I waited.'

'Must be my lucky day.' Dicky cast his eye over her body. She was wearing a tight black dress, red high heels and a huge gold necklace. No wedding ring marred her hand.

'You look more like you're on a night out, rather than providing chauffeur service?'

'I've been out for dinner with friends. I said I'd pick my brother up on my way back. Did your speech go OK?'

Dicky smiled, he could never resist a change to brag. 'Yeah, it always does, people can't get enough of tales of the Merry Men.'

"I bet now that book's out, it's gone crazy again?'

Dicky took a slug of his whiskey. 'That piece of shit? That tosser doesn't know what he's on about. It makes me fucking angry that I get shit for making an honest career out of being a former criminal and yet that prick can write whatever he likes about whoever he likes. It's him that's benefiting from the proceeds of crime, not me.'

Diane smiled. 'No, it doesn't sound very fair, do you know the bloke that wrote it?'

'Yeah, I knew him, he was Governor of Nottingham for a while. Cruel bastard never missed a chance to tell me how he was the one responsible for Stan's death and how the world was better off without him. If you ask me, he was the fucking murderer, not Stan. Anyway, enough about that, are you sure your brother can't make his own way home and you can give me a lift instead?' Dicky ran his fingers up and down the pretty redhead's arm.

Draining the last of her wine, she patted his arm. 'Maybe next time. It was a real pleasure talking to you.'

And with that she was gone.

It only occurred to Dicky the next day that she'd left alone.

The Fixer

1988

Watching Dicky from the other side of the room, the Fixer could see him putting his moves onto the redhead stood at the bar. Flashing her his big white teeth, stroking her arm, laughing; somethings never changed.

The Fixer knew exactly the sort of stuff Dicky would be saying, telling her how pretty she was, bragging about his past, making lewd comments It was frightening how many women fell for it.

The Fixer had been attending Dicky's talks at various points over the last ten years, just to make sure he didn't go too far, but it was always the same old drivel.

The Fixer watched the redhead leave on her own, just as had been the plan.

Chapter 22

1988 – The Avenue, Mansfield.

Sidney 'Babyface' Longshaw threw the paper onto the table knocking a cup of tea into the lap of his girlfriend.

'Oi, Sid, watch it.'

'Watch it? I'll fucking watch it, have you read this? I can't believe that even after all these years, Dicky is still a fucking moron!'

Ce-Ce picked up the paper.

Not So Merry

Former member of the Merry Men, Richard 'Dicky' Yates (65) has slammed Henry Mason, author of the best seller 'Tales from the Gallows', for profiting from crime.

Mr. Richards, who now makes a living as an after-dinner speaker, told our reporter, 'I don't think it's fair, that I get shit for making an honest career out of being a former criminal and yet that prick can write whatever he likes about whoever he likes. Richards added. 'It's him that's benefiting from the proceeds of crime, not me.'

Mr. Richards also referred to Mr. Mason as being a "cruel bastard, who never missed a chance to tell me how he was the one responsible for Stan's death and how the world was better off without him. If you ask me, he was the fucking murderer, not Stan."

Mr. Mason was the Governor of Nottingham Prison between 1964 and 1985, Mr. Richards served various prison terms there, including one for manslaughter following the death of Barry Fox.

Mr. Mason has been unavailable for comment.

Ce-Ce didn't really understand what the problem was. She was thirty years Sidney's junior and had only been dating him a couple of months. Well you couldn't really call it dating. She was more on hand when he fancied sex or needed someone on his arm. People had told her he was a bad man, but she didn't know why, and she really didn't know who this Dicky was.

'I'm going out, get dressed and leave Ce-Ce, I've got business to sort out.'

Sidney grabbed his keys and stormed out.

Chapter 23

1988, Marples Avenue, Mansfield Woodhouse.

Dicky was woken by the phone. He reached out to pick it up. 'Yeah?'

A bright, chirpy voice greeted him. 'Mr. Richards, hi, this is Toni Thomson calling from TV-AM. We wondered if we could book you to come on tomorrow morning's show to talk about the comments you've made in this morning's paper? We'd pay your expenses and put you up in a hotel.'

'Comments? What comments are you on about? I haven't spoken to no fucking reporters.'

'Mr. Richards, I suggest you take a look at the front page of this morning's Daily Chronicle, and I'll call you back.'

Dicky slammed the phone down, but it rang again immediately. 'Hi Mr. Richards, this is Steve Williams calling from the BBC's Breakfast Time. We'd like to invite you onto our show tomorrow to chat to our host Jeremy Paxman about the comments you've made that are in the papers today.'

Dicky put the phone down, it rang again, and he pulled the cord out of the wall.

What was going on? He'd not spoken to any reporters.

Heading downstairs, he could see the red top of the newspaper beckoning him from the hall mat. Picking it up and reading the headline, he noticed the picture of the reporter; it was the redhead who'd approached him at the bar last night.

'Fuck!'

Chapter 24

1988 – The Vicarage, Edwinstowe

Even though he knew some people still doubted his faith, Larry had never felt more at peace.

Ever since he'd acknowledged his calling from God in 1970, he had been happier and more fulfilled. He'd been worried that his past would stop him attending theological college, but it didn't, and he'd excelled and been accepted by his peers and stopped more than a few young men from following in his footsteps.

Now, 58 years old, Larry had decided to take on the easier task of being Vicar of St. Mary's in Edwinstowe. With it came a beautiful vicarage that overlooked Sherwood Forest.

In a morning, Larry liked to put on the radio, make a cup of tea in his favourite mug, and sit in quiet contemplation in his garden, whilst his dog, an English Bull Dog called Moses, ran around.

It was his morning routine. It was simple, it was peaceful, and it was his. It was a far cry from the morning routine of prison. Larry had served various prison sentences, until he finally decided enough was enough in 1960 and went straight. He often thought about Stan and how different life could have been, thirty-five years later and he still missed his friend.

As Larry sat in quiet contemplation, a voice on the radio caught his attention.

'So Nottingham is in the national news again, thanks to the Merry Men... and I don't mean Robin and his band of outlaws, I mean Stanley Thomas. Thirty-five years after his execution and we are still talking about him. This time though, it's his former associate Richard 'Dicky' Richards who has made the headlines.'

Larry ran to the radio and turned up the volume.

'It would appear that Dicky Richards has slammed the best-selling book by former hangman Henry Mason. In true Dicky style he's been very blunt with his comments, accusing Mr. Mason of being the one who is benefitting from the proceeds of crime and also of having taunted him, whilst in prison. We'd like to know your thoughts.'

Larry switched off the radio.

'Fuck!'

Chapter 25

1988 – The Duke, Kirkby-in-Ashfield.

Fiona Potter stood outside her front door having a cigarette. Even in a toweling dressing gown and fluffy slippers she cut a fearsome figure. She seemed to be the only woman in the world whose hair held its perfect peroxide colour; she never had roots showing and her fluorescent coral lipstick never smudged faded or bled. At 65 years old, Fiona was as revered and feared as she had been in her twenties.

'Morning, Mrs. P, here's ya paper.'

'Thanks, Willy.'

Fiona took the paper off the young boy and her cigarette fell from her now-open mouth.

'Billy, get down here, you'll never guess what the silly prick's done now!'

Billy Potter came downstairs. Despite having once been one of the most feared gangsters in Nottinghamshire and Stanley Thomas's best friend, there was no-one Billy was more scared of than his wife. When she shouted, he replied.

'Which silly prick?'

'Dicky. He's been gobbing off to the press about Stan and that book.'

'What? We all said not to say a word about that stupid book!'

'I know, but it's here, front page of The Daily Chronicle; Dicky saying that bloke is profiting from crime and that he was a heartless bastard when he was Governor of Nottingham.'

'I'll get dressed; I best get over to see Sid.'

As he pulled on his trousers, Billy Potter uttered the words...

'Fuck!'

The Fixer

1988

Putting the newspaper down on the table, a wry smile played across the Fixer's lips.

It was showtime.

Chapter 26

1952 – George Street Brothel, Mansfield.

Walter sat at his desk, counting out the money he'd made from the party. Not bad for an afternoon's work. Even once he'd given everyone their 'wages' he was still quids in. Once he'd locked the money away in the safe, he set about updating his records.

His records were his leverage, his security, the thing that protected him and no-one, but him knew about them.

His records were the things that gave him the ultimate power over everyone, and no-one would know it until he chose to cash them in and finally show just how powerful he was.

The very thought of the power that they gave him made him hard.

Smiling to himself, he shouted for his sister. 'Pearl, get up here now.'

One didn't own a brothel and wank oneself off.

He laughed as he unzipped his trousers and waited.

Chapter 27

1952 – Crow Hill Drive, Mansfield.

As Stanley lay in bed, he could hear his wife Hannah downstairs with the kids. He listened as she sang silly songs to the boys and changed words to include their names, the boys squealing with laughter as they joined in with their own silly songs.

Charlie and Eddie were the apples of their eyes. Charlie was five years old, and he was the spitting image of Hannah, with his brown hair and eyes. He ran everywhere and was always inventing games to play with his brother. Eddie was three years old and blond just like Stan. He was never happier than when he was kicking a football or trying to train a neighbourhood dog to give him his paw. Stan made a mental note to talk to Hannah again about getting a family dog.

As Stanley lay there, he realised Hannah's singing had stopped and had been replaced with, 'Stan?'

'What?'

'Billy's here.'

Stan pulled on his trousers and his shirt and headed downstairs, where he found his best friend with a large mug of tea, a bacon sandwich and Charlie sat in his lap telling him about the Stags' latest signing. Eddie was joining in but was really more interested in showing Billy his new toy car.

Stan kissed Hannah on the cheek, and she handed him a mug of tea and a bacon sandwich of his own. Playfully he smacked her bum, and she laughed and flicked him with a tea towel.

'Alright Bill? Boys what you doing to your Uncle Bill?' Stanley scooped both boys up in his arms and planted kisses on their cheeks, both boys screaming with laughter.

Eddie carried on with his gibberish. 'Yes Stan, just thought we could do with a catch up.'

'We'll head into the next room, Han. Boys you be good for your Mam.'

The boys went back to playing with their toys on the kitchen floor.

Stan and Billy took seats in the lounge. 'Now, fill me in.'

"The Fixer's been in touch. They said Dorrell's becoming an issue.'

'Is he now? What makes them think that?'

'He had another one of his parties, which we knew was happening, but they were all there, the Rev, the Doc, the Hon, the Gov, the Politician and a couple of new faces too. Dorrell made a fucking fortune apparently.'

'Did he now? What else did the Fixer say?'

'He's keeping records apparently, thinks no one knows. You know how clever the prick thinks he is. But the Fixer says it's all in there, every last sordid thing that goes on at these party. Photos too, apparently. FYI, The Politician likes it up the arse.'

Stanley laughed. 'There's an image I didn't need. What's the Fixer want?'

'Says it needs sorting. Dorrell's getting above his station, making noises he's about to do us and take over.'

"What a very stupid man Dorrell is. Right, I need to think about how we deal with this. Can the Fixer get me those records?'

'Not sure, I'll ask the question.'

'In the meantime, send Dicky and Babyface to pay Dorrell a little visit, collect some of that money he's made. Make sure they go on a Friday night when the brothels busy. It'll do Dorrell good to remember who's in charge round here.'

'Will do Stan, anything else?'

'Yeah, smash the place up a bit and give him a beating, something he won't forget in a hurry. Oh and tell them to take a slash on those poncy black and red shoes of his. That'll piss him off more than the beating.'

Chapter 28

1952 – George Street Brothel, Mansfield.

Friday nights at the George Street Brothel were legendary.

Everyone had a happy ending at the George Street Brothel.

Walter lay in bed thinking about all the money he was going to make that evening; Gerard was hard at work sucking his cock. A perk of being the boss, Walter felt.

Gerard was six foot two and looked like he'd been carved out of marble. He was toned and muscly, his dark hair and eyes matching his smooth black skin. He was exactly the kind of man Walter liked. It gave Walter a sense of power to be able to have someone as good-looking as Gerard at his beck and call. In some of his wilder fantasies, Walter liked to stare into those dark eyes and fantasise it was Dicky Richards sucking his cock.

Gerard had been at the George Street Brothel for a year. Walter had first met him cottaging in Mansfield Market Place. He'd been hanging out by the Buttercross when he'd approached Walter. Taken by his beauty, Walter had stopped to talk to him and pretty soon, Gerard had moved into George Street and was working full-time for Walter.

Very little was known about Gerard. He'd grown up in Kirkby, liked to suck cock, was good-looking and gave Walter no trouble.

Not long after Walter had arrived at the George Street Brothel, Dennis had turned up looking for a place to stay and work. He and Gerard knew each other. If Gerard was tall, dark and handsome, Dennis was more Greek god; just as tall and muscly, with blond hair and blue eyes. The punters loved him and whilst he could sometimes be a bit moody, he, like Gerard generally gave Walter no trouble.

Chapter 29

1952 – George Street Brothel, Mansfield.

Everyone sat around at the George Street Brothel waiting for the punters to arrive. Walter sat smoking a cigar and sipping on a whiskey, admiring his reflection in his shiny black and red shoes. A Bing Crosby record played in the background.

He watched his staff, sitting at the kitchen table, laughing, joking waiting to get to work. He could see his sister whispering to Dennis. He knew Dennis professed to be gay, but he couldn't help but feel something was going on there. At the very least his sister had a stonking great crush.

His eyes wandered to May. Poor, sweet stupid May. She was the easiest to control as she was so grateful to have a roof over her head that she'd put up with anything and anyone. Tonight, her long brunette hair fell delicately over her shoulders, and she was wearing a pale pink negligee as she sat chatting to Geraldine and Shirley.

Geraldine and Shirley were his dirty duo; they'd have a threesome with anybody. Geraldine was tall and dark with an athletic body; she was the type of woman who looked better out of clothes than in. And as result was currently sat in a skimpy pair of pants and a pair of nipple tassels, her white high heels clashing complimenting her dark skin.

Shirley was tall and blonde with dark eyes, and she was wearing a white bra and matching pants with red heels.

Walter wasn't sure, but he thought Geraldine and Shirley were a couple. He didn't care, they were hardworking, and the punters loved them, and they made him a lot of money.

Cheryl was sat at the far end of the table chatting to Gerard. Cheryl was a total bitch and his resident dominatrix. Sometimes she scared even him. Her fiery red hair fitted her temper, and she was sat in a black basque, French knickers, stockings and thigh high boots, her whip laying on the table. Walter could swear that sometimes she was only seconds away from beating him with it. But she needed somewhere to live so that at least saved him. It was the thought of what would happen when she didn't need somewhere to live that scared Walter.

Every so often, Gerard glanced over in Walter's direction. Everyone knew that Gerard was Walter's favourite and could get away with murder. Walter was half tempted to give Gerard the night off and put him to work on himself, but Gerard earned him a lot of money and Walter wasn't that stupid.

Waving an empty glass in the air, Roy got up and re-filled Walter's glass. 'There you go boss, anything else?'

Walter shook his head.

The doorbell of the George Street Brothel rang.

'Showtime, ladies and gents.'

Chapter 30

1952 – George Street Brothel, Mansfield.

When Walter thought back, it had all happened very quickly. The ringing of the doorbell normally signalled the start of business, only this Friday evening it didn't.

Larry and Sidney 'Babyface', were inside before anyone could stop them, both carrying baseball bats.

Walter got to his feet. 'What the fuck are you two doing here? Roy, Barry, Malcolm, escort these gentlemen off my premises.' Walter looked around frantically, where the fuck where they! 'Roy, Barry, Malcolm!'

Larry started to laugh. 'No amount of shouting is going to wake those three for a bit, is it Babyface?'

'No, Larry, no it's not.' Babyface stroked the baseball bat in his hand. 'They ran into our little friends here.'

'And before you get any ideas, your whores here aren't going to give us any trouble either, are you ladies?'

Everyone at the kitchen table shook their heads.

'Still, let's be sure. Babyface, lock them in the coal cellar for now. Dorrell, you sit the fuck down.'

Pearl, May, Cheryl, Geraldine, Shirley, Gerard and Dennis dutifully followed Babyface into the coal cellar. Walter made a mental note to beat Cheryl with her own whip for not using it to protect him.

Walter took a drag on his cigar and a slug of his whiskey. Larry took them off him, drowning the rest of the whiskey himself. Larry then put the cigar out on Walter's forehead.

'Cunt.' spat Walter.

'Now, now, Walter, there's no need to be a rude boy is there? You know no-one likes a rude boy.'

'They're all locked up Larry.'

'Good, now we can have our chat with little Walter Dorrell here, can't we? Now remind me Babyface, what was it, we came to speak about?'

'Well Larry, I think it was the fact that Walter, here, has been very disrespectful to Mr. Thomas and Mr. Thomas don't take too kindly to that.'

'That's right, Babyface, Mr. Thomas does not take kindly to little pricks in poncy black and red shoes strutting about on his patch and bad-mouthing him, and from what we hear, Walter, you've been doing just that.' Larry poured himself another glass of whiskey.

'I don't know who's been talking, but I would never disrespect Stan. We're all friends aren't we boys?'

"Friends, Walter? Friends? How dare a little cock-sucking wanker like yourself think that Mr. Thomas would ever sully his good reputation by associating himself with a loser like yourself! Babyface, remind Walter here that he's not our friend.'

Babyface took his baseball bat and banged it hard into Walter's groin and Walter doubled over in pain.

'Now, would Babyface do that to one of his friends?'

Walter shook his head.

'I can't hear you, Walter.'

'No.'

'Good. So now we are clear that we are all not friends. Let me be clear about what that does make us. In fact, Babyface, I need three things to demonstrate my point.'

Babyface went over to the mantelpiece and picked up three expensive looking items: a carriage clock, an ornament and a large photo frame.

Babyface threw the first item in the air, and Larry smashed it with the baseball bat, the ornament fracturing all over Walter.

'Point one. Those who are not Mr. Thomas's friends or employees are his enemies and being an enemy of Mr. Thomas is not a good place to be. Babyface. Next point please.'

Babyface threw the photo frame in the air, and once again Larry smashed it with the baseball bat, the fragments again flying all over Walter. This time a shard of glass stuck into Walter's forehead.

'Point two: You become an enemy of Mr. Thomas by not paying him the money you owe him. When Mr. Thomas says you owe him your taxes, you owe him his fucking taxes. Babyface, final point if you will.'

Babyface launched the carriage clock in the air, and with expert precision, Larry smashed it to pieces with the baseball bat, bits of the clock landing all over Walter as his head sunk deeper into his chest.

'Point three; You are nothing, Walter. Absolutely nothing. And this little whorehouse of yours can and will close if you do not start paying what you owe us. So, as a gesture of goodwill, Mr. Thomas would like to meet you in The Boy pub tomorrow night. You will walk over to him and request in your loudest and most polite voice an audience with Mr. Thomas. On being granted the aforementioned audience, you will proceed to beg for his forgiveness at having taken the piss. You will tell him how sorry you are that you thought yourself better than everyone else, that you were misguided, and that you bow to Mr. Thomas and his greater knowledge of everything. You will then pay him a vast quantity of money, whatever you made at that party of yours, and the three thousand you owe will do.'

Walter opened his mouth to protest, but a quick baseball bat to the bollocks soon shut it again.

'You can of course add your own bits of grovelling, you can make up your own script, I'll allow it. But you will grovel.'

Walter nodded.

'Now then, Babyface, lets you and I leave Walter to tidy up and sort out the money and we can look forward to seeing his ugly mug tomorrow night, can't we Walt?'

Walter nodded.

Larry and Babyface turned to leave, but when Walter muttered something under his breath, Larry turned. 'Oh Walter, just one more thing.'

Larry and Sidney unzipped their trousers, and both pissed all over Walter's prized red and black shoes.

As the steam rose off the shoes and Walter choked back his tears, he could hear them laughing long after the front door had closed.

Chapter 31

1952 – The Boy pub, Mansfield.

Stanley Thomas opened the door to The Boy pub and smiled as the room fell perfectly silent. The Boy was notorious. People drank there because they were banned from everywhere else.

A mixture of sawdust, fag ends, and dirt carpeted the floor. Irish Mary sat at the bar, half a gin and orange in front of her. She flicked her peroxide blonde hair and smiled at Stanley and made a show of crossing her legs, so that he could see the bottom of her shoes, which contained a price list of everything she was prepared to do for half a crown.

The Duchess sat in her corner, a Miss Havisham-esque woman, who only ever spoke to order a drink. She would sit in her corner, knitting and watching the world go by, her pint of stout largely untouched.

Snowy the glass collector, stopped in his tracks as he saw Stanley. He bowed his head in deference and then limped off to collect more glasses.

This really wasn't Stanley's usual haunt, full of lowlifes and people who owed him money, but it did people good to be reminded of his presence and that he and his Merry Men could turn up at any time.

Stanley would collect what Dorrell owed him and show anyone else who might be thinking of not paying that it really wasn't a good idea.

Stanley took off his hat and walked towards the bar, the rest of the Merry Men following.

The Landlord of The Boy was a man called Mark Strong, a man in his fifties, he paid his money on time and never gave Stanley any trouble.

'Good evening, Mr. Thomas, gentlemen. What can I get you? On the house of course.'

'That's very kind of you, Mark, we'll all have a pint.'

'Take a seat, Jeannie will bring them over.'

Stanley and the Merry Men walked towards a large table in the centre of the pub, and the man who'd been sat there, got up quickly. 'I was just leaving Mr. Thomas, lovely to see you, have a good evening.'

The man scuttled away, and Stanley and his boys took their places at the table. Jeannie sat down their pints in front of them.

The pub remained silent.

Stanley took a sip of his pint and lit a cigarette.

The only noise was the gentle tapping of pint pots being lifted and placed back on the table and the inhaling and exhaling of cigarette smoke.

In the corner of the pub, a chair made a scrapping noise on the floor and footsteps could be heard making their way towards them.

They stopped when they reached Stanley.

'Stan.'

Billy looked up. 'Mr. Thomas to you.'

Walter ignored him. 'Stan. I hear you think that I owe you some money.'

Stanley took a sip of his pint and continued to stare forward.

Walter continued, 'I spoke with your associates earlier, who said I should come here and pay you what I owe and apologise, so here you fucking go!'

Walter took the carrier bag he was holding and emptied it all over the table. 'A bag of shit, for a bag of shit! You hear me everyone, Walter Dorrell does not dance to the tune of Stanley fucking Thomas and his thugs! This is my town, and I'm in charge now, the Merry Men are done with!'

Billy, Babyface, Larry and Dicky moved their chairs backwards ready to really teach Walter a lesson. Stan shook his head, putting down his pint pot and stubbing out his cigarette, before looking up at Walter.

'Dorrell, you really are a very stupid man.'

The Fixer

1952

From the corner of the pub, the Fixer watched as Dorrell emptied the bag of shit out onto the table in front of Stanley. Walter's eyes blazed in triumph; he really did think he'd shown Stanley who was boss.

The Fixer knew that Walter had just signed his own death warrant. Something had to and would be done.

Chapter 32

1988 – Berry Hill Park, Mansfield.

Henry sat on a park bench in the middle of Berry Hill Park, and unfolded the newspaper, the headline screaming out at him.

Not So Merry... Former member of the Merry Men, Richard 'Dicky' Yates (65) has slammed Henry Mason, author of the best seller Tales from the Gallows for profiting from crime."

Dicky could never keep his mouth shut; he'd always been the same. Henry remembered one incident when he'd been in Nottingham Prison – Henry thought it was for GBH or theft, who knew with Dicky? – But Dicky had decided that he should be top dog and had started a fight with another inmate. He'd dangled the guy by his feet over the balcony, holding a match to them until the guy begged for mercy.

Dicky was so brazen about it, that half a dozen screws were stood watching it happen and did nothing. Henry had marched Dicky down to Solitary himself, and it had been unfortunate that Dicky had fallen down the stairs on the way. Henry remembered the exchange between them, Dicky swearing and cursing and calling Henry all the names under the sun, whilst Henry had simply locked Dicky in the cell, opened the hatch to the door and explained in minute detail the exact details of Stanley's death, how he'd cried like a baby, begged for mercy, pleaded not to die and above all was a fucking coward.

Dicky behaved himself for the rest of his sentence.

But now here he was shouting his mouth off.

Henry put the paper in the bin and nipped in to use the public loo in the park. As he was stood in the cubicle, he noticed something scribbled on the wall.

"The Fixer wants to talk to you, 824173"

Zipping up his flies, Henry looked around the toilet; No-one was there. He scribbled down the number and sat back down on the toilet.

Henry made his way to the phone box on the outskirts of the park. Checking over his shoulder, he put fifty pence in the slot and dialed.

On the fifth ring it was answered.

'You got my messages then?'

'Yes. The mask. Was that you too?'

The voice laughed. 'Of course it was me, who else would have kept such a memento? I do hope it didn't upset Maisy. How is the old girl?'

'She's fine. What do you want after all this time?'

'After all this time? I've always been around, watching from afar, I know all about you, Maisy, Philip, Anna, Toby, and Rebecca. It's nice to see Jerry and Joyce looking well too. So, then Henry, what do I want? Oh Henry, you must have known that this day would come, it was always inevitable. Plus, seeing you all over the telly, hearing you on the radio and of course reading your book made me realise we were well overdue a catch up. I mean with the first book doing so well, the sequel is bound to be a surefire hit. You know the sequel? The one with the truth.'

Henry started to stammer, 'I... I......'

The voice on the other end of the phone sighed, and then laughed. 'Till our next merry meeting, Henry Mason.'

That was the last thing Henry remembered.

The Fixer

1988

The Fixer watched as Henry hung up the phone, before grabbing his chest and falling to the floor.

Henry Mason was not getting out of this that easily. The Fixer dialled 999 and requested an ambulance.

Chapter 33

1988 – Kings Mill Hospital, Sutton-in-Ashfield.

Henry could hear faint voices in the background. He was aware of the fact he was lying in a bed, but it didn't feel like his bed. There was something covering his mouth and he could feel something in his arm. As he tried to work out what was going on, he heard a voice say, 'Mum, he's waking up.'

Opening his eyes, Henry could make out the worried face of his daughter, Anna, Maisy's quickly appearing behind her, followed by Philip and someone he didn't know.

Maisy grabbed his hand. 'Oh my darling, you had us all worried, how are you feeling?'

Henry went to move the mask from his face, but the person he didn't recognise soon took charge.

'Now then, Mr. Mason, you've given us all quite the fright, but you're in the best place and you're on the mend.'

Henry nodded.

'Do you know where you are and what happened?' The nurse gently moved his mask away.

'I'm assuming I'm in the hospital, but the last thing I remember is being near a phone box.'

'That's right, you're in Kings Mill on the cardiac ward, you were found near Berry Hill Park, near the phone box, someone called the ambulance. We aren't sure if you started to feel unwell and tried to call for help yourself.'

'Cardiac ward?'

'Yes, Mr. Mason, you've had a mild heart attack.'

'We've all been so worried Dad.'

'I said you'd been doing too much, that bloody book! You've been all over the place! You'll do as you're told now Henry Mason and rest! We were meant to be enjoying your retirement, not worrying about whether there would be a retirement!'

Henry nodded. Maisy was right, this was definitely the fault of that bloody book!

Chapter 34

1988 – The Vicarage, Edwinstowe

Sidney pulled up outside St Mary's Church in his brand-new Rolls Royce Silver Spirit, which would definitely get Larry's parishioners talking. It still made him laugh, that after everything they'd done and seen, Mad Larry Yates was now 'Father Yates' and spent his days praying and fighting off members of the Women's Institute, as opposed to his previous life where he'd been begged for mercy and spent his day fighting other criminals.

Slamming his car door shut, Sidney started walking up the drive of the vicarage. He could hear barking and a familiar voice yelling, 'Moses, calm down.'

The door opened and there dressed, in a black shirt, trousers and a dog collar was his friend. Older, allegedly wiser, but the same smiling face.

Wrapping his old friend in a bear hug, Sidney realised he really had missed Larry!

'Come in, come in, ignore Moses, his bark is worse than his bite. I should have called him Dicky cos he's always mouthing off with very little action, but I wasn't sure my parishioners would see the funny side!'

Moses appeared to roll his eyes and took a chew off to his basket.

'Now, then my friend, a drink? Tea, coffee or something else?" Larry waved a twenty-year-old bottle of whiskey.

'Is that what I think it is?'

'It certainly is, it's the second one of the lot we bought to toast Stan after he died. It seemed appropriate, considering.'

'Is everyone else coming? What are your parishioners going to think seeing a bunch of old cons invading the vicarage?'

Larry laughed. 'They'll think they need to bake extra cakes!'

Billy was next to enter. 'Knock, knock, your eminence, is that what we fucking call you these days?'

Embracing him, Larry laughed. 'You my friend, can call me what the fuck you like.'

'I knew I was in trouble, but I didn't think I'd have to repent in a fucking church.' Dicky followed Billy in.

Larry laughed. 'I'm not sure even the Church can save you my friend, but I'll put in a word with the Big Man."

As Larry embraced his friend, Sidney noticed, it seemed he couldn't help but smile. However, much he seemed to love his new life, Sidney couldn't help but wonder whether sometimes Larry really missed his old one.

Larry started filling up everyone's glasses with whiskey.

'To Stan.'

The men clinked glasses and drank, taking their seats at the table, and Sidney noticed that subconsciously they'd all sat in the places they had sat when they were the Merry Men.

Whilst some things were very different, other things had remained the same.

The Merry Men sat there in silence. It was comfortable and familiar and for just a few moments, they felt like the men they had been in the 1950's, the ones who were invincible, who lived in the moment, who were fearless and had their whole lives ahead of them.

The bond they shared was unbreakable. They were brothers then and they were brothers now.

The ones that sat round this table had changed, there were the obvious ones, grey hair, lined faces, bones that creaked when they stood up, but now they lived in fear. Fear the that the past was about to infiltrate their present.

The Fixer

1988

From their car, the Fixer watched the Merry Men enter the vicarage, hugging and shaking each other's hands. They all looked so happy to see each other, reunited once again, no matter what the circumstances.

Older, probably not wiser, well certainly not in Dicky's case. This time there was no Stanley to tell them what to do, this time it would probably fall to Sidney to take up the mantel of boss. A thought that made the Fixer smile.

Chapter 35

1952 – Mansfield.

Dorrell strutted across Mansfield Market Place, Roy and Barry scuttling behind him. Malcolm was waiting for him in the car.

'How did it go boss?'

'I think, Malcolm, it's safe to say that Stan and his boys will not be bothering me anymore. It's Walter Dorrell that runs this town now, I know it, he knows it, everyone knows it. I think we'll be having a party tonight and then tomorrow we'll crack on with business.'

Chapter 36

1952 – The Boy pub, Mansfield.

The Boy pub was silent.

Getting to his feet, Stan moved to the bar. 'Mark, clean this up and get me a fresh pint.'

'Yes, Mr. Thomas.'

The Merry Men moved away from the table as well and took their places at the bar. Stan drained half of his fresh pint and stood up to address the pub.

'What you have just seen was very a very stupid thing. Walter Dorrell is the man you should blame when later this week my boys will be collecting double taxes. Anyone who cannot meet payment will address my court at the weekend. Dorrell will pay for his actions, and he's made all of you pay too. Sidney, make a list of everyone who is in here, so we can pay them a visit this week.'

With that, Stan drained the rest of his pint and walked out, Billy and Dicky following him.

Walter Dorrell really was a very stupid man.

Chapter 37

1952 – Crow Hill Drive, Mansfield.

Stan opened his front door. He could hear the gentle hum of the radio and Hannah singing to herself in the kitchen, Charlie and Eddie were playing and laughing in the lounge.

He stood just for a second and took in the normality of it all, he letting the sounds make their way from his ears into his soul. At some point in the future, he had a feeling these sounds would be very important to him.

'That you Stan?'

'Yes duck, it's me, what's for tea?'

***

Hannah felt Stan put his arms around her waist and kiss her. She relaxed into his embrace. This was the Stan that no-one else, but she saw. The family man. Her husband. Her lover. Her best friend.

Hannah had been sixteen years old when she'd met Stanley for the first time, four years his junior. She'd heard stories about him from other girls, but there was something about him. His blond hair, blue eyes and smile that somehow managed to be menacing and endearing at the same time. From the first time he looked at her and smiled Hannah Longshaw as she'd been then, was in love.

The two had married in 1945 at St Wilfred's Church in Kirkby. On the way to the church, Hannah's dad had asked her if she was absolutely sure she knew what she was doing marrying a man like Stanley. It was the only time she'd ever heard her dad offer any form of criticism of Stanley. She said she was one hundred percent sure and that was the last time he'd ever commented on Stanley.

Now twenty-four years old, Hannah was incredibly attractive. Shoulder length brown hair, sparkling blue eyes and a trim figure, which despite having had two children displayed no signs of motherhood. Hannah put up with a lot from Stanley. Whatever people thought, being the wife of a gangster wasn't easy. She lived in constant fear of a knock at the door from the police and Stan being arrested, him being sent to prison for a long time, or worse still being sentenced to death.

Hannah loved Stan and always told herself that whatever happened, the fear of him being taken away from her, would never stop her being with him in whatever moments they had.

They stood in the kitchen together, embracing for what seemed like an eternity. Or until two excited little boys came charging in the room screaming. 'Daddy!'

Hannah knew how much Stan loved his boys, but he kept saying that it was time that they added a little girl to their family. Watching as Stan scooped the boys into his arms, covering their faces in kisses, Hannah thought he might be right.

'Have you been good for your Mam today?'

Both boys giggled and nodded.

'Are you sure?' teased Stanley.

Both boys giggled again, before Charlie insisted, 'Would we lie to you? We've been keeping out from under her feet, so we've been playing gangsters in the garden and then we played cars and then we made a den. Do you want to see our den?'

Grabbing their dad's hands, they dragged him outside.

Hannah smiled. This was her Stan.

Chapter 38

1988 – Kings Mill Hospital, Sutton-in-Ashfield.

Henry lay in his hospital bed. He'd been in a week now and could feel his strength gradually starting to return. The doctors and nurses had all told him repeatedly how lucky he'd been that someone had been on hand to call an ambulance immediately. His family had barely left his bedside and he'd promised them he would take it easier and stop running all over the country doing interviews.

As he lay there, he appreciated the peace and quiet. He'd been moved to a side room, so he had his own space. It was pre-visiting hours so apart from a few beeps of machines and the gentle hustle of the ward, he could just enjoy the peace of his own thoughts.

Henry thought back to the moments just before he'd had the heart attack, that familiar voice on the phone, a voice he hadn't heard for many years. A voice that had ruled his past, been responsible for his present and was now going to take control of his future.

For once in his life, Henry had no idea what he was going to do.

Chapter 39

1952 – George Street Brothel, Mansfield.

Walter Dorrell sat at the head of the table in the kitchen of the George Street Brothel, his 'people' gathered around him. Roy and Barry stood behind him like two guard dogs protecting their master ready to pounce at any time. Malcolm guarded the door. Pearl, May, Cheryl, Geraldine, Shirley, Gerard, and Dennis sat huddled around the table. Walter was regaling them with the events from the pub.

'So, I'm sure you'll appreciate that from now on, I'll be a lot busier. I've a manor to run. Now, I'm not saying I won't talk to Stan and his boys and let them join my firm, but it will strictly be on my terms, do you all understand?'

Everyone nodded.

Walter got up and started walking up and down, his hands clasped behind his back. He rocked back and forth on his brand new black and red shoes; the piss-stained ones resigned to the bin. Walter thought this made him look important. He continued, 'I'll probably put a manager in to run this place on a daily basis as I concentrate on other areas of the business. I haven't decided who, but it will be someone who has my full trust and will run this place just like me.'

Pearl felt a faint taste of blood in her mouth; she was biting her lip so hard to stop herself from laughing in her stupid brother's face. Never in her whole life had she heard him spout anything quite so deluded. There was no way Stan was going to stand for this, no way at all! How could Walter not see that he'd basically signed his own death warrant? Pearl for once was quite pleased her brother was so stupid.

It looked like Stanley Thomas would be the one to solve all her problems.

'Tonight though, we celebrate! Pearl, get out the whiskey.'

Pearl got up from the table, glad of an excuse to move, but just as she headed into the lounge, a brick came flying through the window. Malcolm, Roy and Barry rushed outside to see if they could see the culprit, but no one was around.

Attached to the brick was a note; 'This is your fault Dorrell and we will make you pay!'

Dorrell laughed, going to the back door he shouted, 'Is that the best you've got, Stan? I'm in charge now!'

Just then the phone rang, and Shirley picked it up. 'George Street...' She then went silent, the colour drained from her face. 'I'll tttteeellll him,' she said, before replacing the receiver and turning to Walter. 'Walter, that was someone saying that they're going to make you pay, they said if they all had to pay, then you'd pay too. What do they mean?'

'It's one of Stan's cronies trying it on, they know who's in charge now.'

The phone rang again, and this time Walter snatched it up. 'What?'

Everyone stared at Walter as he slumped down onto the sofa and replaced the receiver.

'Well?' demanded Pearl.

'Get me a drink.'

Barry returned with a large glass of whiskey, which Walter downed it in one.

'What have you done?' Pearl asked her brother.

'That was Mark, the landlord of the Boy. He said that...' Walter held out his glass for a refill, and Barry obliged, '...he said that after I'd gone, Stan said that he was going to make everyone pay double fees 'cos of what I'd done. He said that anyone who didn't, would face his court. Mark said that everyone is furious.' Mopping at his brow with a handkerchief, he added, 'Mark said everyone's after me.'

Just at that moment, another brick came flying through the front room window, only this time the person who threw it stood on the street. 'I know you're in there Dorrell and I'll make you pay for this.'

Walter stood up and went to the window. 'You'll be the one who pays you fucker, I'm in charge now!'

The man laughed. 'In charge? You couldn't charge through an open door, you're done for.'

Pearl looked at her brother. He really was a very stupid man.

Chapter 40

1952 – Mansfield.

Billy Porter had known Stan his whole life. They would finish each other's sentences and they very often knew what the other was thinking before they'd thought it.

Most people thought that shouting, swearing Stanley was the one to be scared of, but Billy knew it was the quiet, thinking, calm Stanley that was the one to be really frightened of. That Stanley would fuck you right up and you wouldn't even see it coming!

Billy watched Stanley, sitting in his chair, starring ahead, smoking. He was thinking. Billy knew trouble was afoot.

The rest of the Merry Men sat quietly, occasionally a mug clanged on the table, or a click of a lighter disturbed the silence. They knew they were waiting.

Stan got up from his chair and stubbed his fag out.

'Right, Larry, Babyface, on Saturday, I want you to head to Ladybrook and collect the money. Anyone who doesn't pay, tell them they are to report to The Boy on Sunday morning. Dicky, Billy, I want you to go to the town centre, same deal. No one is getting extra time to pay.'

'Do you want us to break a few things in the shops of those that don't pay, Stan?' asked Larry

'No, I want you to be calm, I want you to be polite, nothing is to be broken in the shops, no-one is to be harmed.'

The Fixer

1952

Sitting down in Mansfield Market Place, the Fixer took in the hustle of those who moved around them: stall holders selling their wares; shoppers busy getting their weekly shop done; Mothers shouting at children. Chatter of what was for tea filled the air, whilst men made their way to the pub for a pre-match pint arguing about whether Mansfield Town would get three points that afternoon.

The Market Place was just as it always was, and yet the Fixer was aware that in the evening, it would be full of people who were terrified as to what was about to befall them in Stanley Thomas's courtroom in The Boy pub.

Those same people would know that it was Walter Dorrell who had put them there.

A smile crept onto the Fixer's lips, and they laughed out loud.

'Alright duck?' asked a man sat next to them.

'Couldn't be better my friend.'

Chapter 41

1952 – Mansfield

'How did it go?'

'Well Stan, everyone bar Graham Roberts from the butchers, Mags Hall from the paper shop and Old Man Elliott from the cobblers paid double. Those three paid their normal amounts.'

'What about the town centre lot Billy?'

'We had just two who didn't pay in full, John Spencer from the fruit and veg shop and Kevin Lewis from the hardware store. Told him to be in court for eight.'

Stan nodded. 'What did they say, anyone give you any trouble?'

'No, most said they would pay and to send you their respects, most wanted to get back at Dorrell.'

'Good. Reckon they'll all turn up?'

Larry laughed. 'Oh, they'll turn up, Stan.'

Chapter 42

1952 – George Street Brothel, Mansfield.

'Walter! Get down here, there's another pile of shit been posted through the letterbox, and I am not clearing it up again!' Pearl shouted at her brother.

Pearl had always hated her brother.

Her earliest memory was of sitting on the floor playing with some toys as her mum baked in the other room. Walter came in from school and seeing his sister sat all content and happy, he'd trod on her fingers and broken the toy she was playing with.

Betty Dorrell had come running into the room and being a very astute woman, had quickly worked out what had happened. She'd scooped Pearl up into her arms and soothed her tears and then she'd clipped Walter around the ear and sent him upstairs.

From that moment on, it was like an enemy line was drawn between them. Walter would do something to hurt Pearl or break something she thought was precious, but he was never clever enough to pull the wool over his mother's eyes. She could see right through him. Walter never got away with anything whilst Betty was around. In a different time period, Pearl thought her mum would have been the Chief of Police.

If she had been, Pearl was pretty sure the prisons would be empty as no one would dare commit a crime on Betty's watch!

John Dorrell was a gentle man, he saw the good in everyone, working on the bins. He was well known in Mansfield for always having a song to sing, a wave to give and a pleasantry to exchange. A big bear of a man who would get home from work filthy dirty. Once her Mum had given him what for, for getting dirt on her floor, he'd get out of the tin bath his wife had filled in the kitchen clean and tidy and smelling of soap. When Pearl was little, he'd always sit her on his knee and tell her a story, not one from a book, one he'd made up. He didn't go in for stories of princesses being rescued by knights in shining armour, instead, John Dorrell told her stories about princesses who rescued kingdoms and told the knights they were too busy for their nonsense.

John would say to his daughter, 'You, my darling have the power to rule the world and don't let anyone tell you differently.'

Pearl was a bright girl and had excelled at school, she even passed her eleven-plus and secured a place at the Queen Elizabeth's Girls Grammar School. John and Betty had been so proud when she'd got her scholarship.

She'd been doing really well there too, when tragedy had struck. John Dorrell had been at work on the bins when a driver had ploughed into him, and he'd been killed instantly.

Two weeks later, Betty had died, some say of a broken heart, but Pearl knew that she'd decided life wasn't worth living and had overdosed on gin and tablets. Her death was recorded as 'death by misadventure'.

From that moment on Pearl had been left under her brother's care. Walter was twenty-six when their parents died and going nowhere fast. Being the eldest, Walter had claimed that he'd inherited everything, including the house and that Pearl had to do everything he said.

John Dorrell had always seen the best in his son, saying, 'He's not a bad lad, just a bit misguided.'

Betty, ever the realist had said, 'Someone will do for that boy one day. He'll be six feet under before he's thirty.'

Seeing yet another pile of shit posted through their letterbox, and the boards that covered various windowpanes that had been broken by bricks, Pearl couldn't help, but think that her Mum had once again been spot on.

Walter came downstairs carrying a suitcase, 'You can pick that up Pearl, I'm working on a deal.'

'A deal, that's probably going to get you killed, or worse still one of us!'

Walter stopped to admire his reflection in the mirror at the bottom of the stairs, he smoothed his waistcoat and re-arranged what little hair he had. 'Pearl, I know Mum and Dad thought you were the bright one, but you're not. I mean they weren't bright either, were they? Getting knocked over and overdosing? No, I'm the one with the brains in this family!'

Pearl could feel the anger rise inside her, until her mouth filled with bile. If someone else didn't finish off Walter off soon, then she'd do it herself.

Bending to pick up the mess, she fantasised about sticking it in Walter's mouth and making him eat it. Instead, she said, 'I don't think these people are messing Walt.'

'Shut up, no-one's going to harm me, I've got an insurance policy.' He tapped the case in front of him. 'There's a lot of people who are going to want to help me out after they know what I know. Now leave me alone.'

Pearl walked off shaking her head.

The Fixer

1952

'You assured me that Dorrell would be sorted. Instead, it looks like he's made a right laughing stock of you.'

The Fixer sat across the table from Stanley.

Stanley laughed. 'No-one's made a laughingstock of me, it's in hand, Dorrell just doesn't know it yet.'

The Fixer grunted. 'Well, he's making noises about people in high places wanting to help him out and releasing some of the information he has. That cannot happen.'

'I know, and as I said Billy and I have it all in hand. Now stop worrying and let me get on with doing what I do.'

The Fixer nodded, got up and walked out.

Chapter 43

1952 – The Boy pub, Mansfield.

Stanley walked into The Boy pub. It was all set up courtroom-style just as he liked it: A table with a huge chair in the centre, his white wig on the table alongside his gavel and black cloth.

When Stanley held court, he meant business.

To the right of him were three chairs. Billy, Sidney, and Dicky would form the members of the jury. Larry would be chief jailer and deal with prisoners.

To the left was the witness box, to the right the seats where the accused would sit and watch proceedings.

Stanley signalled for everyone to get into position, he put the wig on his head, and Mark, the landlord, handed him a pint.

'Here you go Mr. Thomas, just let me know if you want anything else.'

Billy, Sidney, and Dicky took their chairs, while Larry opened the doors of the pub, and in walked those who hadn't paid their fines.

Stanley smiled. He could see how scared they were, but this wasn't about their fear, this was about their respect.

'The accused' all lined up in front of him, and Stanley banged his gavel on the table. 'Order, order in the court! Now then, jailer who's first?'

'Your Honour, it's the butcher Graham Roberts first.' Larry grabbed the elderly man by his arm and pushed him into the witness box.

'Graham Roberts, you are charged with non-payment of taxes, how do you plead?'

The elderly man started to stutter. 'Guilty, Your Honour, I'm sorry, I didn't have it this afternoon, but I've got it now.' The man reached into his pocket and pulled out a wad of notes. 'It's yours, I've put in a bit extra.'

Larry took the money off the man and put it on the table in front of Stanley.

'Sit down, I'll pass judgment shortly. Next!'

'Your Honour, this is Mags Hall from the paper shop.' Larry shoved the woman into the witness box, she was openly sobbing.

'Stop sniveling, woman, how do you plead to non-payment of taxes?'

'Please don't hurt me, my kids need me.'

'For the love of God woman, answer my fucking question! Guilty or not guilty?'

'Guilty', Mags sobbed.

'Now sit down and shut up! Next!'

Old Man Elliott made his way to the box, he'd been a fighter pilot during World War One and didn't look scared, more bemused. Stanley liked Old Man Elliott and knew that he'd play the game.

'How do you plead Old Man Elliott to the charge of non-payment of taxes?'

'Guilty, Mr. Thomas, Your Honour!'

'Sit down, judgement will be passed later.'

Old Man Elliott nodded and made his way to his seat, where he gently patted the shoulder of Mags Hall.

'Next!'

Larry dragged John Webster from the fruit and veg shop to the box, John looked around him nervously.

'John Webster, how do you plead to the charge of non-payment of taxes?'

'Guilty, Mr. Thomas, but I'll have the money by Wednesday and a bit extra.'

'Very good, now sit down.'

John Webster joined the row of people.

'Next!'

Last to the box was Kevin Lewis who ran the hardware store. He was a big man, and rumour had it he'd once been a bare-knuckle fighter, but he'd swapped the ring for selling hammers. Stan had wanted him to join the Merry Men, but he'd refused. He was however more than happy to supply them with any tools they might need.

'So, Kevin Lewis to the payment of non-taxes, how do you plead?'

'Guilty as charged Stan, I mean, Mr. Thomas.'

'Take a seat! Right, can I have the final defendant please?'

Everyone started to look around the room, slightly confused. There was a gentle hum of muttering. Who else was there? There'd only been the five of them?

Suddenly there was a lot of noise as Larry started dragging someone up from the cellar.

'Fucking move it, you cunt,' were Larry's instructions, as the person he was dragging came into view.

No-one could work out who it was, as they had a potato sack over their head and their hands and feet were tied together, but as they came further into view, the onlookers could see his shining black and red shoes, which were scuffed from being dragged along the floor.

Larry shoved the person into place in front of Stan.

'Remove the hood of the accused.'

'This is a mistake, Stan,' Walter said 'You're messing with the wrong man. But if you untie me, I'll let it go and we can move on.'

'Guard, silence the prisoner!'

Larry obliged with a quick punch to Walter's stomach, and he bent double.

Through gritted teeth and a shortness of breath, Walter stammered, 'Untie me now and I'll let this go.'

Stan laughed. 'I'm not sure our prisoner understands the concept of shutting the fuck up!'

Larry obliged with another punch to the stomach, and this time Walter lost his balance and fell over. Larry dragged him back up on his feet. Walter remained silent.

‘So, then, Dorrell, you are charged with disrespect, not just of myself and the rest of my associates, but that of your fellow man: the good and kind people of Mansfield who work hard every day to run their businesses and pay their taxes. Your crimes have meant that they suffered! They suffered by having their taxes increased and their Saturday night ruined by being dragged in front of this very court! How do you plead?’

‘Fuck you Stan!’

Larry didn’t wait to be asked, he just punched Walter in the stomach. He fell to the floor again and Larry swiftly kicked him the ribs and dragged him back to his feet.

‘Answer the question!’

Walter put his head down.

‘Dorrell, you know I’m a fair man, so this is what I’m going to do. You have a choice, you can either admit your guilt or I can ask your fellow defendants to pass judgement.’

Walter sneered. ‘I’m not admitting anything, you twat, and my people will never betray me, so let them decide!’ Walter stared at the row of defendants in what Stan could only assume he thought was a menacing way.

‘OK, Babyface, hand out the cards.’

Babyface started handing out cards and pens to the defendants.

What I want you to do,’ Stan instructed, ‘Is write a name on the card you’ve just been given. If you think you deserve to be punished for non-payment of taxes, then write your own name on the card. But if you think that Dorrell is a snivelling cunt and should pay for making you and your fellow business owners pay double, then write his name on the card. If you choose yourself, you will not only pay the money you owe, but taxes will remain doubled for you and your fellow business owners for the foreseeable future. Choose Dorrell and you will not pay extra and everyone who has paid double will have the extra refunded. We go with the majority; this court is fair.’

The defendants started to scribble on their paper.

Walter continued to stare at Stan.

Eventually everyone stopped writing.

‘Graham Roberts, please tell me how you have voted.’

Graham turned his card around, ‘I voted for Walter Mr. Thomas.’

‘Twat!’ shouted Walter, causing Larry to stamp on his foot.

‘Mags, how have you voted?’

‘I also voted for Walter, Mr. Thomas.’

‘Good, now you treat those kids of yours with the money you would have given me.’

‘Oh, I will Mr. Thomas, thank you, thank you so much.’

‘Old Man Elliott?’

Old Man Elliott turned his card round. 'Walter of course, no-good piece of shit that he is, this is all his fault!'

'Three votes so far, so it's just a formality, but let's carry on. John Webster, how do you vote?'

'I vote for Walter too, thank you.'

'And finally, Kev, how do you vote?'

'I vote for that prick Dorrell too, the man's a complete liability.'

Stanley slammed his gavel on the desk. 'The defendants have spoken! You are all free to go. Please tell your fellow business owners that their extra taxes will be returned to them within the week.'

The five defendants hurriedly made their way out of the pub.

'Now then, Dorrell, it looks like your people have spoken and have chosen you to take their punishment, so let's get things started. Dicky.'

Dicky produced a bowl and a spoon from behind the bar and placed it on a table, and Larry marched Walter over and pushed him into the chair.

"This, Dorrell, is a bowl of my morning shit and the first part of your punishment is to eat it. Eat it all up now Walter, there's a good boy!"

Chapter 44

1952 – George Street Brothel, Mansfield.

'He's here! The boss is here!' yelled Malcolm. 'He looks in a bad way.'

Roy and Barry rushed to the front door of the George Street Brothel, where they found Walter dumped in a heap on the floor, his clothes and his shiny red and black shoes covered in blood and vomit.

'Get me inside.' He hissed. The men started to get him to his feet. 'Careful!' he demanded. They managed to get him to the sofa, before he snapped, 'Pearl, May, Cheryl, get down here now!'

***

The three women emerged from their bedrooms and made their way down the stairs. Pearl was the last of three and she paused at the top of the stairs, so she could have a look at her brother, she allowed herself a quick smile. Such a shame. Composing her expression into that of a concerned sister, she rushed downstairs after the others. 'Oh no, what's happened?'

'Get some water, some...' Roy paused. 'Errr, bandages, plasters or something.'

'I'll go.' Pearl escaped into the kitchen, where she couldn't stop smiling. Whoever had given her brother a beating had done a good job. Not good enough though, because he was still breathing, but it was a start.

Pearl left the kitchen with a bowl of water and a cloth, and started wiping her brother's face, clearing away the blood.

'You smell of shit.'

'Stan made me eat a bowl of his,' Walter whined pathetically.

'He what?' Pearl turned her face away before anyone could see the tears of laughter that were starting to prick her eyes. 'Oh Walter, how terrible.'

Pearl carried on wiping the blood off his face. The more she cleaned, the more she could see that his nose was clearly broken; he had two swollen eyes and his lips were busted. She applied a couple of plasters to his forehead.

'I think you should go in the bath and then we can see what we are dealing with. May, go and sort him one out. Malcolm, Roy, you'll have to help him into it.'

All three of them did as Pearl said, Walter groaning and grumbling as they moved him. Once they were safely upstairs, Cheryl looked at Pearl and started to laugh. 'Eating shit indeed!'

'I know, fucking hell, I knew Stan wouldn't take this lying down. God knows what else he did to him; I can only assume it was painful!'

'Walt's lucky he didn't kill him.'

'Hmm, pity he didn't, although it's surely only a matter of time.'

Chapter 45

1952 – George Street Brothel, Mansfield.

A week after his beating, Walter was sat on the sofa under a blanket. His bruises were starting to fade to a yellowish colour, but his broken ribs still hurt and when he did move, he hobbled around.

Although he had put on a brave face, he was scared. He knew he'd gone too far and that he was lucky Stan hadn't killed him. He also knew that he'd been made to look like a fool in front of everyone. He needed to do something to regain the upper hand.

Walter would never tell anyone what had happened during that beating, but he fantasised about doing the same to Stanley one day. One day he would make Stanley pay. Once he was healed, he would work on a plan to get back at Stanley and those who had betrayed him, but for now the great Walter Dorrell needed to rest.

The Fixer

1952

The Fixer had, had a full report on what had gone off during Walter's punishment. It sounded like Stan had given it his own flavour, and the Fixer hoped it was enough to slow Walter down, but they doubted it was.

Chapter 46

1952 – George Street Brothel, Mansfield.

Walter sat in the kitchen of the George Street Brothel. For once everyone was out, only Malcolm remained, but he was outside guarding the door.

Walter made himself a cup of tea and opened up the case he'd put on the table. Very carefully he removed a notebook and some photos, before laying the photos out on the table.

His 'insurance policy' he called them. These were going to help him put Stanley in his place once and for all.

Walter started to arrange the photos into piles. He then got out his notebook and started to cross reference so that the photos were in date order and matched the notes in his book. Picking up one of the photos, he put it to one side. It was about time he started to make it clear just who was in charge.

Gathering everything back up he put it back into the suitcase and returned it to its hiding place. Collecting the photo from the table, he walked into the hall and picked up the phone and dialled.

'It's me, I'm going to send you something through the post and then we will have a chat.' With that he hung up.

Chapter 47

1952 – West Bridgeford

Frederick Dykes replaced the phone and smiled at his wife. 'Wrong number,' he said.

Cynthia Dykes smiled at her husband and returned to her needlepoint. She knew her husband well enough to know that they received a lot of wrong numbers at their house.

Frederick Dykes was the High Sherriff of the Nottingham, a position he'd got by lying and cheating his way there. He took a massive pride in the legend that went with the position and liked the fact it was part of his role to administer justice, be that fairly or otherwise.

He liked to be referred to as the 'Sherriff', Cynthia knew, particularly by the women he slept with, normally behind his poor wife's back. It was a generally acknowledged fact that Frederick's brand of justice could be bought, and he generally wasn't bothered whose cash he took.

Cynthia looked up from her needlepoint at her husband, to where was stood staring out the window, gently twiddling his thick black moustache, something she knew he did when he was nervous and thinking something over. Whoever had been on the end of the phone had rattled her husband.

'Are you sure you're OK Fred?'

'Yes, give over bothering me, I'm going out for a bit.'

Cynthia watched as he stormed out. Getting up she poured herself another gin and returned to her needlepoint, and as she sat down, she couldn't help but wish that whichever tart her husband had gone off to see might ask him to move in, so she could be rid of him.

Chapter 48

1988 – Juniper Care Home, Sutton-in-Ashfield.

George Haynes sat by the window of his nursing home with his newspaper, trying to drown out the sound of the old people getting over-excited by a game of whist. He tutted silently under his breath, as he moved his wheelchair! He would have serious words with his son the next time he visited about putting him in here.

'Would you like a cup of tea Lord Haynes?'

George looked up from his paper. 'Yes, Jean, I would, but make sure you don't just wave the teabag at it like you did last time, I want it nice and strong, and I also want a biscuit and not one of your cheap ones, I want the ones with the good chocolate."

'Yes, Lord Haynes.'

George watched as she scuttled off. They'd had the same conversation every day for the last ten years, George liked to think it kept Jean on her toes. He missed having people jump to his every command in his court room, so now he made do with making Jean's life a misery. He positioned his spectacles so that when she returned, he could peer over the top of them and say, 'Is that the best you can do? Well, I guess you've made it now, so I'll have to drink it.'

George had been a High Court judge for many years and still insisted on anyone he considered to be less important than himself calling him Lord Haynes. He pretty much kept himself to himself, although just recently an old army major had moved in and now, he spent some of the time he wasn't making Jean's life a misery swapping war stories and partaking in a glass of scotch with him.

George Haynes had once been a man to be feared and had made it his mission to rid the streets of scum. Despite his smallness of stature, round glasses and bald head, he had once been a terrifying man, he'd bullied people, stamped on anyone who's gotten in his way and done whatever he needed to, to get to the top. Even at the ripe old age of eighty-five, he got a kick out of making the younger nurses cry and delighted if he got them to quit on the spot. He liked to push the senior carers buttons by referring to them as 'his staff' or the 'maids'.

He was dragged from his thoughts by Jean.

'Here you go Lord Haynes, your tea, the good choccie biscuits and today's newspaper.'

He was just about to respond in his usual manner when he noticed the headline of 'The Daily Chronicle'. 'This can't be happening.'

Jean nodded and pointed at the mugshot of Stan. 'Oh, it's that man who's been on the telly talking about that murderer. My fella says that it was quite the story at the time. I think they were from round here somewhere; he's got the book at home.'

The mention of the book seemed to snap George out of his shock. 'Book? Could I possibly borrow it Jean?'

'Yes of course, I'll bring it in tomorrow.'

'Thank you.'

For the first time in ten years, George Haynes picked up his cup of tea and dunked his biscuit, without once making a comment about the colour of his tea or the thickness of the chocolate.

Chapter 49

1988 – Nottingham Prison.

Derek Davies made his final night-time checks, walking along the empty corridors of Nottingham Prison. No one could describe it as quiet, prisoners shouting abuse, yelling threats, mixed in with some gentle sobs.

Derek had worked at the prison since he was twenty-one years old and had seen a lot of changes, some good, some bad. He'd seen people come and go. He'd seen others come and stay and he'd seen some come and leave not necessarily of their own accord.

Occasionally, Derek would wander down to the old, condemned cell and into the execution chamber. Not many people knew that they still existed at Nottingham Prison, it always looked to Derek like the room was stuck in time. Once hanging had been abolished in 1964, they'd simply shut the door, the rope still dangling from the wooden framework and the trapdoor was still in full working order. Derek knew, because occasionally he tried it. The room looked ready to welcome another guest.

Derek had witnessed three executions during his time working at the prison. Jeremy Austin had been his first. Austin had slit the throat of an old lady as she'd been asleep, he then proceeded to rob her. He'd got caught trying to sell her wedding ring. Derek had been responsible for watching Jeremy Austin through the night and then on the morning of his execution had been there to walk with him from the condemned cell to the execution chamber. He'd then simply observed what had happened. Derek had only agreed to do it because he'd been paid overtime and he needed the money for his wedding. He thought he'd be more upset at the sight of a man being put to death, but Jeremy Austin was such a despicable human that it hadn't really bothered him.

The second was Neville Farr. Neville had been involved in a bank robbery that had gone wrong. He'd shot and killed three people, two people who'd been in the bank and the assistant manager. Derek thought he'd seemed quite sorry about it all and was quiet and unresponsive on the gallows, only saying he was sorry over and over again.

The third and last one had been Stanley Thomas. Standing on those deserted gallows, the noose hanging by the side of him, Derek sometimes thought he could hear Stan's voice. He had treated the whole thing like he was going for a pint with his mates, he hadn't been scared or frightened, he simply hadn't been bothered.

After Stan, Derek had refused all overtime relating to executions. He'd earned enough money for his wedding.

Derek still thought about Stan, it was hard not too, particularly with the book coming out and Henry Mason being on every talk show going. Derek remembered Henry and his dad Jerry, they still lived locally from what he heard, but he never went to the north of the county. Derek and his wife Miranda lived in Arnold and tended to stay in and around Nottingham. He wasn't sure what he'd say to them if he did see them anyway.

Derek had worked for Henry Mason when he'd been Prison Governor and he had no intention of ever seeing him again if he didn't have to.

Someone must have tipped the press off that he'd been involved in Stan's execution, because he kept getting phone calls about taking part in TV shows or giving an interview to the papers, but he simply wasn't interested.

At fifty-seven years old, Derek wanted to see out the rest of his career, retire, and then spend his days helping out at his local church and going on walking holidays to the Lake District.

Derek pulled the door shut on the condemned cell and locked the door. Stan and the past were best left where they were.

Chapter 50

1988 – Perth, Australia.

'That you, love?'

'Yes Mum, it's me, where are you?'

'Kitchen.'

Eddie Thomas walked in and kissed his mum on the cheek. 'What you making?'

'Chocolate chip cookies, your brother's favourite.'

Eddie stuck his finger in the bowl and his mum playfully tapped his hand away.

Hannah Thomas stopped stirring the mixture for a minute and looked at her son, he was the spitting image of his dad. Tall, broad shouldered, blond hair, the same piercing blue eyes. Years of living in Australia and working outdoors had given him a permanent tan. That's where the similarities ended. Eddie had none of his dad's cruelness, he was kind and gentle and made his money working at a local riding stable. When he wasn't teaching kids to ride, he was trekking through the Outback on the back of his horse, or on a beach surfing. He was happy, he was healthy, he was funny, and Hannah was incredibly proud of him.

'Where is that brother of mine?'

'He's outside on the decking, can you take him this and make sure he's not getting too hot?' Hannah handed Eddie a cup.

'He's a grown man Mum, he knows if he's getting too hot or not!'

She watched as Eddie headed outside, where Charlie was sat in his wheelchair. Watching through the window, she saw him turn his head at the sound of footsteps.

'That you, bro?'

'Yeah, it's me, Mum sent me out to check on you, and give you this. You OK?' Eddie handed his brother the cup and ruffled his hair affectionately.

'Get off, you great puff!' Charlie laughed at his brother.

Charlie Thomas had been in a wheelchair since he was five years old, a year before his dad had died. Looks-wise the two were very similar, except Charlie had his mum's slightly darker colouring and he was far broader in his shoulders from pushing himself around in his wheelchair and playing basketball.

Hannah had emigrated to Australia with her children in 1954, the year after Stan was executed. She wanted a fresh start for them all, she couldn't bear going to the shops and having people point at her or make assumptions that her children would grow up to be just like their dad.

The comments about herself she could just about stand, but one man had said to her in the street that he bet she was glad Charlie was in a wheelchair as he was less likely to grow up to be a murdering scumbag like his dad, but that Eddie was definitely destined for the hangman's noose.

Her brother Sidney had begged her not to go, promising that he and the rest of the Merry Men would take care of her. Her parents made a half-hearted attempt to keep her in England, but she knew that deep down they were ashamed of the dishonour her marriage had bought on them.

As soon as Hannah stepped onto the SS Orsova, she knew she'd made the right decision. As they left Tilbury Docks and started their long journey, she knew she was doing the best for her children; their children. Ultimately that was what Stan would have wanted.

Hannah had made a real life for them in Australia, she'd trained as a teacher and got herself a job at the local school, where she'd eventually ended up as Head Teacher. Her children had thrived in the sunshine. She'd made sure Charlie had gotten the best care and had gone to the best school and he'd grown up to be a really talented artist. His work was regularly on display in galleries all over Australia and sold quicker than he could paint. He also played wheelchair basketball and was all set to play in the Paralympics later that year.

Eddie too had flourished in Australia, having excelled at school and sports, and he loved being outdoors. Pretty much as soon as they'd stepped off the boat, Eddie had started riding and surfing and doing any outdoor sport he could manage. He'd started working at a local stable after school and had gone on to manage and then buy the stables.

Hannah shuddered at what both of them could have become had she stayed in Mansfield.

It was rare they spoke about Stan. Occasionally one of them would ask a question, but it was normally answered and moved past quickly.

Hannah had kept in touch with the Merry Men, some more than others; then odd Christmas card or phone call, but she knew what they were all up to as she spoke to her brother Sidney every week.

Hannah didn't really know what Sidney did, he said he was a successful businessman and restauranteur, he had a string of restaurants, bars, and clubs across Nottinghamshire. How legitimate he was, was another matter, but he'd successfully avoided prison his whole life, so she could pretend that his business interests were legitimate.

As Hannah popped the chocolate chip cookies into the oven, she smiled to herself and was truly grateful that she'd taken her children and moved halfway around the world.

Chapter 51

1952 – West Bridgford

Frederick Dykes had got up early every morning for a week, patiently waiting for the postman, so he could intercept the post before his wife got up.

Five days after the call from the 'wrong number', a brown envelope landed on the doorstep. Ripping it open, Frederick found a photo and a note. The note said, 'gather the troops, it's time to get rid of Stan.' The photo was from the George Street Brothel's latest party. Fredrick was wearing nothing put a cowboy hat, a gun sling with a Sheriff's badge attached to it and a pair of chaps. His cock was being sucked by one girl as another was ramming his gun up his arse.

Frederick went straight out to the garden and lit a fire; he then made a phone call.

Chapter 52

1952 – George Street Brothel

Walter smiled as he replaced the handset of the phone. The photo had, had exactly the effect he had wanted. He had explained that there were plenty more where that came from of all of them at the party.

The Sheriff had agreed to relay his message and work with him on a plan to get rid of Stan.

Walter's plan was far greater than a few bent officials, he intended to really show Stan who was boss.

'Malcolm, Roy, Barry, get in here now.'

The three men came wandering in, and Walter asked, 'What did you find out?'

'Well, boss, he tends to leave his house on Rock Hill at about nine every morning, sometimes he stops off for a packet of fags and other times he walks straight to meet Stan and the boys at the Town Mill.'

'So, if we're going to get him, we need to do it within a few minutes of him leaving home.'

'Yes, boss.'

'Roy, did you find somewhere we can take him?'

'Yes boss, we can take him to behind where the Stags is, there's some old wasteland there, no-one will find him for a bit.'

'Good, now I want us to do this tomorrow morning, everyone ready?'

'Yes, boss.'

Walter smiled. His plan was coming together, and soon Stanley Thomas would be the one eating his shit!

Chapter 53

1952 – Rock Hill, Mansfield.

Sidney 'Babyface' Longshaw, was the only son of Marlene and John and could do no wrong in either of their eyes.

His sister Hannah had been ten years old when he'd been born, and his dad had all but given up on having a son to carry on the family name. Between any other siblings this would have caused problems, but Hannah worshipped her brother just as much as the rest of the family but was always on hand to tell him when she thought he was making a mistake.

Ever since he'd been a baby, Sidney had charmed everyone he'd met; his beautiful face, mop of curly blond hair and clear blue eyes, along with a smile that could make you forget whatever it was you were about to say had made him a hit. Hannah had given him the nickname of 'Babyface' and it had stuck. Even in his teenage years, it was how he was known.

Sidney was bright, too. Intellectually he was sharp and did well at school, but he was also streetwise, and despite his teenage gangly limbs, he was tall and strong and even at sixteen years old turned ladies' heads.

Despite many attempts to change his mind, Sidney had decided school wasn't for him and he would rather make his way in the world with Stan and the boys. Hannah had pleaded with Sidney not to follow the lead of her wayward husband, but he just laughed at his older sister and told her not to worry. Hannah had tried to appeal to her husband's better nature, but Stan told her to stop mothering the boy and let him make his own choices in life.

In a last-ditch attempt, Hannah had tried to talk to her parents, but they'd simply uttered something about 'boys being boys'.

Truth be told, Sidney was in awe of Stan. He admired the sharp way he dressed, and the respect he commanded, not only from the rest of the Merry Men, but from everyone in Mansfield. Stan always had money in his pocket and the best of everything. Sidney wanted to be just like him.

He knew Stan trusted him and, despite the odd mistake, Sidney was doing well, he was learning the ropes. He'd noticed people were starting to treat him differently too, they'd step aside to let him pass, he had money in his pocket and the prettiest girls on his arm.

Getting ready to leave his house, he shouted through to his mum, 'See you later Mam, I'm off to work, not sure what time I'll be back.'

'Ok love, I'll save you some tea, be careful!'

'I will, love you.'

'Love you.'

Sidney shut the door behind him and started walking down Rock Hill. His thoughts were taken up by the day ahead and a girl who he'd been seeing who was starting to get a bit keen. He thought it might be time to dump her and move on.

He was so lost in his thoughts, that he didn't notice the car slowly driving behind him, and he didn't notice when it gently pulled up beside him and someone got out and bashed him on the head and dragged him inside.

No, Sidney didn't notice that at all.

Chapter 54

1952 – Mansfield.

When Sidney woke up, he was laying on the floor, his hands bound behind his back and his feet tied. He immediately recognized the four faces stood over him: Walter Dorrell and his lackies, Malcolm, Barry and Roy. The four of them looked down on him, their faces a mixture of excitement and fear.

'You, know who I am, you cock sucker?'

Sidney couldn't help but laugh. 'That's rich coming from you.'

Walter landed a kick square in Sidney's stomach.

'I know who you are, Dorrell, you and your bum boys.'

'Oi, we ain't no queers!' piped up Malcolm.

'No, we're not!' agreed Roy.

Sidney lay on the floor amused as a quarrel broke out between them as to whether or not any of them were gay and when they'd last had sex with a woman. It was pitiful really. Eventually Walter stepped in.

'Shut it you lot! Babyface isn't it? Isn't that what they call you? Well, you ain't going to have no baby face by the time we've finished with you!' Walter bent down and started to stroke Sidney's face. 'Pity really, because I do hate to see something so beautiful become so spoilt. Of course, you could stop this by coming and working for me: girls or boys on tap and I'm sure we could form a very special friendship.'

Sidney laughed. 'No fucking way you poncey bastard.'

Walter grabbed Sidney's face. 'Stan's finished in this town, done with, a goner! The rest of the Merry Men will be out of here too, this is my town now and if you're not with me, you're against me and believe me pretty boy, you do not want me as your enemy. One last chance.'

'Fuck you, Dorrell!'

'Shame. Boys, he's all yours.'

Sidney could see the look of confusion in Malcom, Roy and Barry's eyes, and eventually Barry spoke, ''Ours' boss?'

'Yes! Beat him up! Oh, for Christ's sake do I have to do everything myself?' With that Walter landed a boot firmly in Sidney's ribs, and the others seemed to catch on and joined in the kicking.

Sidney kept quiet as the kicks rained down, he could feel that a couple of his ribs were broken and his nose was busted, but he also sensed that these useless oafs had the stamina of a group of a ninety-year-old Nannas. Sidney pretended to pass out and the kicking stopped.

'Now what boss?'

'Leave him here, someone will probably find him and if not, oh well!' Walter laughed and the other three joined in. 'I told you, Stan's done for, this is just a warning shot. There's far bigger things afoot for that twat, he'll be dangling at the end of the hangman's noose before the end of the year. Now let's get out of here."

Sidney lay perfectly still, he heard Walter's car door slam and the car drive off. As he contemplated how he was going to get himself free, he heard a noise and footsteps start to make their way towards him.

Sidney closed his eyes again. Gently someone touched his shoulder.

'You alright mister?'

Sidney opened his eyes. 'Sort of, but I need help. Do you know who I am?'

'No, mister.'

'I'm Sidney Longshaw, I work for Stanley Thomas, do you know him?'

'Yes, mister, we know him, we aren't going to get in no bother, are we?'

'No, but you need to listen to me, I want one of you to run down to the Town Mill and tell Stan that you've found me, and I want the other to untie me, got it?'

'Yes, Mister Sidney. Joe you go and get Mr Thomas and I'll wait here.'

The second boy started running as the first got to work untying Sidney.

Chapter 55

1952 – Mansfield

Ten minutes later Sidney could see Stan's car making its way towards him. Pulling up, the doors opened and out got Stan, Larry and the young boy who'd gone to fetch them.

Stan looked at the other boy who was sat on the floor next to Sidney. 'What's your name?'

'It's Gavin, Mr Thomas.'

'Well Gavin, me and my boys are indebted to you and your mate Joe here, thank you for what you've done. Here's a pound each, I want you to take it and I don't want to find out that you've told anyone else about this, do I make myself clear?'

Both boys spoke in unison. 'Yes, Mr Thomas, thank you, Mr Thomas.' Taking their money and picking up their fishing stuff they headed off.

Stan turned his attention back to Sidney. 'Now then, what happened to you?'

'Dorrell and his boys jumped me as I left home.'

'What damage they done?'

'Can feel a couple of broken ribs and I think my nose is busted.'

'Larry, help me get him up and to the car, we'll take him back to my place and Hannah can fix him up. What the fuck were you thinking letting Dorrell get one over on you?'

'I'm sorry Stan, I just didn't see them, but Dorrell's planning something; they thought I was unconscious and started talking about how you were done for and that this was just a warning shot. I think he's planning on setting you up for something so that you hang."

Stanley laughed. 'We'll fucking see about that! Dorrell really is a very stupid man.'

Chapter 56

1952 – Crow Hill Drive, Mansfield

'Hannah, Hannah, where are you?'

'I'm in the kitchen, what's all the shouting?' Hannah emerged from the kitchen into the hall wiping her hands on her apron. She went deathly pale at the sight of her brother covered in blood and being held upright by her husband and Larry. 'What in God's name has happened? Take him into the lounge, put him on the sofa.'

Hannah went back into the kitchen and emerged with some bandages, a cloth, and a bowl of water. Kneeling in front of her brother, she gently started to mop his face.

'Is someone going to tell me, what has happened to my brother?'

'The stupid prick got himself beaten up by Dorrell and his boys.'

'Walter Dorrell, did this to my brother? I thought you'd dealt with him?'

'I have, he's acting up, needs a gentle reminder.'

'If you don't sort him Stan, I will!'

Hearing their dad's voice, Charlie and Eddie came bursting into the room. 'Daddy, Daddy, Daddy! Uncle Larry!'

Slowly they noticed the blood-stained face of their Uncle Sidney, and Eddie started to cry, while Charlie gently approached his Uncle. 'What's the matter Uncle Sidney, did you fall over?'

Sidney smiled. 'Something like that, mate.'

The Fixer

1952

The Fixer made themselves a cup of tea and sat at the kitchen table. They'd had word about Dorrell's attack on Sidney and the threats he'd made towards Stanley. They'd also heard from Frederick Dykes about the photo and the demands that were being made of him.

Taking a sip of their tea, The Fixer decided it was time.

Chapter 57

1952 – Crow Hill Drive, Mansfield

Hannah quietly opened the door of the spare room and checked on her brother. Sidney was sound asleep. Not even his bruised and battered face could detract from his beauty. Closing the door, she then checked in on her two boys.

Charlie was five years old and a miniature version of her. From the moment he'd arrived, Hannah knew she would fight tooth and nail to protect him and make sure he grew up to be a good person. Charlie was a sweet, kind boy, who spent ages playing games with his brother and loved to draw. Very often, Hannah would find him sat on the floor surrounded by pieces of paper and his crayons drawing anything and everything.

Eddie was three years old and he had the same blond hair and blue eyes as his dad. Eddie was full of energy, which he had by the bucketload. From the moment he woke up to the moment he went to sleep he was charging around. One minute he was pretending to be a policeman, the next a cowboy, then he was playing football or digging in the garden.

Hannah loved her boys, and as she stood watching their little chests rise and fall in steady regulated breaths, she worried what would become of them. Would her little boys follow in their father's footsteps? Would they take over his empire, striking fear into the hearts of anyone who crossed them? Would she worry about the police knocking at her door to tell her that they'd been arrested, or even, worse murdered? Would each marry some woman who would be fall hopelessly in love with them, not realizing what they were getting into, and then spending a life living in fear that something bad would happen?

Hannah wanted the best for her boys, and she was damn sure they were going to get it.

Chapter 58

1952 – Crow Hill Drive, Mansfield

In the future, whenever anyone asked Hannah about the twenty-second of May 1952, she would say it started just like any other Thursday.

Hannah got out of bed and washed and dressed, tying her dark hair into a ponytail. She woke Stan and then went into her boys and woke them up, washing and dressing them. Then the boys sat at the kitchen table whilst she made them breakfast.

Charlie was telling her about a picture he wanted to draw, and Eddie was saying he wanted to play outside after breakfast.

Stan came downstairs to join them, and they ate breakfast as a family, laughing and joking. Breakfast-time was Hannah's favourite time of the day. It was their time.

At nine a.m., Stan kissed Hannah on the cheek, kissed his boys and headed off.

Hannah started to wash the pots and said the boys could go and play in the backyard.

The morning passed as it normally did, Hannah doing chores and popping out to make sure the boys were OK. They were spending the morning playing at cowboys, their laughter and happy squeals filling the air. Hannah loved the sound of them playing, it was the soundtrack to her day.

At midday, Hannah started to prepare lunch for her and the boys, as she sliced and buttered a few slices of bread, she realized the air was silent. As she paused to listen closer, screams replaced the laughter she was listening for, beginning as sobs and soon escalating into wild noisy, pain-filled screams.

At first Hannah thought it was the neighbour's cat, but pretty soon she realised the screams were coming from her own backyard and they were littered with the word 'Mummy'.

Running outside, Hannah found Eddie on his hands and knees clawing at a pile of slabs, his tiny three-year-old hands bleeding and red raw where he was frantically scrabbling at the concrete beneath him.

'Eddie, what are you doing, what's the matter?'

Through loud sobs, Eddie started to point at the slabs, and Hannah was unable to make him stop trying to move them.

As if in slow motion, Hannah turned her head to where Eddie was pointing, and she saw a tiny head poking out from under the slab. It was Charlie, he was laying perfectly still and quiet, but she could see tears slowly rolling down his face.

'Help me, help me!! Call an ambulance!' Hannah started screaming the words over and over as she joined Eddie in trying to move the slab of concrete under which her eldest son was trapped.

Pretty soon a couple of the neighbours came running, Cyril March and Ken Trinder lifted the slab off the young boy, before Ken's wife Pamela joined them.

'An ambulance is on the way,' she said.

Hannah sat cradling the head of her son. 'Charlie, can you hear me, what happened?'

Charlie, sobbed. 'Am I in trouble?'

Hannah noticed that Ken had picked up her youngest son and his wife Pamela was cleaning up his hands.

'No, my darling, not in trouble, I just need to know what happened.'

Eddie stopped crying and said, 'It was the man with the red and black shoes, he asked us if we wanted to play hide and seek. He made me hide in the coal shed, but I peeked so I could see and he told Charlie to hide under there and then he and his friend dropped it. I tried to make him help Charlie, but he laughed and left. I'm sorry

Mummy, I tried to help.' Eddie began to sob loudly. Ken and Pamela comforted the boy.

At that moment, the ambulance arrived, they were closely followed by Stan. Cyril March had been to fetch him.

As Hannah climbed into the back of the ambulance with her son, she could see Stan speaking to their neighbours and making arrangements for Eddie to go to her parents.

As Hannah stroked the head of her oldest son, she knew that one of her biggest fears had been realized: Stan's business had finally hurt one of her children. Hannah swore that someone would pay for hurting one of her own. She wasn't sure who. But someone would.

Chapter 59

1952 – Kings Mill Hospital, Sutton-in-Ashfield.

Hannah paced the floor of Kings Mill Hospital, while Stan sat quietly, his arms folded across his chest. Hannah knew he was angry as her and was trying to keep himself calm.

'Mr and Mrs Thomas? I'm Dr Gibson. I've been looking after Charlie. Would you follow me please?'

'How is he, how's my boy?' Stan's voice was low and calm.

Dr Gibson, showed them into a side room and beckoned for them to take a seat. 'Charlie has undergone some fairly major trauma to the lower half of his body. The slab has broken both his legs and shattered his pelvis.'

'My poor little boy, can I see him?' Hannah started to get up, but Stan gently pushed her back down.

'That's not it though, is it, Doc?'

'I'm afraid not, Mr Thomas. Charlie doesn't appear to have any feeling in the lower half of his body at all. We are running more tests as we speak, and we will make a decision if he needs an operation. The likelihood is that he will need surgery. His pelvis has been very badly damaged, and we think it's affected some nerves in his spine."

Hannah started to cry. 'My poor, poor Charlie.'

'Will my boy walk again?'

'It's too early to say at this stage, but his little body has undergone a massive trauma. He's a brave lad though, he's not complained once, and all the nurses are quite taken with him. If you'd like to see him, I can arrange that.'

'Yes please, we'd like that wouldn't we Han?'

Hannah nodded.

'Give me five minutes and I'll send a nurse to get you.'

Hannah broke down in sobs and Stan put an arm round his wife. 'I'll get the bastard who did this.'

Hannah stopped crying and turned to face her husband, her face red and angry. 'The bastard that did this? You're the bastard who did this, it's because of you, that my boy is in this state! It should be you in that hospital bed, not Charlie."

Chapter 60

1952 – Kings Mill Hospital, Sutton-in-Ashfield

Charlie Thomas lay in his hospital bed. He wasn't quite sure what was happening, but he thought he must be in trouble because his mummy and daddy hadn't been to see him and the doctors and nurses kept sticking things into him to see if they hurt. It didn't, but maybe he should say it did, then maybe he could see Mummy and Daddy.

He thought about his little brother Eddie too. He hoped he was OK. The bad man had made Eddie get into the coal shed, and he hoped he hadn't hurt him too. Charlie started to cry.

'Charlie, baby, it's Mummy.'

Charlie could see his mum's face, and it looked like she'd been crying. He hoped it wasn't because he was in trouble.

'Mummy, I'm really sorry, am I in trouble?'

'Trouble? Of course not, we are going to work with the doctors and nurses and make you all better again, but I need you to be a brave boy and tell me and Daddy what happened.'

'Is Daddy here too?'

'I am son, I'm here.'

Charlie watched as his dad walked towards the other side of his bed and took his hand.

'Daddy, if I tell the doctors I can feel my legs, can I come home?'

'Son, I need you to do me a huge favour, OK? I need you to tell the doctors and the nurses the truth all the time. If you can't feel something, say so, if something hurts, tell them. That way we can bring you home as quickly as possible.'

'Yes Daddy, I promise. Where's Eddie? The man locked him in the coal shed.'

'Eddie's fine my darling, he was very brave, and he tried to help you. He's with Mamma and Pops, they're looking after him.'

'Charlie, can you tell me about the bad man?'

'He said he wanted to play hide and seek with me and Eddie, he said he was a friend of yours and that you'd sent him to play with us while mummy cleaned up.'

'What did he look like son, was he on his own?'

'He wasn't very tall, and he had light brown hair and his teeth stuck out like Bugs Bunny, he had these black and red shoes on, Eddie said they looked like clown's shoes. He said he was your friend Daddy. Am I in trouble?'

'No, son, you're not, I'm just going to have a word with Mummy and then I'm going to nip home and get you some pyjamas and your teddy bear.'

***

Hannah and Stanley stepped outside of the hospital ward.

'It was fucking Dorrell! Dorrell did this to our boy! I'm going to go home and get some stuff for you and Charlie and then I'll make some arrangements.'

Hannah nodded, and just as Stan was about to leave, she reached out and grabbed his hand. Pulling him towards her, she kissed his cheek and whispered in his ear, 'I don't care what you do to him, but he suffers... and he suffers badly!'

Chapter 61

1952 – George Street Brothel, Mansfield

Pearl Dorrell had spent a very rare day by herself. She'd got the bus into Nottingham and had been shopping. She'd savoured the hours of strolling round the shops and enjoyed lunch in the café off Market Square, eating her sandwich and drinking her coffee, watching the world go by.

As she watched the other people going about their business, she could have been a million miles away from the George Street Brothel and her brother.

Pearl knew he was up to something but wasn't sure what. The beating from Stan and the boys had made no difference. If anything, it had made Walter worse. He was determined to get his own back and Pearl had noticed him making furtive phone calls and hiding that ridiculous box of his away which he thought no one knew about.

The whole thing made Pearl feel uneasy.

Arriving back home, Pearl could hear laughter coming from the kitchen. It sounded like Walter was holding court and those idiots Malcolm, Roy and Barry were lapping up every word.

As she opened the door, she caught the words 'Stan' and "had it coming" and her heart sank. What on earth had her brother done this time?

'Alright, Walter, boys? You all seem in a good mood?'

'Sister dear, I am. Lets' just say that when you disrespect Walter Dorrell, you make an enemy for life, and I will make your life a misery.'

The three men laughed out loud again.

'What have you done? Have you caused bother with Stan again? You know what happened last time?'

Walter lashed out at his sister smacking her around the face. 'Pearl, I will not have you question me and my actions, now fuck off.'

Pearl left the room. Her brother was getting out of hand, and she knew it was only a matter of time before someone did something.

The Fixer

1952

News about little Charlie Thomas had travelled quickly. He was still in hospital, he'd had his operation, but the odds of him walking again were slim.

The Fixer knew Stan was itching to get at Dorrell, but they'd instructed him to lay low. Something would be done about Dorrell, but it had to be done in the right way.

The Fixer was managing the situation.

Chapter 62

1952 – Kings Mill Hospital, Sutton-in-Ashfield.

Hannah had spent every moment she could at the hospital with Charlie. She was in awe at just how brave he was. He'd endured test after test, he'd been prodded, he'd been poked, he'd had two operations and he'd smiled through the whole thing.

Every day he'd say, 'Mummy do you think today will be the day I'll be able to walk again?'

It broke Hannah's heart to say, 'Maybe tomorrow.'

The doctors were pretty certain that Charlie would never walk again. They'd explained that they'd tried everything they could, but his pelvis and spine had been too badly injured. They'd started a course of physiotherapy and were organising a wheelchair.

Hannah had balanced her time at the hospital with looking after Eddie, who was struggling to understand why his brother could no longer run around and play with him. Hannah's Mum and Dad had been helping out with childcare and the neighbours had been doing what they could too.

Hannah couldn't work out whether it was because she was Stan's wife, or because they were genuinely shocked that someone could do such a thing to a small child, whoever's son he was.

The gossip around Mansfield was rife as to who would do such a thing to Stan's son. Most people were speculating that it was Walter Dorrell and they were waiting for Stan to exact his revenge. The police weren't really interested, they said they were investigating, but they weren't really bothered, they clearly thought that anyone related to Stan got what they deserved.

Stan had remained quiet on the matter. He had been at the hospital just as much as he could, reading stories to Charlie and promising him the best wheelchair money could buy. He'd been home to tuck Eddie in bed at night and for once in his life, Stan had remembered his 'please and thank you's' whenever one of the neighbours had helped out.

Hannah had tried to talk to him about Dorrell, but he'd only ever say that it was in hand and she wasn't to question his methods.

Chapter 63

1952 – Berry Hill Park, Mansfield.

The last few weeks had taken their toll on Stan, and he needed just thirty minutes to think. Sitting on a bench looking over the lake in Berry Hill Park, Stan took a long drag on his cigarette.

Seeing his boy laying under that slab, sitting by his hospital bed, telling him he'd be OK and then hearing the news that he'd never walk again had made Stan even more determined to put this right. This was all his fault. He felt like he was losing control of the situation. Sidney taking a beating had been bad enough, but to see his son laying in a hospital bed, unable to walk, nearly broke him.

The Fixer had told him to wait, that plans were being made and then Stan could do whatever he wanted to Dorrell. Stan knew the Fixer was right, but it was hard. Every bit of him wanted to go over to Dorrell's and beat him till his stupid bucked teeth fell out and his pale eyes popped out of his scrawny body. He'd beat him till nobody of this earth would recognise him.

But Stan had been told to wait and wait he would.

Chapter 64

1952 – Old Market Square, Nottingham

Frederick Dykes looked out of his office window onto the Old Market Square below. He could see people going about their business, and he felt his lip curl into a sneer. They didn't have a clue.

A knock at the door bought him round.

'Enter.'

'Lord Haynes for you, Sheriff. I've organised you a tea tray.'

'Thank you. George, how nice to see you.' Frederick greeted the judge with a warm smile and a hearty handshake. 'Take a seat my friend.'

The two sat at the table in the office and exchanged banalities about how their wives were doing, what players Billy Walker would bring to Nottingham Forest for the next season and how their golf handicaps were coming along.

The secretary placed the tea tray on the table between them and poured the drinks, quietly leaving the room as the two debated whether Wally Ardron would be their top scorer next season. They appeared like any other old friends, comfortable in each other's company and using their positions for a catch up.

The moment the door was closed, Frederick got up and moved to his desk. Throwing an envelope down in front of George Haynes, he said, 'This is what the bastard has sent me and now he's trying to blackmail me.'

Reaching into his briefcase, George Haynes got out a similar envelope. 'Snap! Any of the others had anything similar?'

'The Doc isn't returning my phone calls, and the Gov has said he'll talk to the Rev, but he's definitely had an envelope.'

'Any news on what Dorrell actually wants?'

'Just says it's something to do with Stanley Thomas and that he wants him gone. I'm not quite sure what that means." Frederick took a sip of his tea.

'We can't have that sleazy bastard calling the shots. We need to deal with Dorrell and we need to do it quickly.'

'Has the Fixer been in touch?'

'Yes, they've said not to do anything rash and that a plan is being formulated. The longer we leave it, the more dangerous Dorrell gets. Have you heard what he did to Stan's lad?'

Frederick nodded. 'Yes, he'll never walk again apparently. I can't believe Stan hasn't done anything yet.'

'So, do we wait, or do we do something?'

Frederick took a deep breath. 'I say we give the Fixer two weeks and then we take matters into our own hands.'

George nodded. 'Agreed.'

Chapter 65

1952 – Nottingham Prison

William Smith replaced the handset of his phone and scribbled a note in his diary.

Frederick – June 30th 7pm

He must tell his secretary to block out that afternoon.

Sitting back in his chair, William looked out of his office window, which overlooked the exercise yard of Nottingham Prison. He wanted the prisoners to know that he was always watching.

William Smith wasn't a man to be messed with. Six feet two 2 in height, he was all muscle, and had a mop of bright ginger hair and matching beard. Even his shadow had been known to strike fear into the hardest of criminals.

Before he'd entered the prison service, he'd been an Army Officer in World War Two and had been awarded the Military Cross and the George Medal. He'd had an incredibly distinguished army career and had been involved in the liberation of Belsen. It had also been rumoured that he had been in charge of looking after the prisoners throughout the Nuremberg Trials and had been present at the executions. Behind his back, some of the prisoners would joke that he'd tapped up the Nazi officers about the best ways to treat prisoners.

William had, had a meteoric rise to be Governor of Nottingham Prison. He was a fierce, tough and sometimes cruel man who did not believe in the rehabilitation of criminals. Given his way, all criminals would be subjected to hard labour, public floggings, and execution. He felt the current laws were far too lenient. Crimes should be punished. In his prison, even the most minor of misdemeanours were treated with the harshest of punishments.

William knew that Dorrell would meet a similar harsh fate and he only hoped he was there to witness it, and even better still, administer it himself.

Chapter 66

1952 – Nottingham Prison

Dr Michael Dunderdale bit into his spam sandwich, crumbs falling onto his protruding stomach. He brushed them away with one hand and continued flicking through the pages of his newspaper with the other.

There was a knock at the door. 'Enter.'

One of the nurses came into the room. 'Sorry to bother you Doctor, while you're having your lunch, but the Governor has asked to see you.'

'Tell him, I'll be there in fifteen minutes, now get out.'

There was no way that he, Dr Michael Dunderdale was jumping to William Smith's tune. He could wait. Michael took another bite of his sandwich and washed it down his gluttonous throat with a swig of tea.

Michael Dunderdale was not a well-liked man. He was known as "Blunderdale" throughout the prison because of his lack of ability to diagnose anything correctly. It was a running joke amongst the prisoners, that men who Blunderdale had pronounced dead had gone on to live long and happy lives.

Thirty-seven years old and single, Michael was grossly overweight with a potbelly that spilled over his trousers, and he insisted on wearing a tight belt, which only highlighted the problem. He always wore a black shirt, allegedly they were different ones, but they all seemed to have the same sweat patches ingrained in the fabric under the armpits. He wore a gold chain around his neck, which had probably once fit, but now looked like if he made a sudden movement, it could strangle him at any minute. His pale blonde hair had prematurely thinned during his teens, but he insisted on keeping the wispy bits that remained. His look was topped off with bottle top glasses. He was not an attractive man in any sense of the word.

Michael knew exactly what William wanted with him, he also knew how worried Frederick and George were, although he didn't know why they were bothered. Dorrell was nothing and a nobody. Michael bit into another sandwich and took another slurp of tea and settled down to read the racing pages.

Chapter 67

1952 – Ye Olde Trip to Jerusalem Pub, Nottingham.

The Reverend Roger Collins sipped his pint and eyed up a woman sat in the corner of the pub; the man she was sat with had his back to him. Roger decided they must be lovers. After all, what kind of bloke bought his wife to a pub on a Thursday afternoon? That was something reserved for mistresses, slags and prostitutes. Roger raised his glass to her. If she was a prostitute, she might fancy a bit of business after she'd finished with this one. The woman lowered her eyed and looked away.

'Slag.' Roger muttered under his breath.

'Afternoon, Reverend.'

Roger turned to see a man he knew from drinking in the pub. He didn't know his real name, just that he was known as 'Dodgy Paul' by all the regulars.

'Afternoon.' Roger raised his pint by way of a greeting.

'Want another?'

'Why not? Bless you, my child.'

Dodgy Paul signalled to the barman and pulled up a stool next to where Roger was sat. 'No work today, Reverend?'

'No, Thursday is my day of rest.' Roger laughed at his own joke.

'Only there's a game going down tonight if you fancy it?'

'Always. What's the stake and where?'

'Hundred quid and we're playing at my place. It's an exclusive game, just six of us, but a chance to win big.'

Roger's eyes lit up, a chance to win back some of the money he'd lost over the last few weeks, his luck had got to change. 'I'm in, what time?'

Dodgy Paul drained the last of his pint. 'Eight. See you later Reverend.'

Roger needed a win; he'd not done well the last few months and he was running out of people to borrow money from. His job as a prison chaplain didn't pay much, and as the Bishop of Nottingham kept reminding him, he was very lucky to still have a job at all. He'd been sent to work in the prison after a series of 'indiscretions' ten years ago. He knew he'd been lucky to keep his job, but if he was honest, Roger really didn't care. He'd only become a vicar because he got a free house and he thought women would find the dog collar a turn on and he'd have sex on tap. It hadn't really worked out that way.

At sixty years old, Roger was biding his time until he could retire. Publicly, to the Bishop he played the game of rehabilitating prisoners. In private it was more a case of beer, women, and gambling.

Roger was not an unattractive man, but years of heavy drinking had left him a red complexion and a bulbous nose, as well as a thickening waist. His once-jet black hair was now salt and pepper grey and his arrogance, once charming was now just plain rude.

His days were spent listening to prisoners bang on about how badly they were treated, or worse still, the ones who'd found religion. They always made Roger roll his eyes, he had to stop himself saying, 'Bullshit, you just want to carry favour with the Governor.' But he'd nod and tell them how happy he was they'd found the Lord and then invite them to pray with him.

If he was honest, his favourite bit of his job was dealing with the condemned prisoners. At least you never knew what you were going to get with them. Some confessed everything, some were really angry, and others were really blasé right up until the last minute.

The execution itself was usually fun too; there was always a buzz around the prison and then someone invariably wanted to interview him about his opinion on capital punishment.

Roger had found it far more lucrative to sell his story to the papers and be an 'inside source'. He'd phone up his favourite journalist and recount all the gory details and be paid handsomely for it. He could really do with a couple more executions to boost his bank account.

Chapter 68

1952 – Nottingham Prison

Reginald Braithewaite slammed the cell door shut. That would be last he'd hear out of that gobby little prick for a few days. Opening the hatch in the door he saw the prisoner huddled on the floor, clutching his ribs, blood pouring from a cut above his eye.

Reginald didn't have the time or patience to deal with criminals who thought they were above the law and gave him lip. He found in cases like that a swift boot to the ribs and a smack in the face normally gave him a bit of peace.

Reginald had joined the prison service when he was eighteen years old and to start with, he'd been full of hope that he'd be able to work with the prisoners to rehabilitate them and show them a new way of life, open them up to a life where they saw the good in the world.

Sadly, after thirty-one years of service, Reginald had become incredibly jaded by the whole thing. He'd been beaten up on numerous occasions once suffering a beating so bad that he thought he'd never return to work. He'd been spat at and had urine and faeces thrown at him a million times. He'd seen prisoners hurt themselves and each other in the worst ways imaginable. He'd witnessed and administered corporal punishment and been present at numerous executions.

He remembered the very first execution he'd attended, he'd been twenty-one years old at the time and still believed in the rehabilitation of prisoners. He was anti the death penalty, thinking it cruel and barbaric, but he'd been told that it was part of his job and that he had to go.

. The criminal facing the gallows was a murderer by the name of Richard Burton. Richard had raped and murdered his landlady, having subjected her to horrific abuse over a six-month period, keeping her prisoner in her own home and abusing her on a daily basis. He'd eventually killed her and chopped her body into pieces and put them in the loft. The alarm had been raised when her friends started to worry that they hadn't seen her for a while, and she always seemed to be out when they popped round. A police officer had eventually gone around to investigate and had noticed the smell of rotting flesh in the house and the fact that Richard Burton had been really vague about his landlady's whereabouts. A search of the house had revealed the grim secret.

Reginald hadn't been sure what to expect from a man who was about to face the gallows. Burton had been aggressive, shouting and screaming proclaiming his innocence and swearing vengeance on everyone. What had struck Reginald was the way in which the hangman, Jerry Mason, had dealt with the situation. He'd been firm and undeterred by the screaming and had completely taken control of the situation. So, although to Reginald it felt like it had gone on for twenty minutes, the reality was it had taken Jerry Mason less than a minute to lead a kicking and screaming prisoner to his death.

After that, Reginald worked with Jerry Mason, or Old Man Rope as he was known on a regular basis and increasingly started to think that the prisoners who met their fate in this way deserved it.

Once, he'd got a few executions under his belt, Reginald started to administer corporal punishment too. It had turned his stomach the first time he'd heard the noise of the birch making contact with a man's bare skin, he'd done the lashes and then promptly left the room to throw up. This too became easier, particularly when the beatings were being dealt out to a prisoner who'd been giving him lip or had thrown something at him. Reginald took his time with those. Sometimes he dished out unofficial beatings too.

At forty-nine years old, Reginald Braithewaite was totally disillusioned with the prison service and wanted to earn as much money as he could and then retire somewhere warm, where he could drink beer and read the paper in peace.

The Fixer

1952

The Fixer watched as George Haynes left the Town Hall on Old Market Square after his meeting with Frederick Dykes. The Fixer knew that the men were getting increasingly concerned about Walter's behaviour and were intent on doing something.

The Fixer had told them to wait, everything was in place and the timing needed to be just right. The Fixer was leaving nothing to chance.

In six weeks, Walter would be no more.

The thought made the Fixer smile.

Chapter 69

1988 – Perth, Australia

Hannah shouted for her boys to come in. It didn't matter that Charlie was now forty-one and Eddie thirty-nine, they were still her boys.

Putting the cookies, she'd just baked onto a plate, she started to pour tea as Charlie and Eddie made their way to the table.

'Four cups Mum?' enquired Eddie.

'Yes, your sister has just phoned. She's on her way over, so make sure you don't eat all those cookies!'

'Or you really will feel the long arm of the law.' Charlie joked and the three of them laughed.

They were still giggling as Jess Thomas walked into the kitchen.

'What's so funny?'

Hannah kissed her daughter on the cheek and said, 'Charlie was joking that if we ate all the cookies, you'd have us arrested.'

Jess laughed and sat down at the table with her family. The irony that a member of the Thomas family had joined the police was not lost on any of them.

At thirty-five years old, Jess Thomas was the youngest of Stanley's children, although he had never known about her. She'd been born five months after his death. Jess had all her father's wit, charisma and intelligence, although unlike him she'd put it to good use.

At eighteen, she'd joined the Australian Federal Police, where she'd worked harder than anyone to achieve her current rank of Sergeant. It was a job she loved and was dedicated to. She had the respect of her colleagues who knew that she wasn't to be messed with, but they appreciated her fairness. It was like she had a sixth sense when it came to catching criminals and would very often work off of hunches; call it feminine intuition or the blood of her dad running through her veins that enabled her to read people so well.

Jess was tall, with a slim athletic build, chestnut brown hair which was normally tied back in a ponytail to keep it out of the way whilst she worked and piercing blue eyes, exactly the same as her dad's. Hannah thought she was the perfect mixture of her and Stan.

Jess, rarely asked about her dad. She knew all about him and what he'd done, but never really asked for extra information. She simply wasn't bothered. As far as she was concerned, her family consisted of Hannah, Charlie, and Eddie and that was it.

Hannah sat contentedly drinking her tea and watching her children laugh and joke with each other, they mercilessly teased each other, and the good-natured insults flew back and forth.

She knew that she was about to shatter that. Well, she wasn't, Stan was.

Hannah got up and poured more tea, sitting back at the table, she reached down and placed a book in front of her. Taking a deep breath, she said, 'Guys, we need to talk, I have something to tell you.'

The room fell silent immediately, and all three turned to look at their mum, worried expressions on their faces.

'Mum, are you OK? You're not ill, are you?' asked a worried Jess.

'No, nothing like that, but I do need to tell you something.' Turning over the book in front of her, she pushed a copy of Tales from the Gallows by Henry Mason in front of them. Eddie and Jess looked confused, but Charlie sighed.

'It's about dad, isn't it?'

'Yes, well partly. It's the memoirs of a hangman, he worked on loads of executions, but Dad's was his first and of course, anything to do with him still causes massive interest, you know what your dad was like.'

Jess reached over and took the book. 'Has it just come out? Maybe no one will read it?'

Hannah shook her head. 'Afraid not, it's topping the best sellers list and the guy who wrote it has been on every talk show going. I spoke to your Uncle Sidney earlier, and he says that it's all kicking off. Dicky Richards apparently spoke to a journalist and so the Merry Men are all over the papers. Sid says they're all getting phone calls about appearing on talk shows and doing interviews and some film producer has been in touch about doing a film. He reckons it's only a matter of time before they track us down here."

‘But we haven’t done anything wrong.’ Eddie said. ‘I barely remember dad and Jess never met him! Charlie you must have limited memories?’

‘I guess, I probably remember him the most. I spent a lot of time with him after my accident. He’d spend ages reading stories to me and playing games.’

Charlie’s voice started to crack, and Hannah reached over and took her son’s hand.

She remembered exactly how Stan had been after Charlie’s accident. Wracked with guilt that his business dealings had left his son paralysed, he’d spent hours sat by his son’s bedside, reading him stories, playing games with him, and sometimes just watching him sleep. In those last few months, he’d displayed a side that even she’d never seen before.

‘I know my darling, he was your dad, he was all of yours dad and he loved you. Jess, I know he didn’t know about you, but he’d have loved you too, he’d have been a nightmare every time you got a boyfriend.’

Tears started to trickle down Hannah’s face. For years she had refused to acknowledge what life could have been like with Stan. If only they’d all been able to move to Australia, how different life could have been.

‘So, what does this actually mean for us, Mum?’ Ever the practical one, Jess obviously wanted to put together a plan.

‘I’m not sure, maybe nothing or maybe we’ll have the press camping on the doorstep.’ Hannah looked over at Eddie who was thumbing through the book, she noticed he’d stopped at a page full of photos. ‘I suppose Uncle Sid just wanted to make us aware of what was happening in the UK. Ultimately, it’s up to us. We don’t have to speak to the press if they turn up, or we can prepare a statement, read that out and refuse to communicate any further.’

Jess nodded. ‘Good idea, I can speak to the boys at the station and get the house put onto a patrol route, that way if the press does start harassing us, we can arrest them, and I’ll have the book thrown at them.’

Eddie was still staring intently at the page of the book he’d stopped at.

‘Eddie love, are you OK?’

Very slowly he nodded, but Hannah could tell he was holding back tears. ‘I’d forgotten him... I mean I wanted to forget him and here he is, look, it’s my face starring out of this photo.’ Eddie wiped the tears away with the back of his hand. He pushed the book back towards Hannah and suddenly there he was, Stan, smiling up at her. Goodness knows where they’d found that photo, it was a rare candid shot of Stan laughing at someone, completely unaware the photo had been taken.

Eddie was right, he really was the spitting image of his dad. Hannah stroked the page with her fingers.

Charlie who'd been sitting very quietly, said, 'We never talk about him, do we? We never get out old photos. Jess do you even know anything about dad, apart from the obvious?' Charlie's voice cracked as he said the word 'Dad'. It was thirty-five years since Hannah had heard Charlie say that word with any kind of feeling behind it.

Jess shook her head. 'No, not really. I just thought that none of you wanted to talk about him, I didn't want to bring him up in case I upset you all. I don't even know where he's buried.'

Eddie looked up. 'Where is he buried Mum?'

'At the prison. In those days, the body wasn't released back to the family, so he's in a prison graveyard somewhere.'

'Did you do anything to mark his passing? Is there anything anywhere to remember him?'

A smile played on Hannah's lips. 'Yes, we did do something. Are you sure you want to hear the story?' Hannah watched as her three children nodded at her, suddenly thirsty for information about their dad, 'I wasn't allowed to see your dad on the day he died, but they did let me in the day before. Me and Billy Porter went to see him. Billy was your dad's best friend; they had been since they were kids. Stan made Billy promise to look after us and told him that he was to open one of the bottles and that I was to be there too.

The day of Stan's execution, I'd arranged for you to be at your grandparents, they'd never really approved of Stan, and I told them I wanted to be alone. I sat in our kitchen along with Billy, your Uncle Sid and Mad Larry Yates. Dicky Richards was in prison for something or other. We just sat there watching the clock, your Uncle Sid held my hand really tight, and when the clock struck 9a.m., we just all sat there crying, all of us, these big hard men and me just sobbing. Then Billy stood up, he went over to the cupboard, got out some glasses and opened a bottle of scotch. Billy said that Stanley had stolen three of them from the High Sheriff's office. We sat there and we drank the whole thing.

'We spent the whole day drunk and talking about your dad. We laughed till we cried and cried till we could laugh no more.

'None of us left the house that day because we knew that the press would be waiting, but about three weeks later, it had all calmed down a bit. Billy pulls up in the car and tells me to get in, we drove out to Edwinstowe and the Major Oak. When we got there, your Uncle Sid and Larry were waiting. Larry was holding a spade, a bit of me panicked at first, I mean he wasn't called Mad Larry Yates for nothing! I could see they'd dug a little hole by the tree, it was weird because there was no one about. Bill said this was your dad's idea. They each got out an item that reminded them of him, Billy had your dad's watch, Sidney his cap and Larry a tankard that your dad always drank out of. Billy said we thought we'd all bury something here that reminded us of him, that way we'd always have somewhere to come to remember him. Stan thought this was fitting, seeing it was the home of the original Merry Men. I was wearing Stan's wedding ring on a chain round my neck, so I put that in there, and we also placed one of the bottles of scotch he'd stolen in there too. Billy said a few words and then Larry covered the hole in.'

Hannah went quiet.

'Did we ever visit there?' asked Charlie.

'We did, I took us all just before we left for Australia. I don't know if you remember, it was a nightmare trying to get your chair through the forest, but I was determined that we'd all see your dad one last time, to say a proper goodbye.'

'Do you have any of Dad's stuff left?' asked Eddie.

'Give me a sec.'

Hannah left the room and returned with a large, battered suitcase. 'I wondered if this day would ever come and if you'd want to know more about him. That – 'she pointed at the book, 'That's not the truth about your dad, that's not who he is... who he was.' Hannah corrected herself, 'These are a few things I saved.'

Opening the suitcase, Hannah let her children start to explore, walking over to the fridge, she got out a bottle of wine and started pouring it in to four glasses.

The kitchen table in the Thomas house was now strewn with all kinds of family memorabilia.

Jess sat with a blue and yellow scarf wrapped around her neck.

'Your dad was a Mansfield Town fan' Hannah told her. 'You know, even to this day, I still find myself checking the score to see how they've done. He'd have been over the moon that they made it to Wembley and won the Freight Rover Trophy.'

Eddie looked surprised. 'You do that Mum? You never say?'

'I know, well as you said, we never talk about him, and I didn't want to upset you.'

Charlie was sat going through a pile of photos. 'Who's this?' he kept asking, Hannah kept throwing names at him.

'That's Billy Porter, that's Dicky Richards, Mad Larry and of course your Uncle Sid, he was a good-looking so and so even back then.'

'What happened to them all? Do they ever keep in touch?' asked Jess.

'I get the odd Christmas card from Billy and his wife Fiona, I don't know her, he married her after we'd moved here, I think they had a pub in Kirkby, which their daughter runs now. Bill's a good guy, he was the only one who could calm your dad down. I haven't heard from Dicky in years, he was always a bugger for the women. Sid says he does some after dinner speaking now, which is odd, because he could barely string a sentence together without grunting. The weirdest one is Larry, he's a vicar now! He's at a church in Edwinstowe, I get a card from him on the anniversary of your dad's death. And your Uncle Sid, well you know all about him!'

'You never mention that you still hear from them, why was it a secret?' Eddie's voice had become frighteningly calm, just like Stan's would when he was about to lose his temper.

'It's never been a secret, I just never wanted to upset you. Growing up, you never asked after your dad, and I didn't want to make you remember him if you didn't want to.'

Eddie nodded slowly. 'Do you miss him, Mum?'

'Every single day.'

Charlie was sat with a pile of newspapers in front of him. 'You saved these from the trial?'

'Yes, I wanted to save as much as I could, so that should this day ever come, we could talk about everything.'

'What about his family, do we have grandparents? Uncles? Aunties?'

'I never met his mum and dad, he never really spoke about them, just said they weren't around. I always got the impression that it was Billy's mum and dad who'd bought him up, and the Merry Men were his family, Billy especially.'

Charlie was holding a jumper of Stan's in his hands. He bought it towards his face and breathed in. 'It still smells of him.' Taking a deep breath, he said, 'I want to meet them, I want to go back to England and meet all these people that meant so much to dad.'

Hannah, Eddie, and Jess starred at him.

Jess was the first to speak. 'So, do I.'

Eddie nodded. 'Me too. Mum.'

Hannah sighed, 'OK, if that's what you want, I'll make some arrangements and we'll go back to Mansfield.'

Hannah took the hands of her children and smiled. She could see the excited looks on their faces, but down in her tummy, she couldn't help, but feel this was a massive mistake.

Chapter 70

1952 – The George Street Brothel, Mansfield.

Walter lay back on his bed, hands behind his head as Gerard sucked his cock. Ever since Walter had orchestrated the beating of Sidney and the 'accident' that befell one of Stan's kids and there'd been no retribution, Walter had felt untouchable. Stan finally knew who was in charge and that was Walter Dorrell!

Walter had spent the last few weeks swanning about Mansfield, demanding money from local businesses. So far no-one had refused him and when he'd asked if they were still paying Stan, they all said they hadn't seen him or any of the Merry Men. Licking their wounds, no doubt! Crying into their pints.

Once Walter had done away with Stan once and for all, he wasn't sure what he'd do with the rest of the Merry Men. If they showed him a suitable amount of respect, then he might let them join his gang, he could do with the muscle. As loyal as Malcolm, Roy and Barry were, they didn't have the presence of Billy, Dicky, and Larry. Plus, what better way to piss all over Stan's memory than to make his gang see what a proper leader should be like?

As for Sidney, Walter had special plans for him. A boy as good-looking as him should be on Walter's arm and working at the George Street Brothel to earn his keep!

Walter knew he was very close to sealing Stan's fate, but he just had one more thing he wanted to do, to ensure that Stan really knew that there was no amount of pain that he, Walter Dorrell, wouldn't and couldn't inflict on him.

Chapter 71

1952 – Mansfield Library.

Wandering around the book-stacked shelves in Mansfield library, Pearl felt happy. Running her fingers along the spines of the books that lined the shelves, she came to rest on the latest Agatha Christie, They Do it With Mirrors. Pearl loved Agatha Christie books, for a few brief hours she could lose herself in a world of intrigue and mystery, where good always triumphed over evil, and the bad guys were always carted away to an unknown fate.

Taking the book, Pearl settled herself down on a chair in the far corner and started to read. Those hours spent amongst the books in the library were her sanctuary, they were stolen moments, where she wasn't the sister of Walter Dorrell, or an orphan, or a prostitute, she was just Pearl, a girl who liked to read, and had a desire to learn.

Pearl was suddenly dragged from the pages of her book, by a voice saying, 'Oh Mrs. Thomas, we were so sorry to hear about your Charlie, how is the little angel doing?'

Just in front of her, she could see Hannah chatting to the librarian. 'He's doing Ok thanks, we're getting there. Six months ago, I thought we'd lost him, but he's a fighter. Do you have the books I asked for?'

While the librarian located the books, Hannah turned around, as if she was aware that someone was staring at her.

Pearl wasn't sure what to do, so she smiled and raised her hand slightly.

Hannah said something under her breath to the librarian and started to walk over.

'You're Dorrell's sister, aren't you?'

'Yes, I'm so sorry for what he did to your boy, I had no idea, if I'd known I'd have tried to stop him.'

'My problem isn't with you. From what I hear, you have enough on, but you can give your brother a message from me. You tell him, I don't care how long, or where or when, but I will make sure that he pays for what he did to my boy. Not Stan, not the boys, me, I'll be the one who makes him pay! It will happen when he's least expecting it and it will hurt. I will hurt him.'

Pearl nodded at Hannah. 'I'll tell him. And Mrs. Thomas? For what it's worth, I am sorry, and I think my brother deserves whatever is coming to him.'

Hannah held out her hand, and Pearl took it, 'Pearl? Is that your name? Pearl, you do whatever you can to get away from him and then run, run far away from here, from him, and you live your life away from all of this.'

Pearl watched as Hannah turned and walked away. As she collected her books, she never once looked back and that was the last time the two women saw each other until Stan's trial.

Chapter 72

1952 – George Street Brothel.

Pearl arrived back home to find Walter sat on the sofa with Gerard and Dennis playing music and drinking.

'Where the fuck have you been, you fucking slag?'

'Nice to see you too, dear brother of mine. I've been to the library if you must know.'

'The fucking library, thinks she's something does this cunt, when we all know you're just a dirty slag who gets paid for her cunt.'

Walter started to laugh hysterically, and Gerard and Dennis joined in, although Dennis mouthed 'I'm sorry', so that Walter couldn't see him.

'Well. This paid for cunt has a message for you from Hannah Thomas.'

Walter laughed again. 'Another slag! What does she want? A real man's cock! A son who's not a cripple!'

'She wanted me to pass a message on. She said she's coming for you, because of what you did to her boy. Not Stan, not the Merry Men, but her, and she says she'll get you when you least expect it. She said she has time, and she will make it hurt.'

Pearl could hear Walter laughing as she went upstairs, and then for the very first time and in a move that she wasn't sure was wholly ethical, she prayed. She prayed to God that Hannah would get Walter and if it wasn't Hannah, then Stan and the Merry Men and if it wasn't any of them, she prayed for the strength to finish Walter off herself. She was pretty sure that even God wouldn't mind answering a prayer like that if it meant riding the world of such an absolute bastard.

Chapter 73

1988 – Fleet Street, London.

'Get the fuck out my office and come back when you have the fucking facts!'

Pearl Dorrell picked up her mug and threw it after the journalist who was scurrying out of her office.

The journalist who'd had many experiences of Pearl throwing mugs at him, managed to shut the door just before it hit him, leaving shards of broken pottery everywhere.

Another mess for me to clean up, thought Pearl.

At fifty-two years old, Pearl was the only female editor on Fleet Street, she'd taken over at The Daily Chronicle five years ago and had sweat blood and tears to get there. She now expected the same level of work from her staff, and anything less she took as a personal insult.

She made a note on the pad on her desk to have the journalist who'd just run out fired; he'd made one mistake too many.

Pearl had worked as a journalist for the last thirty years. Aware that she was a news story in her own right, she'd made the decision that she would live in plain sight. She wouldn't hide from her past, she wouldn't live in fear, waiting for a journalist to bang on the door and threaten to tell her story with or without her consent.

Pearl told her own story in her own way.

After her brother had been murdered, she'd decided that was her cue to leave

Mansfield and start again somewhere else.

With Walter dead, the George Street Brothel had become hers, and she'd promptly given Malcolm, Roy and Barry their marching orders and told the others to make other arrangements as she was selling up.

The house sold for two thousand pounds, which seemed like an absolute fortune at the time. She gave May, Cheryl, Geraldine and Shirley fifty pounds each from the sale and said it was the least she could do after everything Walter had put them through. Gerard and Dennis, she gave ten pounds to, she hadn't seen the boys since. She'd heard rumours that Gerard had continued to ply his trade, but she had no idea if he still did. Dennis had moved to Scotland and had last been heard of working in a bar somewhere in Glasgow.

The girls had all kept in touch to varying degrees. May had got married and moved to Cornwall, her husband blissfully unaware of her past. Cheryl had stayed in Nottingham, working in various pubs and clubs, before she eventually decided she'd had enough and had moved to Skegness to run a guesthouse. Geraldine had eventually gone to work for a charity that worked with girls who'd been forced into prostitution and the last Pearl had heard was running the charity and living somewhere in Derbyshire.

Then there was Shirley. Pearl had come across her fairly recently in her professional capacity. When the George Street Brothel closed, Shirley had used her fifty pounds to rent a house in St Anns in Nottingham, and there she had set up her own brothel, which specialized in S and M. The brothel had been a huge success, with most of Shirley's clients or 'the Mistress' as she was known, taking most of her clients with her.

The tiny, rented house in St Anns, soon turned into a large city centre premises, with an array of celebrity clients. Shirley had hit the headlines a few years ago after the Inland Revenue had investigated her for tax fraud. She had fought back by saying that the only possible way for her to pay the bill would be for her to write her memoirs, therefore exposing some very high-profile people. That's exactly what she'd done, and The Daily Chronicle had serialised it sending its profits through the roof in the process and leaving a trail of devastated careers in its wake, along with a string of embarrassed-looking men holding press conferences trying to appear sorry with their furious-looking wives stood behind them.

Walter had been murdered in November 1952, with Stan's trial taking place shortly afterwards. Pearl had gone along every day on her own to the Shire Hall in Nottingham. At first, because she had to give evidence, she'd had to sit outside while she waited to be called.

The girls had offered to go with her, but it was something she wanted to do on her own. She knew it would be bad enough having people stare at her, but she didn't want the girls to have to go through the same thing, hearing the whispers of 'slag' or, at best, 'prostitute' and 'that's his sister, the poor cow' at worst.

Once Pearl had given her evidence, she sat amongst the crowd in the gallery, waiting to see what fate would bestow Stanley Thomas, her brother's murderer. She was surrounded by the rest of the Merry Men, other people who were there to support Stan and most importantly Hannah.

Pearl hadn't seen Hannah since they'd spoken in the library, and she wondered whether she'd acknowledge her now. The first time Pearl made her way into the gallery, Hannah was sat at the opposite end of the row to her, Billy sat on one side of her, her brother Sidney on the other, both holding her hand, while Larry was at the far end of the row. Billy, Sidney and Larry, all ignored her. They all knew her, as at some point, they'd all slept with her. In fact, Sidney had lost his virginity to her. But today they acted as if she wasn't there.

She'd gone from a girl they shagged to the girl whose evidence was going to send their friend to the gallows.

Hannah met Pearl's eyes only once during the trial, right before the verdict was due to be passed. She'd caught Pearl's eye, given a brief nod, and then returned to looking straight ahead.

Once the sentence had been passed, Pearl had taken her very few possessions, boarded a train at Nottingham Victoria Station and made the journey to London and there she'd stayed.

Chapter 74

October 1952 – Crow Hill Drive Mansfield.

It had been six months since Charlie Thomas had been attacked and every day since, he'd continually amazed his parents. From being a scared little boy laying in a hospital bed being told that he'd never walk again to being back to his normal self, laughing, playing, taking care of his brother. The obvious things had changed, they'd made practical changes to the house and Charlie had to have physio every week and do exercises at home, but he never once complained.

Charlie was a bright imaginative child, and on a daily basis, his wheelchair went from being a racing car to a spaceship to a horse to a million other things. Hannah would hear him and Eddie playing games, fighting, laughing, and plotting adventures. They'd spend hours colouring pictures and telling stories to each other.

Stan had been a changed man the last few months too. He was never far away from his son's side, and in the early days he would sleep by Charlie's bed, calming him down if he woke up frightened, carrying him to the toilet, rubbing his head, telling him stories to get him back to sleep. He spent hours helping Eddie learn to read, playing with his favourite toys, pretending to be a horse so Eddie could be a cowboy. Screams of laughter rang from the Thomas household.

Hannah listened to the laughter floating through from the sitting room and held her tummy. She hoped the new baby wouldn't change things too much. She'd only just found out that she was pregnant and hadn't told anyone yet, unsure how she felt about it herself.

On a few occasions, Hannah had tried to broach the subject of Walter Dorrell with Stan. She wanted justice and was getting impatient. The police couldn't charge him because there was no real evidence. They'd questioned Dorrell, but he'd denied everything, and his henchmen had given him an alibi. Plus, Charlie was the son of a gangster, surely he was just collateral damage in any of Stan's business dealings?

Every time she asked what Stan was planning to do, he told her it was in hand and not to worry and not to mention it again, but Hannah couldn't see a plan. She couldn't see anything happening. It looked like Dorrell was getting away with hurting her boy and she vowed that if Stan didn't do something soon, she would.

Chapter 75

November 1952 – Crow Hill Drive Mansfield

'Stan, I'm nipping over to my mum's, I'll be about an hour, that OK?'

'Yes duck, see you later.'

Hannah needed an hour by herself, she was starting to get morning sickness, and she just fancied a walk, some fresh air and time to think. Stan had been over the moon when she'd told him about the baby, saying he hoped it would be a girl. The boys had said they didn't want a girl because girls smelled and they didn't want a boy, because a boy would steal their toys. Hannah had explained that it was going to be one or the other, so Charlie had asked if they could get a dog instead.

Hannah wasn't quite sure where she was going to walk to, so she just wandered, lost in her own thoughts of the new baby, her sons, her husband and what she was going to do to Walter Dorrell.

So lost was she in her own thoughts, that she didn't hear the footsteps behind her, and she didn't realise what was happening until a hand put a handkerchief over her mouth and told her not to scream.

Before she knew it, she was in a boot of a car being driven away.

Chapter 76

November 1952 – Mansfield

When Hannah woke up, she couldn't work out where she was. Slowly she took in her surroundings: she was in a room, a bedroom she thought, but it wasn't hers. The flowered wallpaper was faded and peeling off the walls, and there was chest of drawers in the corner that was missing a drawer.

She tried to move, but her hands were tied to the bedpost above her head and her legs spread apart each tied by rope to the end of the bed. She tried to scream, but there was a gag in her mouth. She was at least fully clothed.

'Boss, she's awake.'

It was a man's voice, but not one she recognised.

She could hear steps and then the door opened, and a man's face leaned over her. His breath made her gag, a mixture of stale whiskey, fried food and teeth that hadn't been brushed for a few days, none of which were not a great combination for a woman with morning sickness.

As he lowered his face closer, his pale eyes coming into line with hers, he removed the gag.

'Do you know who I am Mrs. Thomas?' He spat the last two words.

'I know who you are, you attacked my son, you fucking bastard.'

'Now, now, Mrs. Thomas, I wouldn't say you were in any position to be calling anyone a bastard, would you? How is that little playmate of mine? Running around I assume?'

Walter Dorrell started to laugh.

Hannah started to thrash around on the bed, desperate to get free, determined that once she was free, she would squeeze the life out of Walter Dorrell with her bare hands, finish what Stan couldn't. Her movements made Walter laugh even more.

'I bet your son doesn't move like that anymore.'

'I swear to God Dorrell, I will finish you myself. That's if Stan doesn't get his hands on you first'

'Stan? That cunt and his band of wankers? He's going to do nothing to me, too scared, he saw what I did to his son, and he did nothing and when he sees what I'm going to do to you, he'll still do nothing. He's finished.'

Walter climbed on top of her.

'What you need is a real man, a man who has you screaming with desire night after night, who makes you cum.'

With every word he spoke, Hannah could feel his spit landing on her face, the stench of his breath making her feel more and more sick. 'A real man? Is that what you think you are? From what I hear you're nothing but a fag, a gay boy, a cock sucker, who likes nothing more than a cock in his gob and one up his arse, you make me sick. Perverts like you should rot in prison.'

Walter grabbed Hannah's face squeezing her mouth open.

'You shut your filthy mouth you whore!'

With that he stuck his tongue in Hannah's mouth.

With sheer brute strength, she bit down as hard as she could, and Walter fell back off the bed, blood pouring from his mouth.

Scrambling back to his feet, he was so angry, Hannah couldn't make out the words that were spilling from his mouth. As various insults tumbled freely, he started to land punches on her, first to her face, hitting her more and more furiously, until eventually he was punching her repeatedly in the stomach.

Fearing for her unborn child, Hannah screamed out, 'Walter, stop, stop, I'm, pregnant!'

Walter froze, seemingly snapped back to his senses, for a second.

Hannah had hope that underneath it all, Walter was a decent man and he'd untie her from this bed and let her go.

'Pregnant? With Stan's child, or don't you know whose it is, you filthy slag?'

'Of course, it's Stan's. Walter, I'm begging you, you've already hurt one of my children, please, please don't hurt another.'

Walter started laughing again. 'What did you call me earlier? A filthy cock sucker?' As he spoke, he started to push Hannah's skirt up. 'A filthy cock sucker who liked nothing more than a cock in his gob?' As he said this, he pulled Hannah's pants down. 'Well how about if the first cock that little bastard of yours sucks is mine?'

Hearing Walter unzip his trousers, Hannah closed her eyes and prayed.

Chapter 77

November 1952 – Mansfield

When Hannah opened her eyes, she found herself still in the room with the peeling wallpaper, but her arms and legs were untied. She could feel that her knickers were still around her ankles, and she felt sore. Everywhere hurt. Her face and body from where Walter had rained punches down on her, and her insides. Her insides ached and a shooting pain seared inside her, her tummy once full of a new life, felt empty and hollow. Raising herself onto her elbows, she could see the sheets beneath her soaked in blood.

Getting into a sitting position, Hannah Thomas straightened her clothes and got to her feet and left. She had no idea where she was or if Walter and his goons would come back for her, but she knew she needed to get to a phone box and get help as soon as possible.

Staggering outside, she realised she was only a few yards from home. Steadily, she started to walk, all the time aware that her unborn child was trying to escape, desperate to keep him or her safe inside her for as long as she could, willing the baby to hold on.

For as long as she lived Hannah would never know how she made it home that day. Letting herself in, Eddie ran towards her screaming, 'Mummy'

A worried-looking Stan followed him. 'Where the fuck have you been? Your mum said you never went over.'

As Stan, finally seemed to notice his wife's bruised and cut face and the blood on her skirt, the last thing Hannah remembered was trying to speak and collapsing into her husband's arms.

***

This time when Hannah opened her eyes, she was in a room she recognized. Her room, her concerned looking husband sat by one side of her bed and Dr. Dalton the other.

'The baby? Is my baby, OK?'

Stan looked at the floor.

'I'm sorry Mrs. Thomas, but at the moment we're not sure, you've lost a lot of blood, the likelihood is that yes, your baby has died. We need to get you to a hospital for tests.'

'You mean was murdered.' Hannah started crying, angry sobs wracking her body.

Dr. Dalton reached down and touched Hannah's hand. 'I'm so very sorry, I've left some painkillers and I'll arrange for an ambulance to come and pick you up. Mrs. Thomas, Mr. Thomas.'

The doctor nodded his head and left the room.

'Where are the boys, Stan? Are they safe?' Hannah sat bolt upright in bed. 'Where are they Stan?'

"It's OK, they're fine, Sid's downstairs with them. He's going to give them their tea, but right now, I need you to do something for me.' Stan's voice cracked. 'I need to know who did this to you and I need to know everything they did to you.'

The Fixer

November 1952

When news reached the Fixer about what had happened to Hannah Thomas, they knew that they could only hold Stan back for so much longer. It was time to end this once and for all.

Picking up the phone, the Fixer dialled a number they knew from heart.

'It's time, I trust everyone knows what they're doing and is ready to go?'

Replacing the handset, the Fixer poured themself a whiskey.

Chapter 78

1988 – The Avenue, Mansfield.

'If that's what you want, sis, I can make the necessary arrangements. Once the flights are booked let me know the details and I'll pick you up at the airport. You'll stay with me. Are you sure about this? It's crazy here with that book about Stan and Dicky shooting his mouth off, you'll be walking into a media shit storm. OK, if you're sure. Love you.'

Sidney replaced the handset of his phone and leaned against the wall. He heard breathing behind him.

'And who the fuck do you think you're saying 'love you' too? You got another bird on the go, you bastard?'

Sidney turned around to see his latest girlfriend stood behind him, Keeley, or Carly or something, he couldn't remember her name, just always called her 'babe' and she appeared not to notice. 'My sister, as it goes, not that it's got fuck all to do with you.'

'You've got a sister? You never said, can I meet her?'

'Yes, I do and no, you can't. Look babe, this has been fun, but it's over.'

'What? You said you loved me!'

'Did I? Truth is babe, I'm not even sure what your name is, could be Keeley or Carly, but I neither know nor care, so get your stuff and fuck off.'

The girl marched straight up to Sidney. 'It's Claire, you bastard.'

Sidney laughed. 'Well then Claire, there's the door.'

Holding the door open, Sidney watched the irate woman walk out, with everything else that was going off, he really didn't have the time for a woman hanging around.

Sidney caught sight of himself in the hall mirror and rubbed his chin. He needed a shave.

At fifty-one years old, Sidney was still a magnificently handsome man, with or without stubble. His nickname of Babyface was still accurate. His face was smooth and wrinkle free, his shaved blond hair and piercing blue eyes made him look like he was more fashion model than a 'businessman' and his smile had been the downfall of many a woman.

Heading to the kitchen to make himself a cup of tea, Sidney's thought about his sister and her plan to visit the UK. Hannah hadn't set foot on British soil since she'd taken the children and left thirty years ago. Sidney flew to Australia once a year to visit her and the family, but Hannah had always said that returning would be too hard.

He adored his nephews and niece but was always surprised that they never really spoke about Stan. Every time he visited them, he expected that this would be the time they'd have questions, want to know about their dad's past, but they never did. He'd often questioned Hannah about it, but she simply said that they didn't seem interested, and she didn't want to push it with them. She'd worried that a trip to the UK would drag up memories and questions, she didn't want to answer, and yet here she was planning on bringing the whole family over when Stan's face was once again all over the papers. He really didn't understand his sister sometimes.

Sidney had hated it when Hannah had decided to emigrate to Australia. He'd begged her not too, promised her that he and the rest of the Merry Men would take care of her. She'd never have to worry about money, or a place to live or being alone with the children. But she wouldn't have it. She said she wanted a new life, a fresh start for her and the children far away from where anyone knew them. She'd asked Sidney to go with them, but he'd refused, told her that his life was in Mansfield.

Sidney had cried three times in his life, the first time was after he'd found out that Walter had raped his sister, the second was on the day Stan had been executed and the third the day his sister had set sale for Australia. Those weeks and months that had followed her departure he'd been lost. His parents were relieved that Hannah had left, they thought her marriage to Stan and his subsequent execution had bought shame on them. They'd tried to encourage him to stop hanging around with the Merry Men, scared that a similar fate was waiting for him, but he ignored them.

Soon after Hannah had left, he moved into a spare room in Billy's house and there he stayed until Billy got sent to prison in 1954. After that, the rest of the Merry Men were in and out of prison for various offences ranging from theft to manslaughter to GBH.

Sidney was smarter than that, and decided that he needed a legitimate business, well one that was seemingly legitimate at least. He'd invested in a nightclub, one nightclub had led to two, then to three, then to a couple of bars and restaurants. Some were on the level, others not so much, but Sidney's operation was slick and smart, and nothing happened in Nottinghamshire unless he knew about it and had given permission for it to go ahead. Sidney had always avoided spending any time at Her Majesty's pleasure.

Sidney had kept in contact to varying degrees with the rest of the Merry Men. He occasionally drank in Billy's pub, The Duke and enjoyed dinner with him and his wife Fiona, who even Sidney was a bit scared of. The dinner invitations had got a bit lessened once Fiona had found out that Sidney had slept with their daughter Marjie.

Dicky popped up occasionally, normally when he needed a favour, or he'd messed up and needed Sidney to sort something or someone out.

Larry, or Father Yates as he was now, preferred to be more discreet about meeting up with Sidney. The two would very often drive out to a pub in the middle of the Derbyshire Dales or the Lincolnshire Wolds and enjoy a pie and a pint as they reminisced. Occasionally Larry would tap Sidney up for some money for the church roof or some equipment for the Sunday school, Sidney always obliged. He figured it was one way of making it right with the Big Man and securing his place in Heaven.

Until a few weeks ago, they hadn't all been in the same room for over twenty years and with Hannah coming back, he knew they'd all be together very soon.

Chapter 79

1988 – Heathrow Airport

Sidney stood nervously in the airport waiting for his sister, nephews, and niece to walk through the Arrivals door. He kept jangling the keys in his pocket. He still thought

Hannah was making a massive mistake coming back to the U.K., but no amount of pleading had made her change her mind.

The rest of the Merry Men were aware she was coming, and Larry had offered to come with him to pick them up, but Sidney had told him there wouldn't be enough room in the car. The truth was he didn't want to draw any unnecessary attention to what was happening. He knew all it took was one for one person to recognise him or Larry, or both of them and then put two and two together and all hell would break lose. This way, he thought, even if someone recognised him, they might think he was picking up a lover or a friend. That was his hope.

He wasn't sure he was going to get away with his plan, there'd been a bloke sat in the café behind him for hours, nursing a cup of coffee, intently watching Sidney. He was either a copper or a journalist and for once, Sidney hoped he was a copper.

Passengers started to file out of the Arrivals doors, carrying suitcases, pushing trollies, looking tired and wearily greeting their waiting friends and family. In the distance, Sidney could see his sister, Charlie in his wheelchair following her, Eddie pushing a trolley with all their luggage on and Jess bringing up the rear with a couple of bags of Duty Free. Sidney had given them strict instructions not to shout his name, but to wave and then they'd make their way to his car in silence and catch up when they were safely on the road.

Waving excitedly, the Thomas family made their way over to Sidney.

At that moment, the guy who'd been intently watching him jumped to his feet and ran forward, while another man who Sidney hadn't clocked ran forward with a camera, clicking away.

'Mrs Thomas? It is you isn't it, Hannah? Are these your boys, Charlie, and Eddie? Who's the girl? Did you marry again? Are you back because of the book? What's your thoughts on it? Will you be doing an interview? My paper will pay good money for your story.'

Sidney pushed the men out the way. 'Fuck off, she's got nothing to say to you.'

Putting his arm protectively around his sister's shoulder, he guided her through the crowd.

Undeterred the reporter turned his attention to Jess. 'Who are you, sweetheart? Is she your mum? Who's your dad?'

Sidney noticed Jess moved forward quickly to make sure that the reporter wouldn't get in Charlie's way. She seemed more than aware that because of his wheelchair, he'd be the easiest to detain. 'Who I am is none of your fucking business.'

'An Aussie hey? Is that where you've all been living? What about you Charlie? Do you know who was responsible for your accident?'

The photographer was still clicking away, while the reporter had stepped in front of Charlie's chair, but Charlie simply wheeled over his foot. This gave the Thomas children the perfect chance to catch up with their mum and Uncle Sidney as airport security finally stepped in to deal with the ambushing reporter and cameraman.

Arriving safely at Sidney's car and loading in their luggage, none of them spoke until his brand-new Rolls Royce Silver Spirit was safely on the M25.

'How did they know we were coming?'

'No idea, the only people who knew were me and the rest of the boys, and not even Dicky is stupid enough to shout his mouth off again! I told you, that books sent everything crazy again, I did warn you.'

'I know, but I... we wanted to come, we needed to come.'

Jess reached over and placed her hand on her mum's shoulder. 'Don't stress Mum, we're all in this together, we won't let anyone upset you.'

Hannah patted her daughter's hand. 'I know, I know I'm safe here. I think it was just a shock and I'm tired from the flight. A good night's sleep and a proper cup of tea and I'll be as right at rain.'

Chapter 80

1988 – The Avenue, Mansfield

Hannah woke up after a deep sleep. For a second, she couldn't work out where she was and panicked. Memories of the day she'd been raped by Walter came flooding back. Even after thirty-six years if she woke up in a room, she wasn't sure of, it frightened her. Gradually she made her breath slow down to a normal rate as she reassured herself that she was safe at her brother's house, and that, although she was back in Mansfield, Walter was dead and couldn't get to her and he couldn't harm her children.

She could hear voices downstairs, the buzz of her children and her brother, excitedly talking about the things they were going to do whilst they were here, questions about Stan flowing backwards and forwards.

Putting on her dressing gown, Hannah headed downstairs, she could see the newspaper laying on the mat and bent to pick it up. The headline of The Daily Chronicle screaming at her,

Stan's Mrs Back in the UK

It was accompanied by a made-up story of how Hannah had told the reporter that she was here to tell her version of events for the first time. The paper had reported that Hannah was joined by two children, her sons Charlie and Eddie. Charlie who had been left crippled by an alleged altercation with the man his dad murdered and an unidentified woman, who was assumed to be Hannah's daughter from another relationship, or the wife of one of the boys. A huge photo of them arriving back at Heathrow accompanied the story. There was some stuff about Sidney, and his businesses.

Walking into the kitchen, Hannah threw the paper on the table. 'What bullshit!'

Sidney picked up the paper and started to read. 'I told you, Stan and this bloody book is still big news, especially for that paper. You know who it's editor is don't you?'

'No, who?'

'Pearl Dorrell.'

'Who's Pearl Dorrell?' asked Jess.

'She's the sister of the guy your dad killed. She worked as a prossy in his brothel, then she "alleges"' – Sidney draw air quotes round the word "alleges" – 'that she saw your dad murder Walter. It was her evidence that did for your dad. I always reckoned she was paid off, because right after she'd given evidence, she hot footed it to London to start a new life and wound up as editor of The Daily Chronicle. The woman's a hard-faced bitch, who'd sell her granny for tuppence.'

Eddie put a cup of tea down in front of his mum. 'We could play her at her own game mum. You could tell your side of the story, tell them what dad was really like.'

Hannah shook her head. 'What's the point? I loved your dad, but he did kill Dorrell, he had every reason to do it, people won't care about why.'

'They might care if Charlie spoke too, told everyone about what happened to him?' reasoned Jess.

'I'll do it Mum, if that's what you want, I can tell them what I remember about that day and about dad afterwards.'

Taking his sister's hand, and speaking gently, Sidney said, 'You could tell them everything. It won't excuse what Stan did, but it might help people understand.'

Hannah shook her head. 'No, I'm not doing it. I came here so the kids could find out more about Stan and that's what we're going to do. I'm not falling into a trap with the press. Now I'm going to have a bath and we can go out for the day.'

Hannah could hear them all talking in hushed voices as she made her way upstairs.

Maybe she shouldn't have come back after all.

The Fixer

1988

Closing the newspaper and putting it back on the table, the Fixer smiled. So, Hannah Thomas and her children were back in the U.K. It amused the Fixer that Jess Thomas had been described as an 'unidentified woman'. Anyone with half a brain cell, could see that was Stan's daughter, she had his smile and his eyes.

It had been a long time since the Fixer had last seen Hannah Thomas. Over the years they'd kept a track of her movements, knowing she had moved to Australia, getting a job as a teacher, working her way up to a headship.

The Fixer was pleased that Hannah and her family had found happiness, but sadly, once again, their happiness was going to be collateral damage.

Chapter 81

1952 – Mansfield

Stanley was ready, everything was in place and today was the day he would have his revenge.

Sitting on a wooden chair in the middle of a deserted warehouse, Stanley chain-smoked, a pile of nub ends surrounding his chair.

Sidney sat on a chair to the left, taking sips from a cup of tea and keeping quiet. Today was not a day for chatter, Stan had made that clear.

'You ready for this Sid? You know what to do and how it's going to go down?'

'Yes boss.'

'You know what to do afterwards? You promise me you'll make sure that Hannah and the boys are always taken care of?'

'I will Stan, nothing will ever happen to them on my watch, and the rest of the boys know that too.'

'She's your sister, Sid, your responsibility. The others will do what they can, but they'll probably end up at the end of a hangman's noose too. You, you're smart, not just street-smart either. Whatever you do, they'll never make it stick.'

Sidney nodded.

Stanley and Sidney stopped talking as they heard a car pull up to a halt outside the warehouse, followed by the sound the door swinging open and Larry, Dicky walking in, dragging Walter in by his feet. Billy followed them.

Walter's hands and feet were tied together, and he was unconscious.

'Did he give you any trouble?'

Billy laughed. 'No, not once Larry bashed him over the head.''Right, now you lot fuck off, this is between me and Dorrell.'

'But...'

'No, 'buts', Bill. You lot are nothing to do with this, now get out, go somewhere you can be seen by lots of people.'

Billy, Larry, Dicky, and Sidney hesitated for a second, before Billy nodded at Stan and then ushered them all out, shutting the door behind him.

Chapter 82

1952 – Mansfield

Walter began to stir. He felt groggy, and for a second, he thought he'd had too much to drink. But as he tried to move, he realised that he was tied to a bed, and he was naked. There was a brief hope that this was something he'd asked for and that Gerard or Dennis were going to appear and there'd be fun times to be had by all. But as he turned his head, he could see Stan sitting on a chair drinking a cup of tea. On the table next to him lay a baseball bat, knife, some electrodes, blowtorch, and a bucket.

Walter started to wriggle, trying to work out if he could get free. He could hear Stan start to laugh.

'Oh no, Princess, there's no getting out of this one. I'll be right here until every bone in your miserable little body is broken and you're begging me to take your final breath. Do you understand me?'

Walter laughed. 'You don't have the bollocks to do this to me and you won't get away with it!'

'The bollocks you say?' Picking up the electrodes, Stan attached them to Walter's testicles, sending a shock through his body.

Walter cried out in pain. 'Cunt!'

'I won't have bad language in my presence.' And with that another shock went straight through Walter's body.

'You see, Walter, there's an easy way to do this, a hard way to do this, and then there's my way of doing this. Do you understand?'

Walter grunted.

'The answer you are looking for, Dorrell, is 'Yes Mr Thomas.'

Picking up the baseball bat Stan swung it into Walter's ribs.

'You see, I was mildly irritated when you didn't do as my boys asked and pay me the money you owed me.'

The baseball bat once again connected with Walter's ribs.

'I was even more irritated with the shit on the table incident, but I thought making you eat my shit would at least calm you down a bit. But that didn't happen, did it, Dorrell?'

Walter grunted again.

'But then, you kidnapped one of my men and gave him a beating. Sidney is not just my friend, he's my brother-in-law, so I was very angry about that, particularly as you left him with broken ribs and a broken nose.'

Taking the bat again, Stan swung it again into Walter's ribs and into his face.

Walter wanted to curl himself up into a little ball, to try and protect himself. His groin was burning, and he thought one of his broken ribs was puncturing his lungs. He was struggling to get air into his lungs and he could hear his breath coming out in little raspy bursts.

'But then, then, Dorrell, you took it even further and you came after my boy, you put my Charlie in a wheelchair and that made me really fucking angry.'

Walter waited for the bat to come crashing down into his ribs, but it didn't happen, instead he heard a little puff of air and the smell of gas. He felt the warm trickle of urine spread down his leg.

'My boy will never walk again; he's lost the use of his legs. Do you know what it's like to not to be able to walk, Dorrell?'

Walter watched as Stan made his way to the end of the bed where he was tied. Stan took the blowtorch he was holding and started to burn the bottom of Walter's feet. Walter screamed in pain, 'Help me! Help me!'

Stan laughed. 'Oh Dorrell, that wasn't it though, was it? Not content with crippling my boy, you then had to go one step further, didn't you?'

Walter whimpered. The burns to the soles of his feet making it difficult to take in what Stan was saying to him.

'What did you do, Dorrell?'

'I... I...' Walter started crying.

'You did what?'

'I slept with your wife.' Walter sobbed.

'You raped her, Dorrell. You raped my wife.' And with that Stan sent more electric currents coursing through Walter's testicles.

The pain so intense, he could no longer scream. His mouth opening and closing, a mixture of tears and snot starting to choke him.

'Do you know what else you did, Walter? You killed my unborn child.'

Stan turned away and picked up the bucket that was on the table.

'Do you know what's in here Dorrell?'

Walter was exhausted and in pain, all he could manage was a slight shake of his head.

'It's clay. I'm going to make you a little death mask, won't that be lovely? I'm going to cover your face in this clay and then the look on your face as you try to take your last breath will be preserved for all eternity.'

Walter tried one final time to break free, praying that Malcolm, Roy and Barry would come to his rescue, despite that seeming highly unlikely.

Stan started slapping the clay on to Walter's face, leaving his nostrils until last. As the clay started to harden everywhere else, Stan filled Walter's nostrils with clay and sat down.

That was the last things Walter knew.

***

Stan made himself a cup of tea and then sat waiting as, finally Dorrell's laboured breathing came to an end.

'Bye, Walter. Rot in hell you.'

Stan got to his feet and touched the clay on Walter's face before walking away and leaving Walter's body to the fate that awaited it.

Chapter 83

1988 – The Major Oak, Sherwood Forest, Edwinstowe.

Sidney's Rolls Royce pulled into a parking space at Sherwood Forest.

'Are you ready for this?'

'Yes, I want the kids to see where we buried Stan's things.'

The five of them got out the car, Sidney helping Charlie into his wheelchair. In silence, they walked towards the huge oak tree, its large branches propped up by scaffolding. The area was largely deserted, the drizzly rain keeping away the Robin Hood-seeking tourists.

'Can you remember exactly where?' asked Hannah.

Sidney nodded his head. 'Yeah, it was in this spot, you can see where we marked the trunk.'

They all held hands and Hannah could feel the tears start to fall down her face. She knew Stan's body wasn't there, and that it was just possessions buried under the soil, but it was the closest she had felt to him in years.

Eddie put his arm around his mum's shoulder. 'Is there absolutely no way we can visit where his body is buried?'

'I don't think so. In those days, their bodies were buried in the prison grounds, so he'll be there, I doubt they'd let us in, what do you think Sid?'

'You want a member of the Merry Men to ask to go into prison? That'll be a first!'

They all laughed.

'They might let us.' Jess said. 'Maybe I could phone them and explain. If we don't ask, then we don't get. I can be really persuasive, Mum." She looked at her mum expectantly.

'OK, why not? The worst they can say is no.'

They continued to stand there in silence, until Hannah felt a tap on her shoulder.

'Here, ducky, aren't you that gangster's wife? Him that killed that fella, who's in that book, that everyone's talking about?'

Hannah shook her head and put on a well-rehearsed Australian accent. 'No, love, I'm just another Aussie tourist.'

Chapter 84

1988 – The Avenue, Mansfield

Hannah knew that her daughter had not risen to the rank of Sergeant at the age of thirty-five by being a pushover. She was determined and insistent and there was no way the person at the other end of the phone was getting away with giving her anything less than what she wanted.

'If you could tell him that Sergeant Thomas is on the phone from the Australian Federal Police C.I.D and that my enquiry is urgent.' Jess put her hand over the phone. 'She's putting me through,' she whispered, and Hannah smiled at her daughter.

'Governor Mitchell?' Jess continued. 'Hello, my name is Jessica Thomas, I am a Sergeant with the Australian Federal Police C.I.D, I am also the daughter of Stanley Thomas and my family and I would like to visit his grave, which I believe is located within your prison walls.' Jess was silent for a few moments. 'I appreciate that it's probably not the norm, but my family and I are visiting from Australia and with all the recent publicity surrounding my father's death, it has been a very distressing time. My mother has never seen my father's final resting place, I never knew my father, and my brothers have limited memories, but we'd like the opportunity to pay our respects.'

Hannah could tell from her daughter's voice that Governor Mitchell was going to agree whether he wanted to or not. Ever since she'd been a little girl, Jess had been adept at arguing her point and getting everyone to agree to things.

After five minutes, Hannah heard her daughter say, 'Governor Mitchell, thank you, we will see you tonight at 9p.m. We'll of course bring identification, and we'll ask for you personally. Thank you, your discretion in this matter is greatly appreciated.'

Jess replaced the handset triumphantly. 'I told you, I'd get us in. He wants us to go this evening, so there's not many people around. He did say there's not a lot to see, that Dad's buried in a grave with others, but at least we can see where he is.'

'Sis, that's amazing! Well done. Mum, I'm going to nip out and get some flowers to take, anyone want anything from the shop?'

I'll come with you, Eddie, I could do with some fresh air.

Charlie nodded at them. 'I'll come too, just let me grab my coat.'

The three Thomas children left the room, leaving Hannah to sit on the sofa and put her head in her hands. 'It's almost a game to them, they have no idea.'

Sidney put his arm around his sister. 'You don't have to go; tell them you can't face it.'

'I can't do that, I owe them. After everything Stan and I have put them through, they need me to be there for them.'

Sidney hugged his sister tighter. 'I'll drive you, but I meant it when I said there's no way I'm voluntarily setting foot in a prison, I've spent my whole life avoiding it!'

Hannah laughed as Sidney hugged her.

Chapter 85

1988 – Nottingham Prison.

Never had Sidney's brand new Rolls Royce looked more out of place than it did as it pulled up outside Nottingham Prison.

'Everybody, O.K? I can drive you all straight back home?'

'No, Sid, we'll be fine.'

'I'll wait here for you, make sure you look after your mum.'

'We will.'

Sidney watched as the four of them headed to the prison gate, unable to shake the uneasy feeling he had in his stomach. He parked his car up and got out, lighting a cigarette. He looked around, he couldn't see anyone, although he was sure he could feel someone, feel their eyes staring at him in the darkness. Holding up his cigarette lighter, he tried to see if he could see anyone lurking in the darkness. He couldn't. He told himself it was just the ghosts of the past, this place always gave him the creeps.

He'd been here a million times, to see Stan before he was executed, and made various visits to the rest of the Merry Men when they'd been locked up for various crimes over the years.

He'd always managed to avoid being banged himself though.

Flicking his cigarette end to the floor, Sidney got back in the car and waited.

Chapter 86

1988 – Nottingham Prison

Shaun Mitchell greeted his guests at the prison door. He was in his fifties with a bald head and a greying moustache and beard. The neck of his shirt was slightly frayed from being worn too much, his tie had made its way to a jaunty angle around his neck, but his shoes shone brightly and were impeccably clean. He spoke in a low, soft, deep voice, that had a slight Birmingham twang.

Jess struggled to imagine the prisoners being scared of him at all.

'Governor Mitchell, I'm Sergeant Jessica Thomas, this is my mother Hannah and my brothers Charlie and Eddie. I just wanted to say again how much we appreciate this.'

Shaun Mitchell took Jess's outstretched hand and shook it limply. 'You're welcome, but as I said on the phone, this really is most irregular.'

'We appreciate that, but all this publicity that the book has created around my father has stirred up lots of memories for us as a family, we just wanted to see his final resting place.'

Shaun Mitchell nodded his head. 'Follow me, I've asked one of our guards, Officer Derek Davies to accompany us, he can help if you need some assistance with the wheelchair.'

It was then, that Jess noticed an even more nervous-looking man lurking in the shadows. She stuck her hand out to him. 'Officer Davies? Thank you for your time to help us.'

Derek Davies swallowed hard and took Jess's hand. 'You're welcome' he stammered. 'If you could follow me, I must warn you, there's not a lot to see. Executed prisoners were buried in the grounds, of the prison and to save space, it's three to a grave, but I can show you where your dad is.'

Eddie took his Mum's hand as they walked down the corridor, a bunch of flowers in the other. Charlie followed in his wheelchair, while Jess walked behind them. She sensed there was something more to Officer Davies than met the eye and she was determined to get it out of him.

'Have you worked here long, Officer Davies?'

'Since I was twenty-one. I retire in a few years.'

'Twenty-one? Where you here when Dad was? Did you know him?'

Derek Davies lowered his eyes, seemingly unable to meet Jess's gaze.

'Well?' she demanded, 'Did you?'

Derek Davies nodded. 'Yes.' His voice broke as he added, 'I was there.'

'There?'

'At his execution.' He still couldn't seem to meet Jess's eyes and strode ahead.

Jess stopped walking. She felt like her legs were going to give way and she leaned against the wall.

'Jess, are you OK? Mum, Eddie, stop, Jess doesn't seem well.'

'Jessica, darling, are you OK?' Hannah held her daughter close. 'We don't have to do this, we can go home?'

'No, I'm OK, I just... It was just...'

'Sergeant Thomas, are you OK? Did Officer Davies upset you in anyway?"'

Jess looked up and saw that for once she'd been wrong. A flicker of a smirk danced through his eyes and around the corners of his mouth. Shaun Mitchell wasn't a weak pushover of a man; Jess could see that he ruled this prison by pettiness and fear. He got his kicks by gently taking a knife and making a small incision, he'd then worrying that wound in any way he could: he'd massage salt into it, let it start to heal and then he'd pick at the scab again until it got infected. He would find a weak spot and exploit it. He'd obviously known that Derek Davies had been present at her dad's execution, and it was no coincidence that he'd been chosen to walk with them to Stan's final resting place, he wanted to mess with them.

'I'm fine, Mum, just not eaten a lot today. Let's carry on.'

They walked in silence, until they reached a door.

Governor Mitchell, paused, before he opened the door. 'I'll re-iterate what I've already said, there's not a lot to see.'

Opening the door, Officer Davies led them to a large grassy area, where there were rows of stones that split it into sections, marking the final resting places of the people who had been executed, had taken their own lives or had no-one on the outside to care where their final resting place was. No gravestones were present.

'As you can see, all the graves are unmarked, as was befitting someone who had broken the law, but we do have a record of where everyone is, by number. Stan is over here; he's buried with two others.' Governor Mitchell started walking.

'Do you know who?' asked Charlie.

'Not off the top of my head, we very rarely come out here these days and we never have visitors.' The Governor stopped walking, 'Here it is, grave one-zero-seven-one-one-one-one.'

Eddie bent down and laid the flowers on the piece of grass, he thought, but he wasn't sure that he heard the Governor snigger.

'Could we have a minute, Governor Mitchell?' Jess was determined not to let him see that the presence of a man who had witnessed her dad's execution had rattled her.

He nodded. 'Officer Davies and I will wait over here and then on our way back, Derek, here can tell you all about the execution itself.'

'What's that meant to mean?' asked Charlie.

'Officer Davies here was present at your dad's execution, so if you want to know all about his final moments, I'm sure Derek will be happy to fill you in. I mean, it's a story he tells any chance he gets.'

Jess could see the Governor's shoulders shaking with laughter as he walked off.

Derek Davies mouthed the word 'sorry', lowered his head and followed his boss.

Chapter 87

1988 – Nottingham Prison

The Thomas family left the prison in silence. Despite the baiting and tormenting of Governor Mitchell, they'd refused to be drawn into his attempts to get Officer Davies to tell them about Stan's final moments.

As they reached the prison gates, Governor Mitchell said, 'I want to thank you.'

'Thank us?' questioned Jess.

'Yes, because of you, I'm able to get the renovations on my house done and take the Mrs on holiday to Spain.'

As he opened the door, the Thomas family were once again greeted by the baying paparazzi.

Chapter 88

1952 – Crow Hill Drive, Mansfield

Murder in Mansfield! Brothel Owner Found Dead!

The newspapers all carried the same headline.

Walter Dorrell's body had been found naked, bound and bloodied in an abandoned warehouse A post-mortem had revealed that the final cause of death had been suffocation. All the papers reported that investigations were ongoing and that no-one had been arrested.

Hannah threw the newspaper on the table in front of her husband. 'Have you seen this?'

'Yes, I'm aware of it. Looks like Dorrell got what was coming to him.'

'Should I be worried Stan?'

'No, I'm just sorry someone got to him before I did. Oh well.'

'Stan?'

'I told you, don't worry, everything's in hand. Have I ever let you down before?' Stan kissed his wife on the forehead, picked the newspaper up and threw it in the bin.

She was just about to follow her husband out the room, when there was a knock at the door. Answering it, she found four policemen stood there.

'Mrs. Thomas? Is Stan in?'

'What do you want with him?'

'A word.'

Pushing her aside, the policemen made their way into the house.

'I don't recall either my wife or myself inviting you into our house.'

'Stanley Thomas?'

'Who wants to know?'

'Stanley Thomas, you are not obliged to say anything unless you wish to do so, but whatever you say will be taken down in writing and may be used against you.'

'You can't take him; he's not done anything!' screamed Hannah.

'He bloody has! I know it, he knows it, and you know.'

'Hannah, call my solicitor! Get Robin Martin to meet me at the station. I'll be home before you know it.'

The policeman putting on Stan's handcuffs laughed. 'I don't think so, this will be the last time you ever see this house!'

And with that, Hannah watched as her husband was bundled into the back of a police car and did indeed make his final journey from the home they shared.

Chapter 89

1988 – Mansfield

The days that followed their visit to Stan's grave at Nottingham Prison were some of the worst Hannah had ever known; far worse than the ones that had followed his actual execution.

For days, the newspapers had been full of the story of her and her children's visit to the prison. The Daily Chronicle spun the story every which way it could, quoting 'unnamed sources', who Hannah presumed to be Governor Mitchell, going into the tiniest detail about what happened when they'd visited the grave. They knew about the flowers Eddie had taken, Jess's wobble in the corridor and the fact that 'by a weird twist of fate, one of the officers that had accompanied them had been present at Stan's execution.'

If they weren't talking about the visit itself, they were full of stories about Jess, making her out to be a tragic character who having grown up not knowing her dad had tried to find an identity working for the police. They flirted with the suggestion that Jess wasn't Stan's at all and had been fathered by another member of the Merry Men.

Charlie's accident was bought up, how it was this that, that had led to Stan killing Walter, and yet Walter's involvement had never been proved, it had just been a tragic accident. They claimed Stan's hatred for Walter was so strong that anything that went wrong in his life, he immediately blamed on Walter.

Eddie fared better in the press. They made reference to his 'movie star' looks and how he was clearly following in his uncle's footsteps as a playboy. They ran stories in which they claimed to have spoken with women he'd allegedly slept with whilst he'd been in the U.K. Eddie said he wished it were true, but if he'd honestly bedded all the women, they claimed he had, he'd have been horizontal since he'd arrived in the U.K a week ago! They'd even managed to track down his ex-girlfriend, who was pictured wearing a bikini on an Australian beach saying how Eddie had broken her heart when he'd dumped her. He had indeed dumped her, but only after he'd found her in bed with a bloke she worked with, a fact that had conveniently been left out of the story.

But it was Hannah that really faced the vitriol of the press. She was painted as a weak, tragic character who had never really known what her gangster husband was up to. She'd married him as a naïve eighteen-year-old, had born his children and then been left widowed at the age of twenty-six. They quoted 'friends' of hers who claimed that she'd decided to flee to Australia in the hope of a better life but had never re-married because secretly she had never gotten over Stan. They harped on about she still idolised Stan, how she regularly kept in touch with the rest of the Merry Men and how she had written to them during their various prison stays, desperate to keep the legend alive.

The latest story was that Hannah was a broken woman following the trip to the prison to see her husband's grave, and how she was now petitioning the Home Office to have Stan's remains dug up so that she could fly him back to Australia and have him buried in consecrated ground, because the Australian's didn't care about stuff like that.

The Daily Chronicle churned out unsubstantiated story after unsubstantiated story, always quoting either an 'unnamed source' or 'someone close to' Hannah and her family. Reporters camped out on Sidney's doorstep, ready for the next bit of the story to unfold, and the whole thing became relentless.

Hannah was in fact far from a broken woman, she was a furious one. The lies about her she could take, the lies about Stan she could take and as for the stories about Sidney, her younger brother was more than capable of fighting his own battles in his own inimitable style. But go after her children and Hannah would come for you and she wouldn't stop until she'd got you.

Chapter 90

1988 – Berry Hill, Mansfield

Henry Mason sat in his office, a copy of the latest The Daily Chronicle lay on the desk in front of him, a pile of older copies to his right and a mug of steaming coffee to his left. He read the latest stories being reported about Stan's family, how his son Charlie had been the catalyst for Walter's murder, how Hannah Thomas was some Miss Havisham-type character living her whole life shrouded in the pain and devastation of her husband's execution.

And those were just the stories from that day.

Henry had spent the last few days reading everything about the Thomas family. He stared at their photos; he could see Stan so clearly in the eyes of Eddie and could tell from his stance that he possessed Stan's same confident cocky nature.

But it was the stories and photos of Jess Thomas that really got him.

Jess was six years older than his own daughter, Anna and yet had the two had lived very different lives. Henry wondered if Jess had always known about what had happened to her dad, whether she'd asked questions about him? Had she felt a stab of pain on Fathers' Day, knowing her own dad was no longer around, that she had no-one to send a card to. Had she been jealous of her friends whose dads had been able to attend parents' evenings, take them to the zoo, teach them to swim? Who had done those things for Jess Thomas?

Henry had been there for every moment of his daughter Anna's life. He'd captured her first steps in a photo, wiped away a tear when he and Maisy had dropped her at the school gates for her first day. He'd taught her to swim on a family holiday to Bournemouth, helped her learn to drive, paced the floor whilst she was out on her first date and thought his heart would burst with pride when she'd graduated from teacher training college.

The lives of Jess Thomas and Anna Mason had been very, very different.

As Henry continued to read his paper, he heard the front door open and a barking dog.

'Dad, Mum, you in?'

He heard Maisy shout, 'In the kitchen love.'

Henry closed his paper and got to his feet. Ever since he'd had his heart attack, Anna had got into the habit of popping round to see them every evening after she'd taken her dog Mitch for a walk. Anna claimed it was because Mitch wanted to see them, but Henry knew the beagle had nothing to do with it! The heart attack had obviously scared Anna, making her realise that her parents weren't invincible and that time with them was special.

Hearing the study door open, Mitch came running to meet Henry, 'Now then, how's my favourite naughty beagle? And my favourite daughter of course,' he added, kissing her on the cheek.

'We're good thanks Dad, Mitch wanted to see his grandpa.'

'I'm sure he did! When are you going to make me an actual grandpa? It's about time that boyfriend of yours made an honest woman of you.'

Henry opened a tin and gave a frantically paw-waving beagle a biscuit.

'I've told you, Chris and I are happy as we are! Plus, what do I want a baby for? I'm surrounded by kids all day every day, Mitch is far easier to look after.'

Maisy laughed. 'As long as you're happy, duck, that's all me and your dad care about. Now how was work?'

Henry sat and listened to the happy chatter that passed between them, occasionally stopping to throw a ball for Mitch. He wondered if Jess Thomas had ever experienced this feeling of family love and enjoyed the easy banter of being a close family.

Chapter 91

1988 – The Avenue, Mansfield

Sidney could always tell when his older sister was plotting something. She went completely silent, starred into space, and started twirling her hair and tapping her foot.

'Penny for them, Sis?'

Hannah turned to her brother. 'I've been thinking. I know the bastard press are watching us, but we came here to meet up with the boys and for my children to find out more about their dad and that's what we're going to do.'

'How are you planning to throw them off the scent?'

'You must have a lady friend who can dress up as me and take your car out for a drive? It's me they're most bothered about, so if they think I'm going out, they'll follow me, that way we can leave by the back door and head to Larry's.'

'I have just the person.' Picking the phone up he started to dial, "Fi-Fi, it's Sid, I need a favour from your Marjie...... No, not that sort of favour. I need her to come over here and pretend to be our Hannah to throw the press off the scent, so Hannah can meet up with the rest of the boys.'

Fi-Fi was clearly not keen about giving in to Sidney's demands.

'Fi-Fi, I'm not asking, I'm telling. Tell Marjie to be here by 9 a.m. tomorrow morning and to come round the back, then tell Billy to meet me at Larry's at midday.' And with that he hung up. 'Fiona Potter is a gobby cow, but it's sorted. Marjie is their daughter and she'll pretend to be you. Are you absolutely sure?'

'Yes, I am, it's what we came here for and I can't let the kids down. I've had enough of being bullied by the press.'

The Fixer

1988

'She's planning what? No, let her have this one.'

The Fixer replaced the phone.

So, Hannah was taking her children to meet up with the rest of the Merry Men, it would be the first time she'd seen them all in one place in thirty-five years. The Fixer felt they owed Hannah this one, a chance to meet them in peace.

Peace wasn't going to be something that Hannah would have a lot of over the next few weeks.

Chapter 92

1988 – The Avenue, Mansfield

'Sid! Sid? Sid!!!'

'Alright, keep your noise down woman.'

Sidney came into his kitchen to see Marjie Potter stood there. Kissing her on the cheek, he said, 'I'm not deaf you know.' Throwing her arms around him, she kissed him back full on the mouth. 'Well, you are getting on a bit and they do say your hearing goes when you get older.'

Hannah walked in to find the two of them locked in an embrace and laughing. 'Hannah, this is Marjie Potter, Billy's daughter.'

'You look just like your dad.' Hannah stuck her hand out to shake Marjies.

"Thanks, I couldn't get my mum's blonde hair, could I? Oh no, I had to get my dad's mop of ginger hair and his freckles.'

It was worryingly obvious, to Sidney, just how stunningly beautiful Marjie was. Whilst she had certainly inherited her dad's colouring and his height, she had her mum's piercing green eyes. She was slim and toned and when she smiled, she lit up the room. Sidney knew she was crazy about him, and if he were honest those feelings were mutual. Not that he'd ever admit it.

'So, how are we going to make the beautiful Marjie look like a slightly dowdy sixty-one-year-old Australian housewife?' Hannah asked.

'Dowdy? You? Behave, you're stunning! Dad said you were a looker. I've bought a long black wig and I reckon if I wear some of your clothes and disguise my face with sunglasses and a scarf no-one will realise. I mean, with the amount your being followed, no-one will think it's weird you're trying to stay incognito."

'Go and get changed Marjie and then we can get you out of here.'

Marjie headed upstairs.

'She seems nice.' Hannah observed.

'Yeah, she is, she's a real firecracker, smart too. She took over running The Duke in Kirkby a few years ago when Billy and Fiona decided to semi-retire. She's turned it around, the foods great, the beers even better and she's capitalised on the Merry Men legacy. There's memorabilia all over the walls and she arranges 'evenings with', where she gets us in to do talks. Place is a gold mine.'

'Very pretty too. Seems to be a fan of yours.' Teased Hannah.

Sidney could feel himself blushing. 'We get on. She's Billy's little girl. Plus, he'd kill me if I went near her again.'

Hannah laughed. 'I think you might have a crush on her, too.'

'Oh shut up.' He threw a tea towel at his sister as Marjie came back in the room, this time dressed as Hannah.

'Well, will I do?' Marjie gave a little twirl.

'Perfect! I was thinking, you should take my handbag too, we don't want to give anyone any reason to suspect you're not me.'

As Hannah and Marjie started to make the swap, Sidney got out the keys to his car.

'Marjie, be fucking careful with my car. I swear if there's even a scratch on it, I'll make you pay to have it repaired. It's a very powerful car, so take it steady, don't speed and don't do anything to draw attention to yourself.'

'Hark at him, suddenly worried about breaking the law. Yes sir! All understood and received! I shall drive her like I was a little old lady taking in the sights on a Sunday. How long do you need me gone for?"

'A few hours. We need time to get to Larry's without being seen. Doesn't matter if they see us coming back, as long as they don't know where we've been.'

'Fab, and you'll take me out for dinner afterwards?'

'Not a chance Marjie Potter, I don't want your dad or more importantly your mum shouting at me.'

'You're not scared of them.'

'Well maybe not your dad, but your mum will have my bollocks for earrings. Now go and drive carefully.'

Marjie blew a kiss at Sidney and just as she was about to leave, she stopped and came back into the room, hugging Hannah she said, 'I really hope it goes OK and you all get the answers you want. They're good blokes at heart and they loved your Stan, my dad's never got over it.'

Hannah hugged her back and Sidney noticed one solitary tear track down her cheek.

Chapter 93

1952 – Shire Hall, Nottingham.

Stanley was sat in his cell underneath the Shire Hall, waiting for his trial to start.

He was already bored by it all.

Since his arrest a month ago, Stanley had been in Nottingham Prison. It had done his head in. The other prisoners largely left him alone, scared of him and his reputation, but the guards were a different story. They never missed an opportunity to tell him he was destined for the hangman's noose. Stan ignored them. There was no way that he Stanley Thomas, was heading for the gallows for doing the world a favour and ridding it of Walter Dorrell.

His solicitor had told him not to worry, that he'd get him off, that there was no real evidence and that pleading not guilty was the right thing to do. There'd been rumours that there was a witness, but nothing had been made formal.

'Thomas, come on, you're up.' The guard gestured for him to stick his hands out so he could cuff him.

'Is there any need for these? I'm not going anywhere.'

'There's every need and the only place you're going is the noose.'

Stan smiled and said, 'Cunt,' under his breath.

'What was that?'

'Nothing, ready when you are... sir.'

When Stan reached the dock, he could see the expectant faces of the jurors who were going to decide his fate. Some of them starred right at him, others looked away. He could see his solicitor Robin Martin and the barrister who would be pleading for his life, Frank Edwards. Turning his head, he could see Hannah sat in the gallery. He thought she looked tired; the worry of the last few weeks etched onto her beautiful face. He was pleased that Billy, Sidney, and Larry were with her. Dicky had gotten himself arrested a few weeks after Stan for ABH. Stan nodded up at them.

Stan watched as Judge George Haynes entered the court room. Stan was aware that this was the biggest trial he'd ever presided over, and he seemed determined that everything would be in order.

Stanley had heard all about George Haynes, he had a tough reputation and was determined to rid the streets of 'scum'. He was fearsome and had a reputation for liking young girls.

Putting his glasses on, George Haynes banged his gavel to bring the court to order.

'Stanley Thomas, you are charged that on the 11th November 1952 you did unlawfully kidnap and murder Walter Dorrell, how do you plead?'

'Not guilty your Honour.'

There was a ripple of noise around the court as someone shouted out, 'Of course he's not fucking guilty.'

'Silence!' Lord Haynes banged down his gavel. 'I will not have noise in the gallery. Any more outbursts and I shall hold whoever is responsible in contempt, do I make myself clear? Now let's continue.'

Both barristers made their opening statements, Stanley's barrister, Frank Edwards painted him as a businessman and a doting husband and father, who did everything within his power to care for his family, particularly his crippled son, who had been injured in a terrible attack, where the culprit had never been brought to justice. He told the court, that Stanley couldn't have possibly murdered Walter Dorrell, because on the day of the alleged murder, Stan had been in a business meeting with his associates over thirty miles away in Sheffield. There were people who were prepared to give evidence to that fact. After his meeting he had returned straight home and spent the evening with his wife and children. Stanley Thomas was an upstanding member of society.

The barrister for the prosecution, Rod Briggs, a weasely-looking man with thinning hair and round glasses, argued that Stanley wasn't a businessman, but a gangster who profited from terrorising people in Mansfield. Walter Dorrell had found himself facing the wrath of Stan when rumours suggested that he had been responsible for the accident that left Charlie Thomas paralysed. Rod Briggs argued that this had been a malicious rumour, and there was no truth in it, but it had angered Stanley to the point where he wanted to harm Walter Dorrell.

He went on to explain that, in fact, Walter Dorrell was the upstanding businessman, who ran an honest and successful business and had refused to pay the illegal taxes imposed by Stanley on the residents of Mansfield. There were witnesses to the fake trial that Stanley had made Walter take part in and the beating he had subsequently taken.

There had also been the matter of the far more tragic suggestion that Walter had been responsible for Mrs. Thomas losing her baby. These were lies spread by people who wanted to harm Walter's reputation, but they were enough to send Stanley Thomas into a rage that would lead to the torture and death of Walter.

Rod Briggs told the jury that he would present them with witnesses who would allow them to get to know, albeit posthumously the real Walter and the career criminal who killed him.

He closed by saying that for far too long Stanley Thomas had run amok around Mansfield, bullying and terrorising its residents, doing what he wanted, when he wanted. Today that would come to an end.

The stage was set.

Chapter 94

1952 – Shire Hall, Nottingham.

Over the next few days, the jury were treated to witness after witness, those who sang the praises of Stanley, and those who argued against him, crying about the tragic end their beloved Walter had faced.

It was a game of tennis, the legal ball bouncing backwards and forwards, the score always seemingly at deuce, neither barrister able to get an advantage.

On the 9th December 1952, one barrister took it to break point.

'The prosecution calls to the stand Miss Pearl Dorrell.'

There were audible gasps from around the room. Stan shifted in his seat uncomfortably and looked over at his barrister, who simply shrugged his shoulders.

'Your Honour, the defence was not aware that this witness was on the list. I'd like to request a short adjournment whilst I confer with my client.'

George Haynes pressed his hands together in a prayer-like movement and rested his chin on them as if he was considering it. 'Adjournment denied, the witness can give her evidence.'

'Your Honour, I really must object. We had no idea the deceased's sister was going to be a witness.'

'Well now you do, Mr. Edwards. Swear her in.'

Pearl Dorrell made her way slowly to the witness box. Her head was bent, and she looked at the floor as she walked. Very briefly, she stopped in front of the dock where Stan was sat and very gingerly looked up. The jurors likely caught a glimpse of the fear in her eyes as she quickly put her head back down and continued forward.

Pearl was dressed in a long black skirt and matching polo neck, with flat sensible shoes. She wore very little make up, her long brown hair tied back in a bun in the nape of her neck, and a large crucifix hanging to the front. Her eyes looked sore from crying. She looked every bit the grieving sister and more importantly, every bit the star witness.

The court clerk took a bible and placed it in front of Pearl. 'Miss Dorrell, do you swear the evidence you are about to give will tell will be the truth, the whole truth and nothing but the truth, so help you God?'

Placing her hand on the bible, in a very small voice she said, 'I do.'

Rod Briggs was straight to his feet. 'Miss Dorrell, or may I call you Pearl?'

Pearl nodded. 'Yes.'

'Pearl, I just want to thank you for having the courage to join us here today. I know that losing your brother must have been a terrible shock, particularly as you only lost your parents a few years ago too.'

Pearl smiled weakly. 'I just wanted to do what I could for Walter, my brother.' Her voice cracked as she said the word 'Walter', and she dabbed at her eyes with a lace handkerchief.

'We all appreciate how difficult this is, so take your time, but can you tell me a bit about your brother, what sort of man he was?'

'Walter is... I mean was – 'more tears and dabbing of eyes with a handkerchief, 'Walter was a kind man. He took me in after our parents died and looked after me, and he made our house in George Street a home, not just for me, but for lots of people. There was always a bed for someone who found themselves homeless, or a brew in the pot or a hot meal for the hungry. He was so kind. He was determined that we would remain a family, and he promised me he'd always take care of me.' Pearl let out a large sob.

George Haynes intervened. 'Take your time, Miss Dorrell, we can do this at your pace, and you must let me know if you need a break.'

'Thank you, Your Honour, I'm OK really, I want to do this for Walter.'

'Very well, Mr. Briggs, you can continue.'

'Pearl, did your brother know Stanley Thomas?'

'Yes, he did.'

'How?'

'Mr Thomas kept trying to get money out of Walter, 'taxes', he called it. Said that Walter was running a brothel and that any business in Mansfield had to pay taxes.'

'Was your brother running a brothel?'

'No, that was a vicious rumour put round by the locals. They didn't understand that because of his kind nature, Walter was happy for people who had nowhere else to go to come and live with us. He was a businessman, but an honest one. He didn't like how Stan and his gang bullied people.'

Frank Edwards was straight to his feet. 'Objection! Miss Dorrell is casting aspersions on people who aren't on trial and deliberately trying to blacken my client's character by referring to rumours.'

'Overruled, sit down Mr Edwards.'

'But Your Honour!'

'But Your Honour nothing, I said overruled. Now sit down, before I hold you in contempt of court. Please continue, Mr. Briggs.'

'Thank you, Your Honour. Pearl, please continue. What did your brother think Mr Thomas was doing?'

'He'd charge all the businesses in Mansfield 'taxes', but it was protection money really, and if you didn't pay up, you got a beating. Walter took a stand once, but Mr Thomas put him on trial, where he was the judge. He beat Walter black and blue and made him eat ...'

'Made him eat what, Pearl?'

'Human faeces.'

Pearl sobbed and there was just a faint titter of laughter from the gallery.

George Haynes banged his gavel down.

'Human faeces? What state was your brother in when he got home?'

'He was broken, mentally and physically. Way after his wounds had healed, he was scarred mentally by what had happened to him, I mean you just don't treat another human being that way! But Walter swore that whatever Stan did to him, wouldn't stop him from doing the right thing by the people of Mansfield.'

'What about the rumours your brother was responsible for the accident that Charlie Thomas had?'

'It was just an accident, a terrible, terrible thing to happen, but as I understand it, he was playing with his brother, when a slab in Mr Thomas's own garden fell on him.'

Frank Edwards was straight to his feet. 'Objection!'

'On what grounds this time, Mr Edwards?'

'The witness is speculating about what happened, she doesn't know, she wasn't there.'

George Haynes looked thoughtful for a second. 'Overruled.'

'You have got to be kidding me!'

'I assure you Mr Edwards as the judge presiding over this court, I am not kidding. No charges were brought or filed against Mr Dorrell for the accident the witness is referring too, so your objection is overruled. And if you challenge me again, you'll be spending the night in the cells with your client.'

Frank Edwards slumped back down. He could see his case disappearing before his eyes. Rod Briggs could suggest that Walter Dorrell had been able to walk on water and this judge would allow it. This case was set up for Stanley Thomas to hang and nothing he could say or do was going to change the outcome.

Pearl continued to give her evidence, pausing to cry at certain points and dab at her eyes with a now sodden lace handkerchief.

Occasionally Frank Edwards got to his feet to object about one thing or another, but he was quickly overruled on each occasion. All Frank could do was sit and watch the noose get tighter and tighter around his client's neck.

Stanley sat there silent and staring straight ahead, not a flicker of emotion showing on his face.

***

Rod Briggs had never had a trial go his way in quite this manner. It was as if everything he said or did was pure gold, and he was wiping the floor with Frank Edwards.

As he strutted about the courtroom, Rod was having fanstasies about becoming a world-famous barrister who was called on to prosecute cases all over the U.K., whilst earning a huge amount of money and then retiring to write his memoirs and give entertaining after-dinner speeches.

'Miss Dorrell, I appreciate everything you've told us so far, but I'm afraid I need to ask you about the day of your brother's murder, can you tell me what happened?'

Pearl nodded and took a deep breath. 'Yes, it was about nine in the morning and Walter and I were sat having a cup of tea. We always tried to find some time in the morning, where the two of us could have a bit of time to ourselves for a catch up. There was a knock at the door and Walter went to get it, I could hear voices, but couldn't make out who the other voice belonged to, so I got up to have a look, and could see Mr Thomas at the front door.'

'What happened then?'

'Well, Walter came back inside, he looked a bit shaken, but when I asked if he was OK, he said yes and that Mr Thomas, had asked him to meet up with him later in the day, but he wouldn't give me any details.'

'Did your brother seem worried? Did the defendant threaten him?'

Frank Edwards made an obviously half-hearted attempt to object. 'Objection! The prosecution is trying to overlook the minutiae of the situation by asking lots of questions!' To everyone's surprise George Haynes ruled in his favour.

'Sustained. One question at a time please Mr. Briggs.'

'Sorry, Your Honour. Miss Dorrell, did your brother seem worried?'

'Yes, he wasn't quite himself when he came back in, I asked him what was wrong, but he wouldn't tell me, he said he was going to have a bath and get ready to go out. I should have made him tell me, maybe I could have helped.' Pearl let out another large sob.

'Did you hear the defendant threaten your brother?'

'No, I didn't.'

'What happened next, take your time.'

'Walter came back into the lounge, kissed me on the cheek and said, 'Button don't worry'. That was his nickname for me. He'd called it me ever since I was born.' Pearl sobbed again and through her tears added, 'I wasn't happy, I was worried about him, about what Stan... Mr Thomas might do to him, so I thought I'd follow him.'

'You made the decision to follow your brother?'

'Yes, Mr. Briggs, I thought, I might be able to help...'

'I know this is difficult, Pearl, but I need you to tell the court exactly what happened that day.'

'I followed Walter to a warehouse, just behind the Mansfield Town ground, it's just off Quarry Lane. Walter didn't see me, but I saw him. He knocked on the door and a man answered.'

'Do you see that man in the courtroom today?'

Pearl nodded. 'Yes, yes I do.'

'Can you point him out?'

Pearl pointed to Stan. 'It was Mr. Thomas, who answered the door.'

'What happened then?'

"I got closer to the warehouse, and I could see through a gap in the wall, so I watched."

'What happened next?'

'My brother and Mr Thomas started to argue. He called my brother all kinds of names and said that he was going to make my brother pay for what he'd done to Charlie and Mrs Thomas. My brother denied it all, but Mr. Thomas just kept getting angrier and angrier, eventually he punched Walter and knocked him out.'

'Did you try and do anything?'

'I didn't know what to do, I was scared. I thought if I went to get help, I'd be too late, and if I went in, I was frightened Mr. Thomas would hurt me too.'

'A very difficult decision for you, please continue.'

'Mr Thomas, then, tied my brother up and started beating him. He hit him a baseball bat, I think. He just kept hitting him, breaking bones in his body, he was relentless. He just kept going. I could hear my brother screaming, begging him not to hurt him. He just kept begging, over and over again, but that just made Stan angrier, and he started shouting at him again, accusing Walter of all kinds of things, blaming him for Charlie's accident and Mrs Thomas losing their baby. He just kept saying, 'Admit it!', but Walter just kept pleading, saying he hadn't done anything, so Mr Thomas got out a blowtorch and started to burn my brother. Walter just kept crying and screaming, and I didn't know what to do.' Pearl started crying uncontrollably, and Rod Briggs handed her his own pocket handkerchief.

***

Frank looked at the faces of the jury. Some of them were looking at Stan with looks of pure hatred, while some looked in shock as to what they were hearing. Others were fighting back tears.

He had lost Stan to the hangman.

Stanley sat perfectly still, staring forward, still not betraying a flicker of emotion.

'Pearl, what happened next?'

'Walter just stopped making any noise, he went quiet. It was like someone switched him off. I just ran then, I thought if I could get back to George Street, I could get some help, but I was too late.'

'One final question, was it just your brother and Mr Thomas in the warehouse that day?'

'Yes, it was, it was solely Mr Thomas who killed my brother.'

'Nothing further Your Honour.'

Frank Edwards could see the jury nodding, and getting to his feet, he began the futile process of cross-examining Pearl Dorrell.

Chapter 95

1952 – Shire Hall, Nottingham

It took the jury just four hours to reach a unanimous decision and Frank Edwards thought most of that time, they'd probably spent having a cup of tea and enjoying the free sandwiches in the jury room.

The jury had made their minds up the moment Pearl Dorrell had walked into the courtroom.

The jury filed back to their seats, none of them looking at either Stan or Frank Edwards.

Rod Briggs sat at his desk; chest puffed out. He clearly knew he'd won.

In the gallery sat Hannah Thomas, once again flanked by her brother Sidney, whose hand she held tightly, Billy Potter and Larry Yates. Pearl Dorrell sat the other side of the row, on her own, still dressed in black, her long brown hair tied in a bun.

The crucifix that had been around her neck was now in her hands and she twiddled it between her fingers.

Everyone got to their feet as Judge George Haynes came in. He seemed quite happy: He too, Frank surmised, knew that he was about to preside over a guilty verdict and send Stan to his death.

'Members of the jury have you reached a unanimous verdict in the case of Stanley Thomas?'

The Foreman of the Jury got to his feet. 'Yes, Your Honour we have.'

'Do you find the defendant, Stanley Thomas, guilty or not guilty of the murder of Walter Dorrell?'

'Guilty.'

There were cheers from one section of the courtroom, and jeers and shouts of 'Cunt!' from another.

Hannah let out a loud sob and buried her head in her brother's chest.

Stanley never even flinched. In the days to come, some people said it was as if he'd been told his favourite ice cream was out of stock; he just didn't seem bothered. He never looked up to the gallery at his wife, never looked at the jury and never acknowledged his legal team either.

The Judge shushed the courtroom, seemingly not even bothering to hide his smile now.

Reaching for the piece of black cloth, he placed it on his head.

'You shall be taken to the place from whence you came, and from there be taken to a place of execution. You shall be hung by the neck until the body be dead. Take him down'

Chapter 96

1953 – Nottingham Prison

Stan had been taken straight back to Nottingham Prison following his sentencing, He'd spent some of the time before his execution in a cell with Dicky, who was in there on an ABH charge. Stan spent those weeks leading to his execution making plans. He made sure Dicky knew what was expected and what to tell the others, when the rest of the Merry Men visited him. They were also given orders for the future.

Hannah visited her husband twice, once just after his sentencing and the second time, the day before his execution.

Stan reassured her that everything would be OK, that she would be looked after, and that she would never struggle. He told her that whatever happened the boys came first, and she should do whatever she could to make sure they grew up to be good and to succeed. Stan told her to move on, to find someone else to fall in love with, a good kind boring man who would look after her. Hannah sobbed her way through both conversations, and although Stan would never show it, seeing his wife's red, tearstained face nearly broke him.

Chapter 97

1953 – Nottingham Prison

Stanley knew that today, the 8th January 1953, was the day of his execution.

He could hear movement in the cell next door, with preparations being made. A priest had been to visit him the day before to hear his final confession, which in true Stan style had consisted of the words 'fuck' and 'off'

Every so often, someone opened the hatch in his cell door and peered at him, making sure he didn't kill himself, before they killed him. He'd been measured up for his drop and he knew that Old Man Rope would be doing the honours, a man who, according to legend was kind, courteous, slick and never made a mistake.

Stan lay on his bed smoking. To anyone who looked into his cell, he was a man without a care in the world, who was simply spending the day relaxing.

At 9 a.m., the partition wall to his cell swung open and in walked a smartly dressed man, he handed him a glass said, 'Now then, son, let's make this quick and with no trouble.'

Waiting for him were the Prison Governor, William Smith, the Sheriff of the County, Frederick Dykes, the Prison Doctor, Michael Dunderdale (who, from what Stan had heard, would probably pronounce him alive after the execution.) the Prison Chaplain, Roger Collins and two guards, Reginald Braithewaite and Derek Davies.

'Thanks for coming boys, nice of you all to turn up.'

Chapter 98

1988 – St Mary's Vicarage, Edwinstowe.

Sidney pulled up in front of St Mary's Vicarage, now home to Mad Larry Yates, or Father Yates as he was known to the many parishioners who turned up every week to hear him preach.

'You, OK? Ready for this?'

Hannah nodded. 'Kids, you, OK? You sure you want to do this? We can go home?'

'No, we all want to do this.' Jess responded.

As they got out of the car, the vicarage door opened, and an English bulldog came running towards them.

'Moses, get back here, our guests don't want covering in your slobber! I'm so sorry, he gets very over excited by visitors.'

Moses sauntered back inside as Larry rushed forward to greet his guests. 'Come in, let's get you inside before anyone sees you and you get even more hassle from the bloody papers.'

'Are Vicars allowed to swear Larry?'

'Yes, we fucking are, Sidney.'

And with that, the tension was broken, and they all went inside laughing.

'Hannah, let me look at you.'

Taking her hands, Larry stared into Hannah's dark brown eyes. He could see the corners were marked by soft laughter lines, but there was a deep sadness behind them, and the stress of the last few days was etched into her forehead. Her dark hair was tied up in a ponytail.

'You don't look a bit different.'

He pulled her into a warm embrace, and Hannah let him hold her, he felt her relax in his embrace.

Hannah had last seen Larry just before she'd left for Australia. He'd been in prison for ABH, and she'd gone to see him to say goodbye. He'd begged her not to leave, saying that they'd all look after her, but Hannah couldn't be persuaded to stay. Over the years, they'd exchanged letters and cards.

'Larry, you haven't changed a bit either. Well apart from the becoming a vicar thing and going all respectable.'

'Bless you, my child, but there's a bit more grey in this old mop of mine these days and I am indeed a respectable God-fearing man. Now then, we are being rude, I want to meet these amazing children of yours. Charlie, Eddie, I haven't seen you, since you were little boys! Oh my, don't you both look like Stan.'

Walking over to where Charlie was in his chair, he reached out his hand to shake it, before apparently changing his mind, and instead wrapping him in a huge bear hug. 'Screw the handshake, any boy of Stan's is a boy of mine.' Walking over to Eddie, he did the same. 'Hannah, these boys of yours are good-looking chaps.'

Taking a step back, he took a long look at Jess. 'Oh my word, you must be Jess. Now you really are your father's daughter." Walking up to her, he very gently stroked her face, his eyes slightly welling with tears. 'I swear, I can see the old bastard looking back at me in those eyes of yours.' He held her in a tight embrace. 'Your dad would have been a nightmare with any bloke you'd have bought home, no-one would have been good enough. Oh Hannah, if only he'd known.'

A comfortable silence filled the air, until a barking Moses ruined it. A knock at the door signaled a visitor, and a visitor obviously meant a treat.

'Knock, knock, you in Your Reverend Highness, or whatever the fuck we call you these days?'

Dicky came into the room. He hadn't changed a bit, still the loud, brash, handsome man he'd always been, jet black hair and eyes, his six-foot six height making him the focus of any room he entered. Hannah had once described him as a wicked Cary Grant, and she'd been right.

Seeing Hannah and Jess stood there, he doffed a pretend cap and said, 'Sorry, didn't realise there were ladies present. Hannah Thomas, aren't you a sight for sore eyes?' He walked straight up to her, picked her up and spun her around.

Hannah had visited Dicky in prison, before she'd left for Australia, but hadn't really heard from him since. Larry and Sidney kept her up to date with what he was up to, and she'd seen the 'interview' he'd done about Henry Mason's book in the newspaper.

Walking over to Charlie and Eddie he pumped their hands up and down. 'Charlie, Eddie, pleasure to meet you! Or pleasure to see you again! Although I suppose you don't remember me? well I guess see you again, you won't remember me? Do you remember me? Of course you do, I'm your Uncle Dicky.'

Charlie nodded. 'Actually, I do, you bought me a toy car after my accident.'

'I did, didn't I? I've always been a good bloke!' He laughed out loud at his own joke, before spotting Jess in the corner of the room, at which point his laughter suddenly stopped. 'Fuck me, it's Stan in a wig!' Walking up to Jess, he looked straight into her eyes, something overtook him and gone was the jovial laughing bloke that walked into the vicarage. Standing in his place was a quiet, thoughtful one who apparently couldn't believe what he was seeing. 'Those eyes, Han, they're Stan's eyes.' He grabbed Jess and held her, and Hannah thought she heard him say, 'I've missed you, you old bastard.' under his breath, but she couldn't be sure.

Larry busied himself putting the kettle on and handing out plates of homemade biscuits and cakes.

'You've never made these?'

'No, Sidney, one doesn't have a Mother's Union and bake for oneself you know.'

They all laughed.

‘What’s so funny?’ Billy Potter was the last of the Merry Men to arrive, shaking the rest of his former crew by the hand. He stopped when he got to Hannah and gave a little bow. ‘Mrs Thomas.’

‘Mr Potter, charmed, I’m sure.’ Hannah stuck out her hand for Billy to kiss it, and they both broke out in laughter and started hugging each other. ‘I’ve missed you!’

‘I’ve missed you too!’

Billy had been Stan’s best friend, ever since they’d been at school. No-one had been able to deal with Stan in the way that Billy had. Billy could calm Stan down, get him to listen to reason. Billy had been devastated by Stan’s death and some say, Hannah suspected that he’d never really recovered.

In 1960, he’d been sent to prison for theft, but since his release, he’d gone straight. He’d married Fiona Aitkens in 1963, they’d bought The Duke in Kirkby-in-Ashfield, a pub they still owned. Their daughter Marjie had been born in 1964 and had taken over the day to day running of the pub.

Despite many pleas over the years to tell his story and the fact he’d been the subject of many films and documentaries, he had never spoken about his friendship with Stan.

The man standing in front of Hannah had changed very little over the years: his bright ginger hair was laced with white, but his freckled face and bright green eyes, still filled her with the same reassurance they always had.

Letting Hannah out of his bear hug, he turned to Charlie. ‘It’s so nice to see you again, I don’t know how much you remember about any of us?’

‘A little bit, I probably remember more than Eddie. It’s nice to see you again, too.’

‘Eddie, I’ve heard a lot about you, all good. It seems you had the good fortune to take after your mum and not your reprobate of an old man or uncle.’

‘It’s nice to meet you too.’ Eddie took Billy’s hand, and Hannah could see her youngest son was starting to feel a bit overwhelmed. She went over to him and put her arm reassuringly around his shoulders.

Turning, to where she’d been waiting patiently, Billy seemed to notice Jess for the first time. ‘Oh wow.’ Just as the others had done, he stopped in his tracks, staring into her eyes, taking in every inch of her face. ‘You are just like your dad.’

And before she knew it, Jess was once again lost in the embrace of a man she’d never met, and yet, seeing her daughter hug her husband’s best-friend just felt all so familiar. A man for whom she had so much unconditional love that she, too, risked becoming overwhelmed.

Chapter 99

1988 – St Mary's Vicarage, Edwinstowe

With the introductions out the way, the Merry Men, Hannah and the Thomas children all sat around a large oak table in the vicarage kitchen.

Sidney took charge. It still made Billy laugh, that despite Sidney joining them as a cocky fifteen-year-old, it was Sidney who now called the shots. It didn't bother Billy, he had no interest in running the gang, never had really. All he wanted these days was a quiet life, although the chances of that were quickly evaporating.

'So, as lovely as it is for me to see your old faces, today, is not about me. Today is about my nephews and niece. They want to know as much about their dad as possible and you old bastards are the best people to tell them about the man Stan really was.'

Dicky piped up first. 'Can you stop calling us old? Ask away.'

Charlie, Eddie and Jess exchanged nervous looks. Billy could tell they'd talked about this moment for the last few weeks, but now it was here, they didn't know what to ask first.

Jess eventually broke the silence. 'How did you all meet?'

'Well,' Bill answered, 'your dad, Dicky and I were at school together, not that we went very often. The Reverend over here was a bare-knuckle fighter. We met him at a fight after he'd beat the shit out five guys in a row and your Uncle Sid used to hang round us all the time begging to join us.'

'I did not beg, I may have asked a few times, but I did not beg!'

'What was Dad like at school?' asked Charlie.

Billy and Dicky answered in unison. 'He was a cheeky fucker!'

They all laughed and after that, the questions flowed easily; lots of questions about Stan as a young man, about his parents – what were they like? What happened to them? They laughed, they cried, and Hannah could feel the unbreakable bond that had once existed between her husband and his friends had now been extended to his children.

Larry and Billy each had some photos, which they spread them out on the table. Charlie, Eddie and Jess worked through them, asking questions about who was who, where they were taken, remarking how good-looking they all were, laughing as they joked back and forth, wanting to know if they could visit certain places. Eddie picked one up of Stan sat on a beach, it looked like he was objecting to having his photo taken, but he was laughing at the same time.

'Where's this, Mum?'

Hannah took the photo and studied it. 'Skeg, I think. Either there or Blackpool. Those were the only places we went in those days. Not exactly Bondi.'

Finally, Charlie asked the question the Thomas children had spent the last few weeks discussing.

'Did Dad, do it? Did he kill Walter Dorrell?'

The Merry Men all looked at each other, and Sidney nodded at Billy.

'Yes, Charlie, yes, he did. But there were very good reasons for it.'

'So, Dad was a murderer?'

'Yes, Jess, he was, but that's just a label, it's not as clear as it was made out. He didn't do it for no good reason. Dorrell was rotten, he was rotten to the core. Do you remember how you ended up in that chair, Charlie?'

'I have a vague memory of a man making me and Eddie play hide and seek.'

'That man was Dorrell. He put you under that slab and he made sure that you never walked again. It drove your dad insane that you'd been hurt. Dorrell had been a harmless prat up until that point, ran the local brothel, wore these stupid red and black shoes because he thought they made him special, a bit of a dirty pervert, with a big mouth and delusions of grandeur, but no real threat. Then, all of a sudden, he tries to challenge Stan. He hurt you and then he...' Billy stopped talking, suddenly realizing what he was about to say. 'He, err, he... Hannah?'

Sidney took his sister's hand, and Hannah could see her three children staring at her. She'd kept her secret long enough. 'Walter raped me.'

Billy took Hannah's other hand, and they all sat in silence.

'When? Why have you never said, Mum?'

'It was thirty-six years ago. I'd just found out I was pregnant with you, and I was really suffering from morning sickness, Charlie had not long had his accident, Eddie was a toddler, and I just needed some time. I told your dad that I was going to your mamma's, but I just needed some air and time on my own. I'd not long left the house, when Walter kidnapped me. He must have knocked me out with something because the next thing I remember I woke up and I was tied to a bed. And then he attacked and raped me. I thought I'd lost you Jess.'

'Oh Mum.' Eddie put his head in his hands. 'We never knew.'

'You weren't to know; you were both babies! I was your mum. This was too much for me to get my head around, let alone two small boys.'

'Is that why Dad never knew about me?'

'Yes, all the signs pointed to me having lost you. Technology wasn't quite as advanced then as it is now. I went to the doctor's a few times to say I thought I could feel you moving, but they told me it was a phantom pregnancy. Then your dad got arrested, then there was the trial and he died and then next thing I knew I was giving birth to you.'

'Is that why Dad did what he did?' asked Charlie.

'Yes, your dad loved his family and the fact Walter hurt you and me and at the time we thought Jess, was too much for him to bear and he had to do something.'

Jess got up and hugged her mum. 'Mum, I'm so sorry you've had to keep this to yourself all this time and I'm even sorrier that we didn't get to meet Dad and that we've never really spoken about him. From now on, let's do what we can to keep his memory alive and remember the real Dad.'

Billy raised his mug. 'Hear, hear, I'll drink to that.'

The others did the same and they all clinked mugs.

Larry got to his feet. 'I think this calls for a proper drink.'

The Fixer

1988

The Fixer sat in their car outside the vicarage. Through the window they could see the Merry Men, Hannah, Charlie, Eddie and Jess sat at a table. There had been hugging, laughing, and crying and they were now indulging in many bottles of wine.

A pang of what felt like jealousy stabbed at the Fixer, seeing them all reunited after all these years, enjoying each other's company, and getting to know each other again, Stan's kids fitting in as easily as if they'd always been around these people.

The Fixer started the engine of their car and drove away, the pang of jealousy replaced by one of sorrow, that once again life was about to come crashing down for the Thomas family and the Merry Men.

Chapter 100

1988 – Fleet Street, London

Pearl sat back in her chair, arms behind her head looking out of her office window onto Fleet Street. It was a view she never got tired of. She loved the hustle and the bustle of journalists running in and out of buildings, desperate to get to a story, or rushing back in to meet a deadline.

There were tourists wandering the streets taking photos of the famous buildings, and the autograph hunters who habitually walked up and down on the lookout for celebrities who might be heading into one of the buildings to do an interview.

Fleet Street had its own soundtrack too, the hum of the traffic mixed in with screeching police sirens as they accompanied the accused to stand trial at the Old Bailey all laced with the pealing of the bells of St Paul's Cathedral. They were sounds that excited and gave Pearl peace all at the same time.

Pearl remembered the first time she'd walked down Fleet Street. She was eighteen years old and had only been in London for a few weeks, and she'd arranged to meet a journalist at Ye Olde Cock Tavern. He wanted her to sell him her story. Pearl had other ideas.

She remembered pushing open the tavern doors for the first time and breathing in the smell of ale, cigarettes, and history. She could see the faces of the tavern's famous clientele starring back at her, Samuel Pepys, Alfred Tennyson, and Charles Dickens. Even now, whenever she was struggling for inspiration or needed some time out, she came and sat in this pub.

That first meeting with the journalist who had later become her boss and mentor had been eventful. Tony Richardson had been knocking around Fleet Street for years. If you'd have looked up 'old hack' in the dictionary, you'd have seen Tony's face starring back at you.

He'd started his career at the age of eighteen. A bout of polio as a child had deemed him medically unfit to be conscripted into the army, so he'd done the next best thing and reported on it. He covered the D-Day Landings, the death of Hitler and the Nuremberg Trials, proving himself to be a fearless journalist who would go wherever the story was and find the person at the heart of it.

After that, he covered the death of George V, the abdication of Edward VIII and the subsequent coronation and death of George VI and most recently the trial of Derek Bentley and Christopher Craig. The huge interest in Stan and the Merry Men even though they resided north of Watford Gap, had meant he'd spent time in Nottingham covering Stan's trial and subsequent execution.

It was there that he'd first approached her to sell her story. She'd liked him instantly: there was something about Tony Richardson that made you want to tell him everything. She'd taken his card and said she'd think about it.

Pearl's plan had always been to move to London after Stan's trial and start again. She'd lined up lodgings on Star Street, just off Tottenham Court Road and had started working in the Kings Arms pub while her plan took shape.

She'd phoned Tony Richardson after a month of being in London: He was the first part of her plan.

She'd found him sat at a table in the tavern, a half-drunk pint of Guinness in front of him, smoking a cigarette and scribbling in his notebook. He'd got to his feet and reached up to kiss her on both cheeks. At five foot three, he'd had to stretch to do it. 'Now then my dear girl, let me get you a drink? What will it be?'

Pearl had ordered a gin and tonic.

'Mother's ruin, good choice. You and I are going to get along famously. Sit down, make yourself comfy.'

Tony had gone off to the bar and started chatting to the barman. This was part of the reason Tony had been so successful, he oozed charisma and charm and had a way of chatting to people that put them so much at ease, they were soon telling him everything.

Tony put a gin and tonic in front of Pearl and another pint in front of himself. Pearl had taken a large swig and had then told Tony her plan. She'd never forget the look on his face: he'd looked her surprised at first, then a big smile had broken out, and he'd laughed out loud and promptly agreed.

Pearl wanted to write her own story, but under his guidance and afterwards she'd be given a job as a trainee reporter with The Daily Chronicle. And that's exactly what had happened.

Her story had been a huge success, and she'd proven herself to be a talented writer. Tony, good as his word had mentored her, he'd pushing her to be the very best journalist she could be. He challenged her, praised her, and filled the air with expletives when she made a mistake. Tony had eventually ended up as the Editor of The Daily Chronicle and Pearl, forever his protégé had continued to rise through the journalistic ranks, proving her worth every step of the way.

Tony had retired at the age of sixty-five and was now happily living in Bournemouth causing havoc at his local Darby and Joan club and writing his memoirs. Pearl visited him whenever she got the chance.

Pearl knew she'd been putting off the phone call she needed to make, so with Tony's words of, 'That story won't write itself, Dorrell,' ringing in her ears, she picked up the phone and dialled.

Chapter 101

1988 – The Avenue, Mansfield

'I'll get it.' Hannah picked up the phone. She'd been back in Mansfield for a week, and it had pleasantly surprised her, how easily she'd adapted back to life there. It was like she and Sidney had never been apart and following on from that initial meeting with the Merry Men, they'd seen each other regularly. They'd stopped sneaking about and met whenever and wherever they felt like.

'Hello, Mansfield 722683... Yes, this is she. Who's this?'

'Hannah, it's Pearl, Pearl Dorrell.'

'What do you want? How did you get this number?'

'I want to talk to you. I want you to tell me your story.'

'I thought your rag of a newspaper just made stuff up! Why do you want to waste time finding out the truth?'

'Hannah, this is your chance to tell your side of the story. What you think? We'd pay you, of course.'

'Pay me? I'm not a prostitute selling my soul to the highest bidder' Hannah heard Pearl take a sharp intake of breath. 'Pearl, I'm sorry, I didn't mean that.'

'I know, please think about it. I'd do the story, you and me and how life has been since. Hannah, think about it. Look, why don't you take some time and then call me at the paper? If you agree, I'll come up to Mansfield.'

'I'll think about it.' And with that Hannah hung up.

The Fixer

1988

Getting Hannah Thomas to tell her side of the story would be the beginning of the end. The Fixer then had plans to get the Thomas children to all make various media appearances: chat shows, breakfast television, a discussion with a publisher.

Billy Potter might prove more difficult. He'd never once engaged with anyone about life with Stan. But the Fixer hoped Hannah might offer some gentle encouragement.

If not, then they'd turn up the pressure.

Chapter 102

1988 – The Boy Pub, Mansfield

Pearl sat in The Boy pub in Mansfield, waiting for Hannah to arrive. There was a bit of her that still couldn't believe that she'd agreed to the interview, but then fifty-thousand pounds was a lot of money to turn down.

The Boy pub seemed a prophetic place to meet, considering the amount of history that it held for both the Thomases and Dorrells.

Pearl took a sip of her gin and tonic and started going through her notes. Eventually she became aware of footsteps making their way towards her.

'Pearl?'

Looking up, she saw Hannah, and met her eyes for the first time since they were in the courtroom at Stan's trial.

'Mrs Thomas... Hannah.' Pearl stuck out her hand for Hannah to shake. Hannah hesitated for a second, but eventually she took it. 'Can I get you a drink?'

'Red wine, please.'

Pearl went to the bar and returned with a bottle and two glasses. Pouring, she set one in front of each of them, debating whether 'cheers' was an appropriate thing to say in this situation.

It was Hannah who broke the silence. She raised her glass and said, 'To Stan and the truth.'

Pearl raised her glass too and clinked it again Hannah's. 'To Stan and the truth. You haven't changed a bit, just how I remember you.'

Hannah ran her hands through her long brown hair, which today hung about her shoulders, 'A bit greyer and a few more wrinkles, but the Australian way of life suits me. You, however, have changed! You're so glamourous.'

Pearl smiled. The last time they'd seen each other, Pearl had been a teenager, long dark hair tied up in a pious bun to give the jury the impression that she was a grieving sister. These days, Pearl was far more herself. Now fifty-two years old, she had retained her slim figure, and to make sure that she cut an imposing figure, despite being five foot eight, she always wore six-inch heels, whether she was on or off duty. Her dark hair had long since been dyed blonde and today was worn in a short bob, very reminiscent of Princess Diana. No-one saw Pearl Dorrell without her make-up and her trademark red lipstick.

'Well, I do try.' Pearl laughed, and to anyone looking on, they would have looked like any two friends having a catchup and enjoying each other's company.

'So, how does this work? I want your assurance that my words won't be taken out of context. And when do I get my money?'

'I have a cheque for you in my bag, which I'll give you when we've finished. There's also a contract I need you to sign, so that we both know where we stand and once that's out the way, I'll get out my Dictaphone, so I can record what we're saying. I'll make notes as we go. I'll write the story from there. Did you bring any photos?'

Hannah nodded. 'Will I get them back?'

‘Yes, of course.’ Pearl handed Hannah the contract for her to look at as she flicked through the photos Hannah had brought.

‘Wow, Jess is really like Stan.’

‘Everyone says that.’ Hannah handed Pearl the signed contract. ‘Right, let’s do this.’

‘Hannah, I want to start by saying, how grateful I am that you’ve agreed to talk to me today. Most people will know Stan’s legend, but not the man himself. Can you start by telling me how you two met?”

‘We met at the Palais de Danse in Mansfield in 1944. I was seventeen at the time and I’d gone out with my friend Lucy. I saw Stan as soon as I walked in. I knew all about him: everyone knew Stan in Mansfield, and I said to Lucy, ‘I’m going to marry him.’ She thought I was crazy, but I knew as soon as I saw him. I also knew I needed to be different, so I walked past him and ignored him and started chatting to a bloke stood near him at the bar. Stan asked if he could buy me a drink and I said no, I had one and walked away. He asked me three more times that night and each time I turned him down. Just as I was leaving, he asked if he could dance with me and I said no, I was leaving. He asked if he could see me again and I told him that if Stanley Thomas really did know everything, then he’d know who I was and where to find me.’

‘And did he?’

‘Of course, he did! He was Stanley Thomas! I was working at my dad’s grocery store Longshaws on Leeming Street, and as soon as we opened, in he walked with a big bunch of flowers and said, ‘Now I’ve kept my end of the bargain, are you going to keep yours?’ I laughed, but my dad was horrified. The last thing he wanted was his little girl dating the local gangster, but he was too scared to say anything, so I agreed, and Stan took me out that night.”

‘Where did you go?’

‘Well, ironically, we came here, to The Boy. It was quite the place to be seen. We had a few drinks and Stan made me laugh with his outrageous stories and that was it, my heart was a goner, it irrevocably belonged to him.’ Hannah took a sip of wine and seemed to lose herself for a minute. ‘There was no-one quite like him. I don’t think anyone saw him the way I did. Well maybe Billy. He was a total bugger. He could make me laugh like no-one else could, his stories about his time as a soldier in World War Two were incredible.’

Pearl looked surprised. ‘Stan was a soldier?’

‘Yes, he lied about his age, and joined in 1939 because he thought it would be an adventure. But he was medically discharged two years later, partly because they found out the truth about his age, and partly because of an injury. He was hit by shrapnel. He had a scar above his right knee. He was lucky it didn't blow his leg off.'

Pearl nodded and made a note. 'After that first date, what happened?'

'We met in the September of 1944, and that was it. We were together all the time. My parents were horrified, they tried desperately to make me find a nice boy, one who worked down the pit and who would provide for me, but I wasn't interested. I knew my dad would never challenge Stan, so I carried on courting him. He proposed at Christmas in 1944 and we married in April 1945. Charlie was born two years later and Eddie in '49.'

'Was it a happy marriage?'

'Yes, on the whole it was. Don't get me wrong, Stan could drive me insane, far more so than anyone I've ever met, but that comes with being soul mates and loving someone so completely. He knew what buttons to press and so did I. Our fallouts were epic, but so were our make-ups.'

'Was he faithful?'

'Most of the time. There was the odd trollop here and there, but nothing I ever worried about, it was all for show.'

'Did you know any of them?'

'No, they weren't important.' Hannah picked up her wine and began drinking, making it clear that, was the end of that particular line of questioning.

'Did you know about his business dealings?'

Hannah took a breath. 'Some of them yes, not all. I kept out of it. Stan was my husband, he provided for us, we had a roof over our head, food on the table and my children were well looked after. It wasn't my place to question what he was doing.'

'How were you treated by the people of Mansfield?'

'With respect. As Stan's wife, it was always going to be that way.'

'What about your family? Did they ever accept Stan?'

'No, not really. They tolerated him and were polite to his face. My mum was distraught when Sidney joined the Merry Men, but my dad just shrugged it off. He'd already had enough of trying to stop either of us from falling under Stan's spell. Don't get me wrong, they were really good with the kids, they loved Charlie and Eddie and were always on hand to help me out with babysitting duties, but I think they were pleased when I emigrated.'

'What about Stan's parents?'

'I never met them. He never really talked about them. He once said they'd disapprove of his lifestyle, so I took that to mean they'd disowned him. I picked up a few bits over the years we were together, though. His dad ran a pub somewhere, I think it was local, but I couldn't tell you where. They never met the kids, and as far as I know, they never said anything after Stan's death. I couldn't tell you if they were alive or dead.'

The two women continued to talk about Hannah's marriage to Stan and the kind of father he was, and another bottle of wine was ordered.

Pearl knew it was time. 'Tell me about Charlie's accident.'

'You know what happened? I'm not going to say any different, we both know it was Walter.'

Pearl nodded. 'Hannah, this is your story told your way, I don't want you to dress anything up.'

Hannah proceeded to tell Pearl about the events of the twenty-second of May and what had happened to Charlie that day.

'How did you know for sure it was Walter?'

'Stan got him to describe him, and we knew it was Walter, he mentioned those stupid red and black shoes he always wore, like clown's shoes Charlie said.'

Pearl smiled. 'I hated those bloody shoes.'

Hannah laughed and carried on with her story. 'Walter admitted it too.'

'He was never charged, though, was he?'

'No, that's not how we did things then. Stan said he was going to sort it and I had to let him.'

''Let' him?'

'Yes, let him. We both knew the police would do bugger all. The son of a gangster gets injured by the local pimp, they were hardly going to bust a gut solving that crime.'

'You don't seem to have a very high opinion of the police. Whoever his dad was, a little boy was still crippled that day.'

'I never had you down as naïve Pearl. The police didn't give a shit.'

'You said Walter admitted what he'd done to you, can you elaborate?'

'He told me what he'd done when he raped me.' Hannah drained a full glass of wine.

Pearl felt the look on her face change.

Chapter 103

1988 – The Avenue, Mansfield

Sidney threw a copy of The Daily Chronicle on the table in front of Hannah. 'I've got to hand it to you Sis, it's one hell of an interview. Most unusual for a member of the Dorrell family to stick to their word.'

Hannah took the paper and saw two photos of herself staring back. The first was of her as a young woman in her wedding dress, holding Stan's hand outside St Peter's Church. Her eyes were full of love and hope, while Stan looked like the cat who'd got the cream. The second photo was a more recent one, taken just before they'd left Australia. Hannah was laughing at something Charlie was saying: her mouth was smiling, but her eyes had lost their sparkle. The headline screamed, My Life as Mrs Thomas.

Hannah and Pearl had agreed that the interview would be serialised over a few days. This was the first part and was all about how Hannah and Stan had met.

'Maybe it'll give people a different take on Stan, plus I can't let that Mason chap think he's the leading authority on my husband just because he met him for thirty seconds in a prison cell.'

Sidney placed his hand on his sister's shoulder. 'I hope people do start to see Stan the way we did, but you know this is going to open the floodgates. You'll have every Tom, Dick and Wogan wanting you to go on their talk show.'

'I know. Well maybe it's time I did.'

As if on cue the phone rang, and they could hear Eddie's muffled voice, before he shouted through, 'Mum, it's some producer wanting to know if you'll do an interview with Derek Jameson.'

Sidney laughed. 'I'd hold out for Wogan.'

Chapter 104

1988 – The Homesteads, Kirkby-in-Ashfield

Jerry Mason sat on his favourite seat in his garden, took a sip of his tea and waited for the paperboy. This had been his daily routine since he and Joyce had moved into the Homesteads fifteen years ago.

Weather permitting, he'd get up, make a brew, and sit outside waiting for the paperboy, he'd then read the paper cover to cover, do the crossword and then head back inside to moan to Joyce about everything he'd just read and the state of journalism and the world in general.

'Morning, Mr Mason, lovely day, isn't it?'

'Certainly is, Nathanial, thank you for this.' Flipping the boy a fifty pence piece, he added, 'you staying out of trouble and doing your schoolwork?'

'Absolutely Mr Mason, got an A in English yesterday. Thanks for this. Say hello to Mrs Mason for me.'

'Good lad, and I will.'

Unfolding his paper, Jerry Mason caught his breath, the headline, My Life as Mrs Thomas jumping out at him. Sighing, Jerry started reading. Stanley Thomas wasn't going anywhere anytime soon.

Jerry wished he'd forgone his morning tea, for a large whiskey!

Chapter 105

1953 – The Wagon and Horses, Kirkby-in-Ashfield

Jerry was straightening his tie in the mirror when his wife Joyce walked in.

'Let me do that for you duck.' Affectionately she started untying with her husband's black tie and re-doing it. 'You OK about tomorrow?'

Jerry nodded slowly. 'Yes, I think so. I know what needs to be done, just another day at the office right?'

Joyce kissed her husband's nose. 'Yes, just another day at the office and then you're done. You promised.'

'It's a promise I'll keep. After this, no more. We'll invest a bit of money into the pub and go on holiday; you've said you always fancied Jersey.'

'Jersey would be lovely. We can get away and recharge our batteries and put all of this behind us. Stephanie and Darren have said they'll watch the bar.'

Jerry took his wife in his arms. They'd been married thirty years and he still couldn't believe his luck of having married such an amazing woman. Whilst Joyce had never approved of his job as an executioner, she'd always kept his secret and always supported him. Joyce was everything to him, she was his best friend, his confident, his challenger and the person he turned to in good and bad times.

Jerry was a seemingly unassuming man. He was five foot six, with greying hair, a moustache, and steely blue eyes, which were sometimes hidden behind horn rimmed spectacles. The truth was Jerry was, far from unassuming. He was, in fact, a very astute man, a keeper of secrets and both a gentleman and a gentle man. He was not to be messed with, either as he stood behind the bar of his pub, The Wagon and Horses, or by the people he faced on the gallows.

He had become a hangman in 1921, following in the footsteps of his grandfather and father. It seemed inevitable that he'd follow in their shoes: he knew what the job entailed, understood the need for secrecy and compassion, and, above all he knew it was just a job, and one that paid good money.

It was the money he'd earned from being an assistant hangman that had allowed him to cement his cover story as an affable publican. Then money had paid for the deposit on the pub, Joyce's engagement ring, their honeymoon, and allowed them to start a family.

Jerry had met Joyce in 1922. She'd come for an interview at his pub and from the moment she'd walked in, Jerry, knew that he'd just met his future wife. They'd married in 1923 and become a family of three in 1925.

While Joyce had never been a fan of her husband's secret career, and even less of a fan when her only son had joined him, she understood that to the Mason men it was important.

Jerry kissed his wife goodbye, got into his black Morris Minor, and started the drive to Nottingham Prison for the final time.

As Jerry drove to take part in his final ever execution, his mind wandered back to his first. He'd assisted his dad in the execution of a killer who the press had nicknamed 'Acid Bath Bobby.'

Bobby Nolan had run a guesthouse in Nottingham, which attracted travelling salesmen. It had appeared that these men had checked in and never left. Bobby would lace their food with arsenic and then strip off their skin, fashioning it into items, which he kept around the home. He'd then dispose of the rest of the body in a vat of acid. He'd gotten away with his crimes for 10 years and killed approximately fifty people. The police couldn't be sure of the exact number of Bobby's victims. but from the items around his home, they'd managed to identify at least fifty different pieces of skin. His crimes had come to light, when his final victim's wife had alerted the authorities to her husband's disappearance. Checking his last known location, they had uncovered a hotel of horrors.

The day before the execution, Jerry had helped his dad get the gallows ready, asking countless questions and taking everything in. On the day of the execution itself, Barney Mason had taken his son to one side and said to him, 'Son, I want you to always remember that whatever that man has done in the outside world, he's about to pay the ultimate price. We are not here to pass judgement or to make this anything other than it is, it's our job. Whatever he says or does, we treat him with kindness and respect, and we do it quickly. Do you understand?"

Jerry had never forgotten those words and would have that same conversation with his own son.

'Acid Bath Bobby' hadn't said a word on the gallows, and Jerry remembered being surprised at how quickly it was all over. Once the body had been cut down and certified dead, it had been part of Jerry's job to get the body ready for the undertaker. After that the body was gone and buried in a numbered grave at the back of the prison.

Today would be Jerry's five-hundred and first execution and he still remembered the names of every man and woman who had dangled at the end of his rope.

Jerry knew that the final name on his list, would be one that would haunt him for the rest of his life.

Chapter 106

1953 – Nottingham Prison

As Jerry drove up Perry Road in Sherwood towards the prison, he could see the streets lined with people holding placards; The same thing happened before every execution, but this crowd were far louder than normal. The street had a carnival-like atmosphere.

They'd got twenty-four hours to wait before the execution took place, but they clearly didn't want to miss anything.

Jerry parked his car behind the back of the prison and rang the bell to be let in.

'How are you Mr Mason? Noisy lot out there, aren't they?'

'They certainly are Officer Evans.'

'Still, I suppose we always knew it would be, what with him being so high profile.'

'Yes, it was inevitable. Is everyone here?'

'Yes, Mr Mason, I'm to take you to the Governor's meeting room.'

The two men set off, Officer Evans talking about everything from the impending execution to the fact he wasn't sure that George Jobey would still be Stags manager at the end of the season. Jerry nodded and made noises at the appropriate points.

'Well, here we are, Mr Mason. I understand it's your last one. I just wanted to say I'll miss our chats, but maybe I'll bump into you at Field Mill one day?'

'Thank you, Officer Evans, and hopefully we will, and if you're ever passing by my pub feel free to pop in for a pint.'

'That I will Mr Mason.' Officer Evans turned to walk away and just as Jerry was about to knock on the door he stopped, turned around and added, 'God speed Mr Mason.' And with that he walked off.

Jerry entered the Governor's meeting room to find everyone else had already arrived.

Despite the fact the execution didn't take place until the following day, it was standard procedure for everyone who was officiating to be on prison grounds the day before. Normally they'd run through the procedure, make final checks and be on hand, just in case a final stay of execution was granted.

William Smith walked straight up to Jerry. 'Good to see you, Jerry, ready for tomorrow? Can I get you a coffee? Something stronger?'

Jerry nodded, he could never understand that when an execution was imminent, there was a buzz around the prison. From the prisoners themselves it was a sense of unease that one of their own was about to meet their Maker; from the staff itself, the excitement was similar to that of a sportsperson about to face their biggest challenge. There could be no mistakes, they had everything to play for and everything to lose.

Jerry accepted the steaming cup of coffee and sat down. 'Can we just run through the final plans please?'

Everyone started to take their seats around the table, 'Can't believe it's your last one Old Man Rope.' Frederick Dykes put a hand on Jerry's shoulder, 'But what a way to go out, eh?'

Jerry nodded. 'Quite.'

Opening his briefcase, Jerry laid a sheet of paper out on the table. 'So, as we all know, the execution of Stanley Thomas is scheduled for oh-nine-hundred hours. The gallows are all ready, but I will carry out my final checks at precisely oh-eight-hundred hours. Warden, Sheriff, I'd like you present as I do this. Dr Dunderdale, I require you to make sure that all medical equipment is present and correct and that all possible circumstances are catered for. I also expect there to be appropriate measures in place once the condemned man has passed and that all required certification is filled out'

'Aye aye Captain.' Michael Dunderdale, saluted Jerry to try and lighten the mood, but Jerry was in full swing. An execution was not a laughing matter.

'Reverend, I'll assume that the condemned man has not requested your presence for his final hours, so as I prepare to make my final checks, I'd like you to enter the condemned cell and distract him from any noise that may be coming from next door. Finally, Reginald you will be in Mr Thomas's cell with him and the Reverend. Derek, you'll be with me. When the time comes, I will tie Mr Thomas's hands and lead him to the gallows, you will be on hand just in case. Is everyone clear on what is expected?'

'Yes, Jerry, crystal clear.' Taking Jerry's coffee from him, William replaced it with a whiskey. 'Now let me chase up the buffet and you wash it down with that whiskey.'

Chapter 107

1988 – The Homesteads, Kirkby-in-Ashfield

Henry arrived at his parents' house to find his dad sat outside reading the paper. Jerry looked up. 'Have you read this?'

'The Daily Chronicle? Yeah, I've seen it. They're running an excerpt of Hannah's interview every day.'

'I know. I don't know why everyone just couldn't let sleeping dogs lie. You caused this, you and that bloody book! We were all just getting on with things, but you couldn't leave it, could you?'

'Dad, it was never meant to be published. Maisy thought it would help me if I wrote everything down, help me move on after I'd retired. She sent it to the publisher, not me! I don't want this dragging up any more than you do!'

'It's not stopped you showing off on all those TV shows and doing all those interviews. We are never going to be free of that fucking man.'

Henry was shocked to hear his dad use such strong language. Jerry never swore.

'It'll all die down. Dad, I promise. Hannah and the kids will go back to Australia, someone else will write another book about something even more salacious; I mean, Jeffrey Archer's bound to be working on something following last year's libel case, he's far more newsworthy than me.'

Jerry rolled his eyes and exhaled. 'Let's bloody hope so! All this stress, it's not good for me or your mother. I want us to see our days out in peace, not worrying about what skeletons are about to come tumbling out the closet.'

Henry put his hand on his dad's arm. 'Know, dad.' Looking down at the front cover of the newspaper, he looked at the photos of Hannah. 'She was always a beautiful woman.'

'Enough!'

'Let me go and get us another cuppa. Mum inside, is she?'

Henry made his way inside. 'Mum, I'm going to put the kettle on, do you want one? Mum?'

'In here, dear, and yes that would be lovely.'

Henry found his mum watching This Morning and knitting. 'Your dad, OK? He's been out there ages today. I was expecting him to come in and have his normal moan at me.' She laughed. 'Mot that I'd have him any other way.'

'Me either. Tea, coffee?'

'Tea please, and there's some of your favourite biscuits too.'

Henry headed into the kitchen to put the kettle on, and as he waited for it to boil, he found himself thinking about Hannah Thomas and her children. Would they go back to Australia, or would they decide to stay here? He'd read that interview. She was clearly still in love with Stan, there didn't seem to be evidence of her having a man waiting for her in Australia.

Handing his mum her tea, he headed back into the garden, where he could see his dad, arms folded across his stomach, head towards his chest; he'd claim he was examining the inside of his eyelids, but Henry knew he got really tired these days, and all this stress with the book and Hannah doing interviews wouldn't be helping. Sitting in the chair next to him, Henry placed the tray on the table between them and gently touched his dad's arm. 'Dad, tea... Dad? Dad!'

Henry started to shake his dad a little harder, but Jerry's head just flopped to one side. 'Mum, Mum call an ambulance. It's Dad, I think he's had a stroke.'

Joyce came rushing outside. 'What did you say?' Seeing her husband slumped in his chair, she let out a wail that didn't sound like it came from this eighty-six-year-old woman but was the more the cry of a wounded animal. Rushing to her husband and falling at his feet, she looked at her son and said, 'He's dead Henry, my Jerry is dead.'

Chapter 108

1988 – St Wilfred's Church

As the hearse pulled into the grounds of St Wilfred's Church, Henry reached over and took his mum's hand. 'You, OK?'

Joyce nodded.

As they approached the church, they could see rows of people all gathered to pay their respects. Jerry had been a popular man. Henry could see that the waiting crowd was made up of people who'd been regular customers at The Wagon and Horses, various ex-members of staff, people he'd watched football with, played cards with neighbours and a few faces from the past.

The undertaker got out and opened the car door for Joyce and Henry, Maisy, Anna, Philip and his wife Eve all followed, each one of them shaking hands and kissing various faces in the waiting crowd.

The undertaker started to usher people inside. 'Mr Mason, if you're ready?'

Henry nodded. He was going to be one of the pallbearers, feeling it was the one last thing he could do for his dad, making sure that he went to his final resting place in peace.

Henry and the rest of the pallbearers started their walk into the chapel, while Joyce followed her husband's coffin, gripping on tightly to the hand of her daughter-in-law, her grandchildren and great grandchildren following on behind. Their walk was accompanied by the soft tones of Frank Sinatra singing My Way.

The vicar got everyone seated and began his service. He talked about what a great man Jerry had been, respected by everyone who knew him. He'd been a loving husband he'd been to Joyce and a doting father to his only son Henry. The vicar spoke about how much Jerry's grandchildren and great-grandchildren adored him, how he was always ready with a kind word or a bit of advice. The vicar spoke about Jerry's career as the landlord of The Wagon and Horses, and how he and Joyce had run a thriving pub, which was the cornerstone of the community in Kirkby, and what a tribute it was that the congregation was made up of former staff and customers.

The vicar said Jerry's death was a true loss to society and the world was a poorer place for him not being in it.

There was no mention of his former career or Henry's book.

The Fixer

1988

The Fixer sat outside St Wilfred's Church watching people filing into Jerry Mason's funeral. The Mason family were all there, Henry putting himself front and centre by insisting on carrying his dad's coffin.

The Fixer wasn't sure if Henry had noticed, but in amongst the congregation were a few familiar faces.

Being pushed in a wheelchair by a lady who the Fixer assumed was his career was the Honourable Lord George Haynes.

Hiding behind a pair of dark glasses and a wispy beard, the Fixer could make out the insipid features of Michael Dunderdale's face, the tight gold chain and pot belly spilling over his trousers being an additional giveaway.

Less obvious and standing almost out of sight was Derek Davies, who as far as the Fixer was aware still worked at Nottingham Prison.

The Fixer wasn't sure if Jerry's death would throw up any problems for their plan, but as far as they could tell everything was still on track. If Henry recognised the faces at the funeral, it might spook him a bit, but spooking Henry was a good thing after all.

Chapter 109

1988 – The Wagon and Horses pub, Kirkby-in-Ashfield

After the service, it felt fitting that the wake was held at The Wagon and Horses. The function room of the pub was soon full of people making the most of the buffet and sharing their memories of Jerry. Henry lost count of the amount of people who shook his hand and told him how sorry they were for his loss. He listened to countless stories about his Dad, some he'd never heard before and others he'd been told a thousand times before, but he still laughed in all the right places.

Watching his mum from across the room, he could see that his daughter Anna was keeping a close eye on her grandma, making sure she had a drink and something to eat and that she wasn't getting too tired.

It played on his mind constantly, about how his mum would cope without his dad, and it felt like someone was crushing his windpipe. He couldn't breathe. It wasn't just his mum who wasn't going to cope without his dad, he wouldn't either. Jerry had sacrificed so much for his son over the years and Henry felt like he'd never really repaid that debt and he couldn't shake the feeling that it was the stress caused by his book that had contributed to his dad's death.

Henry watched as a man approached his mum, from across the room. He couldn't see his face, but he could lip-read as his daughter asked her gran if she was OK as she glared at the man.

The man took a seat next to Joyce and Henry realised exactly who the man was. Dr Michael Dunderdale. Henry felt his throat start to tighten. What on earth was he doing here? He was surprised he was still around and hadn't died from a heart attack long ago. Henry wanted to rush across the room and pull the gold chain around his neck until it cut off his air supply.

Henry chose option two and crossed the room to see what on earth the useless doctor wanted. 'It's Dr Dunderdale, isn't it?'

'Michael, please.' Sticking out his hand, Henry accepted the offer. 'Henry, I was so sorry to hear about your poor dad. As you know, he and I worked together for many years, and when I read about his death, I just had to come and pay my respects to you and your mum.'

'That's really kind, isn't it Henry?'

'Yes, Mum, it is. How are you keeping?'

'Really well,' the doctor replied. 'I retired in 1975 and married the merry widow, my nickname for my wife Janie.' Michael laughed out loud. 'Janie's a multi-millionaire, her husband left her very well provided for when he died, so we travel a lot and spend a lot of time at the villa in Benidorm.'

'How nice.'

'And what about you, Mr Big Shot author? That book of yours is doing very well.'

'Thank you, it's certainly been far more successful than I could have predicted. But I'll be glad when all the publicity dies down.'

'Quite. You must be very proud of your son, Mrs Mason?'

'Oh, I am, he's a good boy, he made me and his dad very proud.'

Henry touched his mum's arm, and Michael stood up to go.

'Well, I must be getting back to my Janie. We fly to Benidorm again tomorrow for three weeks, but I wanted to come and pay my respects. Maybe when I'm back, Henry, you and I can have a proper catch up?'

'Thank you, and yes, that would be nice.'

Henry sat down next to his mum in the newly vacated chair. 'What an odious man he was!' She said, 'I'm surprised your dad was friends with someone like that!'

'He wasn't, no -ne was that man's friend! He was the prison doctor, but all the prisoners called him 'Blunderdale', because he didn't have a bloody clue what he was doing. Dad used to joke that he had to double check that any prisoner that he executed was really dead after Blunderdale had pronounced time of death because you couldn't trust him.'

Joyce Mason laughed. 'That sounds like your dad, he couldn't stand idiots.' Tears started falling down Joyce's face and she took her son's hand. 'I miss him, what am I going to do without him?'

'I don't know what any of us are going to do without him, mum.'

Chapter 110

1988- Television Centre, London

Hannah sat in the green room listening to the producer briefing her again.

'So, Hannah, the show goes out live, so no swearing. One of us will fetch you when it's your turn to go on. Terry is going to ask you lots of questions about the stories that have been running in the papers, so there'll be nothing to trip you up. All the questions will relate to stuff you've said, but remember that we go out at seven p.m., so there's sometimes kiddies watching, so don't be too graphic.'

Hannah nodded but was beginning to regret her decision to come on the show. She felt sick with nerves, and the producer seemed to pick up on that.

'Please don't be nervous, Terry is the best in the business and is just the sort of person that will put you immediately at ease. Everyone loves him.'

Hannah smiled. 'My brother said I was to hold out on doing any TV interviews till O'Brien got in touch.'

The producer laughed. 'Smart man, your brother. No-one has viewing figures like Terry. Now can I get you anything? Tea? Coffee? Water?'

'A tea would be great thanks, milk, no sugar.'

The producer nodded. 'Be right back.'

There was still forty minutes until O'Brien went on air, so Hannah decided to enjoy her cup of tea and try and keep herself calm. The producer had said that as well as herself, there was a pop band called Bros on, which had accounted for all the screaming girls outside when she'd arrived and some actress who'd just joined the soap opera, Eastenders.

Hannah had been back in the U.K. for two weeks and it had been an absolute whirlwind. What had started out as a chance for her kids to get to know more about their dad by meeting his friends and seeing where they'd lived had turned into a media storm, at first not of her making, but now Hannah was fully embracing it and making a lot of money in the process. They'd already changed their tickets for the flight home to first class.

The money from The Daily Chronicle would clear off the rest of her mortgage and give her a lovely nest egg so she could think about retiring and taking it a bit easier.

She'd also been approached by a couple of television companies about doing a documentary about her life with and without Stan. The kids all seemed up for it. In fact, they'd become media stars in their own right. Charlie and Eddie had appeared on various radio and TV shows, although Jess was less keen to do so because of her job. She didn't want to return home to a telling off from the Commissioner of the Western Australian Police Force. She was already unsure how he'd take the news that she was the daughter of a famous criminal, even if she had been born after he'd died.

The press, however, were obsessed with Jess and the papers were full of photos of her. One women's magazine had even approached her to see if they could do an article about her fashion sense. Unsurprisingly, Jess had turned them down.

Hannah had loved being around the Merry Men again. It amazed her how effortlessly they'd all fallen into an easy friendship and how much they'd taken Charlie, Eddie and Jess into their impenetrable group.

But it was spending time with her brother that had been the highlight for her. She had forgotten just how much she loved him and enjoyed having someone take care of her. Being Sidney's sister afforded her the same kind of respect that being Stan's wife had, and whatever she wanted could be easily sourced.

They had two weeks left in the UK before they flew home.

Hannah was snapped out of her thoughts by the producer. 'Ready Hannah?'

Chapter 111

1988- Television Centre, London

Hannah stood waiting in the wings as she heard the dulcet Irish tones of Terry O'Brien say, 'My first guest tonight is lady who has been gracing the front pages of our newspapers for the last couple of weeks and has been telling her side of the story; What life was like being the wife of notorious gangster and murderer Stanley Thomas. Ladies and Gentlemen, please welcome Hannah Thomas.'

The audience clapped as Hannah made her way onto the stage, where Terry O'Brien shook her warmly by the hand and gestured for her to sit down. As soon as he gave her his big smile, Hannah felt her nerves disappear.

'Hannah, first things first, you've been living in Australia for the last thirty years, why choose now to tell your story?'

Just as the producer had promised, Terry's questions were gentle, yet probing throughout the interview and by the end of it, such was his skill that Hannah felt like she'd made a new best friend.

As Terry thanked her for coming on, he seamlessly moved into an introduction for the latest band who were driving the girls crazy, Bros, who were going to play their new single, I Owe You Nothing, before being interviewed.

Terry hugged Hannah goodbye. 'You did grand, Hannah, pleasure to meet you.'

The producer accompanied Hannah back to get her things. 'So, how was it?'

'I really enjoyed it, You were right about him, such a gent.'

'He really is thanks for coming on and hopefully we'll see you again soon.'

Hannah found Sidney sat outside in his Rolls Royce waiting for her. 'Can I have your autograph missus?'

Hannah stuck her tongue out. 'Did you see it? Was it OK?'

'It was brilliant, you're a natural. Whilst you were making your television debut, I was chatting to that producer. They want to start filming with you next week. They want to do as much as they can whilst you're here and then they'll come and do some round up bits in Oz.'

'That quick?'

'Yup, they want to strike while the iron's hot. There's a lot of interest in you and us again, and they're not going to delay when there's money to be made.'

'What about the boys, have they all agreed?'

'Hmm, that's where we have a little problem. Billy's not keen at all, and nothing seems to be able to change his opinion. Larry's having to clear it with God, or the Bishop, or someone, but he thinks a donation to God's favourite charity, and it'll be a goer. The Church love a reformed sinner story. And Dicky's all over it, you know what a star fucker he is, reckons it'll get him one step closer to dating Madonna.'

Hannah laughed. 'Knowing him, he probably will end up dating her. Is it no go without Bill?'

'No, not at all, and ideally, they want all the Merry Men. I'm sure I can get Fi-Fi to put some pressure on him when she knows the kind of money we're talking about.'

'If Fi-Fi can't, I'm sure you can persuade Marjie to have a word with her dad, we know how well you two get on.'

'Shut your face, now let's head back to God's own county.'

They both laughed and said, 'to Nottinghamshire'

The Fixer

1988

'So, everyone, but Billy and Larry are onboard? Bung the Bishop ten grand and that'll persuade the greedy fucker to let him appear. Leave Billy to me.'

The Fixer hung up. It was about time Billy started doing as he was told.

Picking up the phone, the Fixer dialled another number. 'It's me, I think you should pay Marjie Potter a little visit. Let's see if we can get Billy to do as he's told that way.'

Chapter 112

1988 – The Duke, Kirkby-in-Ashfield

'Night, Gilbert, see you tomorrow.'

Marjie locked the door as the last of her customers left the pub. 'Dave, you can get yourself off too if you like, I'll finish off here.'

'You sure boss? There's not much to do.'

'Positive, you get yourself home and get a good night's sleep. I reckon tomorrow's going to be even busier. We always have a peak when there's a mention of the Merry Men and Hannah's appearance on O'Brien will certainly have given that another boost.'

'At this rate, you'll have to build an extension on the back of the pub to get everyone in. Night boss.'

'Night Dave.'

Marjie continued wiping down the surfaces of the bar and loading the last of the glasses into the dishwasher. She heard the door go, assuming it was Dave who must have forgotten something. 'What did you forget Dave? Dave? Dave, is that you?'

Heading into the back, Marjie felt someone grab her from behind and put their hand over her mouth.

'Now listen here, you little cunt, I don't want a sound from you, but I want you to fucking listen, do you understand me?'

Marjie nodded her head.

'I want you to pass on a message to your dad, you tell him, that the Fixer says he's fucking taking part in that documentary, no more pissing about. Now you know how easy it was for me to get in here, and this time, I'm not going to hurt you. But next time who knows? You're a pretty girl, so I reckon I'd have some fun with you.' As he said that, he licked her face.

Marjie took her opportunity and raising her knee, she administered a swift kick backwards into the man's groin.

'You fucking bitch.'

Raising a hand, the man spun Marjie towards him before smacking her across the face and knocking her to the floor.

And that was the last thing Marjie knew until her dad found barely conscious on the floor the next morning.

Chapter 113

1988 – The Duke, Kirkby-in-Ashfield

Marjie sat at the kitchen table, holding an icepack to her aching head.

'I think we should call the doctor.'

'Mum, I'm fine honestly. Stop fussing.'

'You're not fine, you spent all night knocked out cold on the floor of this pub, all because of your fucking father.'

'Mum, I keep telling you, it's not dad's fault, the bloke only hit me 'cos I kicked him in the bollocks.'

'That's my girl.'

'Billy Potter, I swear to God, if you don't start taking this seriously, that bloke won't be the only one getting kicked in the bollocks.'

'I am taking this seriously! Are you sure you didn't get a look at him? Anything about him that stuck out? An accent maybe? Or something on his hand?'

'He was local, definitely and, he smelled of Jazz aftershave and stale tobacco.'

'Hmm, not helpful, every fucker smells of Jazz at the minute. Tell me again exactly what he said.'

'He said for me to tell you that the Fixer said you were to take part in the documentary.'

'You're sure' he said, 'the Fixer'?'

'Positive. Who's the Fixer? Someone from the old days? You've never mentioned him before.'

Getting up, Billy kissed his daughter on the forehead. 'Yeah, the Fixer is someone from the old days, someone I thought was long gone. Fi-Fi look after our girl, I need to go out. Any trouble phone Sid. You hear me? Not the police, you phone Sid. Let him deal with this.'

Putting on his coat, Billy left the pub, getting in his car, he slammed his fist on the steering wheel, 'FUCK!'

Chapter 114

1988 – Sherwood Forest, Edwinstowe

Whenever Billy needed time to think, he always ended up in Sherwood Forest. Sitting beneath the Major Oak, where they'd buried those possessions of Stan's all those years ago, it made him feel close to his friend, almost like he could talk things over with him.

Stan and Billy had met at school. They'd been five years old, and Stan had managed to convince the whole school to sing rude words to a hymn during assembly. Billy had laughed so hard that the headmaster had assumed it was him who was responsible and had given him five of the best with his cane. Stan, outraged that someone had taken the fall for something he'd done had, had plotted his revenge on the headmaster and had substituted his mid-morning chocolates with laxatives. The whole school had witnessed the outcome during an afternoon Bible-Studies class.

Stan and Billy had been firm friends since then. Feared and revered by their peers, they ran every school they attended, selling black market sweets and cigarettes, dishing out a beating to those who deserved it and causing general havoc.

Billy idolised Stan, and from the moment they'd become friends, they'd been inseparable. Billy's childhood hadn't been the easiest; his mum was the local 'lady of ill repute', and only had a vague idea who his dad was. The man she thought it was, who lived with them when he wasn't in prison, was handy with his fists and very often Billy would find himself covered in bruises or with a broken rib. He was always pleased when the police turned up to cart his dad off to prison for something as, he'd always hoped he'd get into a fight with one of the other prisoners and end up dead. But it never happened.

Instead, it was Stan who came to his rescue.

One night when they were fifteen, Stan had turned up just as Buster Potter was taking a belt to Billy. He'd clearly been at it for a while, and Billy was huddled on the floor, blood pouring from him, the fight long gone out of him.

Billy's mum was nowhere to be seen, probably earning Buster's beer money.

Stan came up behind Buster and having the element of surprise, managed to get his own belt around his neck before he realised what was going on. Squeezing until Buster became unconscious, Stan told Billy enough was enough. Between them they sat him in his favourite armchair, bottle of whiskey in one hand, lit cigarette in the other. Stan made sure the cigarette was making contact with the chair, which was soon ablaze.

Stan took Billy back to the Thomas's, where Mrs Thomas dealt with his cuts and bruises as she had many times before.

The following day, Mansfield was awash with talk about how Buster Potter's drinking had finally been the death of him.

The evidence was clear, he'd obviously had too much to drink and had fallen asleep with a lit cigarette which had set the house alight.

Billy's Mum claimed to be heartbroken, but within two weeks, she'd mended that broken heart with a new man and moved into his house. Sadly, there had been no room for her son, so the Thomases took him in.

No-one ever suspected what Stan and Billy had done, and it only served to strengthen the bond between them.

A year later, at the age of sixteen, Stan had decided to sign up to join the army and fight in World War Two. Billy had intended to join him, but after taking one too many beatings from his old man, he had been left with hearing problems in his left ear, and so was deemed medically unfit.

Two years later, Stan had been medically discharged after an accident had nearly blown his leg off, he'd been lucky to get away with a shrapnel wound above his right knee.

Billy and Stan had fallen back into their same easy friendship, causing havoc and getting into mischief. Eventually Mr and Mrs Thomas had suggested that the boys leave and get their own place, which they did.

That just seemed to give them the freedom to do whatever they liked, and before long, they'd met up with another old school friend, Dicky and discovered Larry at a bare-knuckle fight, where he'd beaten the living daylights out of everyone who dared get in the ring with him.

The Merry Men had sort of evolved from there, realizing pretty quickly that there was money to be made from offering protection to the shopkeepers in Mansfield. Additionally, just like their namesakes, when someone in the community needed help then they'd look after their own.

The Merry Men had run a tight ship. Everyone knew not to mess with them and if they did, then they faced Stan's court and took whatever punishment he deemed fit, normally with Dicky and Larry doing those particular honours.

Those had been crazy days, and Billy had somehow managed to stay out of prison until 1958, when he'd been arrested for theft and served a couple of years in Nottingham Prison.

When he'd got out, he didn't have the heart to try and re-establish the Merry Men, nothing was the same without Stan, so Billy had started working in a pub, and it was there he met Fiona, who was the daughter of the landlord. They'd married in 1962, and Marjie had come along a couple of years later. After Fiona's dad had retired, they'd taken over the pub and there they'd stayed.

Billy and Fiona were technically retired, and Marjie ran The Duke on a day to day basis.

Despite numerous requests and many unofficial documentaries and biographies, Billy had always refused to talk about his time in the Merry Men and his friendship with Stan. He just didn't want to dig it all up again.

But now he had no choice.

Deep down, he'd always known that The Fixer would re-appear. There was no way that the secrets they kept could stay hidden.

Billy put his head in his hands and sighed.

He heard the sound of breaking twigs come up behind him as someone made their way towards him, before coming to a stop and sitting down next to him.

'I knew I'd find you here. You're nothing if not predictable.'

'I'm glad I didn't disappoint you then.'

'You got my message then?'

'Yes. Was there really any need to go after my Marjie?'

'Well, you weren't listening to my polite requests, so I needed to get your attention. I take it she's alright?'

'Yes, no thanks to your oaf!'

'Well, if your girl hadn't kicked him in the bollocks, it wouldn't have happened. He was on strict instructions not to harm her, but she's a feisty one, that girl of yours.'

'Takes after her mother. So now you've got my attention, what the fuck do you really want?'

'I want you to take part in this documentary that's being made about Stan and Hannah. I want you to talk about your friendship, your life as part of the Merry Men, your time in prison, life now. Everything.'

'You want me to talk about everything? You sure about that? Why can't we just let sleeping Dorrells lie?'

'Come now, Billy, you must have known this day would always come? Some secrets don't stay buried forever.'

'But, we've all moved on, nothing good is going to come of raking up the past again! Let us all see out our days in peace.'

'Billy, you always were an idealist, but sadly no, that might have been the plan, but then Henry Mason had other ideas. If you're looking for someone to blame, then he's your man. Now tomorrow morning, you will get a phone call from the production company to arrange interviews, you will accommodate everything they want and ask for. Understand?'

'Yes.'

Getting to their feet, The Fixer turned to walk away, before stopping and adding, 'Oh and Billy? Do give my regards to Fiona and Marjie.'

Billy shook his head, there was no way out of this for any of them.

The Fixer

1988 – Sherwood Forest, Edwinstowe.

Getting back in their car, The Fixer smiled at themself in the rearview mirror, everything was coming together. Billy was on board, the Bishop had agreed to Larry taking part, the plan was moving forward.

Whilst Henry Mason may have started this chain reaction, The Fixer had, had this plan in place for thirty-five years, waiting until the moment it needed triggering.

What Stanley Thomas had started, and Henry Mason had re-ignited, The Fixer was going to finish.

Chapter 115

1988 – Crow Hill Drive, Mansfield

Hannah sat having her make up done. It felt really weird to 'be on location' at a place where she'd lived with Stan and the boys. She still wasn't quite sure how the producers had got the current owners to agree, but they had and now here she was, sat in her old kitchen, while someone plastered her face in make-up.

The Crow Hill Drive house had certainly changed. She was sat in a brilliantly white kitchen, with red flowered wallpaper and tasteful red accessories. A big fridge freezer hummed in the corner. In the days when she and Stan had lived there, she'd had wooden cabinets and a huge kitchen table, the boys' drawings adorning the walls.

Hannah wondered if the current owners had known about the house's history when they'd bought it?

The producer, Jacqui, came in to see how they were getting on. 'Looking lovely Hannah. We want you to look like yourself, but we need the make-up, so you look lovely on camera. We want to get as much done in the house as possible, so we thought we'd start with a walk through of the house. I know it's probably very different to how it was, but if you can describe how it looked, and give us some memories of the house and your family life. Are there any original features left?'

'Yes, the fireplaces, they're all mine, I mean the houses.'

'Once we've done the walk through, you'll sit you in the lounge by the fireplace and Eamonn, our director, will ask you more questions and then we'll move out into the backyard.'

'The backyard?'

'Yes, we thought we'd get your memories on Charlie's accident. We've only got the house for one day, so we're going to record Charlie and Eddie too. That all, OK? You did say you were alright with everything?'

Hannah nodded. The last few weeks had been such a whirlwind that she was no longer sure what she had and hadn't agreed to. Being back in this house, which was so familiar and yet, so alien, had affected her far more than she thought.

In her mind, she played back memories of Stan carrying her over the threshold after they'd got married, of those first few weeks of marriage when he'd been the doting husband, making love to her all over the house, them laughing till they cried.

The arguments they'd had when he'd been off with the Merry Men doing something, returning late with no explanation, her throwing his dinner at him, watching as pie and mashed potato slid down the kitchen wall.

Her finding out she was pregnant, Stan being so excited, bringing Charlie and then Eddie home, Stan playing games with them.

Charlie's accident.

Her rape and making her way home, thinking she'd lost the baby.

Stan's arrest.

Sitting at the kitchen table with the Merry Men as they waited for the clock to strike nine, knowing that Stan was being put to death and that he'd be gone forever.

Her shutting the door for the final time, taking her three children to a new life.

All these memories screamed at her. It didn't matter how many coats of paint this house had been given, or that new carpets covered the floor, hers and Stan's lives were embedded in the walls of this house and a bit of her expected Stan to come waltzing in at any minute.

'Hannah, hi, I'm Eamonn, lovely to meet you. Jacqui says she's explained everything to you, so if you're ready, we can get started.'

'Yes, absolutely, do you want to do the walk through first?'

'Yes, I thought we'd film you walking up the street and opening the door first, then we'll move to various parts of the house, I'll prompt you with questions as we go.'

'OK.'

Chapter 116

1988 – Crow Hill Drive, Mansfield

Hannah looked at her watch. It was only one o'clock, but she was exhausted. It felt like she'd gone over the same bits of the story a million times, walked in the Rock Hill house, walked out the house, walked up its stairs, around the rooms, told story after story, and now they'd finally let her break for lunch.

Hannah just wanted a moment's peace to collect her thoughts, but Eamonn and Jacqui had other ideas and just kept talking to her.

'Hannah, you've done brilliantly so far, we've got some amazing stuff in the can already. The plan for this afternoon is we'll film you outside with your boys talking about Charlie's accident. We'll interview you separately and together and the final thing is...'

Just as Eamonn was about to explain, a couple of delivery men arrived.

'Where do you want this youth?'

Jacqui got to her feet. 'Is that the table? In the kitchen please, we've made space.'

'Table?'

'Yes, the final thing we're going to record today is you and the Merry Men sat around the kitchen table, just as you would have done the day Stan was executed.'

'But... I... you never mentioned that.'

'As you were doing your walk through, it occurred to us what a powerful bit of the documentary it would be.'

'Dicky was in prison when Stan was executed.' Hannah heard the words come out of her mouth as a sort of feeble excuse as to why they couldn't do it.

'We know, Mr Richards won't be involved in that bit, we have plans to record something separately with him.'

Hannah opened her mouth to say something else, but Charlie and Eddie arrived.

'Alright Mum?' Eddie kissed his Mum on the cheek, while Charlie touched his Mum's hand.

'You sure you're OK, Mum?'

'Yes, all good, just a bit tired.'

'So, this is the old Thomas Towers, is it?" Eddie started to walk around. 'It doesn't look familiar at all. Do you recognise anything Charlie?'

'Bits of it, but it's been so long."

Eamonn filled them all in on the plan and they all headed outside.

Charlie recorded his bit first recounting his limited memory of playing in the yard with his brother and then a man coming in and asking them if they wanted to play hide and seek.

Eddie had very little memory of the incident, but he did remember the screaming and trying to get the giant slabs off of his brother and cutting his hands, some of the scarring still remained.

Hannah could see tears falling down the faces of the crew as she gave her account of that day. She gave them every detail she could remember; she described her fear and the utter desolation she felt when she realized Charlie was paralysed; how she'd blamed Stan for everything and how she knew Walter had been responsible.

When Eamonn yelled 'Cut!', Hannah was mentally and physically exhausted, the thought of any more filming was filling her with terror.

'Hannah, Charlie, Eddie, that was amazing, so heartfelt and moving. This documentary has award-winning written all over it. Truly, this is amazing.'

'Knock, Knock' came a voice from the hallway. Hannah was relieved to see Sidney, Billy and Larry entering the room.

'Fuck me, I never thought I'd see the inside of this house again.' Spotting Jacqui, Sidney put his hand over his mouth. 'Sorry duck, I didn't realise there were ladies present. You alright Sis?' Sidney kissed Hannah on the cheek.

'Yes, just a little tired, pleased to see you lot though.'

Billy walked over and hugged her. 'So, has this been as terrible as I think it's going to be?'

Hannah laughed. 'Probably worse.'

Eamonn the director shouted from the other room. 'I heard that Mrs Thomas, and you've been brilliant all day. Honestly a dream to work with. I promise, this is the final bit for today. Can you all join me in the kitchen, please?'

The four of them made their way into the kitchen, where a big wooden table was set up with a bottle of whiskey and four glasses. A huge clock had appeared on the wall, which had been set to eight o'clock.

Hannah could see Larry looking over at her, she gave him a half smile and whispered in her ear, 'If this is too much, we can tell them to fuck off... in the name of the Lord, obviously.'

Hannah kissed his cheek and giggled. 'Oh, Reverend Yates, what would I do without you?'

'Now, I realise how painful this might be for all of you,' Eamonn began, 'so I wanted to run you through what I had in mind, and I wanted to say, how much I personally appreciate you agreeing to be filmed in this way.' Eamonn paused for a second, as if wondering whether to say the next bit. 'Look, I've never lost anyone in the same way you have, and I can't really begin to imagine how it feels, but spending the day with Hannah, Charlie and Eddie, I feel like I'm getting to know Stan and I'm really pleased I'm giving you the chance to tell his story.'

Billy walked over to Eamonn and stuck out his hand. 'Mate, I think I speak for all of us, when we say 'thank you' for saying that. Don't get me wrong, Stanley Thomas was a very bad man, but he was our very bad man.'

They all laughed and suddenly the uneasy tension that had been there was gone, and they took their places at the table in the exact same places they had sat thirty-five years ago.

Charlie and Eddie had been joined by Jess, by this point, and they all sat out of shot watching the filming.

'What, I want is for you to do exactly what you did on that morning,' Eamonn said. 'I want you to start to talk about what you remember about that day, how you were feeling, what you said, what you did, how you felt when the clock struck nine. Don't worry too much about the clock; in the edit, we can make it right. We're rolling, so whenever you're ready.'

Billy Potter got to his feet and poured everyone a glass of whiskey, and in his gruff Nottinghamshire accent started to speak. 'That day we didn't really know what to do with ourselves, we'd all been to the prison the day before to say our goodbyes. Stan had made me promise to look after Hannah and the boys and I promised him that I would."

Larry joined in. 'He asked me to do the same. Stan's last thoughts were all about keeping Hannah and the boys safe. He didn't know about Jess, none of us did, we all thought Hannah had lost the baby after...' Larry stopped talking, looking at Hannah.

Hannah reached across and squeezed Larry's hand.

'Walter Dorrell raped me.' Hannah said. 'He did it to take revenge on Stan. 'His attack was so brutal that we all thought that I'd lost the baby. Stan died thinking that and it breaks my heart that he never had the chance to get to know Jess and the fantastic young woman she's turned into. He'd have been so proud of her; he'd have been proud of all his kids.'

Sidney squeezed his sister's other hand. 'We were lucky in that we all got to see Stan the day before they murdered him. I think he made all of us promise to look after Hannah and the kids, his family were his life and leaving them was the hardest thing for him, but he did what he did to protect them.'

'That morning, my parents picked up Charlie and Eddie,' Hannah continued. 'I'm not sure the boys really knew what was happening. I'd told them that Daddy was going away and wasn't coming back. I didn't want them in the house when it happened as I wasn't sure how I was going to react. Mum and Dad picked them up about seven-thirty, I remember my mum saying to me, 'I knew it would end up like this.' She never hugged me or said she was sorry I was losing my husband.'

'Mum was a cold-hearted bitch,' Sid interjected. 'She hated Stan but didn't have the bollocks to tell him to his face. Dad was no better. I think they were ashamed of me and Hannah until the day they died.'

'We all got here about eight o'clock.' Billy went on. 'Well, everyone except Dicky. He was in prison for something or other, probably beating someone up. I know he was in Nottingham with Stan, and he did get to see him before he died. Stan had asked me to bring round this particular bottle of whiskey. We'd stolen two from the Judge's house who'd sent him down. We'd stolen them years before his execution and Stan wanted to save them for a special occasion, he thought this was as good as any.'

'Stan always knew that bastard, Haynes, would be the one to do for him.' Larry added. 'I think over the years he's sent us all down. He definitely did me in 1957. Billy did he send you down?'

'Yeah, he did,' Billy confirmed. 'I think if he could have sent us all to the gallows, he would have done.'

Sidney laughed. 'He never sent me down, I'm a law-abiding citizen, I've never been to prison.'

'Only because you've never been caught, you lucky bastard,' quipped Billy.

They all laughed.

Sidney carried on the story. 'The morning of Stan's execution, we all thought we should be together. It seemed right.'

Billy nodded. 'There's something I've never told you all about Stan,' he said. 'The night before the execution, I drove back to the prison, I don't know why, I don't know what I was expecting. I thought about going in and asking to see Stan just one last time, even though I knew they wouldn't let me in.'

'You went to the prison? Why?' Hannah looked shocked.

'I don't know, I needed to see, or I needed to feel like I was doing something. I ended up just parked by the side of the road. It was lined with people, they were going to wait all night, like it was some sort of pop concert. Some had banners in support of Stan, others were not so friendly, shall we say. I wanted to get out the car and kick the living crap out of those who wanted Stan dead, I just thought, how dare they! They don't know him; he wasn't their friend. Then I saw him pull up.'

'Who pulled up?' asked Larry.

'Old Man Rope, Jerry Mason, the man who was going to kill Stan. I wanted to run to him, beg him not to, but I just watched him get out of his car and walk in, like it was any other day.'

'How did you know it was him? I thought his identity was a secret' asked Sidney.

'It was, I don't know how I knew. Someone had told me that the executioner always arrived the day before and stayed on the grounds, so I just wanted to see if I could see him. I just knew I'd know who it was when they arrived, and I did. He was so ordinary, you'd never have picked him out of a line up, but I knew it was him. I just sat and watched as he walked in, and I did nothing.'

'Oh Billy, what could you have done?'

'I don't know, but I know I've never felt so helpless. My best friend was about to die and there was nothing I could do to stop it.'

Hannah held Billy's hand. 'Bill, you were the best friend Stan ever had, and we all know that if you could have done something you would have done, but there was nothing any of us could do.'

'Hannah's right Bill, me, you, Sid, there was nothing left for us to do. All we could do was sit around this table and talk about Stan and what he meant to us. I remember us sharing stories about him, some we laughed at, some we cried at. I think that morning has helped me when I'm dealing with parishioners who've lost people, I tell them to talk about their loved ones, to share their memories with family and friends. The dead can live on through that. It's weird because I think I've talked more about Stan in the last two weeks than I have in years.'

'Me too, it feels good to remember the old bastard.' Sidney said.

Billy sighed. 'This is just making me miss him even more. It feels like we were literally just sat here talking about him on the day he died, the pain hasn't gone away.'

Larry nodded. 'When you truly love someone, the pain of their passing never leaves you.'

'He didn't pass, though, did he? The bastards murdered him!' Sidney burst out. 'Stan was a hero for ridding the world of Walter Dorrell, for what he did to my sister and my nephew! God knows how many more people he'd have hurt if he'd have lived him and that poxy brothel of his, him and those bloody black and red shoes!"

Larry's big bellowing laugh filled the room. 'Bloody hell, I'd almost forgotten about the George Street Brothel, and those shoes of his! Right fucking bunch of misfits worked there.'

Sensing they were going off topic, Eamonn interrupted. 'This is all brilliant, but can we get back to the day Stan died? Billy, what did you do after you'd seen Jerry Mason?'

'I turned around and left, I went home and got drunk. The next day, I was here for eight o'clock just like everyone else. We sat exactly as we are now, I poured us all a glass of whiskey and we just sat chatting.'

'I'm not sure any of us really knew what to do,' Larry said. 'I mean what do you do, when your best mate's about to be executed? There's no rulebook for that.'

'I remember being so pleased that the boys were with me,' Hannah added. 'I thought I wanted to be alone, but Stan told me I shouldn't be, and that I should lean on them. He was right, I'd never have got through that morning without them.'

'Oh Hannah, I don't think any of us could have been anywhere else that day!' Sidney said. 'I'm not sure what I expected to happen when the clock struck nine. Anyone else?' He looked around the room.

They all shook their heads, and it was Billy who broke the silence.

'I think I hoped he'd walk in on the final bong and take the piss out of us for thinking they'd ever really execute him. I'm not sure I believed it would happen.'

Larry nodded. 'Same, nine o'clock felt like a real anti-climax, almost. It just seemed to come and go and yet our whole lives changed that day in that one moment.'

'Hannah rubbed her temples. 'I couldn't get out of my head what was happening to him. I'd read up on what happens at an execution, and I just kept playing it over in my head.'

'What the fuck would you do that for, Sis?'

'I needed to know.' Hannah's voice started to crack. 'I wanted to know what my Stan's final moments on earth were going to be like, what he'd be going through. I thought it might help.'

'Did it?' questioned Sidney.

'No, it still gives me nightmares." Hannah started to sob, and Sidney got up to hug her.

As she sobbed into her brother's shoulder, Sidney tried to comfort her by saying. 'Oh Hannah, you know what a brave bastard he was, he'd have been fearless to the end.'

'What did they say his last words were?' asked Larry

Hannah gave a little laugh. 'He said, 'Till our next merry meeting'. That was Stan all over. Sid's right, he was a brave bastard.'

***

Eamonn got up from his seat, clapping his hands together, he said. 'This is amazing! Really good, candid stuff, but I want us to move to nine o'clock. What we're going to do, is play a chiming clock and I want you to do exactly what you did on that morning. On the last chime, I want you to stay silent till I say 'cut'. Got it?'

They all nodded. Billy got up and topped everyone's glass up. If he were honest, this was a lot harder than he thought it was going to be. He was saying stuff he'd never told anyone, not even Fiona. She'd never pushed him to talk about Stan and he never had, but he was so scared of what The Fixer would have done to Marjie if he didn't play ball that he was saying all sorts. For all Billy knew, Eamonn was on The Fixer's payroll, and if they didn't like what they were seeing poor Marjie would pay the price.

The chimes of the clock started to play, and Billy lifted his glass. 'To Stan.'

The others all followed. 'Stan.'

As the last chime sounded, they all fell silent, each one of them locked in a moment in their shared history, tears gently falling down their faces.

'And cut! Guys that was amazing, really emotive stuff. Let's call it a day. Tomorrow we'll meet at Sherwood Forest near the Major tree.'

'Oak, it's the Major Oak,' corrected Larry.

'Yes, yes of course, we'll meet there at eight sharp. Dicky is joining us tomorrow. But well done on today, truly marvellous.'

***

As the crew packed up around them, the four of them stayed sat at the table, drained of energy and the knowledge that this truly would be the last time that any of them set foot in the house where Stan had lived.

Charlie, Eddie and Jess joined them, their faces stained and blotchy with tears.

It dawned on Sidney just how hard it would have been for them to witness this and hear all these details for the first time. He got up and put his arms around Eddie and Jess.

'You guys, OK?'

'Yeah, just a bit tough to hear, you know.' Charlie replied.

'I know, I reckon it's time we all got out of here, what do you reckon?'

They all got up to leave and Sidney watched as for the second time in her life, his sister closed the door on her old home for the final time.

The Fixer

1988

The Fixer clicked pause on the video recorder. Hannah had her glass of whiskey in the air, held against Billy's. Tears were streaming down her face, Billy was biting his lip in a desperate bid to stop himself from crying, but you could see the could see the tears glistening on his lower eyelids like they were about to burst through at any time.

It was a powerful image, it gave The Fixer chills, and they scribbled on a piece of paper that it was to be used in the marketing material.

The Fixer was impressed by what they'd seen. True to his word, Billy was doing exactly as he'd been told, and that would save having to organise another visit to his daughter.

Pouring themselves a brandy, The Fixer raised the glass. 'To Stan – till our next merry meeting.'

Chapter 117

1988 – Mansfield

Maisy Mason was starting to panic. She'd nipped out to do some shopping and now she was stuck in traffic on the A60. She'd only wanted a few bits from Safeway and had told Henry she'd be half an hour. Ever since he'd had his heart attack, she'd panicked about leaving him for too long. It made her blood run cold when she thought about what could have happened had that passerby not found him and called the ambulance in time.

Henry had been her life ever since she'd first met him in 1956. She'd been to see High Society at the Regent Cinema in Kirkby with her friend, she remembered saying to her friend, and she remembered saying to her friend Vicky, that she hoped one day that she'd meet a man as devoted to her as Bing Crosby was to Grace Kelly. Moments later, she had quite literally bumped into Henry, and he'd spilt her popcorn. Ever the gentleman he'd replaced it and asked if he could take her out the following day to say sorry properly.

And that was that. Maisy Luther, as she'd been then, had fallen utterly and hopelessly in love. The two had married a few months later at St Wilfred's Church. Maisy had given up her job in the personnel department of the Coal Board when she'd fallen pregnant with Phillip in 1959, their daughter Anna had been born two years later.

Maisy had spent a very happy life being a housewife and mother, she'd joined the PTA, become a school governor, given her time to go in and hear the children at school read, accompanied them on school trips and always had a spare biscuit and a hug for any visiting child who might not have been so lucky.

It had sometimes made her smile that their ordinary family life had been juxtaposed with Henry's career as a hangman and then Governor of Nottingham Prison. Sometimes she watched as he played with the children or read them bedtime stories and wondered how he managed to switch so effortlessly between the horror of his day job and the joy of his family life.

She'd asked him once. It had been 1962 and he'd returned from officiating over a high-profile execution. The story of Daniel Heap had dominated the headlines for months. At first, he was an unknown man, kidnapping, torturing, raping and then murdering women, leaving their lifeless bodies outside police stations across the country. Daniel Heap had killed ten women before he'd been apprehended. His subsequent trial and death sentence had been front page news. On the day of his execution, the streets were lined with people championing his death and only a handful protesting that the death penalty was archaic and cruel.

In the run up to Daniel Heap's execution, Henry had been unusually tetchy, shouting at the children and snapping at her. His sleep had been disturbed too; Maisy would be woken by him talking in his sleep and screaming. Maisy was a patient and kind woman, so she would gently wake her husband and hold him in her arms until the shaking stopped and he returned to sleep.

The day before Daniel Rowe's execution, Henry had left for work at four o'clock, the same time as he always did before an execution. Maisy would always make sure he his shirt and suit were freshly pressed and that he had a substantial lunch and that everything he needed for his night's stay in the prison was ready. This particular day, Henry refused to eat, and only took a quick slurp of his coffee branding it 'slop' and storming out.

He didn't return home until after the execution, and he was completely and utterly drunk. It was one of the only times Maisy could remember losing her temper with him and she'd really laid into him, telling him off for snapping at the children and being rude to her and then she'd demanded to know if this was how he intended to cope with the horrors of his day job, because if it was then she was taking the children and leaving him.

Henry had woken up the following day full of remorse and apologies. They had sat down, and, for the first time, Henry really spoken about what he did, how it affected him, explaining that coming face to face with someone as evil as Daniel Heap really got under his skin. Maisy had held her husband as he'd cried and told him that if he wanted to resign, he could, they'd make it work, she could get a job to help ends meet.

Three years later, hanging was abolished and Henry moved to be Governor of Nottingham Prison and seemed to be a lot happier.

Family life continued, the children grew and moved through the school system. Both went to University, Philip to Leeds to study Marketing and Business, and Anna to Birmingham to train to be a teacher.

Maisy was very proud of her both her children. Philip worked as the Marketing Director for a hotel chain and was married to Eve, they had two children, Toby and Rebecca, who Maisy spoilt rotten. Ever the independent, Anna lived with her beagle Mitch, although she had a long-term boyfriend Chris, who she was in no rush to marry. She was Head of English at Ashfield School, a job she loved.

Both of them had been unaware of their dad's past until he'd written his memoirs. They'd been a bit shocked at first and asked loads of questions, which Henry had patiently answered, but then their curiosity had been replaced by pride and Anna had even invited Henry in to talk to her sixth formers about writing a book.

Opening the front door, Maisy shouted, 'Henry, I'm home! Sorry it took so long; the traffic was awful.'

Henry didn't reply, and for a second, Maisy had a sinking feeling. A knot formed in the bottom of her stomach, and she had to steady herself against the door. Taking a deep breath, she realised that she could hear voices from the study; Henry was on the phone.

Relief gave way to curiosity, and Maisy quietly closed the front door and moved to listen at the door of Henry's study.

'What the fuck are you playing at? You said you wouldn't be a part of it, and now here you are singing like a canary? We've got to put a stop to this, otherwise it's all going to come out and that can't fucking happen... I don't give a fuck, it's my life at risk again, I can't have her finding out, I can't have anyone fucking finding out. Sort it!'

Maisy was confused. The voice sounded just like Henry's, but the words weren't his. Henry very rarely swore, and what was he on about? What did he mean his life was at risk? What didn't he want her to find out about?

Maisy tried to reason with herself. Maybe he was organising a surprise for her. He knew how stressed she'd been about his heart attack, maybe that's what he meant about his life being at risk? Henry was prone to being over-dramatic so maybe he was shouting at someone to get them to do what he wanted and speed the surprise up. Yes! That made sense, that was bound to be it.

Sneaking back to the front door, Maisy re-opened it quietly and then once again shouted, 'Henry, I'm home!', and as she banged the door shut, she chose to ignore the sensation of ice-cold blood that ran through her veins.

Chapter 118

1988 – Nottingham Prison

Ever the showman, Dicky Richards was sat in a trailer outside Nottingham Prison having his make-up done.

'Don't make me look like Dame Edna Everage, will you, mi duck?'

The make-up artist giggled. 'Oh Mr Richards, you are naughty.'

'You don't know the half of it, Princess.'

'There, you're all done. I'll get you a coffee and then either our director Eamonn or our producer Jacqui, will come and get you and fully brief you.'

'Thanks, duck.'

Dicky loosened the top button of his shirt and lit a huge cigar. Having spoken to Billy last night, he knew that this was going to be hard. They'd really try and push him, get him to open up about Stan.

Richard "Dicky" Richards had been born in Mansfield in 1923, the third son of Dot and Claude Richards. Claude had run the local newsagents. They'd been good and decent people, as had their other two sons, Donald and Stephen.

Claude claimed Dot had spoiled her youngest son, letting him get away with anything and everything. He was rarely chastised and was given everything he wanted.

Dicky lacked the intelligence of his brothers, but made up for it in brawn, and would very often hit and kick his brothers until they handed over their sweets or toys. Dot would merely laugh it off as her youngest son's humour. As a result, at the age of thirteen he'd been sent to borstal for beating up a boy who wouldn't let him have his brand-new bike.

Dicky had met Stan and Billy at school, very often acting as their muscle when they needed someone to agree to their way of thinking. It was a role that he had continued throughout his time in the Merry Men.

Dicky had been in and out of prison ever since his first trip to borstal, normally for some kind of GBH.

In 1967, he'd been sent down for the final time for manslaughter and served five years. After that, Dicky had decided to go straight and established himself as an after-dinner speaker, regaling people with his tales. He'd also appeared on numerous documentaries and was generally described as a 'rent a gob' on any debate programme about the death penalty or reformed criminals.

Dicky had never married. There'd been women, but they'd been mainly for show. If he was absolutely honest, he'd fallen in love with Stan on the very first day he'd met him, when he'd been 11 years old, and no man or woman had ever measured up.

Dicky took a long drag on his cigar and closed his eyes for a second. He was disturbed by Eammon the documentary maker coming in.

'Mr Richards?'

Getting to his feet, Dicky stuck out his hand. 'Call me Dicky please.'

'Dicky, if you're ready, we're going to head inside. The prison has set aside a cell we can use to film in.'

Dicky laughed. 'I reckon this will be the first time I've been in a prison, and they've let me straight out again.'

Eamonn laughed and the two men walked inside.

Chapter 119

1988 – Nottingham Prison

Dicky took his seat inside the cell. Despite the fact he was laughing and joking, he was severely shaken up to be there.

On his way in, he'd spotted a guard he knew, and it was as if the man had been waiting for him, lurking in the corners. Although it must have been thirty years since Dicky had last clapped eyes on him, but he recognised him instantly: Derek Davies, he'd have known him anywhere.

A fresh faced twenty-two-year-old prison guard when he'd been one of the witnesses at Stan's execution, he'd become a cruel bastard over the years and had not missed an opportunity to mention Stan's trip to the gallows. On one occasion, when Dicky had earnt himself a trip to Segregation, Derek and another guard had 'accidentally' locked him in the cell where the gallows were. They'd left him with the noose around his neck and his hands tied behind his back, unable to move.

'You can stop in here and rot, just like your mate Stan did, dangled at the very end of that rope.' He'd laughed as he'd locked the door and then left Dicky in there for two days.

Seeing Derek had unnerved Dicky slightly, but he was determined to stay calm.

Dicky joked with the producer, Jacqui, as she fiddled with the lighting.

'Right, then Dicky, how I want this to work, is that I'll ask you some questions about why you were in prison in 1953, and your last meeting with Stan, that OK?'

'Sure.' Just as they were about to start, Dicky noticed Derek Davies appear behind the director. 'Mate, can you ask that cunt behind you to fuck off?'

Eamonn looked surprised and turned around, seeing Derek there. 'Oh, Mr Davies is our official escort, he's just here to make sure we're OK.'

Dicky got to his feet. 'Well either he fucks off or you can stick your documentary up your arse.' He started to pull at his clip microphone and made a move to the door. It ever-so-slightly pleased him to see both Eamonn and Derek take a step backwards.

'Dicky, please, what if I ask Mr Davies to stay out of shot?'

Dicky took another step forward. 'I'm not sure I'm making myself fucking clear enough.' He jabbed a finger in the direction of Derek Davies. 'Either that cunt fucks off to whatever rock he crawled out from under, or I walk.'

Derek Davies took another step back. 'Dicky, look, there's no need to be like that, I'm just doing my job, I was always just doing my job.'

'It's Mr Richards to you and don't you dare address me! You speak when fucking spoken too.'

Sensing that things were about to get out of hand, Jacqui, stepped in. 'Look, Mr Davies, I think that under the circumstances, we should get someone else to be our chaperone. Mr Richards is incredibly important to this documentary, and we can't have him upset in anyway.'

'Yes, Derek, listen to the lady, I'm very fucking important to this documentary, so why don't you run along, there's a dear heart.'

Derek opened his mouth to protest, but Jacqui was too quick for him, she had taken him by the arm and was walking away with him, before he'd had a chance to respond.

Dicky returned to his seat and watched as Eamonn breathed a sigh of relief. 'Is that someone we should talk about on camera?'

'I wouldn't give the cunt the satisfaction.'

Jacqui returned with another prison guard in tow. This time, it wasn't one Dicky apparently recognised, and she calmly fixed his microphone and signalled for the make-up girl.

Eamonn started the camera rolling. 'Dicky, tell me about why you were in prison in 1953.'

'I'd been sent down six months earlier for nutting someone. I can't remember his name, but he was a cocky little sod, tried it on, not wanting to pay his taxes, so I gave him a bit of a slap.'

'It must have been more than a slap, if you got sent to prison.'

Dicky laughed. 'Well maybe it was. Plod arrested me on charges of ABH, Judge Haynes sent me down for a twelve month stretch.'

'Judge Haynes? Wasn't that the man who sent Stan down too?'

'Yeah, Judge Haynes has sent all of us down at some point. Used to make me laugh, 'cos we all knew what a dirty little pervert he was.'

'Care to elaborate on that?'

Dicky laughed. 'He was one of the punters who attended Dorrell's 'special parties' at the brothel. Liked 'em young apparently, filthy bastard. Liked them dressed up in school uniforms.'

Eamonn paused for a second. 'Can you prove this?'

'Course I fucking can.'

Eammon wasn't entirely sure he actually could, but he almost sounded convincing

Eamonn wrestled with himself. Should he continue this, knowing that the whole section would have to be cut if it turned out to be lies? Or should he get Dicky back on track? Knowing what a showman Dicky was, he went with option two.

'So, Judge Haynes sent you down for twelve months to Nottingham Prison?'

'Yeah, I think I've been in and out of here since I was eighteen, I'm surprised they haven't named a wing of the prison after me. In a weird way, I was pleased I was here though, 'cos I got to spend some time with Stan before he died. Proper time.'

'How did you find out Stan had been arrested?'

'I heard it on the news and then one of the guards wasted no time in telling me. He came to my cell and said, 'That mate of yours is done for this time.' When I asked him why, he told me that Stan had been arrested for murdering Dorrell.'

'What was your reaction?'

'I told the guard it was bollocks and that whatever trumped up charges they'd got Stan on, they'd never make it stick, but I think I knew. I knew that this time they'd got him, and they'd got him good."

'Did you know Dorrell?'

'We all knew Dorrell. Weaselly, evil bastard. Proper thought he was someone. Always trying to square up to Stan, reckoning he ran Mansfield. Truth was he ran a piss-poor brothel and pimped out men and women who deserved a lot better out of life. He even put his sister, Pearl, on the game, poor cow.'

'Did you ever visit the George Street Brothel?'

'Not my scene mate, dirty place.' Dicky seemed to shift in his seat uncomfortably. 'I think I knew Stan would have to get rid of Dorrell eventually. He took a few beatings, but he just kept going at Stan. It was him that crippled Stan's lad Charlie and then he...' Dicky stopped.

Hannah's rape had been discussed on camera and was public knowledge, but Dicky seemed deeply distressed about it.

'Dicky, I know talking about Hannah's rape is difficult for you. Do you think Stan could have gone to the police?'

'Could he bollocks! Plod wasn't bothered when Charlie was crippled, and they certainly wouldn't care that a gangster's missis had been raped. Stan had no choice.'

'Did you see Stan after he was arrested?'

"Yeah, he was on remand here. He had a cell on his own, but I saw him at mealtimes and association. It always struck me how calm he was about it all. I asked him whilst the trial was going on if he was worried and he just shrugged and said not really.'

'Did he talk to you about the trial?'

'He'd tell me bits, but he never went into detail. I only know what I do about the trial from after. On the day he was going to be sentenced, I remember him coming up to me before he left and he said, 'Whatever happens today, do not let these fuckers wind you up! Stay calm and I'll see you when I get back,' he said, 'I mean it, Dicky, do not get yourself thrown in segregation, I need you here!'

'Why do you think he said that?'

'I think he knew he was getting sent down, but for once in my life I did as I was told. He was right, the bastard guards did try to wind me up. Once the verdict was out, they wasted no time in telling me that Stan was going to swing. They kept at me, needling me, but I kept calm. I remember laying on my bed in my cell, my arms folded, and my eyes shut, I never once responded.'

'What happened when Stan got back?'

'Well, I didn't see him till the next day. He told me I had to listen to him and do exactly as I was told. He said we'd got three weeks, possibly less if they moved him to get plans in place.'

'What were those plans?'

'He was talking about Hannah and the kids and what he wanted us to do and the future of the Merry Men, stuff like that really.'

'Can you give me specifics?'

Dicky smiled. 'Business-wise no, I don't need to end up back in here again! But with Hannah and the kids, he wanted us to make sure she was always alright, that they had whatever they needed, especially Charlie. He said we should make sure the boys grew up right and that if Hannah met someone else, we should let her marry him and not give her a hard time. He said, repeatedly, she deserves to be happy.'

'Did he mean it?'

'Of course he did! Hannah and the boys were his life! He'd never have left them, and he more than anything he wanted them to be happy and have a normal life.'

'Tell me about the day of Stan's execution.'

'Well, they'd moved him the day before, so that was the last time I saw him. I hugged him, I ...' Dicky's voice broke slightly, and he wiped his eyes with the back of his hand. Clearing his throat, he shook his head as if shaking away the tears and carried on. 'I hugged him really tight. I thought he'd tell me to fuck off, but he didn't, he hugged me back and he said, 'Dicky Richards, you are one of the best friends I've ever had, now stop fucking about and when you're out of here, you stay out, you hear me?' I promised and I said I'd make sure Hannah and the boys were OK and then he said, 'Til our next merry meeting and then the guards walked in and one of 'em said, 'Never had you down as a poofter Stan,' and then they took him away and that was the last time I ever saw him alive.'

'The last time you saw him alive?'

'Yeah. On the day of his execution, I just wanted to stay in my cell, but one of the guards fetched me and said they had a special treat for me. He said Governor Smith gave his very special permission. They took me to a room that had a window in it, and I realised that it overlooked the cell where the gallows were.'

'You saw Stan executed?'

'No, but they knew I'd see him after, when they took his body out. They made me sit and look out that window. When it struck nine, one of the guards said, 'Good riddance to bad rubbish.' I sat looking out that window, and about an hour later, I saw them carrying out a coffin, I knew it was Stan. I just sat there, and they started saying, 'There's your mate, not so fucking hard is he now, is he? That's when I lost it and threw my chair at one of them, I was so angry. I gave them both a beating. I ended up in segregation for a month and got time added on to my sentence, but it was worth every fucking second just to give those twats what they deserved for talking bad of Stan.'

Eamonn switched off the camera. 'Dicky that was brilliant, you're a natural.'

'Thank you, now can you get me out of here before they change their minds and decide to keep me?'

Chapter 120

1988 – Sandbanks, Bournemouth

Pearl saw the sign appear that said, 'Bournemouth 10 miles' and felt herself automatically relax. There was something about being at the seaside, and, more importantly, spending a few days with her old mentor, Tony Richardson, that was good for her soul.

They'd spend the time walking on the beach, eating good food, drinking fine wine and reminiscing about the old days as well as talking about their current projects. Tony was writing his memoirs and Pearl could really do with his advice about the stories she'd been running about Stan and his family.

Pearl had first met Tony at Stan's trial and had gone to work for him shortly after she'd moved to London. Over the years, she'd told him everything about her life as Walter's sister and what she knew about the Merry Men. They'd run many stories in the papers over the years about them and even though Tony had now retired, he was still the person Pearl called when she needed advice.

Pulling up outside his house in Sandbanks, Pearl could see him sat on his balcony waving at her.

'Ahhh Dorrell, good to see you. Now get yourself in here, there's a large gin with your name on it waiting for you.'

Pearl laughed and waved back.

Ten minutes later, she was sitting drinking the aforementioned large gin and was laughing at a story Tony was telling her about upsetting the lady who edited the local newsletter.

'I told her, Madam, with grammar like that you're not fit to be editing a picture book, and do you know what she said? She asked what made me such an expert! So, I told her, I listed every fucking award I've ever won and every news story I've ever covered! She asked me if I wanted to take over editing the newsletter, and I said, no I do not, I've got memoirs to write!'

Pearl laughed. 'I can't leave you alone for five minutes can I, without you causing bother?'

'Speaking of causing bother, I read that interview you did with Hannah Thomas.'

'And?'

'It made me proud.'

The two sat in silence for a while, the only noise the clinking of the ice in their drinks and the sound of holidaymakers on the beach.

'You still sure you know what you're doing?'

Pearl nodded. 'Yes, it's the story of a lifetime, it's the story of my lifetime, it's what I've – what we've worked towards.'

Tony took her hand. 'If I'd have known then what I was getting myself into the day you walked into that bar...'

'You'd have run a mile?'

'On the contrary, my dear, I'd have done everything exactly the same. A story like this comes along once in a lifetime. I thought you'd do a year's apprenticeship with me, I'd get all the dirt I could out of you about Stan, the Merry Men and Walter, and then you'd bugger off, marry a farmer and have lots of babies!'

'A farmer?'

'You know what I mean. But we're in it now, lass, and this is the homestretch.'

'It certainly is.' Pearl raised her class. 'To the final chapter."

Tony picked up his own glass and clinked it against hers. 'The final chapter.'

Chapter 121

1988 – M25

Pearl was almost home following her trip away to see Tony. It was a break she had needed, a chance to re-group, gather her thoughts and plan her next moves.

They'd spent their time together walking on the beach, laughing, and discussing just how she could go about things.

Pearl understood she'd set into motion a chain of events that had put not only Stan and the Merry Men back into the spotlight, but it had also created new media celebrities out of his wife Hannah, and their children, Charlie, Eddie and Jess. If she were honest, she'd thought Hannah would tell her to do one and point-blank refuse to do the interview, but her willingness to talk and her honesty had surprised even Pearl.

Ever the journalist, Pearl had been delighted with the interview she'd done with Hannah. It was certainly one of the best of her career. But it also opened her up to questions and sniggers. She'd caught some of the younger journalists gossiping about her past and how she'd been a prostitute. She'd even overheard one journalist joke that maybe that's how she'd got her job as Editor: by dropping her knickers. Pearl made a mental note to remember to fire that journalist tomorrow, when she got into work.

Pearl had never been embarrassed by her past; in her eyes, it was what it was. She'd found herself in a situation not of her making and had had no choice. Once she'd been able to regain her control of her life, she'd made a change. It hadn't defined her then and it wouldn't define her now. She wasn't the first woman to be put on the game, and she wouldn't be the last, but maybe she could show that there was a life afterwards.

Although Pearl wasn't ashamed of her past life, it did haunt her. Occasionally she'd wake drenched in sweat having had a nightmare, the men who'd abused her forming the narrative of her dreams. The parties that Walter had thrown had scarred her the most. Some loser wanting a blowjob, or a quick shag had never bothered her, but the parties took Walter's level of depravity to another level. The men that attended were told that anything went, and it most certainly did.

Being the youngest, Pearl always had to dress as a schoolgirl and she was the first choice of the men known as the Hon and the Doc. Walter always insisted on nicknames being used, he said that he wanted his guests to be free to be themselves and what happened at one of his parties stayed at his party, it was a place where they could be free.

As well as the Hon and the Doc, there was the Rev, the Gov and the Politician. It always struck Pearl as ironic that they were forced to use these nicknames for the sake of privacy, when everyone there knew that Doc was Dr Michael Dunderdale, Nottingham Prison's doctor, the Rev was their prison chaplain the Reverend Roger Collins, the Gov was Governor William Smith, the man who ran the prison, The Politician was Frederick Dykes, the Sheriff of the County and the man who filled her most with dread was the Hon, or the Honourable Lord George Haynes as he was known to the many men and women he'd sent to prison.

Despite what Walter had told them, every single one of their visits was documented, along with photographic evidence. Walter said it was his insurance policy incase things got 'tasty' and he needed to call in a few favours.

George Haynes still filled Pearl full of dread. He was an exceptionally cruel man, who liked her dressed as a schoolgirl. He and the Doc had always started off with a threesome and then the Doc would head off to someone else. That's when George would get really cruel with Pearl, beating her and abusing her in ways that even the most depraved of people would struggle to comprehend. It was his face that Pearl saw in her nightmares, his fingers she felt around her throat and his whiskey, cigar-laced breath that she could smell.

Pearl opened the window of her car, breathing in the fresh air. She reminded herself that she was the one in charge now, not any of them, and it was her that was about to send the whole deck of cards crashing down.

The secrets of the men who had abused her and many others had not died with her brother. They were sat in a safe in her house.

Waiting.

Chapter 122

1988 – Regent's Park London

Pouring herself a glass of wine, Pearl turned the dial of her safe to enter the combination, and, once open, she removed the battered briefcase that lay inside, revealing the gun that lay underneath it. Pearl touched it gently with her hand.

Heading back into the living room, she started to spread the contents of the briefcase out onto the table. Even though her brother had been a total waste of space, his notetaking and observational skills had been incredible. He had kept pages and pages of notes about the people who had attended his parties, what they'd done, who they'd been with, even what they'd been wearing.

She remembered Cheryl saying to her once that Walter had made her go into every little detail after every party. Cheryl thought he got off on it, but Pearl now knew he was filling in the gaps in his notes. He'd also managed to get photos of his guests in action, which he had developed himself in a darkroom he'd set up in the garage. For a very stupid man, Walter had been quite smart, Pearl begrudgingly thought.

Her hand strayed to a folder labelled Merry Men. Opening it up, she could see the notes that Walter had made about the very few times Stan and the boys had visited the brothel. It was rare they had, but Pearl remembered the day they'd rocked up all slightly drunk with the aim of Sidney losing his virginity. It had been May who had done the honours. According to Walter's notes, Billy had had a blowjob from Cheryl, Dicky had enjoyed the same treatment from Geraldine, Larry had had sex with Shirley and Stan had slept with Pearl herself, or at least that's what they'd told Walter.

Pearl had added to the notes over the years, keeping an eye on what had become of the party guests.

William Smith had left Nottingham Prison, shortly after Stan's execution. He'd taken a role in the Home Office, where his views on the fact all criminals were beyond rehabilitation had landed him in trouble on more than one occasion, but it had gained him some fairly heavyweight right-wing supporters. They tried to convince him to stand for the General Election in 1966, but William had decided that there was more money to be made appearing on talk shows and writing books. William had died of cancer in 1980.

Frederick Dykes, the Sheriff of the County had continued his political career, although rumours of him being for sale to the highest bidder persisted and weren't helped by some questionable planning permission decisions that he'd had a hand in. He'd died in a car crash in 1967. He'd been drinking and wrapped his car around a tree.

Pearl pulled out the article she'd written about his death from the file.

The Reverend Roger Collins, famed for his love of wine, women and gambling had been found stabbed to death in 1955. No-one had ever been convicted of his murder, but it was thought to be over a gambling debt he had owed to a local gangster. Pearl had a photo of his funeral, where William and Dr Michael Dunderdale had turned out to pay their respects to their former colleague.

Michael Dunderdale himself was alive and unfortunately well, living the highlife with his wife known as The Merry Widow, whom, he'd married in 1975.

George Haynes at the ripe old age of eighty-five was also still alive and now living in a care home. He'd retired from the bench at the age of sixty and had taken to the after-dinner circuit regaling, drunk businessmen and lawyers with tales of his time as a judge and the many men and women he'd sent to the gallows. A large portion of his speech centred around Stanley and how he was the man to finally rid the streets of such a gangster. He'd had a stroke a few years ago, which was why he was in a nursing home.

Pearl just needed him to live a few months longer.

The file was also full of clippings of the more recent developments in the story, the book written by Henry and the various interviews he'd done. Dicky's outburst to the undercover Daily Chronicle reporter, who had been placed by Pearl; her interview with Hannah and the various headlines that the Thomas family had made over the last few weeks.

Pearl knew about the documentary that was being made about Stan, his family, and the Merry Men. They were all fully co-operating with the process.

Putting everything back into the battered leather briefcase and returning it to the safe, Pearl could wait a while longer to make her own revelations.

Chapter 123

1988 – The Avenue, Mansfield

Hannah was making the most of a day off. The last week had been a whirlwind of filming for the documentary. She felt like she'd covered the length and breadth of Nottinghamshire. They'd filmed at the home she'd shared with Stan; they'd taken her to Shire Hall, the court where Stan had been sentenced to death; they'd interviewed her sat in the dock where Stan would have stood and also in the seat where she'd sat throughout the trial. They'd visited Nottingham Prison, although she had point blank refused to do any filming in the condemned cell where her husband had spent his last few hours. They'd filmed at the Major Oak and all over Sherwood Forest. The Boy pub had also provided a filming location.

Some of her interviews had been done on her own, some with various denominations of the Merry Men and some with her children. She'd remembered bits of her life that she thought had been lost to her forever. She'd suppressed her feelings for so long that the strength of them had surprised her. The moment she'd stepped on the ship to set sail for Australia, she had told herself that any feelings she had for Stan stayed in England. Because the kids had rarely asked about their dad, she'd been able to fool herself that she had long since fallen out of love with Stan.

Spending the week talking about him, visiting the place they'd lived, been on their first date, even the court and the prison, it made Stan come alive again, it made her remember how much she'd loved him. How much she still did.

No man had ever come close to Stan. Over the years, she'd dated occasionally, and there'd been a fairly serious relationship with an Australian man, called Nate. He'd been everything Stan wasn't; he had a good job, he worked hard, earned honest money, he listened to her problems, was good with her children and had wanted nothing more than to marry her and for them to build a life together. Hannah could still remember the look on his face as he proposed to her. It had been picture-perfect. He'd arranged a picnic on the beach, complete with champagne and all her favourite foods, and then at sunset, he'd gone down on one knee and told her how much he loved her and the kids and how he wanted nothing more than to be with her for eternity.

Hannah had turned him down on the spot, and then she'd gotten up and walked away and had never once looked back at him. She never returned any of his calls and had never explained why. On the grapevine, she heard that he'd moved away to Queensland and had married someone else.

Hannah couldn't explain to him why she didn't want to marry him. How do you tell someone that you will never love them as much as you love your husband who was executed? And how forming a life with someone else felt like a betrayal and like she was cheating? How do you tell someone that?

Hannah had her brother's house to herself, so she'd settled on the sofa with a bottle of wine, a box of chocolates and a copy of The Secret of My Success on video.

The film was just starting when the phone rang. 'Typical' thought Hannah, before answering the call. 'Hello?'

'Is that Mrs Thomas?'

'Yes, it is, who's this please?'

'Mrs Thomas, my name is Laura and I'm a producer on a TV show called News Focus and I wondered if you and your children would be interested in coming on the show?'

'What's the show about? I've never heard of it.'

'It's a weekly news show that focuses on different topics that are making the headlines. We examine a couple of themes per show and our host Matt McFetridge, will interview the guests. With everything that's been in the news recently, we'd like to dedicate one of the shows to you and your family.'

'Well, we are in the middle of filming a documentary and it's a fairly tight schedule, so when and where?'

'Well, the good news is that we film at the Central Television studios in Nottingham, and we'd like you to come on the show, this Monday. You'd be needed from six and we'll be done no later than eight p.m.'

Hannah checked her diary. 'OK, that will work, see you Monday.'

Hannah replaced the receiver and took a sip of wine. She wasn't sure if she'd done the right thing agreeing to go on a show she'd never seen before, but next week was her last week in the U.K. and then she could go back to Australia.

It dawned on her that at some point during her stay, she'd stopped thinking of Australia as home and more as the place she lived.

Mansfield was home.

Chapter 124

1988 – Central Television Studios, Nottingham

Eddie Thomas had an inability to sit still, so he was busily making everyone a cup of coffee in the green room ahead of their appearance on News Focus. Hannah knew he was nervous, he'd coped well with the documentary filming, but live TV was something else.

Charlie was laughing at his younger brother and gently teasing him, telling him to sit down and shut up. Eddie bantered back with his brother, obviously appreciating the opportunity to take his mind off his nerves.

Hannah smiled across at both of them, she was so full of love and pride for her boys. It never ceased to amaze her how adaptable they were and how they looked out for each other.

Charlie and Eddie had an unbreakable bond. They had been through things that no-one would ever understand, not even their mum or sister. No-one, but them would really understand what it was like to grow up being Stan's kids, not even Jess could really comprehend it. She'd never known her dad and for years hadn't been interested in him.

On the day before they'd moved to Australia, her sons had made a pact that once a month they would talk about their dad and remember him. They'd only told her about it since they'd been back in England, they'd said they hadn't wanted to upset her.

They told her about a box they'd put together, which they'd filled with things that had reminded them of their dad. It contained photos, toys he'd given them, drawings they'd done together, even items of clothing. Charlie had snuck it into his luggage and carted it halfway across the world. He'd only been seven when they'd emigrated, and Eddie had been five, but unbeknown to their mum the pact they had made had lasted, and once a month they got out the box, had a beer and talked about their dad. It broke Hannah's heart that they'd not been able to share this with her.

In a weird way, Hannah felt a bit of gratitude towards Henry Mason and the book he'd written. It felt like they were all being honest with each other. It had given her children the opportunity to meet their dad's friends and ultimately had brought them all closer.

Hannah looked over at Jess, who was sat drinking a cup of coffee. Hannah knew that Jess had always been a little bit jealous of the bond her brothers shared. This trip had done a lot to strengthen the connection between all three of her children, and was another thing that Hannah was grateful for.

Jess had spent her whole life avoiding talking about her dad in case she upset someone, another secret that had only recently come to light. Jess had admitted that watching as the dads of her friends watched from the sidelines cheering them on at sports day or putting an arm around them when they'd got a good report, had made her really envious.

Hannah had hated watching her daughter explain that the reason her dad wasn't there was because her dad had died before she was born and then seeing the look of pity flash across their face as they gave a solemn nod towards Hannah.

She knew Jess sometimes felt ungrateful, because she'd often told her mum what an amazing job, she'd done of being both Mum and Dad, balancing her career with being a parent. She'd never missed a parents evening, a sports day, she'd been the one who had spent the nights dabbing at chicken pox spots with calamine lotion and reading stories till Jess went back to sleep following a nightmare. She'd taught Jess to drive, cried when she's graduated from police college and shouted from the rooftops about her daughter's many achievements. But Hannah knew that ultimately it was no substitute for having Stan about.

Hannah had never hidden who Stan was to Jess. She'd always known that he'd committed a crime and had been punished for it. For ages, Jess had thought that that meant that he was in prison in the U.K. When she'd got a bit older, she thought he'd died in prison, and then eventually curiosity had gotten the better of her and she'd managed to find some details about her dad in some old newspaper clippings she'd found in the library, that's how she'd found out the truth about Stan. Hannah hated the thought of her eleven-year-old daughter finding out the truth that way.

Hannah had always thought that the reason Jess had joined the police was to prove to the world that she was nothing like Stan and to try and stop bad people doing bad things so that their innocent children didn't suffer.

After the documentary and the many TV appearances, Hannah hoped her daughter still had a police career to go back to, and that the sins of the father wouldn't damage what she'd worked so hard to achieve.

'Hannah, Charlie, Eddie, Jess, we are ready for you on set now if you could follow me.' A double denim-clad producer, complete with her important headset and her even more important clipboard, ushered them onto set, where someone else started clipping microphones to them.

'Matt will be with you in just a second.'

The next minute, the show's presenter Matt McFetridge strode onto set. He was larger than life in all ways, a six-foot five frame was the home of his equally large personality and smile. Half of his success had been down to the fact that even the wiliest of guests had underestimated him, mistaking his jovial nature for stupidity, unwittingly walking into his journalistic trap.

Matt bounced onto set, ruffling the hair of camera men, jovially punching them in the ribs, making cracks about their respective football teams. Spotting Hannah, Charlie, Eddie and Jess, he stopped in his tracks, spread open his arms, let his face break into the brightest smile and said. 'Ahhh, family Thomas! What an absolute pleasure to have you here! I can't tell you how excited I am to get to know you and find out what you've been through.'

Walking over to them, he shook their hands and gestured for them to take their seats. A make-up girl quickly powdered Matt's nose.

Hannah noticed that there appeared to be a spare chair, but just as she was about to mention it, Matt started talking.

'Thank you so much for coming on, I'm sure my team has briefed you, but to be clear, the topic of tonight's show is what it's like to be the family of a criminal. For you Hannah, we will focus on being Stan's wife and for you three, what it's like being his kids, how you were treated growing up, did it affect you, that sort of stuff. Jess I believe you're a policewoman now?'

'I'm a Sergeant for the Western Australian Police Force.'

Matt nodded and scribbled a note on a piece of paper. 'Impressive.'

The double denim-clad producer was back. 'So, as I mentioned this is live. We go out just after Corrie, so we're currently in the advert break leading up to our show. As we're about to go live, I'll give the signal and then you must be quiet. The red light will go on, you'll hear the title music and Matt will do his intro. Remember no swearing.'

The double denim-clad producer retreated to the side of the camera, looking at her watch and pressing her right headphone to her head listening intently. 'Thirty seconds to transmission.'

Sure enough, a red light popped on and music started playing, and Matt turned his chair to face the camera directly to begin his introduction.

'Tonight, on News Focus, we investigate what it's like being the family of a well-known criminal, and whether growing up knowing your dad is a convicted murderer affects your chances in life. Is it a case of nature or nurture?

'My guests are the family of a criminal who still dominates the headlines despite having been executed in 1935. Stanley Thomas and his band of 'Merry Men' have been the subject of films, documentaries and books, but what is it like being his family? Knowing that the blood of a man capable of such heinous crimes flows through your veins? Knowing that you chose this man as the father of your children? Over the last few weeks, you'll have read about his family in the papers, and tonight his wife Hannah and children Charlie, Eddie and Jess join me.' Matt swung back in his chair to face them. 'Good evening to you all. Hannah, if I can start with you, at what age did you tell your children who their dad was?'

'They've always known who he was,' Hannah responded. 'Charlie and Eddie have clear memories of him, although they were young at the time of Stan's death, they still remember him. I was pregnant with Jess, when Stan died.'

'I notice, you refer to it as 'Stan's death' but the truth is that your husband was a violent criminal who was executed. Many say he'd escaped the hangman's rope too many times and was responsible for many more deaths and violent acts that he was never charged with.'

For a second, Hannah was at a loss as to what to say. She could feel her cheeks start to go red, the heat rising from her chest and up her neck and although her mouth seemed to be opening, no sound would come out.

Charlie took hold of his mother's hand and took charge of the situation. If the presenter, Matt, lured his guests into a false sense of security with his jovial nature and big smile, Charlie had long since learnt that his wheelchair had the same effect. Although physically Charlie resembled his mum, mentally he was Stan. He was tough, calm and he would fight to the death to protect his family.

'Listen here Mike,' he began.

'It's Matt.'

Charlie continued to talk, ignoring the presenter completely. 'What you've just said is, to an extent perfectly true. Stanley Thomas, my father was a murderer. He was a gangster, and he was executed, but he was only ever charged with the one murder, so whatever rumours do the rounds, they are unsubstantiated and I'm not sure what Mickey Mouse school of journalism you went to, but 'unsubstantiated' means, unsupported, unconfirmed, uncorroborated, not backed up by evidence. i.e., Not true, which means you have just slandered my father on live television, a fact that will not go unnoticed by our lawyers.' Charlie sat back in his wheelchair, as she squeezed her son's hand, Hannah noticed that it was Matt's turn to turn red and open and close his mouth.

Matt soon regained his composure. 'I'm sorry if my question caused any offence, I was merely stating some of the accusations that have been levelled at Stan over the years, and not suggesting they were statements of fact. Hannah, tell me what it was like to be married to Stan.'

Hannah had by now completely recovered her composure, and as she'd spent the last week talking about life as Stan's wife and so answered the question easily.

For the next ten minutes, the interview went smoothly, Hannah, Charlie, Eddie and Jess answered questions easily. The earlier animosity seemed to have disappeared and everyone had relaxed slightly.

As they went into an advert break, the double denim-clad producer re-appeared with some water for everyone. 'You're all doing brilliantly. When we come back from the ad break, there'll be another twelve minutes left of the show. I'll give you a countdown to the red light and going live.'

Taking everyone's water off of them, she returned to her seat.

Matt started the second half, just as he had the first, talking to camera. 'Welcome back. On tonight's News Focus, we are talking to the family of Stanley Thomas, the gangster executed in 1953 for the murder of businessman Walter Dorrell. The recent interest in Stan has been prompted by a new book. Tales from the Gallows is the memoirs of hangman Henry Mason, whose first job as assistant hangman was at the execution of Stanley Thomas. I'd like to welcome to the panel, Henry Mason.'

Hannah grabbed Charlie's hand again. No-one had mentioned that one of the men responsible for Stan's death and the author of that bloody book would be joining them.

Charlie, Eddie and Jess looked at Hannah, accusatory looks on each of their faces. Had she known about this? Had she set this up?

Eddie mouthed to his mum, 'did you know?'

Hannah shook her head; she was as clueless as them.

Matt got to his feet and shook Henry by the hand before gesturing for him to sit.

Henry was a tall, broad man with greying hair and beard and glasses. He sat down in the chair nearest to Jess and Hannah noticed that she involuntarily moved her chair away.

Henry nodded to the Thomas family.

'Henry, is this the first time you've met the Thomas family?'

Henry nodded. 'Yes, it is, although I feel like I know them, I've read so much about them in the papers.'

Charlie shook his head, wincing as his mum gripped his hand tightly.

Why was this man sat talking about them like they were long lost family members who were being reunited by Cilla Black? This man seemed to have no concept of what he'd done or what he was doing to them.

Eddie stared at the floor, and even though she'd moved her chair away, Jess turned her body so that she could fix Henry with a stare.

'Henry, you've been listening backstage to everything the Thomas family has been saying about Stan and what it's like being the family of a criminal. As well as being present at Stan's execution, you were also the Governor of Nottingham Prison for many years. Do you believe that being the family of a criminal can have an effect later on in life?'

'Of course, it does Matt. There is no doubt that the families of criminals go on to have difficult lives, many of them turn to crime themselves, because they know no better.'

Hannah could tell from the look on Jess's face that she was getting really angry, she hoped her daughter wouldn't do anything stupid.

'Over the years, I saw many members of the same family come through the doors of my prison. They're bought in as young children to visit their dad and it becomes 'normal to them. Prisons are like an extension of the family home.'

Jess jumped in before Matt could ask his next question. 'So, are you saying that mine and my brother's birth right was a life of crime, because our dad was a criminal?'

'That's exactly what I'm saying.'

'Well, for your information, our lives have been as far from my dad's as possible! Charlie is an artist who has work displayed in galleries all over Australia, he'll also play basketball in the Paralympics later this year. Eddie, here, runs his own stables and teaches kids to ride and I'm a Sergeant for the Western Australian Police Force. So, we are just three examples of where your unfounded theory falls down.'

'I said many of them turn to crime, not all of them.' Henry sat back in his chair, apparently undeterred by Jess. 'Look your mum, knew the score, she took you halfway around the world so that you wouldn't end up like you dad. She took you away from everything that you knew.'

Hannah, how would you like to respond to that?'

'I took my children away, because I wanted a fresh start for all of us.' Hannah answered. 'I wanted my children to have the very best and I didn't want them to live with their father's legacy and other, ignorant people, like yourself making assumptions about them! My children are good and decent people and they're also half me and half Stan and if you knew Stan, you'd know he was a good and decent man who protected his family and he'd have been fully onboard with my decision. Family first... always!'

Henry laughed and turned in his chair to face Hannah. 'So, I'm right, is what you're saying? You took your kids halfway across the world because you knew if you stayed here, they'd end up in prison.'

'I said nothing of the sort, a good person is a good person, wherever they grow up!'

'You're naive Han.'

'It's Mrs Thomas to you! And no, no I'm not, but I know my children, I know how they were bought up, and I know the conversations that me and my husband had about what we wanted for them.'

'You carry on like Stan wasn't a murderer, like he didn't do terrible things!' Henry retorted. 'You make him sound misunderstood! That man was –'

Eddie jumped in. 'That man was our dad and we loved him, and he loved us, and he'd never have left us if you hadn't killed him!'

''Killed him'? I didn't kill him,' Henry replied. 'He committed a crime and was punished, and you left him! You abandoned him and moved halfway around the world, never giving him a thought until my book came out and you thought there was money to be made from him!'

'Us make money out of Dad?' Eddie cried. 'Are you for real? You're the man who killed him and is now pimping himself out to the highest bidder! How much money have you made from your book?'

'I don't think that's relevant, young man. All I've done is write my memoirs. It's not my fault that people are interested in what I have to say.'

'You patronising old bastard!' Charlie burst out. 'Do you know what, you can stick this TV show up your arse! I think I speak for all of us when I say we're off.'

Charlie started to move his wheelchair and the rest of the Thomas family got up too.

Henry smirked as they left. 'Go on, run away, just like your bloody mother.'

In the corner of the studio, Hannah noticed the double denim-clad producer was frantically waving to get Matt's attention, and in the end, she gave up and just shouted, 'Do something!'

Matt smiled and turned to the camera. 'Well, firstly I'd like to apologise for any bad language. As you can see, tonight's show has been highly charged, so I'm sure you can understand the emotion behind those words. I'd like to thank my guests tonight and leave you once again with the question I asked at the beginning of the show: Does growing up knowing your dad is a convicted murderer affect your chances in life? Is it a case of nature or nurture? Thanks for watching.'

***

Matt McFetridge had never been happier.

He knew that his show would be front page of all the papers tomorrow, and clips of the show would make news channels around the world.

Getting to his feet, he shook Henry's hand. 'Thanks for coming on, Henry. Laura will show you out.'

Matt smiled all the way back to his dressing room. He was pretty sure that show had made someone very happy, and he was looking forward to the phone call that would be coming his way.

The Fixer

1988

The Fixer clicked off the TV. Well, that had been eventful.

They'd doubted that Matt McFetridge could pull it off, but he'd kept his end of the bargain and had got the Thomas family and Henry in the same place at the same time. Henry, true to form, had been his usual arrogant self, although even The Fixer had to admit he had been even worse than even they could imagine.

The Fixer now had to stick to their end of the bargain: Front page news for Mr McFetridge and headlines all over the world. It was amazing what you could get someone to do when they were annoyed that Richard Madeley had been offered This Morning and not them.

The Fixer picked up the phone. Time to tickle the talent's tummy. 'Matthew, darling, you were marvellous...'

Chapter 125

1988 – Central Television Studios, Nottingham

The Thomas family were collecting their belongings and getting ready to leave the TV studios. After what they'd just been put through, Hannah was surprised to find herself thinking that she really must talk to her sons about their colourful language.

The double denim-clad producer was trying to placate the situation, but Charlie and Eddie were hell bent on getting solicitors involved and demanding a public apology. Ms Double Denim-Clad producer was clearly out of her depth and Hannah was pleased.

Looking round, she realised Jess was missing.

***

Jess was exhausted, she needed a minute to herself, before they headed home and they went over everything with her uncle. Uncle Sid was no doubt already on the phone to his solicitor, or someone less law-abiding to sort the situation.

Seeing Henry Mason had genuinely shaken her. She'd read his book, and, truth be told, she knew it about it way before her uncle had phoned to tell them about it.

She'd gone over his account of her father's execution a thousand times: how he'd been unafraid and almost nonchalant about the whole thing and his last words had been, 'Till our next merry meeting.'; the account of Stan's execution, and those of the others who'd faced Henry on the gallows; all mixed in with tales of Henry the family man, the doting dad who'd always made sure his kids were safe and protected from the truth about his job. Effortlessly combining the executioner with the dad who read bedtime stories, never missed a parents evening, took his son to football practice, cheered his daughter on as she swam for the county, bought them their first cars, taught them to drive.

All the things that he'd robbed her and her brothers of the moment that trapdoor had swung open.

Splashing her face with cold water, Jess headed back to the greenroom. Coming the other way was Henry. She contemplated going back into the toilet and waiting for him to walk by, but she knew he'd seen her, and he'd probably just wait for her. The best thing she could do was walk by him, head held high, and ignore him.

She almost managed it, but as she'd just passed him, Henry turned and grabbed her arm, 'Jess, I wanted to...'

'Wanted to what? Apologise for being a total cunt? Apologise for taking my dad away from me? Apologise for hurting my mum, my brothers? Apologise for making a fucking fortune out of my dad? What did you want?'

Henry lowered his gaze first and took a deep breath, and for a split-second Jess saw a glimpse of someone who wasn't the arrogant man who'd just sat beside her spouting his ridiculous opinions, the man who'd sat there proud of himself. For a second, Jess got a glimpse of something she couldn't explain. She couldn't say it was the look of a man who was sorry, it wasn't that of a man who regretted his actions. But Jess couldn't help but think that Henry seemed like a broken man, he was a man who had lost something and was desperately trying to replace it.

Jess realised that he still had hold of her arm. 'Get off me.'

Henry tightened his grip. 'Jess, I...'

'I said, get off of me.'

'Jess please, I just need to say –'

But Jess had stopped listening. 'I warned you.'

With that, Jess grabbed Henry's fingers from her arm, and twisted his arm behind his back, and pushed him up against the wall. 'Stay away from me, stay away from my family.'

Jess headed back to her family.

Chapter 126

1988 – St Mary's Church, Edwinstowe

Larry took in the cool fresh night air as he and Moses walked around the grounds of St Mary's Church. It had been a long couple of weeks and although it had been lovely being reunited with Hannah and the Merry Men, reliving memories of Stan and their past, it had taken its toll.

Larry Yates, vicar of this parish, was a very different man to Larry Yates, the punisher of the Merry Men. It had taken a lot of praying and repentance for Larry to make peace with the sins of his past, but he was largely at peace with them now. There was still the odd night where he woke up screaming, Walter Dorrell's murder haunting his dreams. He'd never truly understand why Stan hadn't asked for the Merry Men's help that night, why he'd insisted on going it alone. The murder, Stan's execution, haunted his dreams, but the thing that caused him the biggest amount of pain was the fact that he was secretly glad Stan hadn't asked for their help that night, that he'd escaped the hangman's noose.

Walking in the grounds of his church with Moses calmed his nerves, he felt safe and at peace. Making his way to the old oak tree that stood at the very bottom of the church yard, there was a bench that wrapped around it and Larry loved to sit there and seek guidance.

No-one had been more surprised than Larry when he'd received the calling to the church, but during his final holiday at Her Majesty's pleasure, he had been laying in his cell one night wondering what on earth he was going to do when he got out, when he had a dream. In this dream he could see a man who looked like Jesus, he was sat at a long table and telling him, there was room for him too. Initially, Larry had dismissed it, but on getting out of prison, Larry had found himself sat in a café in Mansfield, when a man asked if he could join him. The two got talking, and it turned out that the man was the vicar of the local church.

Noel Brynn was to become a very important person in Larry's life. The two had spent that afternoon drinking many cups of tea and chatting. Noel invited Larry along to church that Sunday. Larry had refused at first, saying he wasn't sure it was his thing. Curiosity got the better of him, however, and that Sunday, Larry had put on his best suit, the one he normally wore to court and headed along.

Sitting at the back, Larry had been surprised at how at peace he felt and a sense of being home filled his body.

After that, Larry attended church every week. He struck up a firm friendship with Noel, and they spent hours talking to him about his past and, more importantly his future.

Larry had stuck to his promise to himself to go on the straight and narrow and after he left prison, he got himself a 'proper job' and trained as a plumber. He worked hard, kept out of trouble, and only saw the rest of the Merry Men occasionally.

Larry could still remember the day he decided to pluck up the courage to ask Reverend Brynn, if he thought he could become a vicar. It was following the Christingle service. Larry was picking up discarded hymn books. Larry could still remember the look on Reverend Brynn's face: he broke out into the biggest smile, and he'd said, 'Larry my boy, you are just what the church needs, and I think more than anyone I've ever met, you will be a fine vicar.' And that was that, off Larry went to theological college and once he'd qualified, he'd worked at some of the inner-city churches in Nottingham, before finally settling at St Mary's in Edwinstowe.

Reverend Brynn had long since passed, but one of the final things Larry had asked him was if he'd known who he was the day he'd come to sit with him in the café. Even the massive amount of pain Reverend Brynn was in at this time, couldn't dim his smile. 'Of course I did, my dear boy, but I think God told me to sit with you, and as I got my tea, I had this thought: What if me coming and talking to you changes the course of your life?'

Larry had held his mentor's hand until he had taken his final breath.

Sitting on the bench underneath the oak tree, Larry could hear Moses barking, the deep throaty bark of a bulldog alerting his master to someone approaching. Larry heard twigs breaking under the approaching footsteps.

'Hello? Hello? Anyone there?'

Getting to his feet, Larry could make out the approaching dark outline of an approaching figure starting to come into focus, and before he could make out the features of the man standing in front of him, he heard a voice that, the last time he'd heard it, had been saying, 'Goodbye.'

Larry fell back onto the bench beneath him.

'Holy, mother of God.'

Chapter 127

1988 – the Duke, Kirkby-in-Ashfield

Billy switched off the TV and threw the remote on the sofa next to him. 'That McFetridge is a prick!' he shouted through to his wife Fiona, who was in the kitchen.

'Who's a prick?'

'That bloke that hosts News Focus, Hannah and the kids have just been on and he only had Henry fucking Mason on as well! Spouting his bollocks about Stan, you'd think he'd keep his mouth shut. I mean, what possessed the stupid fucker to go on the same show as Hannah?'

'Maybe he was set up?'

'Maybe. That McFetridge bloke just sat there smirking. Never realised just how like Stan, Charlie is. He told Mason to do one and then they all walked off. Sid will be furious. I might just give him a call.'

Getting to his feet, he kissed his wife on the top of her head.

***

Fiona watched her husband walk into the hallway. She was worried about him and she wasn't a lady who was easily worried. Having grown up as the daughter of a publican and then taken over as landlady when her dad had retired, Fiona had been sorting out barroom brawls her whole life. She was a fearsome figure and even the drunkest of punters knew not to mess with Fi-Fi Potter. With her peroxide blonde hair and trademark coral lipstick, even at sixty years old, she was still the most glamourous lady in the room.

She'd met and married Billy after his time with the Merry Men and although she knew of him and Stan, most of her knowledge of her husband's past had come from the many conversations they'd had over the years. Billy had been devastated by the loss of his friend and even though their pub did a healthy trade off the legend of the Merry Men, Billy had for years refused to speak publicly about Stan. He'd turned down thousands of pounds to appear in documentaries, do after-dinner speeches and write tell-all books, so it seemed odd to Fiona that her husband had agreed to appear in this documentary. She knew he'd been worried about the attack on Marjie, but she also knew that her husband wasn't one to be bullied. Over the years, various threats had been made against both her and Marjie and Billy had never once backed down, always 'sorting it', in his own inimitable style. He'd never say how, but the threat always went away and no more was said about it. It bothered Fiona, that this time was different somehow and she couldn't work out why?

Hannah and her children being back, Billy spending time with the Merry Men again, it all seemed to be taking its toll on her husband. It was all he spoke about. They were meant to be planning a trip to Italy, they'd promised to travel more now they were retired, but every time she bought it up, Billy told her they'd talk about it after the documentary was finished.

These days his vocabulary seemed to feature the name 'Hannah' every other word. Fiona wasn't a jealous lady, but she'd be very pleased when Hannah Thomas headed back to Australia.

Fiona got up and poured herself a vodka and tonic, quietly pulling the door ajar so she could hear what her husband was saying.

He was laughing at something Sidney was saying, and Fiona relaxed a little bit.

Taking a sip of her drink she continued to listen.

'OK, Hannah, well as long as you and the kids are alright, I'm sure Sidney will sort that prick out. Yeah, see you tomorrow.'

Fiona took her drink and sat down, turning on the TV and the volume up, she refused to spend another of her evenings talking about 'poor Hannah Thomas. She was going to watch The Bill. There were two reasons for this: firstly, she liked it and secondly it would really piss her husband off.

Chapter 128

1988 – St Mary's Church, Edwinstowe

'Hello Larry, it's been a long time.'

Larry closed his eyes and said the Lord's Prayer under his breath.

As he said the words, waiting for them to bring him comfort, he could hear the man fussing Moses.

'Well, aren't you a handsome chap? What's your name? We'll just wait for your fucking owner to stop chanting and we can get down to business.'

Larry finished his prayer, but kept his eyes firmly shut, giving himself a talking to. He'd been very stressed just recently, he was in a dark graveyard, he'd spent the last few weeks reliving his time as one of the Merry Men. Maybe he was having a panic attack? Maybe it was a ... what did they call them, a psychotic break? Maybe he was having a breakdown?

Larry told himself to focus. He needed to remind himself what was real and what wasn't. Taking a deep breath in, he touched the bench. Yes, that was real. He took another breath in and leant back against the tree. Yes, that was real too. Another breath. He could feel the ground beneath his feet. On his final breath, he reached down to stroke Moses's head, and as he rubbed the ears of his furry companion, he found another hand doing the same, and the bench beside him moved as the owner of the voice he hoped he'd imagined sat down next to him.

'All this time, and all you can do is say the Lords fucking Prayer and sit there breathing? I expected a better fucking welcome than that, Yatesy'

Larry opened his eyes and allowed himself to look at the man sat next to him. Turning his body to face him, he reached out his hands and started to touch the man's face. He traced the lines that had formed in the corners of his eyes, ones that hadn't been there when he'd last seen him; he stroked the man's beard, new to Larry, but the flecks of grey denoted that the owner had had, it a while. Larry's hands came to rest on the man's shoulders, and he could feel the tears streaming down his face, hot and burning like the ones he'd cried when he'd thought his friend had died.

Eventually, Larry said. 'Stan?'

Chapter 129

1988 – The Avenue, Mansfield

Jess Thomas was sat upstairs at her uncle's house. She could hear him shouting at someone on the phone and her mum telling him to calm down, and Charlie and Eddie saying that their uncle was right, and that Matt McFetridge shouldn't be allowed to get away with it. Her Mum had taken a phone call from someone else, and whoever that was had made her laugh.

Jess just sat there listening. She needed some space from her family tonight. The last few weeks had been intense. It had been a rollercoaster of coming to the U.K., meeting her dad's friends, being hounded by the press, filming the documentary, TV appearances, meeting Henry Mason and finally getting a real understanding of what it was to be the daughter of Stanley Thomas.

It had been relentless, Jess was used to busy, but this was next level and she needed time to think and process.

She couldn't get Henry out of her head. She could still feel his touch on her arm, the smell of his aftershave seemed to linger on her clothes and in her hair and the look in his eyes had haunted her. Why did a man like Henry look so broken? It was a look that seemed to reflect his soul.

Jess got up and pulled her suitcase out of the wardrobe. Opening it, she unzipped the pocket and pulled out a copy of Tales of the Gallows. Turning it over, she looked at his photo on the back.

This man didn't look like he was hiding something. But the man she had met did.

Chapter 130

1988 – St Mary's Church, Edwinstowe

Larry couldn't believe what he was seeing.

Sitting in front of him was one of his very best friends, a man who he believed had died on the gallows.

Alright, this man was older, his blonde hair long since turned grey and he had a beard, but those dark eyes were unmistakable. They were the eyes that Larry had looked into a few weeks earlier, when he'd met Stan's daughter Jess.

Larry knew that what he was seeing, what he was thinking was crazy, there was no logical explanation as to why a man who had died years ago should be, or even could be sat in front of him.

And yet here was.

Stanley Thomas was sat right next to him.

Larry had been faced with many difficult situations over the years. He'd had to find the words to say to avoid being stabbed in prison. He'd had to find ways to explain to worried parishioners that he really was a changed man and had dedicated his life to God. He'd comforted families, when their children had died, and they were looking for answers. He'd even found the words to train his stupid bulldog Moses.

But he was buggered if he could work out what to say now.

So he went with the obvious.

'I don't understand! You died! You're dead! You've been fucking dead for thirty-five bastard years! We're making a fucking documentary about you and the fact you died!'

'Larry, out of all of the Merry Men, I would have thought you'd get the concept of rising from the dead, even if it has taken me a bit longer than three days!'

Chapter 131

1988 – St Mary's Vicarage, Edwinstowe

Larry, Stan and Moses had walked in silence back to the vicarage. Larry had suggested they head back there so they could talk properly and avoid anyone seeing them.

Stan had laughed at the suggestion but agreed.

'Tea? Coffee? Something stronger? I think something stronger.' Larry got out a bottle of whiskey and two glasses and gestured for Stan to sit on the sofa before pouring them each a glass.

Moses settled himself in his basket by the fire.

Larry raised his glass. 'To being alive.'

Stan knocked his glass against Larry's. 'To being alive.'

'So, are you going to explain, or are you Mansfield's equivalent to Bobby Ewing?'

'Well, I'm not in the shower, am I?'

The two men laughed. 'Stan, I'm serious. How?'

'They never hung me! They were never going to! That was never the plan.' Stan laughed.

'The plan? There was a plan? Stan, we've all spent years mourning you! And all the fucking time, there was a plan in place? A plan none of us knew anything about. I thought we were family?' Suddenly Larry stopped, putting his glass down, he put his head in his hands. 'Hannah!'

'What about her?'

'Hannah and the kids, they're here, they're in Mansfield with Sid. Stan, you have a daughter!'

'I know, I know all about Jess.'

'I don't get it, how could you just leave them? Leave us? We could have all helped you, kept your secret.'

'I didn't have a choice and keeping you all in the dark was the only way. Well, most of you.'

'Most of us? Did one of us know?'

Stan nodded and took a huge slug of his whiskey. Billy knows.'

Chapter 132

1988 – The Duke, Kirkby-in-Ashfield

Billy lay in bed. He lay perfectly still. Fiona lay next to him, also perfectly still, her gentle snores filling the air at intermittent intervals. Even though his wife was asleep and snoring, he knew she was mad with him. He'd known the moment he came back into the room after speaking to Hannah and Sid on the phone. She only ever put The Bill on when he was home when she wanted to annoy him. She knew he hated any TV show that showed the police in a good light.

He was trying to work out why she might be mad at him. Even after all these years, his wife could still be a mystery to him.

Still, tomorrow, he'd get up, make her a cup of tea and tell her they could start planning their trip to Italy.

Once Hannah went back to Australia and they were done filming the documentary, his life could return to normal. He was used to avoiding the publicity of films and TV shows about the Merry Men and this one would be no different. He'd once been door-stepped by an actor who'd been playing him in a film. The actor had turned up at the pub, with a photographer in tow. Billy had worked out what was going on immediately and had escorted both of them off the premises and smashed the photographer's camera for good measure.

A trip to Italy would be the perfect way to escape the fuss, and it would stop Fiona being mad at him. Billy took a deep breath and felt the stress melt away. Now he had a plan he could sleep.

Just as he was nodding off, he heard the phone ring. He could hear Marjie's muffled voice, then the bedroom door creaked open.

'Dad, Larry's on the phone, says it's urgent.'

Getting out of bed, he felt Fiona stir.

'Everything OK?'

'Yes, well I think so, Larry's on the phone.'

Fiona grunted, farted, and promptly rolled over and went back to sleep, her bodily functions expressing what she couldn't with words.

'Larry? What's the matter?'

'You knew!' Larry's voice was calm, but there was an edge to it. It was a tone that Billy hadn't heard him use since he'd been explaining to the people who'd disobeyed the Merry Men what punishment was about to befall them.

'Knew what?'

'He's here.' And with that Larry put the phone down.

Billy sat down, still holding the phone receiver in his hand.

'Dad? Everything OK?'

'Not really love, I've got to go out. If I'm not back by the time your mum wakes up, tell her there was an emergency with Larry and I'll explain when I can.'

Chapter 133

1988 – Kirkby-in-Ashfield

Billy got into his car and started the engine. Normally he'd have had music blasting out, but he didn't want any songs to remind him of this journey.

It was a journey he always knew he'd have to make. It had just been a matter of when. He'd known at some point the truth would come out, but now it had, he couldn't work out if he was pleased the burden was about to be lifted or fearful of what path the truth would lead them down.

He was about to find out.

Chapter 134

1952 – Crow Hill Drive, Mansfield

'You can't be fucking serious.'

'I am deadly serious Bill, it's the only way.'

'Stan, these people can't be trusted, they'll get you to do their dirty work and then they'll fuck you over! I'm telling you!'

'They won't, I've talked it through with The Fixer and it's all in place. It's win-win, we get rid of Dorrell for good.'

'Yes, but it also means getting rid of you! You've not thought it through, what about Hannah? What about your boys?'

'Bill, this is the best thing for them. If I don't do this, I'm destined for the hangman's rope at some point for something, you know that these people won't rest until they get me. They will keep on at all of us! You know as well as I do, that Judge Haynes wants to hang the lot of us! This way it keeps you boys safe, and he gets to look like the Big Almighty that rid the world of Stanley Thomas. And I get to give Dorrell what's coming to him. I'm going to kill him anyway, so I may as well get away with it.'

Billy shook his head. 'You're putting a lot of faith in people, who I think will screw you over, the first chance they get.'

'The Fixer's got it all sorted. I'm not the only one with a lot to lose, they all have, too. Getting rid of Dorrell solves a lot of problems for everyone.'

'But Hannah, the boys?'

Stan shook his head. 'Hannah will meet someone else, and he'll be a better dad to those boys than I ever could be. You've got to encourage her to move on.'

Billy exhaled. He knew he was fighting a losing battle; it was clear Stan had made his mind up. It was just the sort of plan that set Stan's soul on fire, a chance to commit a crime, get away with it and put two fingers up to authority. If things went to plan, it would be one of the greatest cover-ups of all time. 'Are you absolutely sure about this? We can trust The Fixer?'

'Abso-fucking-lutely!'

Chapter 135

1988 – St Mary's Vicarage, Edwinstowe

The drive to Larry's seemed to take forever. Billy thought back to the day that Stan had first told him of the plan to kill Dorrell. He'd thought Stan was mad, that someone would betray him at the last minute and that he'd really be hung.

After Stan was arrested and charged, Billy had waited for the six o'clock knock at his door, for the police to come and arrest him and the rest of the Merry Men, for them to be charged and sentenced to death too.

But it never came.

All through Stan's trial, Billy sat in the gallery of Shire Hall, barely daring to exhale, waiting for someone to expose Stan's plan.

But it never happened.

On the day before Stan's 'execution', he'd told the truth to the others. He had driven to the prison, he sat outside, he had waited, he had seen Old Man Rope go in, he had been waiting to see if Stan would walk out the front door, tell everyone it had been a big old joke, but that never happened either.

Billy thought about sitting around the kitchen table with Hannah and the rest of the Merry Men, listening to the clock chime nine, everyone raising a glass, the tears, the devastating grief that had filled the room. He had held Hannah tight that morning, let her sob uncontrollably into his shoulder, his shirt soaked with her tears.

He had stroked her hair, telling her things would be alright, when all he wanted to say was that Stan was alive and well and about to start a new life. But he couldn't.

Stan had told Billy to wait, and he would be in touch with him when he could. He'd taken that call six months later.

Billy pulled up outside the vicarage. Turning off his engine and switching off his lights, he wondered what Larry's parishioners would think if they saw one of the Merry Men creeping in to see their vicar in the early hours of the morning, and just what they'd make of the knowledge that the leader of that motley crew who was allegedly been dead, was currently also inside sat by the fire enjoying a nice glass of whiskey?

Billy let himself in. Moses barked to signal his arrival, and walking into the living room, he didn't know whether to laugh or cry.

Sat there enjoying a glass of whiskey and chatting away like any two long lost friends who hadn't seen each other for ages were, Larry and Stan.

'Room for one more?'

Larry got to his feet and poured Billy a drink. 'I should knock you out for not telling me.'

'You should, but you won't.'

Larry laughed. 'I just don't know how you kept it to yourself all these years. mean I understand you not telling Dicky, that idiots got a big mouth, he'd have got drunk and told some reporter. I can even understand you not telling Sid. There's no way he could have known and not have told Hannah. But me? I keep secrets for a living! You could have talked to me.'

Billy sat down on the sofa next to Stan. 'I promised I wouldn't. We couldn't risk it getting out.'

'But what about now? Are we going to tell Dicky? Sid? What about Hannah and the kids? Stan, you have a daughter, she's amazing.'

'Well, she's a copper, but Larry's right, she's amazing. Your boys are incredible too, and they're here Stan, they're in Mansfield, not halfway round the world like they have been. You can't use that as an excuse anymore.'

'I know, I know they're here.'

'So?'

'So what? I'll see them in my own time. I can't just walk up to my wife and say, 'Hey guess who's not dead? The poor old girl will have a heart attack.'

'What about Dicky and Sid? Are you going to tell them?'

'Larry, calm the fuck down, one step at a time.'

'One step at a time? You turn up here, out of the blue, thirty-five fucking years after your fucking death and say, 'Hey I'm alive!' then I find out, my other so-called mate knew about it and I still don't have a clue, how it all happened, so if someone could kindly fill me in?'

Stan took a slug of whiskey and Billy could tell; he wasn't about to say anything.

'It was a need-to-know basis,' Billy said instead. 'And The Fixer had us by the balls. They were the one running things. You don't think it was a coincidence that Frederick Dykes and Roger Collins met untimely ends? They were about to blab. Frederick was about to land himself in prison for his dodgy dealings, so went to

The Fixer for help, threatened to sing like a canary for a lesser sentence, so they arranged for the brakes on his car to fail. Roger Collins was always up to his neck in debt, that stupid fucker thought he'd try to blackmail The Fixer. It was easy to pass his death off as punishment for a gambling debt, no-one was going to ask too many questions about either of them.'

'I still don't get it. What did the Sheriff of the County and the fucking Prison Chaplain have to do with it, and who the fuck is The Fixer?'

Stan swirled his whiskey around in his glass. 'They were all in on it. The plan only worked if everyone was on board, and they all had a lot to lose. So, they went along with what The Fixer had to say. They'd been planning it for years. They've been in charge of everything for years, and now I want to take back that control.'

Chapter 136

1988 – St Mary's Vicarage, Mansfield

Stan, Larry and Billy had stayed up talking till the following morning. They'd all eventually fallen asleep in Larry's lounge, only to be woken by the sound of Moses scratching at the door to be let out for a wee and his breakfast.

Larry got out of his chair. 'I'm coming boy.'

Last night still felt a bit of a blur.

He flicked on the kettle before going out to the garden to wait for Moses to do his business. The cold autumnal air seemed to ease his hangover. At least by the end of the bottle of the whiskey, the three of them had come up with a plan. Stan had always joked that there was no problem that couldn't be solved by a bottle of whiskey and last night, that seemed right; but putting it into action today might prove a bit more difficult.

Moses wandered back inside and went and sat by his bowl waiting for his food. Larry dutifully dished up, and as the bulldog snaffled through his meaty breakfast, Billy joined them in the kitchen.

'I'll go a brew, if there's one going. What time is it?'

'Eight-thirty. Here you go.' Larry handed Billy a cup of coffee.

'Fi-Fi is going to kill me. She was already mad at me for spending so much time with you lot and Hannah. When she finds out I snuck out in the middle of the night to drink whiskey with you guys, she will go fucking apoplectic!'

'The phone's there if you want to call her, try and temper the situation.'

Billy laughed. 'Nah, she's already mad, so I may as well be hung for a sheep as a lamb. Probably an unfortunate turn of phrase considering!'

'Speaking of which, is the Holy Ghost still fast asleep?'

'No, he went to the loo.'

Stan walked in just at that moment, looking as fresh as a daisy. There were no sign of last night's revelations or whiskey showing on his face.

'Brew?'

'No, thanks, I need to get back. But we're clear, yeah?'

Larry and Billy nodded.

'OK, I'll see you later.'

Stan smoothed his beard and put on his jacket. Reaching inside his pocket, he pulled out a flat cap and a pair of glasses. Doffing his cap, he left Larry and Billy standing in the kitchen.

***

Straightening his cap and adjusting his glasses, Stan walked out of the door.

As he was about to close the door, he heard Larry exclaim, 'You've got to be fucking kidding me!'

It looked like one more bit of the puzzle had finally dropped for the Reverend Yates.

Stan laughed. If he were honest, it was his favourite detail.

The Fixer

7th January 1953 – Nottingham Prison

The Fixer watched as Stan walked into the interview room. He was accompanied by one of the prison guards Reginald Braithewaite. The two had clearly been sharing a joke as they'd made their way to the room.

Any other condemned prisoner would have been in handcuffs, and this meeting would not have been allowed. The day before a prisoner's execution, visits would have been confined to final goodbyes with family, and a possible last bid attempt by their solicitor to get the sentence commuted.

But Stan wasn't any other condemned prisoner, and The Fixer wasn't any other visitor.

'Give me a shout Stan, when you're ready to head back.'

'Will do, Reg.'

Reginald nodded at The Fixer and shut the door behind him.

Stan sat down at the table and sat facing The Fixer.

The Fixer stared back at him, barely recognizable; it was amazing what hair dye, glasses and a change of outfit could do.

'Everything in place?'

'Yes, everything will work exactly as I said it would. Everyone knows the plan. I see Reg is treating you well'

'Yeah, he's alright, keeps bringing me proper food, so I don't have to eat that muck they serve in here. I think he's just glad of the extra money, doesn't really give a fuck about what's going to happen to me.'

'What I need to know, Stan, is that you know what's going to happen? This will be our last meeting and our paths will never cross again. Stanley Thomas dies tomorrow, he is no more, is that clear?'

'Crystal.'

'You will make no attempt to contact anyone from your old life: Hannah, your kids, the rest of the Merry Men, they're gone to you. Forever. I don't care what the rest of your life brings you, but after tomorrow our connection is done, understand?'

'Totally, I knew the deal when I agreed to all this. A chance for me to start over. Move away from this.'

'Good, everything you need will be waiting for you once you're clear of this place.' The Fixer stood up. 'Right, I think that's it.'

Stan got to his feet too, and the two starred at each other. The Fixer stuck out their hand, and Stan laughed. Moving around the table, he took the Fixer into his arms.

'You are one hell of a crazy bitch to think we can pull this off, but it looks like we're about to make it fucking happen. All of them have underestimated you, every single one of them'"

The Fixer smiled, and Stan took her face in his hands and pressed his forehead to hers. The two of them stood still for what felt like forever. Neither of them really wanted to move, knowing that once that touch ended, it would be their last.

Finally, Stan spoke. 'Till our next merry meeting.' He bent his head and kissed her.

Breaking apart, Stan headed for the door. He was just about to leave, when The Fixer spoke.

'Stan, you were right. Everyone has always underestimated me, don't make the same mistake.'

Stan smiled, nodded, and left.

It was to be the last time she was in the same room as him for thirty-five years; until he did exactly what she had told him not to do.

Underestimate her.

Chapter 137

1988 – St Mary's Vicarage, Edwinstowe

Larry and Moses returned from their walk, and Larry was starting to feel as though his hangover had finally gone.

The walk had helped clear his head not only of whiskey fog, but had also allowed him some time to process the events of the last twenty-four hours and the plan that they had come up with.

Walking through Sherwood Forest with Moses at his heel Larry had thought back over the last four decades of his life.

Larry had last seen Stan a few days before his 'execution'. He had played that conversation over and over in his mind so many times. Had there been any clues he'd missed? Had Stan tried to tell him what was happening? Had there been cues that Stan had urged Larry to pick up on? It didn't matter how many times he went over it, there was nothing that he could remember.

The conversation had been normal, they'd said their goodbyes, Stan had asked him to make sure that Hannah and the kids were OK, thanked him for being a good friend, told him to stay out of trouble, shook his hand, hugged him and left.

Nothing.

No hint.

And all this time, Stan had been alive.

Hiding in plain sight.

The moment Larry arrived home, he picked up the phone and dialled.

'Dicky, it's Larry. Eamonn, that documentary bloke, has asked if we can all meet here later to talk about the next bit. Yeah, shouldn't take long. Seven? Brilliant, see you later.'

Cutting Dicky off, Larry re-dialled. 'Sid, it's Larry, you OK to come here later to finalise a few bits for the documentary? About seven. No, just you, this bit is just about us. OK mate, see you later.'

Larry hung up. He'd done his bit.

Chapter 138

1988 – The Avenue, Mansfield

'I'm off to Larry's later. That Eamonn bloke wants to run through some bits for the documentary.'

'Do they need me and the kids?'

'Larry says not.'

'Oh good, the kids were on about going out for a meal or something, but I think I might stay here, have a bath and chill out. It's been a hell of a few weeks don't you think?'

'Just a bit. Are you sure you're OK with everything?'

'Yeah, I think I'm ready to get this documentary finished and then I can head back to Oz with the kids and carry on with my life.'

'Not tempted to stay here?'

Hannah shrugged. 'More than you know.'

Sid hugged his sister. 'Han, if you want to come home, you can stay here, you know that.'

'It's not just me though, it's the kids. We all have lives there and I can't ask them to give up what they've achieved.'

'Then, you move back. They're adults now, they'll understand.'

Hannah shook her head. 'I can't, they've already had one parent leave them, I'm not doing the same.'

Chapter 139

1988 – The Duke, Kirkby-in-Ashfield

Billy had, had one hell of a day. He'd returned home to find a furious Fiona sat at the kitchen table, wearing a floral dress, her peroxide hair piled on top of head, and her face fully made up. On the table was a cup of coffee, a packet of cigarettes, a lighter and an ashtray that had coral lipstick-stained stubs in it.

She had clearly been sat there for hours waiting for him to return.

Billy still didn't know what he was going to tell her, but he knew that under these circumstances, the truth wasn't an option.

'Fi-Fi, I'm sorry, there was an emergency with Larry. Did Marjie tell you? I asked her to when I left.'

Fiona looked at her husband and took a drag of her cigarette, flicking the dangling ash into the ashtray.

Billy wasn't sure if she'd heard him; she wasn't as much looking at him, but through him.

'Did you hear me Fi-Fi?'

Fiona took another drag of her cigarette, picked up her coffee and took a sip.

'Fi-Fi?'

'I heard you.'

'Larry had an emergency.'

'Larry had an emergency, did he? Is that what you're calling her now?'

'Calling who?'

'Hannah Thomas.' Fiona Potter spat the words.

It dawned on Billy that his wife thought he was having an affair.

In a weird way it was a relief. She had no clue as to what was going on. Still getting her to believe that he wasn't having an affair was probably going to be easier than getting her to believe that his best friend was still alive and well.

'Don't be silly! Marjie answered the phone! It was Larry who needed me, he'd gotten drunk and fallen over.'

'You expect me to believe that bullshit?'

'It's not bullshit, ask Marjie. Marjie! Marjie! Get in here now.'

Marjie emerged from the next room. 'Morning Dad, everything OK? How's Larry? He didn't sound right on the phone last night.'

Billy pulled an I told you so face at his wife, but Fiona merely shrugged and stubbed her cigarette out.

'He's OK now, but he was in a bit of a state. He'd had a bit too much to drink and fallen over, I think he's got himself in a state over this documentary.'

'Had he hurt himself?'

'No, not really, more bruised pride, and I think he just wanted to talk. We sat up all night, just going over things. He's worried about what the Bishop will say, whether it will cause him any bother, being so closely associated with Stan again. I think he just needed a mate.'

Fiona had got up from the kitchen table and was putting the kettle on. 'Coffee?' she asked her husband.

'Yes, please, love.'

'I still can't believe that you all agreed to be involved in this documentary, after all this time. I know they threatened Marjie, but you've never bowed to pressure to talk about Stan, so why now?'

'I couldn't have Marjie hurt, you know that and I'm not as young as I once was, I haven't got the energy to be fighting scrotes. Plus, maybe it's time.'

'Time?'

'Time, I put my side of the story out there, told everyone what Stan was really like.'

Fiona walked over to her husband and put a cup of coffee down in front of him, before putting her arms around his shoulders and kissin g the top of his head. 'I wish I'd met him, the Stan that you knew, not the one they all talk about.'

Billy touched his wife's hand, thinking about how he should respond to that.

Marjie saved him the trouble.

'I'm not being funny, but all this is great for business, and Dad, once this documentary is out, you are doing an 'Evening With' here, I won't take no for an answer! Takings will go through the roof.'

Marjie took her coffee and headed out the kitchen, and Billy smiled. It might be he could provide his daughter with a real exclusive and takings that night would be more than she'd ever dreamed!

It didn't take long for Fiona to eventually forgive him. Especially once he'd taken her to the travel agent in Kirkby to get some brochures for their trip to Italy and told her to pick the places that she wanted to go, and then agreed with the travel agent that they'd return in a week's time to finalise the arrangements.

Billy was getting ready to head to Larry's, when he found his wife once again sat at the kitchen table, travel brochures spread out all over the table, with a notepad and a bottle of red. Fiona was in her element and even though, he knew this trip was going to cost him a lot of money, it would be worth every single penny.

'I'm off, love.'

'OK, have fun.'

'Will do. Don't forget to add Rome to that list.'

'It's already on!' Fiona blew her husband a kiss.

Heading to his car, Billy half-wished they were heading for the airport tonight and he didn't have to go and tell Dicky and Sid what had really been going on.

Chapter 140

1988 – The Avenue, Mansfield

Hannah was alone. Sid had left to go and meet the rest of the Merry Men to talk about the documentary, and her children had gone out for dinner and to the pub.

Someone had told them about a club in Mansfield called Digby's, so they'd said they might try that.

Hannah had decided that she would spend her evening having a long hot bath, a glass – well maybe a bottle of wine, box of chocolates and a film. She was actually quite looking forward to the peace.

Hannah lay in the bath, the hot water enveloping her whole body. She closed her eyes and breathed in the lavender scent of the bubble bath. Her mind wandered to what life could have been like with Stan.

Would they still be living in Mansfield? Probably.

She daydreamed that he'd have left behind a life of crime and set up a reputable business, one that was successful, but legitimate, one where he could have worked with his sons, teaching them a trade, eventually allowing them to take over the reins when he retired to spend more time with her. They'd travel, all over the world, enjoying each other's company, delighting in the different sights they'd see, creating memories; returning home with armfuls of gifts for the kids and grandkids. Happy to be together. A happy, secure family.

Hannah sighed, aware that the water was starting to turn cold. Getting out of the bath and drying off, she heard a noise downstairs. It sounded like the backdoor. Maybe the kids had decided not to make a night of it after all, or maybe Sid was home early.

Putting on her dressing gown, she shouted downstairs, 'Hello? Sid, that you? Kids?' There was no answer. Maybe she'd imagined it. She still wasn't used to the sounds this house made and it always seemed a lot noisier when Sid wasn't around.

Picking up her glass of wine, she made her way downstairs. Heading into the kitchen, she topped up her wine glass and made the executive decision to take the bottle into the lounge with her, as it would save her getting up.

Opening the fridge, she took out the box of chocolates she'd bought earlier. She noticed it had been opened. Bloody kids, she bet they'd sneaked one before they'd left. Opening the lid, she saw that only the coffee cream was missing.

Hannah dropped the box.

Stan was the only person she'd ever known that had liked the coffee creams. She used to tease him about it.

Bending to pick up the box, she chided herself. 'Silly cow.' The sooner this documentary was over, and she could return home to her life in Australia, the better.

'I never could resist a coffee cream, Han.'

Turning round, Hannah and the box of chocolates collapsed to the floor.

Chapter 141

1988 – St Mary's Vicarage, Edwinstowe

The Merry Men all gathered around Larry's kitchen table, and Larry put a glass down in front of all of them, along with a bottle of whiskey.

'Should we be drinking if we've got to speak to Eammon about the documentary?' Dicky asked.

'When did you get so sensible Dicky Richards?'

They all laughed, and Larry opened the bottle and started to splash the dark liquid into the glasses. 'Eammon isn't coming, and believe me, you're going to need a drink.'

'Don't tell me, after everything they've decided not to do the documentary? For fucks sake.'

'Dicky, shut up for a second, sometimes you give my arse a headache.' Sidney joked. 'Larry, are you going to tell us what's going on?'

'No, Billy is.'

They all turned to look at Billy, and Billy picked up his glass of whiskey and drained it, before sticking it out for a refill.

'You're not dying are you, Bill?' asked Sidney.

Billy shook his head. 'No, it's not that. it's just well. Oh Christ.' Draining the refill, he took a deep breath. 'It's about Stan. You see... it's that... he's... he's not dead.'

Sidney started to laugh, he looked across at Dicky, who kept going to open his mouth, before shutting it again and was rubbing at his temples. Larry, just stared into his glass of whiskey.

Finally managing to find some words, Dicky asked. 'What do you mean he's not dead? Not dead how?'

'This isn't some 'he lives on forever in our hearts' religious bollocks, is it?' Sidney demanded. 'Has Larry put you up to this?'

'No Sid, I haven't, and Billy means what he says.' Larry said slowly. 'Stan isn't dead. He was here last night.'

'Have you two gone fucking insane?' Sidney's voice was getting louder, the angrier he was getting. 'They hung him thirty-five bastard years ago! My sister moved halfway across the world because of it! And we've all spent the last few weeks making a documentary about the fact he's fucking dead! How can he not be dead?'

As Sidney raged, Dicky sat very quietly, gently sipping his drink, and Larry wondered if he'd understood what was being said.

Sidney's rage continued to explode. 'One of you better start talking and you better start talking quickly.'

Larry topped up everyone's glasses and sat down. 'Bill, I really think you should take it from the beginning.'

Billy nodded. 'Stan came to me not long after Dorrell paralysed Charlie. He said someone had approached him about dealing with Dorrell, but Stan said he wanted to deal with it in his own way. Then after Hannah was raped, they approached him again, said they wanted Dorrell finishing for good. Told Stan that if he did it on his own, everyone would know it was him and that him and us would swing for it. Said if they did it their way, Stan would be able to start a new life and we'd never be charged with anything. Stan agreed. He told me; he couldn't see another way.'

'You expect me to believe that Stan was prepared to leave my sister and the kids?' Sidney demanded. 'Who approached him? Did Hannah know about this? Was everyone else in on it but me and Dicky?'

'Stan said it was the perfect crime,' Billy continued. 'He could kill Dorrell and get away with it. He said it was the only way to get proper revenge and make sure that none of us ever faced charges for it. Hannah didn't know, I'm sure of it. You saw how upset she was, she broke her heart over him.'

'How could you stand there and let her, when you knew all along?' Sidney continued to rage. 'How could you let us all mourn a man who wasn't dead?'

'I didn't have a choice, I thought I was protecting everyone. Plus, the Stan we knew was dead, he was never coming back to us. We had to mourn him, to let him go. Even when you see him, you'll see he's not our Stan.'

'Bill's right, he's not our Stan,' Larry agreed. 'He's a different man. He's colder, he's harder, he's capable of stuff that we'd never imagined. He's lived a life we'll never understand.'

'And yet he's walked amongst us all this time, and no-one has ever put two and two together?'

Larry shook his head, 'Nope, no-one's had a clue. As I said, this Stan is harder, smarter, capable of all kinds of evil.'

'You never answered my question, who was the person who approached Stan, got him to do this?'

Billy shook his head. 'Now that I don't know. Stan only ever referred to them as The Fixer, I know that those blokes who attended Dorrell's sex parties had something to do with it, but I don't know how it all fits together.'

'That Reverend bloke, Roger Collins.' added Larry, 'he got stabbed to death a couple of years after Stan died... Or didn't die.'

'So, was one of them The Fixer?'

'No, I don't think so. I always got the impression that there was someone Stan was protecting.'

Sidney had calmed down and was now seemingly trying to make sense of everything. 'Have you seen him over the years?'

Billy shook his head. 'No, that was part of the deal, he wasn't allowed to see any of us. He called me a few times, normally when he'd had a few. Larry only found out yesterday.'

Billy and Larry were answering Sidney's questions the best they could.

Larry was worried about Dicky. He hadn't said a word and was still very slowly sipping his original glass of whiskey.

The four of them sat quietly for a few moments, and to everyone's surprise, it was Dicky who broke the silence.

'Where is he now?'

Chapter 142

8th January 1953 – Nottingham Prison

Stan lay on his bed. He knew it was happening today. He could hear movement in the next cell, them getting set up, making their preparations. Or at least making out that's what they were doing. But everything was set.

Every so often someone opened the hatch in his cell door to peer through at him, but Stan just lay there. In a couple of hours, he'd be out of here. He'd no longer be Stanley Thomas, gangster, leader of the Merry Men, husband and father, he'd be someone else.

Stan lay on his bed, smoking.

He knew they'd have to go through the motions, so that, for some reason, it would look on the face of it that things were going as planned.

At nine a.m. on the dot, the partition wall to his cell swung open and in walked a smartly dressed man, who handed him a glass and said. 'Now then son, let's make this quick and with no trouble.'

The man winked at Stan and Stan winked back.

Stanley's hands were bound, and he was marched to the gallows. The partition door was quickly closed and the men inside the room waited.

The men all stood around the gallows; Stan, Jerry Mason, Governor William Smith, Fredrick Dykes, , Michael Dunderdale, Roger Collins and prison guards Reginald Braithewaite and Derek Davies.

Five minutes passed, and then Stan said, 'Dad, I think you can untie me now.'

Jerry began to untie the rope around his son's wrists. 'Right, let's at least make something about this official. Governor Smith, Sheriff Dykes can you confirm that the execution of Stanley Thomas was carried out in a legal and fair manner and in accordance with the laws of this country?'

William and Frederick nodded in unison. 'We can.'

'Thank you for your co-operation. Dr Michael Dunderdale, can you declare time of death?'

'Stanley Thomas, is dead, date of death, eighth of January 1953, time of death 9.05 a.m., place of death Nottingham Prison.'

'Thank you, Dr Dunderdale. Reverend Collins, if I can call on you to say a few words on behalf of the deceased.'

'Certainly. God Bless Stanley Thomas for ridding the world of that parasite Walter Dorrell, may Dorrell rot in hell.'

'Thank you. Stan, I need you to get into this coffin, so we can get you out of here, and then I think that's it, everyone. Governor, will you phone Judge Haynes and inform him the plan was successful and I'll speak with The Fixer.'

Everyone nodded.

And with that the body of Stanley Thomas left Nottingham Prison.

Chapter 143

1988 – The Avenue, Mansfield

Hannah woke up to find herself laying on the sofa. She gradually started to take in her surroundings: her wine glass was on the table, so were her chocolates, so maybe she'd been dreaming. She reached up to touch her head, it felt tender, like she had banged it. Re-focusing her eyes, she realised that there was another glass of wine on the table, and someone was sat in the chair opposite watching her.

'You OK now, Han? I suggest sitting up slowly, you've had a shock.'

Sitting up very slowly, Hannah looked across at the man sat opposite her. 'What are you doing here? How did you get in?'

The man smiled at her. 'Han, I think you're going to need a glass of wine, for what I'm about to tell you.'

Hannah reached out and took her glass, a million thoughts were racing through her head. She did a quick mental check of her body: all her clothes were intact and only her head hurt, and that was from where she'd fell and banged it. So maybe he wasn't here to rape her, if he was, he'd probably have done it already.

If he wanted to hurt her at all, she thought, she'd have been tied up. But he'd laid her on the sofa and waited for her to wake, so maybe that wasn't it either?

She knew she hadn't been particularly nice to him the last time they'd met, but if he'd really wanted to talk to her, there were better ways of doing it than breaking in and scaring her half to death.

She took a sip of wine.

'Better, Han?'

'Why do you keep calling me 'Han'? No-one calls me that anymore, and certainly not someone I hardly know!'

The man laughed, 'Hardly know? Han, who do you think I am?'

'What do you mean 'who do I think you are?' You're Henry Mason!'

Chapter 144

1988 – St Mary's Vicarage, Edwinstowe.

'You mean that Stan is with Hannah now?'

'Yes, he wanted to be the one to tell her, thought he owed her that at least.' Billy explained. 'He knew that if he saw you guys first, you'd get to Hannah before he could. But he knew that if he saw her and didn't tell you what was going on, that would cause problems too. He thought it best, if we told you, while he was speaking to Hannah.'

'Typical fucking Stan, still calling the shots after all this time, drip feeding bits of information and getting everyone dancing to his tune. Well not this time.' Sid stood up and grabbed his keys, "I'm going back to check on Hannah and to confront the bastard! He's going to start talking and tell me everything!'

Billy ran to the door. 'No, you'll stay here. Stan wants to see you all, but when he's ready. Sit down.'

'I will not sit down, I'm not a kid anymore, and Stanley Thomas does not tell me what to do. I am Sidney Longshaw, and I run this manor now. Billy, you move out of my way, or I swear I'll knock you clean out.'

Billy hesitated for a second, before Larry interceded and got between him and Sidney.

'Billy, I think you've got to let Sidney go. You've had thirty-five years to get used to this; Sidney's had thirty-five minutes. And he's right, he should be with Hannah.'

Billy reluctantly stepped aside, and Sidney pushed him anyway.

Just as he was leaving, Dicky stood up. 'Wait up, boss, I'll come with you. I can drive, I've barely touched my whiskey.'

Sidney handed him his car keys and the two started to walk out.

Billy looked at Larry, 'Wait up, we'll come too. After all, it should be all or none of us.'

Chapter 145

1988 – The Avenue, Mansfield

'Ahh yes, Henry Mason, that's how you know me these days.'

'What do you mean, how I know you these days?' Hannah burst out. 'I've only met you once and I only know you because of that stupid book you wrote. Look, I don't know what you're trying to do, are you looking for material for your sequel? Do you intend to write about me this time? Make more money out of my Stan? Exploit his widow, exploit his kids? You're a cunt, do you know that? And I want you to fuck off out of this house, before my kids get back, because believe me if you hurt them or cause them pain, I will cause you pain, or more importantly my brother will cause you pain!'

'I always liked feisty Hannah. You're still a good-looking woman. That Aussie sunshine must agree with you. I must admit, I was disappointed you moved halfway across the world, it made it so much harder to keep a track of you and the kids.'

'Keep a track of me and the kids? What are you, some kind of psycho? Were you so obsessed with Stan that you had to stalk his widow and his kids? I want you out of here and I want you out of here now!'

Hannah was at a complete loss. Why was this man stood here talking about her as if he knew all about her, making out there was a history there? Hannah decided that she would give him one last chance to leave, and if he didn't, she was calling the police.

'Look, Mr Mason... Henry. Why don't I call your wife and she can come and fetch you? I think you might be a bit overwhelmed by everything. Someone told me you'd had a heart attack a few weeks ago, maybe it's taken more out of you than you realised.' Standing up, Hannah headed to the phone. 'Now, what's your wife's number and I'll call her.'

'You don't need to call my wife, because she's stood right in front of me and yet because of a fucking pair of glasses and her own inability to see what's right in front of her, she still doesn't fucking recognise me?'

Chapter 146

1988 – The Avenue, Mansfield

'Hannah! Hannah! Are you here? Where are you?' Sidney came bursting through the front door, Dicky, Billy and Larry behind him.

'Sid, I'm in here!'

At the sight of her brother, Hannah ran into his arms. 'Sid, Henry Mason broke in, and now he's saying all kinds of weird things! He won't leave, I think he's had a breakdown.'

Stan started to walk towards them, but Billy had had enough. 'Right! Everyone sit down! Stan armchair. Sid, Hannah: sofa. Dicky, Larry, sit!'

Larry was about to argue that he wasn't Moses, but by the look on Billy's face, he could tell he wasn't messing.

Everyone did as they were told and sat down.

'Wait a second,' Hannah said slowly. 'You just called that man 'Stan'. What's wrong with you? It's Henry Mason!'

Billy shook his head. 'No, Hannah, Henry Mason is Stanley. Stan's alive and sitting right opposite you!'

THE FIXER

1953

'Thanks Jerry, I'm glad it went smoothly.'

The Fixer replaced the handset and smiled to herself. She'd done it! Part One of her plan had worked! Walter Dorrell was dead, Stanley Thomas was now on his way to a new life, the Hon, the Rev, the Doc, the Gov and the Sheriff were out of her life for good and she was finally free.

Free to live her own life.

Time to put Part Two of her plan into action.

Removing the towel, she had wrapped around her head, she shook out her now blonde hair and started to dry it.

Her packed bags were by the door ready for her to leave the George Street Brothel for good.

It was time for Pearl Dorrell to live her own life.

Chapter 147

1988 – Regent's Park, London

Pearl poured herself a large glass of red wine and switched on her record player. As the needle of the record player made contact with the vinyl, a gentle crackle filled the air for a few seconds, before Frank Sinatra started singing, In the Wee Small Hours of the Morning.

Pearl settled on the sofa.

On the table lay a photo album, and picking it up, she flicked open the pages. The first few photos were of her and her parents. John and Betty Dorrell had been good and decent people, they were so proud of her and her talent. Her Mum used to tell her she could be and do anything. She knew that had they lived, Betty would have filled the house with framed newspaper articles that her daughter, the newspaper editor had written. John Dorrell would have sat in the local café every morning reading his daughter's paper, no doubt telling anyone that would listen that his daughter had written the whole paper.

There were no photos of Walter in the album. Pearl very often wondered what would have happened to him, had he lived. She always reached the same conclusion: someone would have murdered him. It might have taken five years, it might have taken twenty years, but someone would definitely have finished him off. Pearl had merely helped speed up the inevitable.

Hidden behind the family photos, were ones of a sixteen-year-old Pearl. She was sitting on the beach in Skegness, her brown hair long and flowing around her shoulders. She wore a bathing suit and she was laughing at the person taking the photo.

Pearl remembered that day. It was one of the very few days she'd been able to escape the George Street Brothel and go to the seaside. Walter had been 'on business' in Birmingham for a few days and the other girls had covered for her with Malcolm, who was meant to be watching the brothel in Walter's absence.

It had been a warm summer's day, and she'd somehow managed to make a picnic without Malcom realizing. She'd then waited patiently at the top of George Street, his car had pulled up and she'd got in. he was wearing a big fedora and dark glasses, she'd laughed when she saw him, particularly when he'd said, "I didn't want anyone to recognize me, so I thought I'd wear a disguise!"

The two of them had laughed all the way to Skegness. They'd spent the day playing on the arcade machines and had then sat and eaten the picnic on the beach, before they'd paddled in the sea, looking just like any other couple. Young and in love.

The next photo showed the man with his trousers rolled up above his knees showing the scar from an injury he'd gotten during the war. He was wearing a vest, and he was reaching towards the camera and laughing, his blonde hair catching the sun. His eyes had lost their hardness. He'd been telling her not to take a photo, but they'd both known that he hadn't meant it.

The next one was of the two of them. They'd asked someone on the beach to take it. His arm had been casually draped around her shoulders and they'd both been smiling, huge toothy grins, which could not hide their happiness at having spent a stolen day at the beach together.

Pearl shut the album and wiped a tear from her.

Even after all these years, Stanley Thomas was still the love of her life.

Chapter 148

1988 – The Avenue, Mansfield

'Is this some kind of sick joke? Are you all in on this?'

Sidney took his sister's hand. 'Dicky and I only found out earlier, Larry's known a couple of days and Billy's always known.'

Hannah rubbed her forehead. 'Billy's always known Henry Mason?'

'No Hannah, I've always known Stan wasn't dead.'

'Of course, he's dead! They hanged him; I've been to the graveyard where he's buried! I moved me and my kids halfway round the fucking world, because he – 'Hannah pointed a finger at Stan, '- died!'

'That's what we were all meant to think,' Billy confirmed, 'but it wasn't true, none of it's been true.'

Sidney had, had enough. 'I think you better start talking, Stan, and you better do it now, I mean do we call you 'Stan'[or are you 'Henry' now?'

Stan laughed. 'Well, technically, Stanley did die, and no-one's called me Stan for years, but seeing as this is a special occasion, you can all call me Stan.'

Dicky had said very few words since they'd been at the vicarage. 'This isn't a laughing matter, Stan,' he said. 'Now I suggest you do as the boss said and start fucking talking.'

'The boss? Who's put fifty p in you, Dicky Richards? I'm the boss of the Merry Men, always have been, always will be.'

'Stan, as much as I want to get into a dick measuring contest with you, I... well we all want you to start talking!'

'It was quite simple really,' Stan obliged. 'Everyone wanted Dorrell dead, especially me. After what he did to you, Han, and Charlie. The way The Fixer suggested it meant I could kill Dorrell and get away with it.'

'But it meant you leaving me, leaving the kids.'

'We all knew I was going to kill Dorrell at some point,' Stan said 'and I'd have swung for it, you'd all have swung for it. This way it meant I got away with it.'

'So, you did it for all of us?' questioned Sidney.

'Yeah, if you like.'

So, we get why you wanted Dorrell dead, the guy was evil, but you keep talking about The Fixer and saying, 'they all' wanted him dead; who's 'they'?'

'You remember those sex parties that Dorrell used to throw at the George Street Brothel? Well, they started to attract the likes of Judge Haynes, Frederick Dykes, William Smith, and he bought along Dunderdale, and that twat Collins. The lot of them were proper depraved fuckers, did all sorts to the guys and girls that worked there, and Dorrell let them, charged them a fortune. As long as they paid, anything went.'

'I remember those parties, he kept trying to get us to go.'

'Yeah, he did, Dicky, but we never went. Anyway, unbeknownst to those who did, Dorrell was taking photos and documenting everything that went on.; He had files of stuff on everyone, called it his 'insurance policy'. Anyway, after he – 'Stan paused and looked over at Hannah, and she nodded at him, 'after he – he raped Hannah and we thought she'd lost the baby. He knew I was coming for him. He knew there was no way I'd let what he'd done to Charlie and Hannah go, so he went to Frederick and told him that he wanted me dealt with. Frederick told him to fuck off and that's when he started talking about his 'insurance policy' and told them, that if they didn't get rid of me in some way, he was going to the papers with all the stuff he had on them.'

'Do you remember when Dorrell had me beat up?' Sidney said. 'He started going on about how he was taking over and how you were done for. I just thought it was more of his bollocks.'

'There was no way, that, they could have their dirty little secrets exposed, so The Fixer got in touch with me and came up with the plan. I was to murder Dorrell, I'd be arrested, charged and convicted and sentenced to death. Only they wouldn't execute me, they'd let me go. The deal was that I had to leave behind my old life and start again, I couldn't have any contact with any of you.'

'But yet, you chose to tell Billy what was going on?' Hannah pointed out. 'Not me, your wife, oh no, you left me alone with three kids.'

'I didn't leave you alone,' Stan disagreed. 'I asked all the boys to take care of you! How was I to know you'd choose to move halfway around the fucking world?'

'Well, I felt pretty alone, when everyone went home on the day, they 'executed you'' Hannah made quotation marks in the air with her fingers when she said the word 'execution'. 'I felt pretty alone when I had to try and raise two young boys who missed their dad on my own. I felt pretty alone every time I went shopping and someone told me that you deserved what you'd got and that my boys would probably end up the same way! I felty pretty alone in the delivery room giving birth to a baby I thought I'd miscarried! It was pretty fucking lonely bringing her home, knowing she was part of the reason you'd done what you'd did, and I tell you something else, stepping on that ship with three kids and sailing halfway across the world was pretty fucking lonely too! So, at which point of your masterplan was I not alone?'

The room was quiet, not even Stan seemed to have an answer for his wife.

Hannah stood up. 'Well? You seem to have an answer for everything else?'

'I was scared that if I told you, you'd be in danger.'

'Danger? That's bollocks! I was in danger from the moment I married you. You wanted a new life, more like, you took the easy option, Stanley Thomas!'

Stan got to his feet, anger contorting his previously calm features. 'Easy option? Easy fucking option? Do you think this was easy for me? I had to leave everyone I loved and start again! I didn't think I'd ever see any of you again.'

'Hannah, I think Stan's telling you the truth.' Billy interjected. 'I saw him beforehand, and he was broken, genuinely terrified that he'd be double-crossed, that they'd really hang him, or come for him at a later date. It broke him to leave you and the kids.'

'Typical Fucking Billy Potter, always defending Stan, whatever the fuck he's done!'

'Han, it's true!' Stan agreed. 'I was terrified! You've no idea, just how many times I picked up the phone to call you or wrote you a letter I never sent! I was terrified, they'd come for you.'

The room fell silent again.

Sid looked across at Larry and Dicky, who so far had remained quiet through the whole thing. Knowing them as he did, he figured that Larry was taking it all in, weighing up all sides of the argument, before he said something insightful. With Dicky it was hard to tell. He'd never been the sharpest tool in the box, and he looked genuinely confused by everything that was going on. Sid wasn't overly sure that he'd fully gotten his head around the fact that Stan was still alive.

'I swear, Han, I asked the boys to make sure you and the kids were always provided for. I told them that I wanted you to move on and meet someone else, I told them they were to support you and not stop you. I wanted you to be happy!'

'It's true, Sis, he did say that, to all of us.'

Larry nodded. 'Yeah, he said we were to make sure that you and the kids wanted for nothing financially ever and that we always looked out for you.'

Stan sat forward in his chair. 'See? I tried to make as many provisions as I could for you and the kids, I just hadn't banked on you moving to Australia.'

Hannah nodded. 'I couldn't stay here. It was the looks, the comments, I wanted to make sure I did the best for my kids, you know? I wanted them to grow up without being in the shadow of their dad the 'murderer'. I wanted them to have the very best in life.'

'I know,' Stan said. 'You did the very best for them, I know that. Han, they're amazing, you've done...' Stan's voice cracked. '...Han, they're a credit to you. I can't believe how handsome the boys are! I mean, Charlie, oh my God, Charlie is a legend, I can't believe how he's dealt with his injury! And Eddie! Eddie's so like me. And Jess... I... The first time I saw her... She has my eyes. I didn't know about her.'

Stan moved even further forward in his chair, till he was perched on the edge, and Hannah did the same. There was only the coffee table separating them, and they were just staring at each other.

The rest of the room was still and silent.

Stan stood very slowly and moved around the table. Pulling Hannah to her feet, he took her in his arms for the first time in thirty-five years. At first her body was stiff, but as Stan very softly began to stroke her hair, she very slowly moved closely to him, he continued to stroke her hair, but moved his lips to the side of her face and was saying something very gently into her ear.

Hannah suddenly grabbed him and held him tight in an embrace, tears flowing down her face. She was saying something back to him, but her tears were so fierce the words were inaudible.

The rest of the Merry Men sat still and were silent. Sidney realized that no-one wanted to break the scene they were seeing before them.

No-one, but Dicky, anyway.

'What I don't get, is why, if you wanted to keep everyone safe and start again, did you choose to work at Nottingham Prison and live in fucking Mansfield?'

Chapter 149

1988 – The Homesteads, Kirkby-in-Ashfield

Joyce Mason pricked the top of her pie with a fork and popped it in the oven. She missed her husband Jerry terribly, but she'd promised herself that standards wouldn't slip just because she was on her own now. Tuesday had always been pie day and pie day it would remain.

Taking her afternoon gin and tonic back into the lounge with her, another tradition she had kept in honour of her husband, she sat down in her favourite chair and raised the glass to a picture of him that hung over the fireplace. 'Cheers my darling.'

Taking a sip, she got out a box of papers she'd been sorting out. Jerry's death had made her realise that her affairs weren't quite as in order as they should have been, and she wanted to make everything as easy as possible for Henry to sort when the time came.

She began putting pieces of paper into piles of 'Legal documents', such as Wills', 'certificates – births, deaths, marriages', 'sentimental', while throwing away the stuff she didn't need.

Finding her marriage certificate, she held it in her hands and smiled. She had been the happiest woman in the world when she'd married Jerry in 1923 and even happier when they'd become a family of three in 1925.

Putting the marriage certificate on the pile, she opened another document, this time a birth certificate. She started to trace the words with her fingers.

HENRY STANLEY THOMAS MASON – BORN 27TH JULY 1925

Her beautiful baby boy. He'd been such a sweet child; his white-blond hair, sparkly blue eyes; he had been a charmer even from a young age. A trip to the shops with baby Henry in his pram would take a couple of hours. Everyone they met would want to stop and talk to her and admire Henry. 'What a bonny baby he is!' they'd exclaim! Henry would dutifully coo, gurgle and smile. He had the ability to melt even the hardest of hearts.

Joyce knew she had spoilt him growing up. He'd gotten away with anything and everything. She'd never really scolded him and had showered him in gifts. She'd laugh at the mischief he'd cause, sometimes howling with laughter when she should have been telling him 'No' and sending him to his room!

As Henry had gotten older, his mischief had turned into truly terrible behaviour, and she'd been forever in the headmaster's office defending her son's actions. Occasionally she and Jerry would try and inflict stronger punishments on Henry, but they never worked. He'd either climb out his bedroom window or just openly laugh in their faces.

One time, Jerry had told Joyce he'd had enough, and he was going to deal with Henry once and for all. When Henry had got home, Jerry had been waiting for him. Without a word and before Henry could work out what was going on, Jerry had pinioned his arms behind his back, tied them with a strap and done the same to his feet. He'd then put the white linen hood over his head and a noose around his neck.

The whole task was completed in less than five seconds, and Jerry had told Henry that unless he bucked his ideas up, this was exactly the ending that was coming to him: he'd dangle at the end of the hangman's rope and break his poor mother's heart.

The incident had actually worked. Well for a few days at least and then Henry had been back to his usual ways.

Jerry had washed his hands of his son.

Putting the birth certificate down, Joyce took a letter out of an envelope, it was on prison letter-headed paper.

Dear Mrs Mason,

I just wanted to write to you and say I'm so sorry I let you down, I could see you sat in the courtroom, and I knew you were crying when they sent me down and I felt really bad.

You have been like a Mum to me, and you've taken care of me when no-one else was bothered about me and I feel bad for letting you down cos you're a good person.

I promise to do better and make you proud of me.

Love

Billy

Joyce shook her head, Billy Potter had been like a son to her, and she'd half-hoped that he'd have a positive effect on Henry, but together the two of them were a nightmare. Billy at least had an excuse for his behaviour. He'd had a rotten homelife, his mum had been a prostitute and his dad had beaten him black and blue, after Mr Potter had died in a housefire, Mrs Potter had done a runner, never to be heard of again.

Joyce and Jerry had taken Billy in, and he'd lived with them for a few years. Henry had joined the Army and Joyce had been so proud. She'd hoped that this would be what her son needed to straighten him out and had allowed herself to daydream about her son, the Army Major. A knee injury had put paid to his army career, and he'd been medically discharged. On his return home, Henry and Billy had both moved out and Jerry and Joyce had heard very little from them. She knew her son had become known by the name 'Stanley', but he'd moved to Mansfield, and Joyce was keen to distance herself, her husband and the pub from her son's criminal activities.

When Billy had been arrested and charged with theft, she had attended his trial. Jerry had warned her not to, but she couldn't help herself. To her, he would always be the scared, ginger, freckly little boy whose cuts and bruises she had cleaned of and made everything better with her homemade sticky toffee pudding. Billy had written her the letter the first time he'd been sent down.

She'd kept track of him over the years and was pleased that he had eventually kept to his word and 'gone straight'. He had created a happy life for himself with his wife Fiona and daughter Marjie. She wanted to tell him he had made her proud, but Jerry had told her to stay away from him.

Occasionally, Joyce would broach the subject of her son with Jerry, but Jerry would simply say, 'He's made his bed, let him lie in it. We've warned him of the risks enough times and if he's to dangle from the end of a hangman's noose then so be it. I won't put my career at risk for him.'

Jerry and Joyce hadn't heard from their son in nine years, and Joyce could still remember the day he'd wandered in as though nothing had happened. It had been mid-November and the pub had closed. They were busy tidying up and getting things ready for the following day, and Joyce had been telling Jerry that she intended on putting up the Christmas decorations that weekend and he'd been laughing saying it was too early. They'd been joke-arguing when Henry had walked in.

'Mum... Dad... I need your help.'

Joyce had wanted to run to her son, grab him in her arms and never let him go, but Jerry put out his arm to stop her.

'What have you done now?'

'I need you to execute me.'

Henry had then sat and explained that he'd killed Walter Dorrell and was about to be arrested and charged, but it was all a set up. Some very important people had paid him to do it because Dorrell was blackmailing them. They'd said if he did it, they'd pave the way for him to escape and start a new life. He needed Jerry to be the executioner, he needed Jerry to get rid of Stanley Thomas, and then he'd return to being plain old Henry Mason, the son his parents deserved.

Jerry had shaken his head, told him he was ridiculous, that if he'd killed a man then he deserved to die. That was the law of the land.

Henry had explained all about Dorrell, told them how he'd crippled his son, raped his wife, and caused her to miscarry their third child. Henry had pleaded with his dad; Joyce had pleaded with her husband.

'Please, Jerry, do it! Do it for our boy, bring him back to us!'

Eventually, Jerry had agreed. He'd be involved, but he had a couple of conditions of his own.

Firstly, Henry left behind his criminal past and moved home. Secondly, he joined the family profession and became a hangman.

'It's a noble profession son, but it's a secret one. No-one will ask too many questions and I can keep my eye on you!'

Henry had agreed.

Joyce opened another envelope. There were some cuttings she'd taken from the newspapers over the years, they were of the daughter-in-law and grandchildren she had never known. Over the years, if ever Hannah or one of the children had appeared in the papers, she'd cut the story out and kept it. It was the closest she thought she would ever get to them.

Knowing that they were back in the U.K. and only in Mansfield, every bit of Joyce was fighting the urge to go and see them, to try and make up for the time she'd missed with them. But she knew she couldn't.

Looking over at the mantlepiece, she saw a picture of Henry, Maisy, Phillip and Anna. It had been taken when the kids had been younger, and they'd been on holiday. Next to it were pictures of Philip and his wife, Eve on their wedding day, Anna in her graduation gown, and school photos of her great-grandchildren Toby and Rebecca.

Henry had grown into a good man and a good father. The death of Stanley Thomas had given her, her son back.

Chapter 150

1988 – The Avenue, Mansfield

Everyone stopped and looked at Dicky.

Hannah pulled away from Stan, and Dicky wasn't sure they'd heard him, so he repeated himself.

'I mean, if I was starting a new life, I wouldn't choose to do it where I'd been living for years, and I certainly wouldn't choose to be a bloody screw!'

'Dicky's right, why did you stay here?' Sidney asked.

Stan pulled away from Hannah but kept his arm around her shoulder. 'Because of my family.'

Hannah smiled up at him. 'Me and the kids?'

'No, my old man was involved, and I needed him and my mum to make it work.'

'Your mum and dad? You told me they were dead?'

'My dad is now, he passed a few weeks ago. My mum still lives in Kirkby.'

Billy smiled. 'I miss Joyce. So many times, I wanted to visit her.'

'You knew his mum and dad?'

Yes, they virtually bought me up.'

'I don't believe this.' Hannah pulled away from Stan and sat back in the chair. 'It's lie after fucking lie. Have you ever told me the truth?'

'Stan's dad was Old Man Rope.' Billy said.

'The hangman?' Sidney questioned.

Stan nodded. 'Yeah, it's a family trade. My grandad did it, my great grandad. I was such a disappointment to them, running round getting into trouble all the time and then I signed up for the Army. They finally seemed a bit proud of that, but then I got medically discharged and they were back to being disappointed, so Bill and I moved out and I never saw them again till I needed their help.'

'So, you only stayed because of your folks?' asked Sid

'Well, yeah, my old man said he'd help, but there were conditions, one of them being that I joined the family business. In fairness he was right. It meant keeping out the way and it paid well. Dad couldn't hack it anymore after a while and he retired, but I carried on and then when they abolished hanging, they asked me to take over as Governor and I thought why not? Do you remember me having a go at you Dicky? I thought for sure you'd work out it was me! Thick fuck that you are, never suspected a thing, yet there I was right under your nose.'

'I suspected you were a cunt!'

Stan laughed.

Sid shook his head. 'I don't get it; I'd have moved halfway across the world if I'd been you.'

'Now, where's the fun in that? I thought where better place to hide than in plain sight. I grew a beard, wore glasses, changed my hair. Everyone thought Stan was dead. No-one really knew me as Henry Mason, so no-one questioned it. No-one expected to see Stanley Thomas wandering down Clumber Street, did they?'

'So, just what is your real name? Who did I marry?' Hannah asked.

'Well, my full name is Henry Stanley Thomas Mason, I started going by Stanley Thomas to piss my folks off. I pretty much kept myself to myself. By the time I met Maisy, I was a good upstanding member of society.'

'Maisy. You're married, you have a different family.' Hannah sobbed, and Sidney put his arm around his sister's shoulder.

'Yes, Maisy. Gold old Maisy. She's safe and dependable and I can do no wrong in her eyes. Philip, my son takes after his mum. Good sort really. But Anna is all me. Jess reminds me of her, I think they'd get on.'

'Does Maisy know?'

'Christ, no! She'd have a shit fit! The book's all her fault really. After I retired, all I wanted to do was watch the Stags play, play golf, and fish. She said I should channel some of my energy and keep my brain active and write my memoirs. I thought, what the hell? Without me knowing she sent it to a bloody publisher, and of course, any mention of me is still worth a fortune, so before I knew it, I'd got a book deal and was off on a book tour and doing TV interviews. It all felt like a bit of fun and then when I found out you and the kids were coming back to the U.K., I couldn't resist the opportunity to see you. Look, it's late and I need to get back, so can we chat tomorrow. I'd like to see my kids, Hannah?'

'Yeah, maybe.'

Chapter 151

1988 – Berry Hill, Mansfield

Putting his key in the door and taking a deep breath, Henry took a deep breath. Time to leave Stan behind and become Henry again, husband to dependable Maisy. Maisy, who had been a loyal and faithful wife, who'd given him two children, who'd been at his side every step of their thirty-one-year marriage, supporting him, encouraging him, there by his side... boring the tits off of him!

For years, Henry had tried to come up with a plan to be able to see his family and friends again, to have that feeling of being his true self, and not this sugar-coated good bloke, 'family man' stereotype he'd been forced into. He could ne never work out how he could do it. The Fixer had told him she'd always be watching and that if he ever even attempted to break their agreement, she'd finish him.

What he'd told Hannah and the boys was true. So many times, he'd tried to find a phone number for her, and had written letters he'd never sent. Occasionally, he'd dialled Billy's number and burbled something at him down the phone, normally after he'd had a few, but Billy would always pretend it was a wrong number and hang up. He'd once even gone to The Duke for a pint. Fiona had served him, she'd exchanged a few landlady pleasantries with him, but left Henry thinking that Billy had married a total battle-axe.

When Larry had been the vicar at a church in St Ann's, he'd once gone and sat at the back of the congregation. At the end of the service, Larry had shaken his hand as he'd left and thanked him for coming but was none-the-wiser as to who Henry really was.

He'd been to one of Dicky's after-dinner speeches too and laughed at the poetic license he'd taken with some of his stories.

Sid owned a number of businesses in town, and Henry would very often take Maisy for dinner at one of his restaurants. He had a knack of timing it for when Sid was in, either entertaining his latest squeeze, or doing business. Not once had Sidney acknowledged him or realised who he was.

The only thing he hadn't been able to do was justify flying to Australia to see Hannah and his kids. Whilst Maisy would never question a boy's night out, or a trip to a restaurant, he figured that even she would baulk at him heading to Australia for a few weeks on his own.

But now he had his chance, and he was going to do whatever he could to grab it.

Opening the door, he could hear the TV on in the lounge. 'Sorry I'm late love.'

Maisy muted the TV and got up to kiss her husband. 'Drink?'

'Yes, please.'

Ever the doting wife, Maisy headed to the kitchen and returned with a glass of whiskey with three ice cubes. 'Here you are. Everything OK?'

'Yeah, it's fine, although the publisher wants me to go down to London for a few days, discuss a few ideas.'

'Maybe I could come with you, make a proper break of it?'

'That would have been lovely, but I think it'll be pretty intense, so I wouldn't get to see you much.' Henry saw the look of disappointment flash across his wife's face.

'But why don't we look at booking a few days away in a couple of months, just the two of us?'

Maisy smiled. 'I'd love that, I feel like I don't get to see you, now you're a big-time author.'

Henry laughed, and just about stopped himself from saying, 'Pretty soon you won't be seeing your big-time author husband at all!'

Chapter 152

1988 – Nottingham

Having managed to secure himself some time away, Henry had booked himself into a hotel in Nottingham, where he'd managed to convince Hannah to meet him, so they could talk things through properly.

She hadn't taken much persuading and had even agreed to keep their meeting a secret.

He'd set out a bottle of wine and two glasses on the table, as well as some snacks. He was amazed at how nervous he felt.

There was a gentle knock at the door, and opening it, he saw Hannah dressed in a dark coat, a headscarf, and a big pair of sunglasses. He laughed. 'Why are you dressed like a spy?'

'I didn't want anyone to recognise me!'

She pushed her way past him and into the room, and Henry closed the door.

'Wine?'

Hannah nodded and started to remove her disguise. Taking the wine glass, she raised it: 'Cheers.'

'Cheers.' Henry motioned for her to sit. 'I thought we should talk on our own. You must have a million questions for me.'

Hannah took a sip of wine. 'Just one really. Why?'

'Why what?'

'Why did you do it?'

'I explained that the other day. I was going to kill Dorrell, one way or another, this just meant I got away with it!'

'But why didn't you tell me the plan? We could have gone away together? We could have started a new life together in Australia.'

'I was told that I had to break all contact. I was too scared that if I got in touch, they'd do something to you and the kids, and I couldn't risk that. I thought I was doing the right thing. Other people that went against The Fixer ended up dead, I couldn't, I wouldn't risk you or the kids.' Henry got out of his chair and knelt before his wife, taking her hands in his. 'I never, ever stopped loving you. So many times, I wrote letters, I fantasised about turning up on your doorstep, but every time I thought I'd worked out how that could happen, there were a million holes in my plan.'

'The man who managed to get himself executed and return to live a full and happy life as someone else, couldn't come up with a plan?'

'This was never my plan. It was The Fixer's plan. She controlled everything, every fucking step of the way, and I knew she'd waste no time in hurting you if I went against her.'

'So, why now? Why not just leave things as they are? You have a new life... a new family.' Hannah spat the word 'family', 'and I have my life in Australia, my kids. None of this ever needed to come out. We never needed to know any of this!'

'Because I can't go on without you! Who knew it would be Maisy who would make this happen? After the book came out and there was so much interest, and I found out you and the kids were coming back, I knew that if I was ever going to be with you again, then I had to take my chance. I knew I'd never get another one.'

'So, why aren't you scared now? What about this Fixer person?'

'I don't care anymore. I can't be without you, or our kids anymore.'

'You mean you don't care if we get hurt?'

'That's not what I'm saying. I'm saying that I will do whatever it takes to be with you. I want to come back to Australia with you, I want to live the life we should have had!'

Hannah shook her head. 'Stan, I'm not sure, it's too complicated, the kids, what will people say?'

'Who gives a fuck what people will say? No-one you know in Australia will question you coming back with a new fella! We'll tell everyone that I'm an old school friend, and whilst you were away, we rekindled our relationship. Everyone loves a love story!'

'But the kids? Jess is in the police!'

'The kids will be fine! Plus, Henry Mason is a good law-abiding citizen, it won't affect Jess.'

'But what about your wife? Your family?'

'Fuck them! I've spent far too long with that dreary cow. The kids will look after her, I deserve to be happy... To be with the woman I truly love.' Henry took Hannah's face in his hands. 'I know you love me, too. Every time you give me an excuse, I will have an answer.'

Very slowly, Henry moved forward to kiss Hannah's lips. Very softly he pressed his lips to hers and for a second, she pressed hers back, but then she pulled away and Henry could see the tears pouring down her face. 'You're right, I do love you, I've always loved you.'

And then for the first time in thirty-five years, Stanley made love to his wife.

Chapter 153

1988 – on a train to London

Henry settled himself back into his seat and closed his eyes as the train gently rocked and gobbled up the miles to London.

He thought back over the last seventy-two hours. It had all gone far better than he had expected, and despite Sidney getting a bit lairy at times, Stan had managed to stay in control and manipulate the situation.

After much talking, the Merry Men were pleased he was still alive and had accepted the situation. Hannah had finally given in to her feelings and in the end had been easy to win over. A few 'I love yous', tears, both hers and his, and pleading and she'd totally given in, agreeing to let him move to Australia with her to start a new life. Plus, she'd spent last night in his bed and had been delighted to find that even after all these years, she was still an excellent shag! There were still his children to tell, but he wasn't worried about that.

He just had one more thing to do and then he could be free to live his life. He could leave dreary old Henry Mason behind and his perfect life behind and get on with things.

Chapter 154

1988 – Regents Park, London

Pearl was pleased to be home and even more pleased to finally take off her shoes. It had been a very trying week. Between ensuring the newspaper went out on time, and full of first-class stories, trying to pull together the threads of the documentary about Stan, and generally stop her life's work going tits up, Pearl was ready to lock the door of her flat, order a takeaway, and drink a lot of wine.

But first, a hot bath.

Laying in the hot, scented, soapy water, Pearl tried to rationalise the week's events.

Firstly, the paper had gone out on time and full of highly newsworthy stories, including some about Stan's documentary, which were full of quotes from 'sources close to' the persons involved. Plus, Distribution had told her that sales were at an all-time high.

She scolded herself for worrying too much.

The documentary itself was slightly more troublesome. Despite numerous phone calls to Eamonn, he kept saying that he was struggling to get hold of Hannah to complete her final segments. She simply never returned his phone calls and was always out when he called.

Pearl told herself that maybe Hannah was just busy making her plans to fly back to Australia, and was trying to squeeze in all the final bits she wanted to do. All of Hannah's footage was nearly in the can, and Pearl had told Eamonn to go over to Sid's house and wait for Hannah to come home.

Pearl ignored the niggling feeling in her stomach.

Pearl put on a pair of silk pyjamas, dialled her favourite takeaway and poured herself a large glass of wine. Putting on a Frank Sinatra record, she settled on the sofa. Five minutes later, there was a knock at the door. Record time even for her favourite takeaway! Grabbing some money from her purse to pay the delivery man, she opened the door.

'Wow, that was quick.'

'Quick? If you call thirty-five years quick.'

Pearl dropped her purse. Standing in front of her was Stan.

'Aren't you going to invite me in?'

'What the fuck are you doing here?'

'Now, now, Pearl, is that any way to greet an old friend?' Bending down to pick up her purse up, he handed it over. 'I know you're a big deal these days, but I figured even you wouldn't want to lose your purse.'

With that he barged past her.

Pearl's head was racing. Everything was and had always been on her terms. Stan, here in her flat wasn't part of her plan. She needed to re-evaluate and quickly.

'You've got five minutes to say what you need to, and then get out. I don't want to see you again, I thought I made that very clear?'

'Aren't you just a bit pleased to see me?' Walking over to a chest of drawers, Stan started looking at the framed photos that adorned it. Picking one up, he smiled. 'You see I think that anyone who keeps a framed photo from a day out that they had when they were sixteen, might be a bit pleased to see the person they had the day out with!'

Pearl grabbed the photo from Stan's hands. It was one of her on Skegness seafront. She was eating an ice cream, and holding a teddy bear that Stan had won on the fairground. She slammed the photo down.

'I've got to say, you look good, Pearl.' He took a lock of her hair in between his fingers. 'I like you as a blonde, it suits you.'

The two of them stood close together, and Pearl was determined not to move first or show by any slip of her body language, just how out of control she felt.

Stan released her hair and laughed. 'Still the same ballsy Pearl, you always have to be in control, don't you?'

'I thought I'd made that clear?'

'Well, I've been having a think, and I think it's time that someone else got to be the boss for a while. I mean, I, for one, am sick and tired of being bossed around by some two-bit prostitute.'

Pearl laughed. 'Oh Stan, it was this two-bit prostitute that has masterminded the last thirty-five years of your life! From allowing you to murder Walter, to allowing you a new career, a new family, a whole new life. This two-bit prostitute allowed that.'

'Well, now it's my turn to allow you a few things! I'm going to allow you to carry on living your sad and pathetic life, writing your crap news stories, living alone, because no one in this world wants you, drinking to forget your pain; but you'll always be the sad little prostitute who was fucked by anyone and everyone, selling her arse to the highest bidder. I'll allow that. But, from now on, I will now do whatever the fuck I want, and you won't do a damn thing about it.'

'You'll do as you're fucking told.' Pearl snapped. 'I told you never to underestimate me, and I fucking meant it! And yet here you are, giving it the big 'uns like you're still someone! You're pathetic do you know that? You and Walter, running around playing at gangsters, who's got the biggest dick, do as I say everyone, I'm the hard man. Blah blah, fucking blah. If I'm still a two-bit prostitute, you're still a pathetic Mummy's boy, who had to go and do some 'naughty things', just to feel alive. You don't scare me, you've never scared me, all of you were far too easy to control. Even as a sixteen-year old I knew how to get you all dancing to my tune.'

Stan moved forward, standing even closer to Pearl. She could see the rage in his eyes, the redness spreading across face.

'You know nothing,' he said. 'You think you've been controlling me all this time? You know nothing.'

Pearl's calmness was in direct contrast to Stan's anger. Very slowly she said, 'Stan, I know everything.'

Stan laughed. 'No, you don't.'

'Frederick Dykes, threatened to tell everyone you were still alive unless you paid him. You knew he liked a drink and so you waited until he'd been in the pub drinking, cut his brakes and he smashed into a tree. Everyone knew he was involved with all kinds of dodgy people, so no-one thought too much of it. Problem solved.' Pearl could see the look of shock on Stan's face, warming to her subject, she continued, 'The Reverend Roger Collins, a corrupt, evil bastard with a gambling problem to boot. He wanted money from you to pay off a gambling debt, threatened to go to the papers, told you he could get a fortune for the story. You waited till he left one of his poker games one night and stabbed him in the back -quite literally. The police assumed he was murdered over a gambling debt, so didn't bother to investigate too much. Another problem solved for you! How am I doing so far?'

Stan slumped to the sofa and put his head in his hands.

'Oh dear, Stan, not quite the reaction you were expecting? I'm not sure at what point, you are going to finally believe me when I say, never underestimate me! You look like you need a drink.'

Heading to the kitchen, Pearl picked up another glass and the bottle of wine, but as she turned round to head back to the lounge, she bumped into Stan, who had followed her. He knocked the glass and bottle out of her hand and before she could react, he put his hands around her throat.

'It looks like you're the one who has underestimated me this time!' He spat. 'I told you, I was taking back my life and I meant it. I enjoyed every second of killing that cunt of a brother of yours, and I'm going to enjoy every second of killing you.'

Pearl tried to fight him off, she frantically trying to grab at Stan's hands, clawing at him to try and get him to let her go, but every time she did, he squeezed just a little tighter and every breath, every movement became agony.

'You see Pearl, you made a very big mistake. You knew I was capable of murder, hell, you set one of them up for me and yet still you thought I wouldn't hurt you. It's such a shame, because I was hoping you'd see sense and that we could have a bit of fun together. You always did intrigue me, I could never work out just how you managed to pull it all together and what you were trying to achieve, but it's done now, it's over.'

For a second, Stan gently released the hold he had on Pearl's throat, and she fell to the floor, gasping for breath. Frantically she started looking around for something, anything she could use to take back control of the situation. If she could only stun Stan long enough for her to get away.

Gradually, Pearl's breathing returned to normal, and Stan grabbed her under her armpits and dragged her to her feet. 'Poor Pearl Dorrell, did you really think I was going to kill you?'

Pearl nodded, very slightly.

'Oh, Pearl, my beautiful, little Pearl, I could never hurt you, you know I've always loved you. Ever since I first saw you at the George Street Brothel, wearing that bloody school uniform that Walter made you wear, glaring at everyone, giving Walter attitude, but I saw you. I saw the real you.'

Pearl gradually started to relax, and Stan moved his hands from her shoulders and began to gently stroke her face, tracing the lines on her face with his fingers.

'We both might be older, maybe a little bit wiser, but when I look at you, I still feel like that crazy reckless young man I was, the one who risked everything to take you to Skegness for the day, the one who made love to you, showing you what sex should be like.' Stan told her. 'I'm still the man who went along with your crazy plan. I'm the man whose heart broke knowing he could never see you again. You were all I wanted; all I've ever wanted. I followed your career. Every time I saw your picture in the paper next to a story you'd written, my heart would burst with pride. So many times, I wrote you letters, I picked up the phone and called your office, hell, I even waited outside your office once hoping for a glimpse of you. I saw you too. You were walking with a man, and you were laughing. I wanted to run up to you, knock him out, scoop you up in my arms and never let you go again.'

'Stan,' Pearl murmured, 'I don't know what to say! I love you too.'

Stan took Pearl in his arms and kissed her, very slowly at first, but becoming more insistent.

'Let's go into the bedroom.'

Pearl nodded, and, taking Stan's hand, led him to her bedroom.

The two made love into the early hours of the morning.

***

Pearl lay back in the bed and looked up at Stan. 'Oh Stan, I honestly didn't think this would ever happen.'

He smiled down at her. 'Are you happy Pearl?'

'Yes, I really am.'

'Good. I couldn't leave you without having a final shag, and at least I know you'll go happy.'

Stan laughed as he saw the look of confusion flash across Pearl's face.

Picking up his pillow, he pressed it across Pearl's face, laughing as her legs and arms thrashed around and she frantically tried to claw at the pillow, scratching his hands and his arms.

The more she panicked, the harder Stan laughed, until eventually she stopped moving, her left arm falling lifelessly by her side.

Stan kept the pillow there for a few more minutes just to be sure. Checking her pulse, he was happy that Pearl Dorrell was gone.

Kissing her cheek and pulling the duvet up around her shoulders so she looked like she was sleeping, he whispered, 'Till our next merry meeting, Pearl Dorrell'

Chapter 155

1988 – Heathrow Airport

Stan and the kids were sat having a cup of coffee as Hannah was grabbing some last-minute bits from the airport shop.

Stan was still amazed at how well his kids had taken the news. Obviously, they'd been shocked at first, they'd been scared, there'd been a lot of tears and then they just seemed to be really happy. Jess kept holding his hand and breaking into random stories. Eddie kept talking about all the places he was going to take his dad, most of them seemed to involve having a pint whilst they were there; and Charlie couldn't wait to have him cheering him on at the next Paralympics.

They were all on board with the story that he was an old friend of their mums and that they'd gotten together during the trip.

Hannah returned carrying a Boots and a WH Smiths carrier bag. 'Have you seen this?' She threw a copy of The Daily Chronicle on the table.

The headline read:

NEWSPAPER EDITOR FOUND MURDERED!

The story went on to say how their very own Editor, Pearl Dorrell, had been found murdered in her bed the previous day. There was an eye-witness report from Ms Dorrell's cleaner, who had found her when she'd gone in to clean her flat. There were also tributes from famous TV presenters and journalists, Terry Wogan, Derek Jameson, Matt McFetridge as well as a heartfelt tribute from Tony Richardson, the man who had been her mentor.

The article also mentioned her association with Stan and the Merry Men.

'I can't believe it, Pearl's been murdered, I wonder who did it?'

Stan shrugged his shoulders and flicked through the article. 'No idea, I mean, being a journalist, she must have a fair few enemies? Not everyone's going to like being headline news, are they? Plus, she's reported one some pretty massive stories. Have they said they've got any suspects?'

'No, just that they're waiting on the post-mortem results, but they're treating it as suspicious.'

An announcement came over the Tannoy: 'British Airways Flight 2870 is now boarding for Perth, Australia, please make your way to gate forty-seven.'

'That's us. Come on time for us to start our new life as a family... finally.'

Stan nodded at the air hostess as he handed her his passport. Taking his boarding pass and looking quickly at him and then his photo, she smiled, handed it back and said, 'Enjoy your flight, Mr Mason.'

Hannah followed him, and he took her hand and smiled. 'Ready?'

She nodded. 'Ready.'

***

They began to walk down the tunnel towards the plane, Charlie, Eddie and Jess had already boarded.

As they made it closer to the door of the plane, they became aware of a huge scuffle behind them and raised voices insisting, 'Excuse me, let me through!'

Turning round, they saw two men heading towards them, Stan and Hannah moved to one side to let them pass, but as they drew level, they stopped.

'Henry Mason?'

'Yes, that's me.'

'Henry Mason, I'm Detective Inspector Webster and this is Detective Sergeant Booker.'

'Can I help you?'

'Henry Mason, I am arresting you on the suspicion of the murder of Pearl Dorrell, you do not have to say anything, unless you wish to do so, but what you say, may be given in evidence.'

The first policeman had spun Henry round and had him in cuffs, before he realised what was happening.

'You can't do that; he hasn't done anything!' Hannah protested.

'Madam, please step aside, or I'll have to arrest you for trying to obstruct a policeman from performing his duty.'

'You can't take him away, we're going to Australia, my kids are on board.'

'I'm sorry madam, but he's going nowhere. What you choose to do, is up to you!'

The policemen started to walk Henry back down the tunnel towards the airport, and he looked back over his shoulder and cried, 'Call Sid. Tell him what's happened, he'll know what to do.'

Hannah watched helplessly as, for the second time in her life, she watched as her husband was arrested and taken away for the murder of someone with the surname Dorrell.

Chapter 156

1988 – Sandbanks, Bournemouth

My name is Tony Richardson, and I had the very great pleasure and honour of being Pearl Dorrell's mentor, although the fact you are reading this means that my heart is broken as my beautiful Pearl his gone.

What you're about to read are Pearl's memoirs, and the real story of Stanley Thomas, which I have been working on for the last thirty-five years.

I first met Pearl when I was working as a reporter for The Daily Chronicle, and I was covering her brother's murder trial. I approached her and asked her to sell her story, and she refused.

I thought no more of Pearl Dorrell, until she contacted me and told me she wanted to talk. I met her in Ye Olde Cock Tavern on Fleet Street with the intention of getting her story and never seeing her again.

However, Pearl had other ideas. She asked me to be her mentor, to help build her career and in return she would gift me the story of a lifetime. Being an old hack, I agreed!

What follows, is that story.

Pearl Dorrell was an incredible woman. At sixteen years old having faced true horrors at the hands of men who should have known better, she plotted to have her brother murdered. She used the evidence that her brother had been collecting against the men who had abused her to blackmail them, into doing what she wanted. She promised to never expose them, as long as they facilitated her plan to allow Stan to murder her brother and then let him walk free.

So desperate were they to protect their perversions and places within society that they agreed and Stan, who never turned down an adventure or the chance for revenge, also agreed.

Pearl has always known that at some point the truth would be revealed. She had a premonition that her death would be part of that revelation and so, in accordance with Pearl's wishes, here is my life's work, the true story of Stanley Thomas.

Epilogue

Henry Mason sat in the dock waiting for his trial to begin.

Henry Mason wasn't a bad man; he just wasn't a very good one.

THE END

Printed in Great Britain
by Amazon

83389269R00142